# SHADOW
# OF
# ATHENA

# Praise for
## *Shadow of Athena*

*A story of adventure and love that transports you to ancient shores. It takes hold from the first pages and never lets up until it reaches a shattering and shocking climax.*

**Bud Gundy, author, two-time Emmy award winning producer, PBS**

*An enchanting love story with compelling characters and suspense that keeps you turning the pages. Authentic details bring ancient Greece to life. A must-read for lovers of historical novels.*

**Patricia Elmore, mystery writer and Edgar nominee**

*A fast-paced intriguing story with vivid characters set in the ancient world. The suspense never lets up and builds to an unexpected and satisfying ending.*

**Charlene Weir, mystery writer, winner, Malice Domestic Award**

*The far past comes alive in this historical novel with a cast of unforgettable characters. A story that lingers in the mind long after the book is closed.*

**Cleo Jones, author of *Sister Wives* and *The Case of the Fragmented Woman***

# SHADOW OF ATHENA

ELENA DOUGLAS

**KNOX ROBINSON**
**PUBLISHING**
London & Atlanta

# KNOX ROBINSON PUBLISHING

34 New House
67–68 Hatton Garden
London, EC1N 8JY
&
3104 Briarcliff Rd NE 98414
Atlanta, Georgia 30345

ISBN PB 978-1-910282-66-3

Typeset in Bembo

Printed in the United States of America and the United Kingdom.

www.knoxrobinsonpublishing.com

*To Tom, André, Lula, Tazia, and Erik*

*You're the best!*

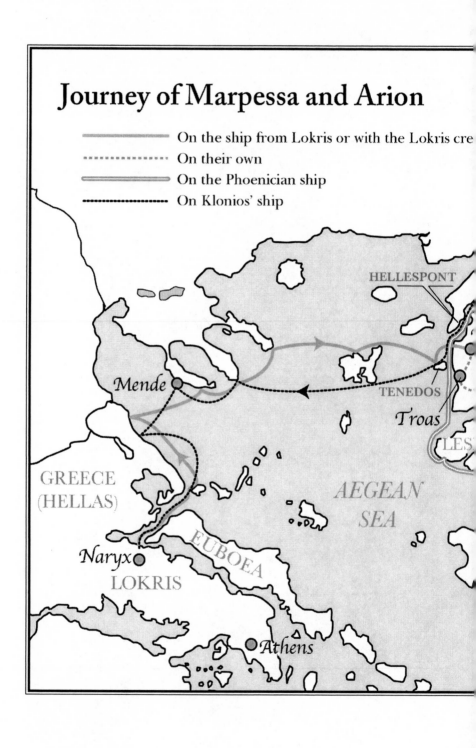

# Journey of Marpessa and Arion

On the ship from Lokris or with the Lokris cre[w]
On their own
On the Phoenician ship
On Klonios' ship

HELLESPONT

Mende

TENEDOS

Troas

LES[

GREECE
(HELLAS)

AEGEAN
SEA

EUBOEA

Naryx
LOKRIS

Athens

BOSPHORUS

EUXINE SEA

Heracléa Pontíca

PROPONTIS

Kysikos

MOUNT IDA

Pergamos

Kaikos R.

IONIA

EUXINE SEA

Detail area

Greece
(Hellas)

AEGEAN SEA

Ionia

Greece and the Aegean

N

0                                    100 miles

100 kilometers

# PROLOGUE

## AJAX: THE LEGEND

During the sack of Troy, the Greek warrior Ajax of Lokris committed a terrible sacrilege. As the Trojan princess Kassandra sought refuge in the temple of Athena, Ajax tore her brutally from the sanctuary and raped her. When his own warriors threatened to kill him for it, Ajax saved himself by vowing to expiate his sin. But on his homeward journey, the unappeased Athena wrecked his ship near the coast of Greece. Ajax managed to scramble onto a rock near the shore and, in his arrogance, shouted defiance at the gods, enraging Poseidon, who split the rock and sent Ajax plunging into the sea. He drowned without ever atoning for his sin.

Deprived of her revenge, Athena turned the full force of her wrath against his homeland, Lokris.

# PART I

# I

## THE CHOOSING

Once a year at midsummer, the Hundred Houses of Lokris gathered in the agora with their marriageable daughters for the dreaded ceremony of the Choosing. Anguished mothers, and even a few fathers, clutched their girls by the arms, knowing that regardless of the tightest hold, the most loving embrace, Athena would have her way. This year, as every year, the blind hand of the goddess would pluck two maidens from their midst like fledglings from a nest.

This year Marpessa's name was in the drawing for the first time. As the somber crowd waited beneath the statue of Athena, she stood numbly with her mother and her nursemaid in the heat-shimmer glare of noon. In all her sixteen years she had never feared anything but her father's rages, his hard hand striking her face. *And Mother would never let him really hurt me.* The fear she felt now was different, unearthly. An invisible goddess-shadow hovered, raising the hairs on her arms and the back of her neck. Her future, until now so secure, was suddenly an all-enveloping fog that could swallow her. She smelled the stink of her own cold sweat and clung to her mother's hand, realizing that for the first time in her life Amaltheia could not protect her. *Oh, Goddess,* she whispered in her mind, *please not me, not me, not me.*

But that was cowardly, shameful. *If you choose me, Athena, I will accept my lot and try to serve you well,* she amended silently, knowing the words were hollow. Gently she released her mother's hand and reached into her sash to pull out the downy white feather she'd found in the woods yesterday. She stroked it with a finger, but its softness failed to soothe her. Above her, dominating the agora, loomed the immense marble Athena with shield and spear, brought out of the temple for the ceremony. The blazing sun pooled the statue's shadow onto part of the crowd. As Marpessa gazed up, the goddess's fixed stone smile became a menacing rictus, the painted eyes boring right into hers as if the goddess could read her thoughts. The knot of dread tightened in her stomach. She turned to Amaltheia for reassurance and caught an unguarded look on her mother's face that rendered it suddenly haggard and old.

All at once someone shouted, "The High Priestess has arrived!" A lightning bolt of tension skittered through the throng. Shoulders tightened, breaths were sucked in. One young girl clinging to her mother's arm seemed about to weep. A woman with a hard, weathered face enveloped her daughter in her cloak and pulled her close, hiding her from sight. Marpessa felt her mother's hands come to rest on her shoulders. *Oh, Mother, take me away from here!* But she knew better than to say it. Its very futility weakened her knees.

"What's happening?" someone demanded, straining to see.

"The High Priestess is approaching the altar, followed by the other priestesses," answered a man taller than the rest. People craned their necks to catch a glimpse of the woman with the power to speak the goddess's will. Marpessa stood on desperate tiptoes but was too far back to see either the High Priestess or the makeshift altar.

An unseen hand struck a gong, and a silence fell that had weight and substance. Marpessa couldn't breathe. She was sure the shadow of Athena had grown darker, more forbidding. The High Priestess's voice rang out. "We're here to choose the two maidens who will this year appease the goddess for Ajax's sin and the curse he brought to our land."

An uneasy rumble greeted her words. Glances came Marpessa's way. She wanted to run, to hide. *They know I'm Ajax's direct descendant. Oh goddess, please—* But she couldn't finish the thought.

The hands gripping Marpessa's shoulders began to tremble, sending coldness through her instead of comfort. Never before had her mother shown fear. Marpessa turned to her and tried a smile, but her lips were stiff as wood. "Mother—"

A loud clattering began on the altar.

"What's that?" a woman nearby asked in a hushed tone, and the tall man said, "The High Priestess is reaching into the caldron on the altar, stirring the ceramic pieces. She's about to draw a name."

"There are more than two hundred names in that caldron—" the hard-faced woman said, her voice trailing off, leaving unsaid the hope of every mother there: *Out of all those names, let my daughter not be chosen.*

*Two hundred*, Marpessa thought. *Not me, not me, not me.* She couldn't stop repeating it. She did not see the priestess lift out the first square of baked clay, but she heard the woman's strident voice call out a name. "Haleia, daughter of

Polites!"

*Not me.* She exhaled, her knees going even weaker. Cries came from the middle of the crowd. Heads turned. Hands reached sympathetically to the family whose daughter had been called. At first Marpessa couldn't remember who this girl was. *Though I must know her.* The priestess commanded, "Haleia, come forward to stand before the Goddess," and through the parting crowd Marpessa caught a glimpse of a tall young woman with a high, proud forehead and straight brown hair. Then she saw the girl's stricken face. *Her! The one with the ailing mother and all the younger brothers and sisters. She's a few years older than I, perhaps eighteen,* Marpessa remembered. *What lies ahead for her now?* But she knew. A dangerous journey. A year of harsh servitude. A lifetime of virginity.

A weight fell on Marpessa's heart. *I'll never again talk to her over the washing at the spring.* Then a shiver ran through her. *Why did I think* never? *It's only for a year.*

"Mother," she whispered, "what will happen to her?"

Amaltheia murmured something inaudible and her hands ran through her daughter's unbound hair. The gesture should have been calming, but her movements were jerky, frenetic. A crackling sound came from the altar, then the smell of smoke. Marpessa's nose caught the spicy fragrance of incense. Faces looked up as a white plume of smoke rose straight into the clear sky. "An auspicious sign," the High Priestess intoned. "The goddess finds Haleia acceptable." A pause. The priestess added, "I will now seek the other who will accompany her."

Again the crowd went deathly still. Again the clatter of ceramic pieces in the bronze caldron. Breaths were held. Marpessa's muscles clenched tightly enough to snap. *Only one more. After that, please gods, I'll be safe.* She was afraid she might be sick.

Then came the summons from the priestess, so loud and terrifying it seemed to issue from the goddess herself. "Marpessa, daughter of Thrasios, come forward! You have been chosen."

# II

## THE CURSE OF AJAX

Amaltheia flung her arms around her daughter. "Oh, no, not you, my darling!" she cried. Marpessa felt her mother, the mainstay of her life, crumpling against her shoulder.

"Mother, it's only for a year," she tried to reassure them both. "It's all right."

But Amaltheia's face was pale as ashes. "No, it isn't. You don't know what—"

"Hush!" said the nursemaid Eumene. "The priestess is speaking."

They heard the insistent call from the altar, louder this time. "Marpessa, of the house of Thrasios, come forward."

Amaltheia grabbed Marpessa's arms. "I won't let them take you!"

Shocked faces swung around to stare at them. "That's blasphemy!" Eumene said. "Let her go."

Marpessa's knees felt as if they were filled with sand and would crumble. "Go," someone urged her. The throng parted, and as all eyes watched, she made her way on trembling legs to the altar. It was the longest journey she had ever taken. Each step carried her a world away from her mother, her home, her life.

*My life no longer. The goddess's now.*

She would spend a year of servitude in a distant land. And when it was done, forbidden to marry, she would live out her life in shameful dependence on male relatives. *It can't be. I don't believe it.*

But it was no use to think of it. *It isn't life or death,* she told herself. *I must keep up my courage. That's what matters now.*

At last she reached the altar. Through a blur she saw the white-robed acolytes gathered behind the High Priestess and the small priestess who tended the smoking censer. Then her gaze was drawn to the huge stone Athena, her helmet pushed back, her long crimped hair flowing over her shoulders. Once more Marpessa looked up into the goddess's eyes, searching them for meaning. *Why?* she asked silently. *Why me?* Then across the altar she saw Haleia. The other girl was visibly shaking. Her eyes locked with Marpessa's, the pain in them striking her like a wave, and Marpessa knew that her own eyes looked back at Haleia in exactly the same way.

*So it's the two of us,* Marpessa thought. *Alone together.*

The High Priestess, a stern figure swathed in white, gestured to the small woman at her side who sprinkled handfuls of incense onto the charcoal in the censer. Once more, white smoke plumed skyward. The High Priestess, watching it with evident satisfaction, raised her voice to the crowd. "Athena finds Marpessa acceptable." Then she directed the two girls to join hands across the altar. Marpessa reached out to Haleia, feeling as if some force outside her will were commanding her movements. She squeezed the other girl's hands in hers and found them cold and damp with fear. *Like mine.* The priestess wrapped a woven band around the girls' wrists. Marpessa stared at the bright, intricate design on the band, geometric owls worked in purple thread. The owl was sacred to Athena. A memory jolted Marpessa. *The white feather. An owl's.* Yesterday morning, rambling in the woods, she had found it caught in shrubbery and stuck it in her sash as a talisman. But it was the wrong kind of talisman. It had drawn the goddess's notice just as a tall tree attracts the lightning.

As the priestess looped the band once, twice, thrice around the girls' wrists, Marpessa felt her hands as numbed and immobilized as a prisoner's.

The priestess's next words were almost superfluous. "Now you are bound to Athena. You belong to her for life."

Amaltheia watched through a blur of tears as the High Priestess held up the bound wrists of the two girls. Raising her voice to be heard in the farthest reaches of the crowded agora, she called out, "People of Lokris! Behold the two maidens who have been chosen to keep Athena's wrath from us for another year!" All were familiar with the story. All knew that, hundreds of years ago, because of Ajax's sacrilege, the goddess had sent drought, plague, and famine to his homeland Lokris. The oracle at Delphi had decreed that, to atone for his sin, two maidens must be sent every summer to serve as menial slaves in Athena's temple at Troy. Every year for a thousand years.

A clamor of applause broke from the crowd. *Of course they're cheering,* Amaltheia thought bitterly. *Their own daughters are safe for another year.* "My Marpessa," she whispered. "You don't know what lies ahead for you."

She feared she might faint. Clinging to Eumene's hand, she begged the old woman, "Don't let me disgrace myself." With all her being she focused on the distant figure of Marpessa standing by the altar.

Amaltheia began to push forward through the crowd.

"My lady, what are you doing?" panted Eumene, rushing to keep up with her.

"I must see her before they take her away!"

"Wait! Everyone is staring at us." The old nursemaid grasped her mistress's arm. "I'm sure they'll let you see her when the ceremony is over."

Amaltheia stopped and drew a deep breath. She was near enough to see her daughter clearly now. At that moment Marpessa's eyes flew to meet hers. *I must be strong for her,* Amaltheia thought. Words she had often said to her daughter came back to her. *To show weakness is shame, dishonor.* She straightened, tried to radiate courage. She even forced a smile. The faintest answering curve touched her daughter's lips. Then the girl lifted her head and faced the High Priestess, who embarked on a long-winded prayer.

Amaltheia's eyes clung to her daughter. Marpessa's brown hair, tinged with gold from the sun, cascaded down her back. Her skin was brown as a boy's, her arms and legs slender but well muscled from climbing and running. *An Amazon,* Amaltheia thought, but with love and pride. *Why did Athena pick her? She's more Artemis's child than Athena's.* Whenever she could, Marpessa escaped from the women's quarters and ran to the orchards and woods to listen to the birds, to watch wild animals. She found happiness there and often brought home creatures to care for: a fledgling with a broken wing, an orphaned baby hare. Thrasios despised what he called her unwomanly ways, and Amaltheia often defended her daughter against his heavy hand. *This dreadful servitude to Athena will stifle her.* But that was the least of it.

*Once you reach Troy, my love, they will hunt you like prey. You could be broken with rocks or speared to death. And they will count themselves heroes if they kill you.*

As part of the ritual, until they reached the temple the girls were at the mercy of Trojan men who stalked them with murderous intent. Two years ago one of the girls had been killed. *We had another drawing and sent a replacement,* Amaltheia remembered. But Marpessa didn't know. *I forbade the servants from talking in front of her. And how can I tell her now?*

Then, for the first time, her eyes fell on the other girl, Haleia. A horrifying premonition struck Amaltheia. *Something will happen to these two in Troy.* She'd had the same nightmare for the last three nights. A harpy swooped down and carried Marpessa off to a far land, and then came a message that her daughter was dead. Amaltheia went cold at the memory. Everyone knew that dreams were prophetic. It was as if her daughter were already lost to her. This was Marpessa's first summer of womanhood, her first time in the drawing. *The Fates are cruel,* Amaltheia thought. *By this time next year I could have had her married and never again in danger from the curse of Ajax.* Her husband Thrasios had hoped to wed Marpessa to the powerful merchant Klonios. *Not him!* she had vowed. *Someone who will care for her and make her happy. As I never was.*

But now it was too late.

Amaltheia stood frozen until the end of the ceremony. Then as the crowd started to disperse, she strode with determination toward the altar. Several acolytes stood in front of the two girls and barred her path, but Amaltheia said, "Let me through!" and thrust her way up to the High Priestess. "I must see Marpessa. She's my only daughter, my youngest child." *My most beloved.* But she did not say it aloud.

"It is not permitted," said the High Priestess. "The maidens must be tested and purified. Then they must swear the oath before the goddess."

"Tested?" Amaltheia whispered.

"It must be determined that they are virgins," the High Priestess answered sternly.

Amaltheia was speechless at this indignity. She strained to catch a glimpse of Marpessa, but the acolytes were leading the girls toward the great black open doors that led into the temple.

"Let me at least speak to her!" Amaltheia cried. *And hold her in my arms,* she added silently.

But the High Priestess shook her head. "Go home, lady. Your daughter will be returned to you. For a brief time. In five days the ship will sail."

Only the eyes of the watching bystanders kept Amaltheia from crumpling to the dusty ground. *I've lost her,* she thought. *How will I live?*

11

# III

## THE VINTNER

Marpessa's father's warehouse was a long way from the agora, and his mind a long way from the Choosing. In fact, he had forgotten all about it. When Klonios came charging into his counting room, Thrasios the vintner looked desperately around, wishing he could escape. He knew why Klonios had come.

"You don't have my quota of wine!" Klonios slammed his fist onto the table. "How *dare* you default on our agreement?"

Thrasios's gut clenched. Then he lifted his head to return Klonios's glare. "It wasn't possible. An early frost ruined many of my grapes."

"*It wasn't possible!*" Klonios mocked. Deep-cut lines surrounded his narrowed eyes and down-turned mouth. He was taut, wiry, muscular, his skin weathered and his black hair shot with gray, about Thrasios's own age of sixty winters. All his movements were quick and abrupt. "So," he demanded. "Just how many amphorae do you have ready for my trading voyage?"

Thrasios gulped, his throat dry. "Twelve, my lord."

"*Only twelve?*" Klonios's words stung like a blow. "Last fall you promised at least twenty. You swore by the gods."

Thrasios made his voice hard. "It was the best I could do." To produce even that amount, he'd gone into debt buying mature vines from other vintners. *What a reckless gamble,* he thought now. "I can make up the losses next year."

"Too late!" Klonios snapped. "I overestimated your abilities. I was sadly mistaken. And to think I was going to make you an oligarch!" Klonios's malicious eyes glared so fiercely that Thrasios's gaze fell, but his whole being ignited with fury at what he had lost. Klonios shrugged, turned toward the door. "Fortunately there are other vintners in Lokris."

Thrasios's stomach plunged. *I'll be ruined if he doesn't buy my wine!* He put out his hands imploringly. "My lord, please! Take the twelve amphorae at a reduced cost!"

Klonios made no reply. In a sudden change of mood he sat down at the table. Thrasios hastily pushed aside scrolls and tally sheets to make a place for him and produced two bronze goblets and a wine jar. "Will you at least sample this year's vintage?" His voice sounded servile, yet he couldn't help it. Klonios was the richest, most powerful man in Lokris, and his ships plied the seas between mainland Hellas and all the colonies, carrying goods from Lokris to the far corners of the world. He was one of the six oligarchs who governed the Council of the Hundred. Every man on the council feared him.

Thrasios poured wine, mixed in water, and watched tensely while the other man sipped. "Not bad," Klonios pronounced grudgingly and fell silent. He seemed to be waiting. *He came here for something other than the wine,* Thrasios realized. He searched his mind desperately. *What does he want?*

All at once he knew. A memory filled his head. The Dionysian festival last year. His daughter Marpessa dancing in the maidens' dance. All the other girls kept their gazes cast down, but not Marpessa. Her eyes shone, and her hair flew about, loosened from the vigor of her movements. So immodest, dancing with abandon like a Maenad! The shame of it—he wanted to strike her. Then, glancing across the crowd he saw Klonios staring at her with naked desire. Thrasios was stunned. Klonios's wife lay ill with a wasting sickness. *When she dies, I can offer him Marpessa. Praise the gods, daughters can be of some use after all!*

Klonios was watching him expectantly. *How ill is the wife?* Thrasios wondered. "I have a marriageable daughter," he blurted.

The other man sat back, gratified, and gave a lascivious smile. "How interesting that you should mention her! How old is she?"

"Sixteen. Blossoming into womanhood."

"I like them young." Klonios lowered his gaze to drink, but not before Thrasios saw his greedy look of lust. "Has she a sizeable dowry?"

"Aye!" Thrasios prayed Klonios wouldn't ask how sizeable, for much of it had gone into this reckless venture.

Klonios gave a cold smile like one on a mask. "My wife won't live to see me return from this voyage. When I come back, I'll offer for your daughter's hand."

The blood rushed to Thrasios's head. All was not lost. Klonios's marriage to Marpessa would be an undreamed-of distinction, and it would also save Thrasios's neck. He smiled. "I would be most honored!"

"And the girl's mother? Will she be equally honored?" Klonios asked with biting sarcasm.

Thrasios's face heated at the implication that Amaltheia was not under his control. When he'd made the mistake of bragging to her about his secret hope, she had snarled like an enraged cat. *Not that old villain! And his wife not even dead yet. Have you considered Marpessa's wishes at all?* A blow across her jaw had served to silence her. *What foolishness!* Thrasios thought. Neither his wife nor the girl had any say in this, and they would know nothing until the time came.

"My wife," he said stiffly, "agrees completely with all my decisions."

Klonios gave a rude snort, then rose. "That is well. Let us swear a solemn oath on it and offer libation to Zeus."

Thrasios lifted his untouched goblet. "I swear before Father Zeus and all gods that my daughter will belong to Klonios and no other." He poured the libation onto the dirt floor. Both men watched the purple stream sink into the earth. "May the gods steal the breath from my body and the light from my eyes if I do not honor this vow."

Klonios gave a dark smile, his eyes like stones. "Let it be so."

# IV

## BROKEN VOW

>꧁꧂

Klonios walked to his house from Thrasios's warehouse well satisfied with how things had gone. The daughter was his, and he'd maneuvered Thrasios into offering her, so that he hadn't even had to ask. His thoughts dwelled on the girl. He remembered her dancing at some festival last year, her sparkling eyes and graceful movements so full of life. As if it were yesterday he saw again her slim, lovely body, her loosened hair with the shimmer of sunlight. How different she was from the other maidens of the town, pale, insipid, hiding in their mothers' shadows, afraid to raise their eyes! And how different from his cold-blooded, barren wife, grown old and ill, for whom he felt nothing. He would teach this new young bride how to please a man. And what a pleasure her education would be! He looked forward eagerly to the end of his upcoming journey.

A passerby jostled him, and he came to himself with a start. He realized the street was crowded. People were streaming away from the agora. Some kind of ceremony, he recalled, involving girls and women. He hadn't paid attention.

Then he heard someone mutter, "—saw her at the Choosing, and—"

*The Choosing!* Though he spent many months journeying on his trading ships, Klonios prided himself on knowing everything of importance that happened in Naryx and the countryside of Lokris. How had this slipped his mind? When he reached his house, he quickly sent a manservant to the temple to find out whose daughters had been chosen for the yearly ritual.

Some time later, when the servant returned with the report of the two names drawn, Klonios sat for a moment, stunned. *It couldn't be.* Then he leapt up. The servant looked astonished when a huge bronze tripod came hurtling at his head. Ducking barely in time to avoid having his skull crushed, he fell to his knees and begged, "Master, with your leave—"

"Go!" Klonios snarled. Without waiting to see the creature crawl from his presence, he slung his mantle over his shoulder and stormed out of the house.

Thrasios, working on his accounts in the warehouse, knew nothing until Klonios burst into his counting room like an angry bull. Thrasios jumped to his feet.

"Deceiver!" Klonios bellowed. "Your vow meant *nothing!*"

"W–what?" stammered Thrasios.

"Don't tell me you don't know! Your daughter—chosen by the priestess for a long journey to Troy."

Thrasios went cold all over and for several heartbeats couldn't breathe. *The Choosing! It was today*, he remembered. The High Priestess had reached into his household and taken his daughter. With the girl no longer his to rule, his power over his family was undermined. He lowered his eyes quickly and for long moments was speechless. Then at last he sputtered, "I didn't know. I—I forgot. How could I have—"

"Silence!" roared Klonios. His fists clenched. His eyes shot flames. He turned and paced. "Who else knows that we spoke of a betrothal?"

"No one," whispered Thrasios.

"I won't be a laughingstock." Klonios stopped before the table and snatched up a goblet, which Thrasios hastened to fill. "She'll be gone for how long? A year? Then she'll return?"

"Aye. If she survives."

Klonios gave his mask-like smile. "Then I'll wed her in a year. Just as we planned."

Thrasios swallowed hard. "The rules of this—this rite we perform for the goddess demand that, once chosen, the girls belong to Athena. They must remain maidens all their days."

Klonios's eyes narrowed dangerously. "I care nothing for the rules. They were made by men. They can be changed."

Thrasios shook his head, forced himself to say, "This pact between the Hundred Houses and the goddess has been in place for untold generations. Since my daughter has been chosen, I am honor-bound to uphold that choice."

"Honor!" Klonios spat. "Say rather *fear*."

"We can't displease the goddess," Thrasios said pleadingly. "As a consequence of her wrath, we risk—"

"What? Drought? Famine? As she sent us before? I don't fear these things. They won't ruin me. I've holdings all around the Great Sea." His mouth twisted scornfully. "Out of all the wine-makers I chose *you* for my partner—and my future father-in-law. You—the most weak-kneed man in Lokris."

"I–I— It wasn't my fault." It came out almost as a whimper.

"Oath breaker! You've betrayed me." Spittle flew from Klonios' mouth. "You knew it could happen! I *will* have your daughter—with the goddess's will or without it! And for the lying promise you gave me this day, I will destroy you!" He stood still, letting the words sink in. Then he upended the table and sent it crashing to the floor.

Thrasios' eyes fell away. "The wine—the amphorae are ready for you." He silently cursed the beseeching note in his voice. "Ready to be shipped." *Please, Zeus and Dionysius, god of the vine,* he thought. *I'll be impoverished if he doesn't take them.*

"I'll send my men for the amphorae." Klonios turned and strode out. Thrasios stared after him, sick with dismay.

*Curse Thrasios! I had what I wanted from him—and now this! Curse the whole city of Naryx for continuing this whole damnable yearly ritual!* Klonios raged. As he went toward the door, he viciously kicked at objects that lay in his way.

He came upon a slave carefully stacking piles of empty wineskins. He kicked the pile, scattering wineskins all over the warehouse floor. The slave looked at him in distress. "Sir, you—" Then, seeing Klonios's eyes, he changed his mind about whatever he had been about to say. He hastily bent down and began to pick up the wineskins.

Klonios was wearing heavy, hard-toed sandals. Waiting until the slave straightened, he launched a vicious kick at his shin with all the force of his rage.

The slave fell to the ground with a muted groan. The sound gave Klonios a small measure of satisfaction as he strode outside.

He did not return to the warehouse. He sent his workers with wagons to collect the amphorae and take them to his ship.

He had no intention of paying for them.

17

# V

## PREPARATION

Marpessa had never been so miserable. With Haleia next to her, she sat wet and shivering on a stone bench within the temple precincts. Inside she was numb. They had just undergone the rite of purification, which meant having icy water poured all over them, their hair washed, their skin scrubbed and scraped with pumice. Then, with all the priestesses in the temple as witnesses, they had knelt naked before the altar of Athena and sworn the sacred oath of obedience to the goddess. Marpessa could still feel the cold flagstones pressing into her knees and hear the words issuing from her mouth, her voice strange and unreal as she repeated after the High Priestess: "I swear to dedicate my body and soul to the goddess from now until death, and to obey her every wish and command." Now, wrapped only in a large white cloth, their drenched hair tumbled down their backs, they sat where they had been told to wait.

Marpessa shook her wet hair and attempted a laugh. It came out as a choking sound, more like a sob. She held up her reddened arms. "That pumice hurt. If they purify us any more, I won't have any skin left!"

Haleia nodded in agreement. "And this is only the beginning," she said. "Next the priestesses will examine us to make sure we are pure. To see if we are maidens."

Marpessa shivered. Her mother had not told her of this, but the servants had. "I've heard the test is very unpleasant." Then, determined to lift the older girl's spirits, she said, "Never mind! We'll face many hardships, but we'll endure. And in a year, with the will of the gods, we will return."

"If we survive!" With a shuddering sigh, Haleia gave in to weeping.

Marpessa reached for her hand and clasped it hard for a moment. "Of course we'll survive! We'll have skillful sailors and capable guides who—"

But Haleia raised her head to interrupt. "When we reach the Trojan shore, we're considered a defilement. Before we reach the temple they will try to—to kill us." Her voice fell to an almost inaudible mutter.

"Kill?" Marpessa breathed, thinking she must have misheard, but Haleia shook her head. "I don't want to talk of it, or I'll never be able to keep my courage up." She straightened and tried to smile. "I'm sure you're right. The guides will protect us. They must." She wiped her eyes on the edge of the cloth that wrapped her. "My mother is very frail and counts on me to look after all the little ones."

"I know," Marpessa said. "You're the oldest, aren't you?" She put her arm around Haleia's shoulders, but this brought on fresh tears.

"Why did I have to be chosen?" Haleia asked in a broken whisper.

Marpessa had no answer. She echoed the question in silence. *Why me?*

But swift upon that thought came another question. *Why not me? I come from a proud family, one of the Hundred Houses who willingly undertook this sacrifice to save Lokris. Why should I shirk from this duty? I'm young, I'm strong, and I can keep my wits about me.*

Haleia was bent so that her damp hair completely covered her face. Marpessa brushed that hair back comfortingly out of the other girl's eyes. *I'll help her,* she thought. *I'll be strong for both of us.* Aloud she said, "We're setting out on an adventure, like the heroes of old." But the words sounded hollow to her own ears.

Later the High Priestess sent the chosen girls home, along with a message to the two households telling them to prepare for the journey. When she received it, Amaltheia summoned Thrasios and their three older sons to meet after the evening meal. Now, the meal having been cleared away, the family gathered around the hearth, where the fire had burned down to glowing coals. The servants had lighted lamps and set them on the low tables before departing. As Amaltheia studied the faces of her family in the dim, flickering light, she thought how strange it was to be together like this. Indeed it had never happened before.

Thrasios sat in his great chair. Though he was silent, it was clear that he was in a towering fury. His glare shot from one face to another, boring hardest into Marpessa, as if this were her fault. Even after all their years of marriage, Amaltheia still feared his unpredictable moods and rages. When his furious gaze came to rest on her, she dropped her eyes. Then her own anger flared. *All my life I've never been good enough for him,* she thought. *Nor has Marpessa. But how dare he be angry now?*

She looked at her daughter, who sat between them. As if clinging to the comfort of her childhood, Marpessa wore a faded, outgrown gown that came

19

only to her ankles. Yet something in the girl had changed since this morning. She seemed composed, less like a child. Her calm gray-green eyes met Amaltheia's, and she gave a small smile. That smile did not reassure her mother. Instead it made her sad, as though her daughter were already flown far away from her, never to return.

Amaltheia looked past Marpessa to her three sons, who sat to the left of Thrasios. She felt a surge of pride. Leukos and Mydon, both tall and lean with dark beards, had wives and had come from their households on the northern edge of the vineyards to take part in this meeting. Diores, the youngest son, curly-haired, smiling, and handsome, was twenty-four, unmarried, and still lived in the house of Thrasios.

After Eumene handed around warmed wine and withdrew, the family sat still, waiting. Thrasios continued to glower. Leukos, the eldest, opened his lips to speak, but at the same instant Marpessa shot forward in her chair and broke the silence.

"We should be proud," she said, looking right at her father, defying his anger. "The Hundred Houses have been making this sacrifice for generations, and now it has fallen to *us*. It is an honor. I accept it willingly."

Diores waved a mocking hand. "A fine speech, little sister!"

"Be silent, Diores!" Thrasios growled. "You cannot know what a disaster this is for our house." The others all stared at him in surprise, but he did not explain. He swung in his chair to face Marpessa. The look in his eyes could have melted iron in the forge. "What provisions must be made for the journey?"

Marpessa clutched her hands together. "A ship will be provided. I need the clothes I will travel in, but when I am there I will need nothing. In the temple of Athena I am to wear one garment, the robe of a slave, and go barefoot, my head shaved."

Amaltheia gave a stifled gasp. Thrasios, ignoring her, said, "This ship. Are we to send a crew? Slaves?"

"Nay, Father. It is the ship that goes every year. There are to be two guides to take us from the shore to Troy." Amaltheia tensed, wondering if Marpessa knew how perilous this part of the journey would be. But the girl gave no sign of it as she continued, "They should be men who know the country well and can get us there safely, but—" She paused and swallowed hard.

Impatiently, Thrasios stared at Marpessa. "But what?" he snapped.

"Two experienced men have served as guides for years, but this year one of them died in a hunting accident. And the other—" Marpessa hesitated. Amaltheia found she was holding her breath.

"Speak, girl!" her father ordered. "What of this other?"

"Well, he's old, Father. More than your years, but not strong like you. His back is bent and his legs are frail. The High Priestess says that we must find another guide to go with him. One who knows the country. Or at least one who is strong and able. And Haleia's family—they have no one. She is the oldest, her brothers are all too young, her father cannot leave, they have no slaves, and—" Her voice trailed into silence.

Thrasios scrubbed a hand through his already-disheveled gray hair. Then he said, the words pulled from him, "Well, we have a slave or two who might be spared. Though the timing couldn't be worse."

"*A slave?*" Amaltheia burst out. "What of our sons! Marpessa must be protected. Surely Leukos or Mydon could go. Or Diores."

"Silence, woman!" Thrasios slammed his fist into the arm of his chair so hard that she winced. "I can't spare my sons from the vineyards at this time! And I won't have them risking their necks."

Amaltheia met his eyes. "Not even to keep Marpessa safe?" she challenged.

Thrasios turned the full force of his venomous rage on her. "This is a useless venture! Worse than useless. I will not waste one valuable life."

*And Marpessa's life isn't valuable?* Amaltheia felt hatred growing within her, bitter and cold as steel. Her body shook with the strength of it. She shot Thrasios a look, wishing it could wound him with its force, but he turned away and did not even seem to notice. As they all sat in silence, not one of the men looked at her. She sank back in helpless fury, tightening her clasped hands until the knuckles ached.

When the silence seemed to become too weighty even for Thrasios, he said reluctantly, "There's that slave we have. The one from Ionia. He must know his way around, since Ionia is not far from Troy. He's a hard worker, but I suppose I could spare him for a little while."

Amaltheia felt sick. Over the years several maidens had been lost, though most had lived. But how would Marpessa survive with only a crippled old man and a slave to protect her? She could hardly look at Thrasios. "Which one is he?" she asked.

"Arion," Thrasios said shortly. Amaltheia had a vague image of a tall, brown-haired young man she had occasionally seen working in the warehouse or the vineyards, but she had no memory of his face.

Leukos made a scornful noise. "That one? He doesn't know anything! He's sullen, contentious, cares only for himself. Why, he'd murder us all in our sleep if he thought it would win him his freedom!"

Thrasios narrowed his eyes. "Be silent, Leukos. You're exaggerating as usual and frightening your mother needlessly. It's Arion, or no one."

# VI

## THE SLAVE

The next morning, Leukos walked through the vineyards to the edge of the woods, where he came upon a small shack. The slave Arion lived here. Leukos opened the door, looked in. Empty. He glanced around, then walked a few paces into the woods where the trees were still spaced apart, and the sunlight shone through, dappled with leaf shadows. But Leukos was in no mood to appreciate the beauty of the morning.

"Arion!" he shouted.

After a pause a reluctant voice answered, "Here." There was a thrashing of leaves and branches, and Arion appeared from behind a thicket, carrying a cloth sack. Leukos stared at him in silence, noting the large ugly bruise just below the slave's knee. He wondered what foolishness the slave had done to get that bruise.

Arion was tall, almost as tall as Leukos himself and somewhat broader in the chest and shoulders. He wore the plain tunic of a slave. His beard was short, and his unruly brown hair was held off his brow with a thin strip of dark red cloth. His eyes, the same oak brown as his hair, held Leukos' gaze with an expression that reminded Leukos of a stag—a mixture of fearlessness and subtle menace. *Feral* was the word that came into Leukos's mind. Arion waited for Leukos to state his business. Not overtly defiant, he refused to be subservient. And it rankled. *He's a slave*, Leukos reminded himself.

"What's in that bag?" he demanded.

Arion gave a slight shrug, continued staring with that stag gaze, and made no answer. His thoughts were as clear as if he had said aloud: *It's not your business.*

Leukos backed away from a confrontation he feared he wouldn't win. "My father sent me to tell you," he began, "that his daughter Marpessa was chosen to go to the temple of Athena at Troy. The ship sails in four days. You're to be one of the escorts to guide the maidens to Troy."

Not a muscle of Arion's face moved, but his eyes registered surprise. "I know nothing of Troy."

"You came from Ionia."

"Nowhere near Troy. And I was only a boy when I was sold into slavery." Arion frowned. "I understand the girls' lives are forfeit on their way to the temple. She's your sister. Why don't *you* go?"

*How dare he?* A burst of fury sent the blood rushing to Leukos' face. "I'm needed here. My father has decided he can spare *you*. So that's the end of it." He turned abruptly and walked away.

After Leukos left, Arion stood still, his arms fallen to his sides. Then he lifted the sack, stared at it, shook it futilely. Just like that, his masters could change the course of his life. He crossed the clearing to his hut, went in, and closed the door hard.

As his eyes adjusted to the dimness, he went to the rough table and dumped out the contents of the sack: wild mushrooms. He'd found a place where they grew in plenty and had barely started gathering them when Leukos appeared. *The Furies take him, and his father and brothers too!* Arion thought angrily. He looked down at the meager harvest. If he could have collected the lot of them, they would have fetched a goodly amount in the marketplace for some rich man's table. Now Arion wondered if there was any point in going back to finish the harvest. In a short while he would be expected to work in the vineyard.

Arion pushed his pallet aside and dropped to his knees behind it. He scraped away the loosened dirt that hid a sack with his small store of silver and copper pieces that he had been earning whenever he could over the years. What a pitiful handful he had saved! By the time he had enough to buy his freedom, he would probably be an old man, too old to earn his own living.

Arion replaced the sack, shoved the bed back against the wall, and sat down on it. *Thrasios's daughter.* He had barely been aware that Thrasios had a daughter. He'd seen her a few times with her mother when the lady Amaltheia visited the warehouse on some errand. He tried to remember what the girl looked like: a slender young thing with a springy stride. Arion was surprised that she'd been chosen in the drawing. He'd thought she was too young. But then, he had not seen her for some time.

Because of her, his whole life had just been turned upside down. Arion had not left this place, these fields and vineyards since he'd been brought here as a boy. He could barely remember his home in Ionia. His mother had been a widow with several children and no means of sustenance. When she became ill unto death and they were all in danger of starving, she had no choice but to sell them as slaves to the Lokrian and Boethian merchants who came periodically in ships to Ionia.

Arion, the youngest, had been seven. Terrified and lonely, he learned not to show it. Nobody cared. For much of the journey by ship he'd clung to the rail in utter misery. He didn't know if he was more seasick or homesick. At the journey's end he was sold to an old man and his wife to wait on them and help around the house. Easy work, and they were not unkind. When his master died several years later, the destitute widow sold him to Thrasios, who was seeking another worker for his prosperous wine business.

Now he was twenty-three or twenty-four, he calculated. And all he owned was this meager pile of precious metal scraps, a tiny portion of what he needed to buy his freedom.

Perhaps this could all be turned to good account. He did not yet see how, but an idea might come to him.

It was time to report to Thrasios for work. Arion stood up and walked thoughtfully out of the hut. He never contemplated escape because most slaves who escaped were caught, punished, often branded or maimed to prevent a recurrence. Or sometimes put to death.

But...*a sea journey*. It would take what? Seven or eight days? Many more than that if seas were rough or the winds unfavorable. Sea travel was perilous, and many things could happen. He smiled bitterly to himself.

Perhaps the slave Arion would somehow be lost at sea, never to return.

A stone was crushing Amaltheia's heart, pressing on her day and night, stealing her breath. The weight of it grew more unbearable as the hour approached. Now she stood with the crowd outside the temple, waiting. Marpessa and the other girl had gone in there hours ago for the final consecration, then the ceremony of adornment, the giving of gifts. For the two maidens would be sent forth as brides to a wedding.

Outside the temple were four horse-drawn wagons that were being made ready for the trip to the port where the ship awaited. Men were piling the wagons with goods for the journey. The slave Arion was helping load supplies along with Gortys, the other escort, a strongly built but stooped man with a wrinkled face and gray hair. Also accompanying them were two middle-aged priestesses who would chaperone the maidens to ensure that every part of the ritual was carried out according to the goddess's will.

Once Marpessa emerged from the temple, there would be time only for a farewell embrace. Then the journey would begin. A sigh burst from Amaltheia, and her lungs hurt with it. A timid hand touched her elbow. Amaltheia half-turned. She had forgotten Eumene at her side. Now she squeezed the older woman's hand in acknowledgement, but her thoughts were far away, thinking of last night when she had been awakened by the soft pad of Marpessa's bare feet. After looking to make certain Thrasios wasn't there, she crawled into her mother's bed. *You curled yourself into my arms,* Amaltheia remembered, *as you used to when you were a little girl awakened by a nightmare. Neither of us spoke. As I held you, I relived your childhood so swiftly gone. In comforting you, in caring for you, in drying the tears you shed over small sorrows, I was the one who was comforted.* Amaltheia's weeping had surged up like a burning tide, yet she held it back, squeezing her eyes shut. *How can I ever let you go?*

Suddenly there was a blare of trumpets from the temple guards who stood on each side of the double doors that led to the inner precinct. Amaltheia started. All at once she couldn't breathe. *So soon.* Her knees shook and threatened to give way. She willed strength into them.

*A few more precious moments only. I must not burden her with my grief. When she is gone, I can weep.*

Marpessa and the other girl came out, led by the High Priestess. They halted at the top of the temple steps. The High Priestess lifted her arms.

"Behold our gift, the maidens Lokris sends forth consecrated to Athena! They go with our blessing, and they bring the good will of the goddess to our land."

The crowd cheered. Amaltheia stared, barely able to recognize her daughter. Both girls wore long flowing robes with loosely draping sleeves. Each had a gossamer veil concealing her face and hair. The veil was held in place by a crown of wildflowers and hung almost to the knees. Amaltheia could not see Marpessa's face, but the girl's back was straight, her head held high. The other girl, Haleia, drooped, her chin sunk on her chest. Both girls were adorned with necklaces of gold and gemstones—like brides. *A mockery, a sham,* Amaltheia thought savagely. Marriage was a woman's lot, but these two were not granted this right. The gold, the gems, the fancy gowns, all would be taken from them soon, along with their hopes of a normal life—or perhaps any life at all. Amaltheia knew her thoughts were blasphemy, but she could not help them.

"Make way! Make way!" shouted the High Priestess, and as the crowd parted, she led the girls down the steps toward the wagon that awaited them. Amaltheia knew that this was the only moment she was allowed. She rushed forward and caught Marpessa in her arms.

"My love, my little one!" she whispered.

"Mother!" Marpessa hugged her. A tremor ran through Amaltheia's body. "Mother, you mustn't weep. Be strong for me. Give me your strength."

Amaltheia forced back the tears. "Very well, my darling!" She held her daughter a bit apart and lifted the veil so that she could look one last time at the beloved face. She managed a feat greater than all the labors of Herakles: a smile, though her eyes were wet. "Marpessa, my strength is yours, and my love goes with you always."

Marpessa smiled back, a heartbreaking smile. "I will return, Mother, if the gods will it."

That was all the time they had. The High Priestess drew the two girls from their mothers' arms and ushered them away. Marpessa managed a quick kiss on Eumene's withered cheek, a last brave smile at her mother. Then she climbed into the waiting wagon.

Before the cavalcade could leave, Amaltheia moved quickly. She had another important errand. She sought out the slave Arion, who was still helping to load the supply wagon.

"Arion! Come here. A moment, please."

He glanced her way, handed up the water jar he was holding, and came toward her. He looked different from the slave she had seen laboring in the vineyards, as if this errand had given him dignity and importance. Someone had provided him with a better tunic, of finely woven dark red wool. A wide leather belt encircled his waist.

"My lady?" he inquired.

She looked up into his brown eyes: impassive, nothing to be read in them. She gripped his arm. "Take care of her!" she whispered fiercely. "Make sure no one harms her while she is in your care." *Don't let them kill her.* But she dared not say the words aloud. She reached quickly into her girdle and pulled out three heavy silver pieces saved over many years from her dowry. She held them out to him. "These are all I have, but they're yours," she said. "Protect her well. Promise me!"

Arion's eyes widened. His hand covered hers in a quick movement as he took the silver. "Thanks, my lady. I'll do my best."

"If —" Amaltheia's voice quavered. "If she comes home safely in a year's time, I will contrive to secure your freedom."

Arion merely looked at her. Nothing moved in his face. She felt a fool for having spoken thus. What she promised was impossible, for they both knew that, as a woman, she had few more rights than he, and no say in how Thrasios handled his business, his property. Arion's eyes softened into an expression of pity. He opened his mouth to speak, but there was a whistle, a shout. The wagon convoy was about to start moving. He gave Amaltheia a quick nod, then ran to climb into the supply wagon.

Amaltheia hurried back to the wagon that held Marpessa. The girl was standing, her veil thrown back so that Amaltheia could see the smile held firmly on her lips. Marpessa lifted her hand and waved as the wagon rolled forward. Their eyes remained locked, Marpessa turning her head to keep her mother in her sight. Amaltheia watched the wagon grow smaller and smaller in the distance, the golden sunlight washed in a bath of tears.

Slightly apart from the crowd, Klonios was standing in the shadow of the statue of Zeus so that he could watch the maidens' departure unseen. While he waited for them to appear, he unobtrusively observed the faces around him. Some onlookers were avidly curious, others impassive, preoccupied with their own lives. People were transparent to him, but none noticed him, and none would ever guess *his* thoughts and plans. Klonios smiled to himself. It was the eve of his departure, and he looked forward to this trading journey as well as one or two more he planned to take this year, the time during which the girl would be gone, serving the goddess. The year would go by fast, he was sure.

When the trumpets announced the presence of the girls, he saw them come forth from the temple swathed in veils. He had no trouble discerning which one was Thrasios's daughter. Aside from her slighter stature, there was a grace and fluidity to her movements. Inflamed with lust, he imagined the youthful body hidden beneath that voluminous gown. He watched her climb into the wagon, never taking his eyes off her until the cavalcade rolled down the road and out of sight.

*My sweet bride!* he thought. *I'll be waiting when you return.*

# VII

## THE JOURNEY BEGINS

Marpessa kept her head up and her back straight until the wagon rounded a curve in the road and her mother could not longer see her. She felt tears coming and fought them so fiercely that her throat clogged and her eyes burned. Barely aware of the clopping of the horses' hooves, the bumping of the solid wooden wheels over ruts in the road, or the girl next to her patting her shoulder timidly as the convoy of wagons made its way to the shore, she slumped in the seat and pressed her hands over her eyes, while deep, silent sobs shook her, all the stronger for her efforts to hold them back. After a time, she felt the comfort of Haleia's hand and lifted her head. Both girls had discarded their veils and crowns of flowers. In Haleia's clear hazel eyes Marpessa saw a reflection of her own pain.

She knuckled away the last of her tears and smiled sheepishly. "I don't cry often. I haven't cried since—since the drawing," she explained.

"I've cried for the last five days." Haleia's eyes were red and swollen. "What will my young brothers and sister do without me?" Marpessa said nothing but took the other girl's hand in hers. Tears pooled in Haleia's eyes. Her head drooped forward, her lank dark hair falling like a curtain around her face. "The youngest, Pyrrhus, is a year old. He took his first step yesterday. I'm worried that I'll never see any of them again."

*They will try to kill us,* Haleia had said in the temple but then had refused to say more. *Death.* That she would cease to exist was unimaginable, yet so terrifying to Marpessa that it cut off her breath, squeezing sorrow to the furthest corner of her being. *Mother!* she cried in silence. *Did you know of this? And why didn't you tell me?*

When she could breathe again, she asked Haleia, "You said 'they' could kill us. Who? Why?"

"I—I don't know much," Haleia answered hastily. "Most girls survive, though, so it's likely we'll be safe. We have guides—the old man, Gortys, has been guiding the temple maidens for years, and that slave of your father's is young and strong."

But Gortys was so infirm he'd barely managed to clamber into the wagon.

As for the slave Arion, she hardly knew him. She had only seen him from a distance. This morning when she'd watched him load the wagon, his stolid face had been like a hand held up, palm out, to prevent anyone from approaching. Leukos didn't like him and thought him disloyal. The slave probably hadn't even wanted to come on this journey. This cold, distant man was now her only link to her home—and her only able-bodied protector. *He doesn't care what happens to us,* she guessed. It was a lonely and frightening thought.

For a time they bumped along in silence. Marpessa looked at the grassy hills, the olive trees with their silver-green leaves, the ancient gnarled oaks adorned in new green foliage, vibrant in the summer sun. But it all looked gray to her. She who loved wild creatures heard with indifference the clamor of birds hidden in the trees.

Suddenly Marpessa made a sound of disgust. *Stop it!* she told herself. Best not to dwell on something that might never happen. That would only serve to make her miserable. "We might have died at home," she said to Haleia, "stricken with some disease, or stung by a scorpion, or bitten by a snake. Any of us could die at any time."

"Is that meant to be comforting?" Haleia asked.

Marpessa shook her head. "We're going on an adventure, and there's honor to be gained. Like the heroes of old. Surely you've heard their stories? They did not know whether they would come back from their journeys. But they—" She paused, searched for the right word. "—embraced their fate."

*I will not be a coward,* she decided. *And I will make the most of each day.*

Immediately she began looking around, observing their surroundings, their traveling companions. Leading the convoy were two wagons that carried the sailors who would crew the ship. Third in line, directly in front of the girls, was the supply wagon with the two guides. In the girls' wagon, on the seat behind them, sat the two sour-faced priestesses who would accompany them as far as the Trojan shore. One was short and stout, with dust-colored hair and an upturned nose that she held high, as if everything was beneath her notice. Her name was Anteia. The other was thin, dark-haired with a small, prim mouth. Marpessa could not remember her name. The two women ignored the girls but made occasional comments to each other.

At long last the oak trees gave way to wind-shaped cypresses and pines. There was a salty tang on the breeze. Leaning forward, Marpessa sniffed. "The sea!" she said excitedly to Haleia. "I've never seen it before!" They rounded a curve, and there it was, a flat, blue-gray sheet of water reflecting the sun in blinding silver. She stood up, shading her eyes. As she stared at the boundless horizon, she could believe she was looking at the edge of the world.

A hand behind her grabbed her gown and jerked her to her seat. "Sit down!" Anteia snapped and struck her sharply on the arm. "You're a lady, not some rude peasant boy. A fine servant you'll make for the goddess if you don't learn manners!" Dismayed, Marpessa bit back the retort that sprang to her lips.

The wagon convoy drew to a halt near a small harbor surrounded by a few houses. At once she saw the ship, propped up by beams on the sides, its prow resting on the sand. Its stern rocked gently from the small waves that struck it. Until now Marpessa had only seen painted ships on the red clay amphorae at home. This ship was larger than she'd imagined. She was curious about how it would float.

The men jumped down from the wagons and formed a line to the ship. They began unloading amphorae, bundles, and chests, handing them along the line to be put in the depths of the ship. Two men led forward a dozen sheep and goats and carried them bleating aboard. Marpessa watched as they were lowered into the hold. At last the guides came to the women's wagon.

"We are ready to take you on board, ladies." Gortys extended a hand to Anteia, then the other priestess. Arion assisted Haleia, and Marpessa watched as the tall girl clambered down awkwardly.

Then Arion stood before her. Startled, she found herself looking into eyes as clear a brown as a stream pooling over fallen leaves. She couldn't read their expression. He reached up his hand to her, but to show him that she was agile and needed no help, she jumped down on her own from the high wagon. To soften her rejection, she smiled up at him. He said nothing, only turned away and followed Gortys to the shore.

A plank, with narrow wooden cleats nailed across it, rested against the side of the ship. Arion helped the priestesses climb up it to the ship, then Haleia. The footing was tricky, and the women moved slowly, clinging to his firm handhold. Then Gortys, who had climbed up first, led them across the gangway to the aft part of the ship, and it was Marpessa's turn to board. Arion made no move to help her. She set her foot on the plank and started in surprise as it moved beneath her. She glanced at him. The look in his eyes seemed to say, *Go ahead on your own, since you're so capable.*

But Marpessa was an adept tree-climber. She sprang up the plank and, without looking back, went to join the other women in the stern where a small area had been set aside for them: a square tent covered on four sides with undyed cloth, and two boards outside it that served as benches. As she sat down next to Haleia, Marpessa glanced at the tent in distaste. It looked hot and stuffy, barely large enough to stand in.

Arion went to sit near the fore. Marpessa saw the crew sitting on thwarts on either side of the ship, oars at the ready. The captain, a short, swarthy, grizzled man, stood on the foredeck. He lifted a large, two-handled libation cup.

"O Lord Poseidon, god of the deep, hear our prayer and grant us a safe journey!" he intoned. "Protect us and bring us safely across the Aegean Sea, that we may deliver these two maidens to Athena's service in Troy." He poured the dark wine into the waters of the harbor. Then he gave a sharp command, and the men on the shore shoved the ship off the sand until it floated free. "Start rowing, men! Pull! Together! Pull! Bring her about!" shouted the captain, and the ship swung around until it faced out to sea.

Someone began beating on a drum to keep the rowers in rhythm. The ship surged forward. Marpessa sat up in excitement, listening to the swish and splash of the oars in the water. As the men pulled and strained, the dock slipped away, and the land began to lose its features.

"Unfurl the sail!" the captain shouted.

Four men tugged on a series of ropes. With a creaking noise, the sail opened downward and billowed out in the wind. The men shipped their oars, and soon the only sound was the slap of waves as the hull cut through the water. The breeze tore at Marpessa's hair, whipping it around her face. The land behind them became no more than a wavy green line. On the far horizon she could see another line of land, faint and hazy. *The island of Euboea.* Until this moment it had only been a name her father mentioned when discussing his wine shipments. Now there it was. The whole world lay before her, deep blue water with a white foam wake swirling out behind. A few gulls floated on the wind behind them. The beauty of it all filled her soul.

*Mother, do not weep for me,* she thought. *If I had stayed all my life in Naryx, I would have never known this moment.*

Watching the land slip away, Arion drew a deep breath. How life had changed! No more harsh master. No more toil in vineyards and warehouse. Instead he would lend the sailors an eager hand and learn all he could of sailing and the lands they would see. So far neither captain nor crew had treated him like a slave. Perhaps they did not even know he was one.

His hand slipped furtively to his leather belt. Some of his hard-won silver had gone toward buying it. He had sewn a secure inner pocket to store his earnings, including the silver pieces given him by the lady Amaltheia this morning.

The thought of that precious metal gave him a pang of guilt. He planned to leave this expedition the instant it became possible. To slip away on the Trojan shore, or perhaps even earlier if the chance presented itself. To disappear. But the silver from Amaltheia seemed to burn against his skin. He remembered the pain on her face and thought of his own mother, forced by illness and poverty to give up her children. Even Amaltheia, rich and privileged, could not control her daughter's fate. Gortys had told him what danger lay ahead for the girls from the armed men on the Trojan shore.

"I've been doing this for a long time, and I've seen many girls killed in spite of all we could do," Gortys had said. "Then the Trojans drag the poor corpse off and burn it."

Arion didn't want to think what might happen to the girls. It would be better to leave their fate to Gortys, who had experience with this yearly mission, since he, Arion, had none. Even if he stayed with them and did his best to protect them, he might not succeed. He knew nothing of fighting or warfare.

And his own life would be at risk.

He stared at the horizon in bitter anger. No one ever worried about *his* fate. Yet he was expected to put the safety of these girls before his own. Well, he would not. He had his own plans.

With the wind steady, they made good speed. When the sun's rays slanted long and golden, the wind slackened. They had reached the channel between Euboea and the mainland. The helmsman guided the ship into a small cove where they would stay the night. There was no beach to run the ship up on, so the captain called, "Drop anchor!" Several sailors unwrapped a large log attached to a rope. It was so heavy it took four men to lift it and heave it over the side. Later Arion learned the log was hollowed out and weighted with lead.

The men began unloading provisions into a pair of skiffs, which they would ferry back and forth until all the men were ashore. As he climbed into a skiff, Arion saw Gortys speaking to the priestesses. The two girls remained sitting on their bench. "Have food sent on board for us," the dark-haired priestess said. "We'll spend our nights on the ship in the modesty and privacy of the pavilion."

Arion was glad not to have to bother with them. On the shore someone had kindled a blazing fire. The smell of grilling lamb filled his nostrils. The sailors beckoned him to join their circle around the fire. After eating, they told tales of their adventures and passed around a wineskin. As he drank with them, listened to their talk, and watched the sparks from the fire shoot up into the sky, Arion could almost believe he was already a free man.

With full bellies and wine warming their blood, the men settled down to sleep. But Arion thrashed restlessly where he lay under the stars. *Those girls.* Just as he was about to win back his freedom, those two were destined for slavery—if they were lucky enough not to be killed. An unwelcome thought came to him. Perhaps the hand of some god had put him here—and entwined his fate with theirs.

He pounded his fist into the soft dirt. *Never,* he told to himself. *I'll never return to slavery.*

# VIII

## CROSSING THE SEA

They were heading northeast, two days out of Euboea when they ran into rough seas. Gale winds pushed the ship broadside, tilting the deck, so that Arion had to grip hard on the rail. He spread his feet, struggling for balance. The waves were as big as hillocks. He was sure the ship would capsize. As the sailors rushed to the oars and brought the ship around, one of the men shouted to him, "Come help with the sail!" Struggling on the swaying gangway, Arion hurried to the ropes. He was glad that he had the knack of it now. And he added a fervent prayer: *Thank the gods I'm not seasick!*

From the corner of his eye, he saw the two priestesses and Haleia go white-faced into the tent. Marpessa watched them with a wicked grin. As soon as they were out of sight, she jumped up from her accustomed bench and went to the railing, leaning into the wind. With the sail now furled, Arion saw Gortys make his way to her across the heaving gangway. "Mistress, you should go inside now. It's not safe out here."

"Safe?" Marpessa scoffed. Clearly she was not prepared to move. "This trip is not safe! But I promise not to fall overboard."

Gortys flapped his hands helplessly and went back to his place near the stern. Arion turned away to hide his smile.

Marpessa loved the gale wind, the cold salt spray on her face. She felt a wild defiance. Poseidon, lord of the sea and shaker of the earth, was making his presence felt. Her ancestor Ajax had died at sea, scoffing at the gods. It was his sin that had brought her to this pass, yet for the first time she felt a kinship with his spirit.

She looked over her shoulder at the tent where the other three women had retired. She was sorry for Haleia's seasickness but glad to be free of the two priestesses. With their watchful, disapproving eyes on her every moment, she was forced to sit still on the bench, to modulate her voice, to behave with decorum, when all the while she wanted to explore the ship, to stand next to the men raising and lowering the sail so that she might learn its workings, to lean on the railing and watch the dolphins leaping in the ship's wake. When the ship anchored for the night, she wanted to go ashore to explore their new surroundings. Instead of being confined to the hot, stuffy tent, she wanted to eat and sleep under the night sky like the men.

A wave hit the ship with a force that made Marpessa lose her footing. Clinging to the rail for dear life, her heart thudding, she barely managed to regain her balance on the slanting beam where she stood. She glanced around quickly, but Gortys hadn't noticed. He was busy helping the man at the helm. The rest of the men rowed with furious effort toward the distant shore, fighting the seas and the wind, while the captain stood near the bow, searching for a sheltered place to drop anchor. The ship could make no headway in a gale of this force.

Marpessa saw that Arion had taken his place at an oar now that the sail was down. The muscles in his brown arms swelled and bunched. He rowed as strongly as any of the sailors. Out here he seemed a different man from the one she had seen laboring over the vats in her father's warehouse.

*He must be happy to have left all that behind,* she realized. *Though he is a slave, he now has far more freedom than I.*


It was just past noon when they found anchorage in a small sheltered cove to wait out the storm. The ship had sustained minor damage. Since Arion was handy with tools, the captain put him in charge of repairs. They were able to set out the next morning without having suffered much delay. Though the wind was now favorable, the seas were rough, and the three women were too weak and sick to come out of the tent. Arion knew this would make Marpessa happy. She had abandoned her sandals, and he saw her often at one rail or the other, or gazing outward near the bow or stern. The ship was not large; the captain ordered her sharply out of the way when the men were trimming the sail and told her to stay away from the helm, but otherwise, so long as she did not interfere with the eight pairs of oarsmen, she was allowed to roam freely from fore to aft along the gangway.

Arion had known very few girls or women, since they rarely ventured farther than their home or the market place. However, he began to suspect that Marpessa was different from most. She had the eyes of a young, wild hawk, restless eyes that ranged the seas and skies, taking in everything. Those eyes spoke to his spirit.

36

A day or so after the storm, one of the gulls that followed their ship became tangled in the ropes that held the sail to the spar, high above the deck. It flapped wildly but could not get free. Its foot had caught in one of the bronze rings through which the ropes were looped.

For a frozen moment the eyes of all the men were on the bird as it flapped and struggled.

"It'll get hurt!" Marpessa cried.

One of the men scrambled below, coming back with a hunting bow. "Best get rid of it now." He nocked an arrow and took aim.

*"No!"* The cry came from Marpessa. Before any could stop her, she kilted up her skirts and began climbing the mast, nimble as a squirrel.

"Stop! Come back!" It was Gortys, but she paid him no heed. The captain made a quick gesture in the direction of the man with the bow, and he lowered it. Arion held his breath. He had a swift, flashing glimpse of her slim legs, muscled like a boy's, as she pulled herself up. No one spoke, no one moved. She was now high up on the mast, which was swaying back and forth in a wide arc as the ship dipped and rose in swells. For a heart-stopping moment she froze, several arm lengths from the spar. The gull, which seemed to have given up, drooped limply. The captain took a few steps along the gangway to stand just beneath her.

"Come down," he called softly. "Just back down. I'll catch you if you slip."

Marpessa made no reply. She began to creep upward again, a hand, then a foot, until at last she reached the gull. She made soft crooning noises to it as she swung herself over the spar and gripped the beam with her legs. Leaning forward, she reached one hand to grasp the gull's foot. Gently she eased it out of the ring.

The gull flapped its wings furiously, then suddenly realized it was free and soared into the air. As Marpessa watched its flight, Arion saw her exultant smile. His heart lifted in response. After a moment she let herself slowly down the mast. When her feet touched the gangway, Arion took a deep, painful breath, realizing that his throat had been caught in a knot.

The captain descended on her angrily. "Why did you do that? You could have killed yourself!"

Marpessa looked up into his eyes. "It had a chance to be free—to live. Besides, it was brown."

"Brown?" the captain asked, mystified.

"It was a young gull," she told him.

All the men were staring at her, but Arion turned aside. Along the horizon ahead, a thin dark line of land was barely perceptible. The shore of Troy, the captain had said. Their goal was now in sight.

Arion lowered his head, tasting shame. Death might lie just ahead for this brave girl. And the other one. While he, cravenly, sought his own escape.

Then he straightened, filled with resolve. When those girls stepped on shore, he would go with them. He would protect them as best as he was able. Whatever it took, he would make sure they arrived safely inside the walls of Troy. Until then, he would think no more of his own escape.

# IX

## THE LANDING

The following afternoon, the ship reached the island of Tenedos just off the coast of Troy and anchored there. As she leaned against the rail looking at the island that blocked most of the mainland from her view, Marpessa mourned the end of the sea voyage. The crew had come to seem like family. They had teased her and smiled with affection in the carefree days when she had wandered among them unsupervised. The captain had become a doting uncle. He came to stand next to her now.

"A tiny island." He gestured at Tenedos. "It's shaped like a triangle. This is the very spot where the Greeks hid their fleet from the mainland when the Trojan horse was being dragged into the city, just before the sack of Troy." He turned to her with a smile, but his words reminded her of her ancestor Ajax and the reason she was here. A queasy dread crept into her belly. Soon she and Haleia would be on their way to that hostile citadel. She would even miss company of the sour priestesses.

At that moment, Anteia called her name and beckoned to her from the tent. It was time to prepare. With a nod at the captain, Marpessa went reluctantly along the gangway and stepped into the darkness of the women's quarters.

After she disappeared inside, Arion and Gortys went to the foredeck where they stood staring at the island and the mainland beyond.

"This is where we always stop," Gortys said. "We can't be seen from the mainland. It's a good place to wait while the girls are being prepared in keeping with the ritual." He gestured toward the tent. Arion followed his gaze but could see only the closed tent flaps. He was not sure what the ritual involved. Nor was he concerned with it at this moment, for Gortys said, "Our real work begins now."

Arion leaned forward, grasping the rail, tensing his muscles. He hoped he was ready.

Gortys gestured in the direction of the mainland. "We must go in at night. It's part of the ritual and the only hope we have of avoiding the Trojans. They'll be expecting us, and there'll be groups of them on the watch for us. So we land under the cover of darkness."

As the picture formed in his mind, Arion asked, "How will we find our way? Can we light a lamp?"

Gortys shook his head. "It would be seen immediately. I know the countryside, and we'll find our way by moonlight. He pointed to the land northward of the ship. "We must round that point and go in at the place called Rhoeteum. Again, it's demanded by the ritual. But the shore is barren and there's not much cover. Just some shrubs and a few rocky outcroppings."

Arion was aghast. "And they know we'll land there?"

Gortys shrugged. "It has always been thus."

"Then they're waiting for us. We'll be walking into a trap."

Gortys shook his head. "There are many places to make land on that shore. And they don't know exactly what day we're coming in, nor what time."

*It's very chancy,* Arion worried. Still, Gortys had been a guide for many years, and no doubt he knew the best way to evade the Trojans.

"Moonrise will be several hours after sunset," Gortys said. "We'll wait until then. The ship will bring us close enough to launch a skiff, and with luck we can bring the girls in without being seen."

"A skiff?" In the moonlight they would be in plain sight of the shore for the time it took to row in. "Can't the girls swim?"

Gortys looked at him as if he had taken leave of his senses. "Girls can't swim."

Arion checked an angry retort and turned away. He had learned to swim as a small child in the streams of his home, before his slavery. It was a necessary part of survival. If they could have swum ashore, they could have made land completely unseen. *Why hadn't the girls been better prepared for this?*

Inside the tent, the priestesses made Marpessa and Haleia discard their gowns. They poured spring water over the girls' naked bodies. Marpessa tried not to flinch. She gritted her teeth as the dark-haired priestess, with rough, vigorous strokes, passed a wet cloth along her belly, down her back, and between her legs. Anteia was doing the same to Haleia.

Then Anteia opened a chest and took out a sharp blade to cut Haleia's hair. Marpessa watched piles of dark brown hair falling to the floorboards. The knife scraped close to Haleia's scalp, and Marpessa could see white patches of skin through the sparse hair that remained. When the priestess finished, Haleia looked like a bald boy. Marpessa suppressed a shiver when Anteia began hacking off her hair. She watched the pile growing on the floor—a lighter brown than Haleia's, with a sheen of burnished gold from the sun. Haleia looked at her with an expression of horror. They were allowed no mirrors, but each girl could imagine her own reflection in the other.

The dark-haired priestess drew out of the chest a pair of loose, coarsely woven gowns. "You must wear these, and nothing else," she said. "No girdles or sashes. You may keep your sandals for the trip to the citadel. But once you reach the temple, you must discard them and bury them. When you are there, you are to be barefoot always."

"Now you are ready," Anteia said, but Marpessa felt far from ready. "Go on deck—the captain will offer a libation to the gods. Then we wait for his orders. The ship won't approach the landing place until moonrise, so you may as well rest."

Marpessa drew a deep breath, willed her knees to stop trembling, and stepped out of the tent. At that moment Arion and Gortys, standing on the foredeck, turned. She saw the shock register in Arion's eyes.

Arion forced himself to look away. To stare at the girls was to share in their shame. Marpessa looked particularly small, pale, and defenseless with her naked head. Arion did not want to think about the dangerous journey and the eventual abandonment that lay ahead for her and Haleia.

The sun was setting, dropping into the sea in a fiery glow. The captain called for his two-handled libation cup to be filled with wine and brought to him. Lifting it over the side of the ship, he cried out, "O Father Zeus, Athena, Apollo! We come before you from across the sea to bring these two maidens to the temple of Troy. Accept their servitude and grant success to our mission, and safety to Lokris for one more year!" He poured the wine into the sea.

As twilight deepened, one of the sailors came up from the galley and handed round baskets of bread and meat. As Arion joined the other men who sat on the thwarts to eat, the mood on the ship was somber and silent. The ordeal that lay ahead for the maidens hung like a pall over everyone. When the meal was finished, Gortys said to Arion, "Now comes the hard part. Waiting." He settled himself along a thwart, his feet up and his head resting against the rail. He closed his eyes, then opened them to say, "You might as well rest while you can. It's going to be a long night."

Arion awoke with a start. Moonlight silvered the eastern sky, and he heard Gortys say to the captain, "We should set out for Rhoeteum now that there's enough light to steer the ship."

The captain called for the men to pull up anchor. Arion got to his feet and glanced toward the tent where the girls had gone to rest. The flap parted, and one of the priestesses looked out questioningly. "We're on our way," Arion told her. "Perhaps you should awaken the girls."

As the men took their places at the oars, nobody spoke. It seemed as if nobody breathed. The sea was calm, the air still, and the men made an effort to slip their oars soundlessly into the water. The ship glided around the northern tip of Tenedos. The mainland was still far away, a long black shape slightly humped above the dark glow of the sea. Arion could see no lights, no ships, nothing moving, but he feared they would soon become all too visible to any hidden watchers.

Gortys glanced at the helmsman and pointed northeast, to the point of land around which they must navigate. The oarsmen pulled with silent strength, and for a long time there was no sound but the creaking of the oars and the soft, rhythmic splash of the blades as they sliced the water. The ship angled in on a long northward diagonal that would take it close to the shore. Arion, leaning into the prow, felt every muscle and sinew in his body stretched unbearably tight.

Suddenly the helmsman, his voice loud in the dark, said, "Level with the tip of the cape."

The captain called out, "Bear to starboard!"

"What are we doing?" Arion asked Gortys.

"We're pushing in as close as we can. Then we go ashore in the skiff."

The oarsmen on the left rowed furiously, and the ship turned slowly toward the land on the right.

"No! Tell them to go straight!" shouted Arion.

Everyone looked at him with surprise, the rowers with their oars poised at the apex.

"Keep rowing north," he urged the captain, "only parallel to the mainland past the point. Pause just long enough to let us to launch the skiff on the seaward side. We can row in from here with less chance of being seen."

Gortys said, "It's a good plan."

"A decoy!" the captain agreed. "If they're watching, they might not know it's us." He gave the order to the rowers, and the boat swung northward again until at last the captain called a halt. The rowers paused, and there was a splash as two sailors dropped the skiff into the sea. Arion and Gortys made their way to the stern, where the girls and the two priestesses waited.

Gortys straddled the rail with difficulty and boarded, stowed some supplies, then reached up an encouraging hand toward the girls, while the two sailors kept the small boat moored to the side of the swaying ship. Arion saw at once that the difficulty would be in loading Haleia into the unsteady skiff. She clutched the ship's rail, frozen with fear, though the distance to the water was not great. At last Arion, impatient, jumped overboard. Treading water, he held the skiff steady and looked up at her.

"Easy now!" he encouraged her, much as he might have reassured a skittish horse. "Keep your weight near the center of the skiff. Then, when you're in, take a seat quickly." She clambered over the rail and stepped down, overbalancing, causing the boat to rock. In panic she took a misstep—and fell in.

The priestesses, watching from the side, screamed. "Hush!" Arion hissed at them. He steadied the rocking boat as he looked around for Haleia, but she had vanished in the dark sea.

There was another splash. *Marpessa.* Arion watched in horror. How could he save them both? Then he saw that she was swimming in quick, sure strokes to the place where Haleia had gone under. She dived and came up gripping the back of Haleia's gown, holding the girl's face above the water as she maneuvered her to the skiff.

Gortys hauled Haleia up, with Arion pushing, and she flopped into the boat like a large fish. Arion turned to help Marpessa, but she launched herself over the side into the skiff, leaving Arion to follow.

"All's well!" Gortys called to the captain. "Keep going north to divert them. We'll be on our way."

He and Arion hauled on the oars. Marpessa and Haleia sat opposite them, Haleia shivering and obviously frightened. Marpessa, equally cold and wet, clutched her arms about herself and rocked gently to warm herself.

Arion marveled at her quick action but said nothing. It was Gortys, almost accusatory, who asked, "How did you learn how to swim?"

"I taught myself. In the woodland streams near my home," she answered, still breathing hard. "I went there often. Alone."

Gortys gave his attention to rowing, and for a time no one spoke. Arion took deep slow breaths, letting the rhythm of rowing calm him.

*By the gods!* he thought. *We've barely started, and already we've almost lost one girl. How will we ever keep them safe?*

Marpessa huddled close to Haleia and looked toward the dark strip of land, still faint and hazy. Gortys said there would be Trojan men hidden in the darkness, men who wanted to kill them. A knot tightened in her throat. Next to her Haleia continued to shake. Marpessa put her arm around her and rubbed her shoulders. She wanted to reassure the other girl but was almost too frightened to speak. *I won't be a coward*, she reminded herself. To take her mind off her fear, she looked around at the others in the small boat, their faces outlined in moonlight. What an ill-assorted group they were! A slave, an old man, two bald girls. And three of the four were soaking wet! A half-hysterical giggle rose in her throat. She suppressed it, knowing how odd it would sound to her companions. Still, a small noise escaped her.

She felt rather than saw the gaze of Arion the slave, and glanced up. He had barely spoken to her on the sea journey, but now his eyes, black in the darkness, probed hers. She caught her breath in astonishment. She felt him look deep into her heart, her spirit. No man or woman had ever looked at her like that. She returned his look unflinchingly and found kindness there, understanding, and a profound respect. Even a kind of comfort, though there was no comfort in her fate.

Any words would have diminished what had passed between them, and Arion spoke none. After a moment he let his gaze slide away without ever breaking the rhythm of his rowing.

*I was wrong about him,* she thought wonderingly.

As they drew close to land, Gortys surrendered his oar to Arion and crept into the bow to search the darkness ahead. He whispered, "From now on we must be absolutely silent." He gave almost inaudible directions to Arion, who steered the skiff parallel to the shore, close in. Then at a signal from Gortys, Arion veered up a shallow stream. Marpessa heard the rough scrape of rocks along the bottom of the boat. Arion steered into some reeds and low, overhanging willows where they were completely hidden, blackness all around them. Gortys grabbed a branch to hold the boat still, and they sat not breathing. Listening. Moments passed that felt like hours. Marpessa heard no sound above the thud of her own heart.

At last, after an eternity, Gortys whispered, "All's well."

Arion slipped over the side and stood in knee-deep water, steadying the boat while Gortys climbed out. Marpessa followed, and she and Gortys helped Haleia. Arion secured the skiff with rope. He and Gortys slung small bundles with food and water onto their backs. Then, trying not to splash, they waded through reeds onto the shore.

"So far so good," whispered Gortys. "Follow me."

He led the way past reeds and mud to flat ground. Marpessa felt dirt, rocks, dry weeds under her feet. Gortys looked around. "No one," he whispered. Marpessa let out a sigh, realizing she'd been holding her breath. No Trojans—*yet.*

"This way." Gortys beckoned. "There's a stream we'll follow." Marpessa felt its sandy bottom as water swirled around her ankles. The brackish stream was wide and shallow where it flowed into the sea. She could make out the shapes of reeds and bushes, even some low-bending willows that grew along its banks. Gortys led the way, finding a path on one side, and the other three followed. The gibbous moon shone brightly above the low black hills in the east. As Gortys and Arion scanned their surroundings, Marpessa found herself staring at every shadow, every small movement. The little stream was peaceful. All was quiet save for their muted footsteps. But it could change in the blink of an eye.

After they had walked for perhaps an hour, Arion stopped suddenly. The others froze, listening. In the far distance Marpessa heard voices. A faint thrashing of branches, as though heavy footsteps plowed through them. Coming closer. An icy tingling swept through her. Her stomach sickened with fear.

"Quick!" Arion's command was no more than a breath. He steered them into a huge thicket. "Be silent!"

As they crouched in the darkness of a prickly nest of leaves and branches, trying not to breathe, they heard a noisy approach.

The Trojans. *Looking for them.*

# X

## TROY

Sticks and thorns pressed into her skin as they hid in the heart of the thicket, motionless, the voices suddenly quite near. Marpessa couldn't see anything—was afraid to breathe. Afraid they would hear. Her heart was racing—galloping. Two or three men, she guessed. No more than a few paces away. She couldn't understand their words, though she knew they must be speaking Greek. Finding Haleia's hand, she held on as if to life itself. Her knees were coiled springs. She wanted to leap up, to flee. As if he sensed it, Arion, behind her, suddenly gripped her arm. His index finger moved up and down along her skin in a gesture that was oddly comforting. Gradually her knees relaxed. At last the sound of feet through underbrush moved away. The voices diminished. Marpessa breathed again. The four of them remained still, frozen, until all the sounds faded in the distance.

Arion released her arm. "They don't know we're here yet," he reassured them.

"We'll wait till they're far away." Gortys's voice came out of the dark.

"The stream dips between steep banks," Arion whispered. "I saw, just before I heard them. We'll have cover."

"That was only one small group," Gortys cautioned. "There'll be others."

When all they could hear was the burbling stream, they crept from their hiding place. Marpessa stretched her cramped legs. The landscape was stark and barren in the moonlight, but true to Arion's word, the banks became high, and they could walk along the sandy streambed hidden from sight, sometimes wading in shallow water. After a time Arion made them pause while he strained to listen. "Voices," Arion said, "but far away." They continued. "Faster," he urged them, and though they were all breathing hard from effort, their progress seemed impossibly slow. Soon the terrain became rocky, and they slowed to a snail's pace, Haleia picking her way with difficulty. Arion took her elbow to help her.

The moon was dipping toward the west. A cold night wind gusted. Marpessa heard crickets chirping and Gortys breathing noisily behind her, but otherwise only their footsteps crunching on pebbles. Then a shout, faint in the distance.

They froze and looked at Gortys, but it was Arion who hissed, "Down! Lie flat against the bank."

Marpessa flung herself prone on the ground, her face in sand, her heart hammering against her ribs. She heard scraping and rustling beside her and looked up to see Arion tearing down branches and reeds and flinging them over her and the others. Then he hit the ground and pulled some over himself. "Put your head down!" he whispered. "Lie still." She obeyed. The voices grew louder. She could almost make out words. Now footsteps, nearer, nearer—stopping. *Oh, gods!* A man was standing just above her. She could hear his harsh, noisy breaths.

"—which way did they come?" she heard. She couldn't breathe. Then came a rustling, and a shower of pebbles struck her. Had he thrown them? Only an animal instinct kept her from jumping out of her skin. She waited for the fatal strike of sword or spear. Her head was bursting. She was going to die, but first she was going to be sick.

A cruel laugh. "They always follow the streambed. We'll get them!" Then more pebbles falling. Shuffling steps. The man's foot must have dislodged loose dirt from the bank. Another voice muttered, "Let's move on." Slowly her darkened, numbed mind realized the men were leaving. *We're safe, they didn't even see us.* Her body went as limp as if she had melted. "Don't move," came Arion's whisper. They waited an eternity until the voices and the steps faded from their hearing. And waited some more. At last Arion got to his feet and helped Haleia up as Gortys scrambled to rise. Then Arion stood over her. She was so weak that she accepted his hand and let him help her up.

"All right, girls?" Gortys asked them.

"The gods tested my courage, and I failed," Marpessa whispered.

"Courage doesn't mean you're never afraid," Arion said, lifting the pack with their food and water. "Let's go." He climbed up the bank and crouched, his head just above ground level as he scanned the landscape. "I can see the citadel," he said when he came back. Then he added, "We must leave the streambed."

"The land is open and flat," Gortys objected. "We won't have any cover."

"But this is where they'll be looking for us." Gortys had no answer to that. "We must spread out and walk crouched over as much as possible so that we're less visible. And no one talks! No sound at all," Arion continued. "I'll lead, then Haleia, then Marpessa, Gortys last. If I make this signal—" he slashed down with his arm— "drop to the ground and don't move. Now let's eat and drink. We'll need our strength. This next bit will be the hardest."

Gortys nodded. He seemed content to let Arion take command. Marpessa was glad. His quiet strength reassured her. They ate some bread and dried fish, drank from the stream, refilled the water skin, then set out across the barren terrain. A faint glow in the eastern sky made them all too visible. Dawn was not far off. Her stomach tightened. This place was too open. They could be seen from afar. Each time Arion scanned the landscape, she looked around and listened but heard nothing above their own labored breathing. Gortys, in obvious pain from his stiff legs, was falling behind. Marpessa whistled softly to Arion, who signaled a halt. They rested on the ground, but Arion did not allow a long stop. Soon they began walking again, almost crawling. Marpessa could see the citadel of Troy looming on the horizon, its walls outlined in moonlight.

All of a sudden Arion made a slashing movement. They dropped to the ground. Marpessa's heart thudded. She heard nothing. Then—a distant voice carried on the breeze. A faint shout, another. They waited, heard nothing more. Arion crept back to them. "They're far away toward the shore," he whispered, pointing. "Keep low. We must hurry."

But the terrain became deeply rutted, littered with clumps of dried dirt and rocks, making their progress difficult. Marpessa's legs ached from the awkward pace. Suddenly Haleia gave a stifled cry and crumpled to the ground. Arion, looking alarmed, ran back to check on her.

"My ankle—twisted." Haleia clutched her leg, grimacing.

Arion crouched down to examine it. "I'm going to bind it." He untied the strip of cloth that he wore around his head. As he wrapped it tightly about her ankle, his loosened hair, damp with sweat, spilled over his brow. "Is that better? Can you walk?"

Haleia scrambled awkwardly to her feet, tried a step, and winced. Arion lifted her arm over his shoulder. "Lean on me. Hop if you need to. We'll walk upright, but we must hurry."

Gortys seemed relieved to be upright. Marpessa took Haleia's other arm over her shoulder to help bear the girl's weight. Their pace was agonizingly slow with Haleia in obvious pain, her lower lip caught between her teeth, her face frozen in grim determination. Her ankle swelled against the tight cloth of Arion's improvised bandage, and she gasped sharply at almost every step. The sky was far too light. Marpessa looked around fearfully. Nothing. No other sounds. What did it mean? Would all their pursuers be waiting for them at the citadel?

"A little bit more," Arion exhorted Haleia. "We're getting close. You can do it."

Marpessa looked toward the citadel, too far away. Haleia gave a moan and stopped. "I can't," she whispered, almost crying.

Arion unslung the water skin from his shoulder and handed it to her. After she caught her breath and took a swig, he looked into her eyes. "There is no can't," he said. The words rang through Marpessa's mind. Haleia put out her arms to lean on Arion and Marpessa and started forward with new resolve.

"Good! Another step, another," Arion encouraged her as they struggled on.

All at once he stopped abruptly. Marpessa felt a shock pass through his body from Haleia to her. "Voices," he hissed. "Nearer."

They froze, listening.

"We must run. Haleia, I'll carry you. Marpessa, keep up. Gortys, follow." He swept Haleia over his shoulder like a sack of grain and began to run as fast as his awkward burden would allow. Marpessa followed. She could hear Arion's labored breaths. Behind her Gortys was losing ground. She could not hear over their noisy progress how far away the pursuers were. In an agony of worry she pushed on.

*Where are they? Have they spotted us?*

The ground grew rougher and began to slope up. Large rocks impeded their way. Marpessa stumbled over a jagged stone. She looked up. These rocks had once been pieces of a crumbling wall. They had almost reached the citadel.

"A bit more—a bit more," Arion gasped. His ragged breaths tore the air. Marpessa longed to help him with Haleia. They reached the base of a high wall of massive blocks of stone. The lower part slanted in a steep slope. The upper part was vertical. Marpessa looked up at the ancient stonework, said to have been put in place by the gods themselves. Some of it had crumbled. Some rocks were newer, smoother. She felt a shiver of awe and fear. Her ancestor Ajax had been among the men who tried to storm these very walls uncounted generations ago.

Arion reached a place in the wall with some concealment from the plain. He set Haleia down and listened for several moments. Over the gusting of the wind, Marpessa was sure she heard voices, sounds of pursuit, but Arion gave no sign. He scanned the uneven walls, broken in many places. She wondered how they would enter the citadel.

"We wait here for Gortys," Arion panted, pulling the girls behind some shrubs.

"He knows the way in."

At last Gortys, limping, caught up with them. They had to wait while he stood rubbing a sore thigh and knee. Then he said, "This way, quickly. We must find the secret entry way." Arion lifted Haleia again. Gortys led them among tumbled stones around the eastern side of the citadel toward the north. After a short time he stopped, searching the wall, which looked impenetrable to Marpessa. "There's a gap—a passage through the wall, once part of a well. It's somewhere near here." Marpessa looked up and down the wall frantically. There were depressions, shadows, but no opening that she could see. Then she heard a voice—a distant shout. She glanced at Arion, who was watching Gortys intently, as if exhorting him in silence to find the entrance. But the older man shook his head. "It must be farther on."

"Hurry!" Arion whispered fiercely. They started up again.

At last Gortys stopped, pointed upward to a deep black opening in the sloping part of the wall. "There it is!" *So small!* Marpessa thought. They could have easily missed it. Would they all be able to crawl through it? She could. But the others?

"Come on!" Arion said. They heard a shout close by, just around the curving wall. "*Quickly!*" He began scaling the wall, one arm holding Haleia, the other hand steadying his way. Marpessa followed. Gortys crawled up behind her, breathing heavily. The uneven slope provided plenty of handholds and footholds. As she climbed toward the gap, she saw that it was bigger than it had looked from the bottom.

Suddenly, a harsh shout came from just below. "*There they are! Stop them!*" Marpessa froze. They were only halfway up. A group of men came into sight around the wall. Some brandished spears. One hurled a stone. It struck the wall and shattered close to them. She looked back. More men came running from the opposite direction.

"*Keep going!*" Arion yelled. A terrifying volley of rocks and spears came at them. Most of them hit the wall and fell harmlessly, but a sharp rock struck Marpessa's calf. She barely felt the sting of pain. Arion was near the opening. He moved Haleia off his shoulder and shielded her with his body. "Climb!" he hissed at her. As they reached the opening, he flung a desperate look over his shoulder at Marpessa. With Haleia out of range, she had become the only target. "*Duck!*" he shouted. Just in time she ducked as a spear struck the wall so close to her head that she felt a breeze on her bare scalp. She shinnied up faster than ever. The barrage of rocks stopped, and she hear more ominous noises, grunts and shouts and the scrambling of many men scaling the wall below her. *Oh, gods, they're climbing after us!*

Arion shoved Haleia toward the gap. She disappeared into the hole. He turned, reached for Marpessa. A rock struck the wall near her, releasing a shower of fragments. "Quick! Get in the passage!" Heart pounding, she thrust herself into the opening.

The sudden profound darkness blinded her. She crawled forward over a rocky surface by feel alone. Soon her knees were sticky with blood. Just ahead she could hear Haleia scrabbling, grunting, moaning. "Go!" Marpessa shouted. She caught up with the other girl and pushed her backside unceremoniously. She heard sounds behind her.

*Let it be Arion and Gortys,* she prayed. *Let them be safe!*

She called over her shoulder. "Arion? Gortys?"

"Here," came Arion's voice, echoing in the dark. "Hurry! They're behind us!"

Marpessa pushed on through a black void, straining her ears for noises behind her. At last the darkness thinned. She nudged Haleia forward, and tried to see past her. "We're almost there," she called back to the men. When she rounded a curve in the passage, light spilled in, blinding her. Haleia crawled into daylight and collapsed. Marpessa wriggled past her, got to her feet.

They were on a narrow street between rows of stone houses. A few people wandered around in the early morning light. An old woman carrying a burden looked at them strangely. Then she gave a shriek. Other women came running. From nowhere a small crowd gathered.

"The temple girls! They've arrived!"

Before Marpessa could catch her breath, a veiled woman near the opening of the tunnel sprang forward. "Quickly! Follow me!" she said. "You're not safe yet!"

# XI

## PARTING

❯❯❯❯❯❯❮❮❮❮❮❮

"I'm a priestess. I'll take you to the temple." The veiled woman grabbed Haleia's and Marpessa's arms. Haleia took a few limping steps, but Marpessa hung back, looking over her shoulder for Arion and Gortys, who had just crawled out of the passage. "Quick!" Gortys said. "Go with her. We'll follow."

He and Arion turned to face the tunnel, ready to fend off the attackers, and Marpessa had no choice but to go with the priestess. She took Haleia's arm over her shoulder and helped the injured girl hobble up the street as best she could. Their guide, observing them, said, "It's only a short walk."

Marpessa's heart pounded. At any moment the armed men might burst through the tunnel and overcome Gortys and Arion. And what of the crowd of women that followed? "Don't worry about *them*," said the veiled woman, seeing her anxious glance. "It's only the men who hunt you. We women can't bear the bloodshed. And the men will give up once we reach the temple."

They hurried along the inside of the curving wall, then up a narrow sloping street deep in shadow. Smells wafted to Marpessa's nostrils: the stench of offal and human waste, the smoky scent of early-morning cook fires. At last they entered a gate into the courtyard of a gray stone edifice of several levels. It was far larger than any building in Naryx, and it was—*forbidding*. Marpessa felt a pang of yearning for the familiar house on the edge of the meadow where she had grown up, a world away.

Inside the gate, their guide relaxed visibly. "Here in the temple precinct you're safe. Wait here. I'll inform the High Priestess that you've arrived." But as the woman disappeared through the yawning blackness of the temple door, Marpessa looked back through the gate. Where were Arion and Gortys?

At last they appeared, Arion with scrapes on his arms and a bruise under his eye. He must have had to fight to keep the Trojan men from pursuing them. She looked a question at him, but he said nothing. It was Gortys who spoke. "It's over, girls. You're safe." He smiled. "From now on no one will try to kill you."

Haleia let out an audible sigh, but Marpessa could not feel any relief. Jagged shards pierced her heart at the thought of what lay ahead. A parting, a year of hard servitude. It was the thought of the parting that bothered her most. A chasm opened within her. She looked at the others, wanting to put her arms around all of them, to hold them, but instead she lowered her head until she had mastered her tears.

Gortys turned to Arion. "Our job isn't done yet. But the next part will be easier."

Arion looked surprised. "What remains to be done?"

"Have you forgotten? We must escort the others to the ship."

"Others?" Marpessa looked up, puzzled. Then she remembered. "Oh! The other two maidens! The ones who came last year and have completed their servitude."

She saw Arion's face clear as he too remembered.

"At least we can go without fear," Gortys reminded him. "Nobody will be trying to kill them."

Arion made no response. He seemed strangely distracted.

At that moment a stout woman in a white robe and rounded headdress under a gossamer veil came out of the door. Her imposing manner indicated that she was the High Priestess. "Welcome. We are glad you have arrived," she said formally, looking the two girls over from head to toe. Her eyes lingered on their shorn heads. "It is well that you have been prepared. We can begin initiating you right away." She turned toward the men. "I regret that we cannot offer you food or shelter. You must escort the other maidens to your ship without delay so that you can begin your journey home. I will bring them to you." Her eyes swung again to the girls. "This may seem hasty, but it's for the best. Now is your chance to send messages with these men to your families. Do so and be quick about it. Then make your farewells." With a brisk nod, she turned on her heel and marched back into the dark doorway.

The four of them stood in awkward silence. At last Gortys stepped forward and took first Haleia's hand, then Marpessa's. Marpessa clung to the comforting warmth of his callused hand and didn't want to let go. "We will tell your families that you came here safely," he said, "and that you send your love. Farewell, my dears! If the gods will it, I will see you both in a year's time when I come on the same errand with your replacements."

Haleia murmured something that sounded like "Farewell," but Marpessa's throat was clogged. They were all looking at her. At last she managed to say, "Thanks to both of you for guiding us so well."

Taking his cue from Gortys, Arion grasped Haleia's hand. "I trust that your ankle will mend," he said. "You should try to rest it."

Haleia laughed shakily. "If I can!"

"Farewell," Arion said to her solemnly. Then he turned to address Marpessa in the same formal tone. "Farewell."

Her mouth was trembling. Her eyes flooded again and she knew they could all see her tears. She bit her lip, furious at herself for this show of weakness. Arion's gaze met hers, steady and serious. He made no move to take her hand. Those brown eyes willed her not to cry. "Be strong," he said.

At that moment the High Priestess came through the doorway followed by two thin, stooped creatures that at first sight did not even look like young women. Their hair was shorn and wispy, their eyes hollow and ringed in dark shadows, their skin as pale as if it had never seen the sun. A stale odor arose from them. Marpessa's heart dropped. *Will we be like that in a year's time?* She had a faint memory of two girls setting out last year, robust and healthy. She could not remember their names. And now they looked as if they had no names.

"Praise to Zeus, Apollo, Athena, and all gods! It is good to see you safe." Gortys gave the two a forced smile. "We must go now. You will want to start your journey home." He took the wraithlike girls by their arms. "Come," he said to Arion. "We are no longer being pursued. We can leave by the main gate."

Though he knew he had no choice, Arion thought it heartless to just walk away, leaving Marpessa and Haleia standing there with the priestess. They were probably as shocked as he was by the sight of the two returning girls. What unimagined hardships had they endured? These same hardships now lay ahead for Marpessa and Haleia. *At least they will be safe,* he tried to console himself. As he followed Gortys and their new companions down the street, he did not turn back for a farewell glance, for he could not bear the look in Marpessa's eyes.

Gortys led them around a corner out of sight of Marpessa and Haleia. Arion lowered his head. He felt an emptiness, a sense of uselessness. He had a sudden vivid memory of his seven-year-old self standing on the dock among strangers while his ailing mother walked away, drooping. He had known from that moment that he was alone in the world. Did Marpessa and Haleia feel that same terrible aloneness? Then he reminded himself that they were not seven years old, and in a year's time they would return to loving families. Besides there was nothing he could do for them. Best put all thoughts of them out of his mind. He had his own fate to think about.

*Now is my time, my chance to escape. How will I do it?*

He plodded along with the other three around a curve, down a sloping street toward a large, open portal. As they walked, Gortys spoke bracingly to the two girls.

"We will cross the plain to Rhoeteum," he said, "where we left the skiff. The ship will be waiting for us just offshore. If you are strong enough to walk, we can make it there in two or three hours. Just think! Soon—in a matter a few days, if the gods are willing—you will see your families. Are you hungry? We have food in our packs."

"We have just eaten a meal," one of the two informed him.

"What are your names?" Gortys asked. "I should remember from last year, but my memory isn't what it once was, and—"

But Arion wasn't listening. He pulled his mind away from thoughts of these two girls and the ones they'd left behind.

*How?* he wondered. *It must be now, before we board the ship. When we reach the skiff, I'll disappear into the shrubbery, and—*

But that would never serve. Gortys would wait for him, look for him, then alert the crew of the ship. There would be a widespread search. If they didn't find him, he would be reported as a fugitive to all the nearby Greek colonies in Aeolia and Ionia. Many on these shores would be pleased to catch him, to collect a reward.

The four of them went out of the citadel onto the plain, following a well-trodden road. As they walked, Arion gnawed on his lower lip, his thoughts leaping ahead to what would happen once they reached the ship. Gortys had instructed the captain to anchor just offshore from where the skiff had landed and to await them there. Once they boarded, the plan was to sail to an island northwest of Tenedos, where they would anchor for the night.

An idea came to Arion, a possibility so full of peril that he grew cold with fear. It would be difficult, and there was a good chance he would not even survive. But though it went against every instinct, it was the only way.

He must get back on that ship.

# XII

## ESCAPE

Thankful that he had not been asked to row, Arion watched the men raise anchor, haul the oars, and swing the ship around. He, Gortys, and the returning girls had found the skiff without difficulty and had rowed to the ship. Now the air's chill pierced him to the core, and tension gnawed at his gut. He drew deep, calming breaths. As the men hoisted the sail, Arion moved in to help. Then, when they were done, he slipped away to the railing near the stern. A brisk wind lifted white-capped swells on dark blue seas. The sun came from behind a cloud to throw down blinding lances of light. On such a bright, cloudy day, it would be hard to see an object in the water.

*Good,* Arion thought. He tightened his leather belt around his waist, making sure his silver pieces were secure against his body. His sturdy sandals would weight him down, but that couldn't be helped. He would not give them up. Ruefully he discarded his cloak, for that would hamper him. As he watched the shore slip away on his right, his muscles clenched. He must wait for just the right moment, when they were farther from land but not too far. As the wind caught the sail, the ship bucked like a frisky horse and shot forward. The land's features began to grow indistinct.

*Now.* He waited until no one was near, no one paying him any attention. Then, standing on a narrow thwart near the rail, he took a misstep and tried to regain his balance, making it look awkward in case any were watching. He overbalanced and swayed, his arms flailing. With a cry, he pitched into the sea.

He sank deep under. The sea was colder than it had been last night, and the shock of it stunned him, held him motionless for several heartbeats, his mouth and nose full of salt water. He fought to the surface, feeling as if he were in a nightmare where the sea was thick as syrup and his limbs were paralyzed. At last he came up choking, amid waves that slapped over his face and stole his breath.

He heard yells from the ship. "Man overboard!"

"Arion!"

"Can he swim?"

A wave washed over him. He went under—surfaced again, sputtering. It was not hard to feign difficulty staying afloat. "Help!" he shouted.

Someone yelled, "Here's a line! Catch it!"

But the ship was already moving swiftly away. A rope came snaking toward him. The wind whipped it aside. Arion swam hard toward the rope, made a grab for it—missed.

He gulped a breath and sank under. Beneath the surface he paddled furiously away from the ship. Then he came up again gasping and struggling.

He heard a faint shout. "Too far—losing him!"

He went under again, swam away, raised his head. His lungs felt swamped. He was already tired from fighting the swells. He floated on his back, keeping his face just above the surface while he recouped his strength. The ship was speeding farther away, propelled by the full sail. In these waves, with the sunlight and cloud shadows dancing over the surface, he would be all but invisible.

With a strong wind driving them, they would debate furling the sail and going back to look for him. He hoped they would decide that it would be too hard to find him to be worth the effort. By the time they could bring the ship about, they would think it likely that he had drowned. Besides, they needed to make land on that far island before nightfall. They would remember that he was only a slave after all, one who had already served his usefulness on this journey, and therefore expendable. If supplies ran low, there would be one less mouth to feed. The seas were dangerous, the outcome of any voyage unsure. Their survival was of more importance than the life of one slave.

*Let them sail on!* Arion prayed. *Let them return to Naryx and tell Thrasios that his slave has been lost at sea.*

He lifted his head to look. The ship had not come about. It was growing smaller in the distance. They had given him up as lost. In profound relief, he floated on his back and breathed deeply.

But the most perilous part of his escape lay ahead. The land was far, and he had never swum a distance this great, and never in strong surf. When he had rested, he turned toward shore and began to swim in steady strokes. Soon his body grew numb from the cold. He tried to find a rhythm in the waves so that he could get a breath between each one. But this proved so hard that every few strokes, he had to roll onto his back to rest and catch his breath.

His arms grew heavy as stone. He lost all sense of time. Surely hours had passed. He'd been swimming forever, yet the shore was no nearer. He was already drained from his exertions last night. The surf thrashed him, cut off his breath. The sky clouded over, the waves became rougher. If he didn't reach land soon, his weariness would overcome him.

Bizarre shapes and images possessed his mind. He didn't know what was real any more. The dark line of land ahead blurred and became the tail of a sea monster, then slid away to nothing. All around was endless malevolent sea. Vague darting shapes in the water appeared and vanished when he looked. Lights floated in the waves like eyes staring at him, hostile spirits of the deep come to bring him doom, but when he blinked they were gone. He was losing his mind to cold and exhaustion.

A huge wave swamped him. He went under, couldn't find the surface. His lungs near to bursting, the cold, dark sea was taking him, pulling him under to a place where he would find warmth, where nothing mattered. He couldn't fight any more. It was easy. He would let go, slip away.

*No!* a faint, urgent voice in his head insisted. *No!* He kicked desperately to the surface and gulped air. Something soared over his head, a shadow flashing past. A seagull! Suddenly Marpessa was his mind, springing up the ship's mast to rescue the young gull. A seagull meant land was near. *Only a little more. One more stroke, one more...* He had encouraged Haleia's pained steps with words like these. When strength was gone, there was still a small reserve. *There is no can't.* Over and over he repeated the words he had said to her. *I* will *reach the land. I must.*

Ahead lay the land's deep gray-green shadow. He could see the shore's shape now, its vegetation. He launched himself forward, put his feet down. Nothing. Still too far. Somehow he kept swimming closer, closer to the shore, that last reserve of strength almost gone. Then at last his toes groped rocks and sand. *Solid ground.* Too cold and exhausted to feel relief, he dragged himself from the sea and staggered up the strand like a drunken man. He crawled out of the wind into a clump of bushes and collapsed. It was only late afternoon, but he was too spent to think of finding food. As he curled in on himself to stop his shivering, he made one last move, reaching into his sodden leather belt. Aye, it was all there, the silver he had saved. Not much, not enough, but—

Sleep overwhelmed him, the thought unfinished.

As darkness fell that night, Marpessa lay on a thin pallet in the room where the girls had been taken to sleep, a small cell-like room with a dirt floor, one small window opening, and a door that led to the temple courtyard. Next to her, Haleia, on her own pallet, was breathing deeply and evenly. The priestess had given her a poppy draught for her injured ankle, and the exhausted girl had fallen into a profound sleep that Marpessa envied. She turned her thoughts to what the priestess had told them. "Tonight you will rest, but tomorrow you must start your duties, which will be to sweep and wash every stone in the floor of the outer temple chambers, the portico and the steps every day. Never will you enter the inner sanctuary; never must you come before the image of the goddess herself, for, as part of the atonement to Athena, you are considered unclean during the time you are here. You are slaves, the lowest of the low."

She paused, and Marpessa blurted, "Why did the men try to kill us on our way to the temple?"

"Because you are taking the role of Ajax himself. They tried to kill him for his sacrilege until he sought sanctuary in the temple. But to the goddess Athena he was a defilement. As you are now." The word left a stain on Marpessa's soul. Then the priestess added, "And remember, you are never to go outside in daylight— not even in the courtyard."

This made Marpessa want to weep, but she was beyond the relief of tears. A dark desolation filled her, a weight pressing on her chest. *Never stand in the sun? Never feel the breeze on my face? How will I endure a whole year?*

Arion's words returned to her. *Be strong.*

*Arion.* Strangely it was his face that she saw now in her mind, while the faces of her mother, her father, her brothers, and her old nurse, had faded into shadows, their features blurred. She pictured Arion where he surely was now, on the ship. All day she had thought of them, the men and the two other girls walking across the plain, making their way to the skiff, rowing out to the ship. She imagined Arion sitting in his favorite place near the fore as they sailed away to that distant island where they would anchor for the night. Then they would continue the long journey across the Aegean Sea.

It made her feel too lost and alone to think of them on their way home without her. Then it was as if Arion, sitting on the ship, turned to meet her eyes. She sat up in the darkness. Determination filled her. *Arion, I will endure,* she said to him in her mind. *I will go home again. And I will not look like those two poor girls, broken and defeated.*

# XIII

## ALIEN LAND

"Where are you from, stranger? I haven't seen you in these parts before."

As he was digging into his belt in search of coppers, the question came at Arion like an arrow. He was in the agora of a small town near the shore—he did not know its name—and his inquisitor was a merchant who proffered a fine woolen cloak that Arion needed badly, though it would cost him most of his copper pieces. Any question could be a trap. But this man surely could not know he was a runaway slave. Arion did his best to look confident even though his tunic was stiff with salt, his hair most likely disheveled, and his stomach growling audibly.

"I am recently come from Ionia, sir." Arion gestured vaguely south. "This is a fine cloak. I'll take it, but for a lesser price. My old one was blown overboard while I was crossing the gulf." After haggling the man down by several coppers, Arion put the pieces in the man's hand, gave him a "Good day," and turned away quickly. He found the stall of a baker woman who regarded him as suspiciously as if she thought he would steal her bread. Handing her one of his coppers, he took the round, flat loaf she gave him and fled before she too could question him.

During the next days he wandered from village to farm, hiring himself out for building or making repairs, helping with crops or tending the herds of sheep, goats, and cattle that roamed the flood plain. He worked for food, copper pieces, and tools until he had enough to live on while he built a hut. He found a place between two willows near the banks of a river. It was a deserted stretch of land, separated by the stream from the nearest farms and grazing grounds. Though it took him many days to build, he was proud of his small home. It was just large enough for a low pallet and the rough-hewn chest he made from olive wood to store his few belongings. Now he had a shelter while he roamed as an itinerant worker during the days. But few who hired him had coppers or goods to spare. He often earned his bread only. He hunted for meat or fished in the shallow, meandering river. His store of coppers and silver dwindled, though he managed to save the silver pieces given him by Amaltheia.

The wooden rod struck Marpessa's back again and again as she knelt on the dirt floor of her cell, her body bowed over, her hands flattened against the wall for support. Each thud of the stick was a lightning bolt slamming through her. Never had she known such pain. But she would not cry out. She squeezed her eyes shut, braced for each blow, and waited for it to end.

At last it stopped. She straightened, drawing shaky breaths, realizing she *could* straighten, could still breathe. Her cheeks felt wet. Tears had seeped through without her will. Her back burned and throbbed. Almost worse than the pain was the humiliation, the wound to her soul. She turned to look at her tormentor. The Mistress of Temple Discipline, a stone-faced priestess of middle years, stood staring down at her, the smooth-planed stick resting against the floor. Malice shone from her narrowed eyes. "Do you promise never to go out into the courtyard again?" she demanded.

Marpessa, still having difficulty catching her breath, managed a nod and staggered to her feet. Then she gasped out, "For going in the courtyard—I was flogged?"

"You were not flogged," said the priestess sternly. "Men—prisoners, slaves—are flogged and sometimes die of it. I did not use my full strength, and you will not die. But we do not tolerate the slightest disobedience. Now turn around. Let me see your back." Before Marpessa could protest, she bent and lifted the hem of the girl's shift from the back of her knees all the way up to her neck, leaving her completely bare. Marpessa hugged her arms around her chest and cringed from the cold air on her aching flesh.

"Only bruised," the priestess grunted. "No broken skin." She let the shift fall back into place. "To make sure you have learned your lesson, you will be confined to your room for three days with nothing but dry bread and water."

Three days in this tiny hole! That was almost worse than the beating. "Who will do my sweeping?" Marpessa asked.

"Haleia will do the work for both of you. See? She too is punished! Make sure it never happens again." She struck the floor with her stick for emphasis, then turned and left. Marpessa fell prone on her pallet and gave in to bitter tears.

*It was my own fault,* she acknowledged, *but I thought it would do no harm.* Weeks—she'd lost track of how many—had passed since their servitude began, and she had been obedient and had followed every rule. But yesterday she had succumbed to temptation. Looking longingly out of her window at the sunny courtyard and seeing no one nearby, she had crept outside to catch the warmth and feel the breeze, only intending to stay for a few moments. But someone saw her and reported her.

Alone in her room, Marpessa yearned for activity. Even scrubbing the steps would have been a relief. She missed Haleia, who endured these days without complaint, doing Marpessa's job as well as her own. She had told Marpessa that at home she ran the household and took care of her ailing mother and the younger children. She had accepted their lot far better than Marpessa.

*I thought I was the strong one*, Marpessa recalled. But there were different kinds of strength, and Haleia's was not to be scorned.

The confinement ended at last but left an inner wound that wouldn't heal. The next day as she resumed scrubbing the temple portico at Haleia's side, a heaviness dragged her spirits down. Haleia, perhaps in an attempt to divert her, asked, "At home did you ever think about marriage?"

Marpessa replied, "Not much. Only as something far distant, something I knew would happen eventually." But the subject did not cheer her. "If I had not come here, Father would have found me a husband in a year or two."

"I didn't have much chance of marriage," Haleia said. "We were too poor to afford a dowry."

"It doesn't matter now, does it?" Marpessa said. "Still, I wonder who my father would have chosen." A sudden memory surfaced. A year or more ago when she had been dancing with the other maidens at the Dionysian festival, she felt someone's eyes upon her. A man was staring at her, a hard, wizened man about her father's age, his eyes like glowing coals in a cruel face. A predator's face. *Evil.* Dismayed, she stumbled in the dance. It was as if those eyes had stripped her down to her bare body, her naked soul. The memory sent a shudder through her. She said to Haleia, "My father would have chosen a wealthy man, but perhaps not someone with a kind heart, someone I could love."

"Love!" Haleia scoffed. "A man's job is to put bread and meat on the table. To provide a home."

Marpessa dipped her rag in the pail of water. "My mother taught me that happiness doesn't matter, only duty and honor. But still, I think she wanted me to be happy."

With that they fell silent. Marpessa thought of the wraithlike girls whom Arion and Gortys had escorted back to the ship. "Those two girls," she said. "They'll never be able to get married either."

Haleia shrugged and went on scrubbing.

Women who never married were disgraced, forever dependent on the charity of fathers, brothers, uncles. *How can I endure it?* Marpessa wondered, *if after this I am denied the only honorable life a woman can have?*

A quick, darting movement caught the corner of her eye, and she turned to look. Not far outside the colonnade, a small sparrow hopped about the courtyard looking for grain between the paving stones. *Poor little thing,* she thought. *It must be starving to come to this bleak place looking for food.*

But the bird took flight and left Marpessa longing for wings.

There were days when Arion tramped for hours, footsore and weary, finding no work, only doors closed in his face. Many nights he went to bed hungry. Then fear gripped him. *I can't work if I'm starving—if I have no strength.*

Sometimes the men who hired him asked questions. "Who are you, young fellow? What are you doing here? What *polis* are you from? How do I know you are not a brigand?" Or: "You say you are Ionian, but in your speech I hear more of Hellas."

Word of him, this stranger in their midst, would spread. Some merchant ship from Lokris might come to this shore. Someone might recognize him. Perhaps his former shipmates did not really believe he had died. If he was caught, he would be taken back to Lokris and punished, perhaps put to death. And he had another looming fear. In the cold weather, the season of rain, the river would flood its banks. His little hut would no longer be habitable. But where would he go? There was a gnawing ache within him, a mixture of loneliness and dread.

He often thought of Marpessa and Haleia. How were they faring? As a distant dream he recalled how protective he had felt when they crossed the Trojan plain, even willing to risk his life for them. He remembered binding Haleia's ankle, then putting his arm around her to bear her weight. That contact, flesh against flesh, now seemed like something rare and precious. He remembered Marpessa jumping in the water to save Haleia. The strength and spirit she had! He had wanted to say to her, "You have the courage of the ancient heroes." When they hid in the thicket as the Trojans searched for them, she had borne herself well, but he had felt her fear. It surprised him that he could know her very feelings. In comparison, his existence now seemed almost meaningless.

He found work with an old widow, alone and helpless. She needed a man to lift heavy things, repair fences, pull the brambles from her garden. "You can work for me from time to time when I need it," she'd said, "harvest time, sheep-shearing, repairs. I can't pay you in silver. Only in food. And not a lot." But he was glad to help.

The widow made him think. He wanted someday to find a wife, yet no freeborn maiden would ever have him, a fugitive, a man with nothing but the skill of his hands, the strength of his back and limbs. But perhaps a widow, an older woman, with children, it didn't matter. Someone who would be glad of his company, his usefulness.

Someone who could offer a home, an escape from his present existence, caught between the harsh struggle of living and the fear of dying.

The longing to escape overpowered Marpessa. She needed to walk under an open sky, to feel the breeze on her face. *If I could have freedom, just a little, it would help me endure.* An idea came to her. The day was forbidden to her, but perhaps she could steal part of the night when all were asleep. At night she would be invisible. She could go outside and look at the moon and stars, feel the cool night air. *Outside the temple gate.* The very thought of it made her heart pound with fear and excitement. *I would come back before they even know I've gone.* She understood the risk and accepted it willingly. *I was beaten, and I endured. I was imprisoned, and I endured. It's the lack of freedom I cannot endure.*

She thought of little else. She toiled at Haleia's side without uttering a word. She could not share her thoughts, for the other girl would never understand. As her plan formed, she envisioned herself climbing over the gate in the dead of night, slipping down the dark street on the other side—just for a short time, just a taste of freedom. But it would be enough.

Still, something held her back.

Then one day at the noon hour, when all the priestesses had retired for the midday meal, as she and Haleia were sweeping and scrubbing, their stomachs growling with hunger, she straightened, shook the stiffness from her knees, and looked around. She stood directly in front of the open door to the temple, the very place she was not supposed to enter. Peering in, she saw several dark rooms at the end of which was the inner sanctum, which she knew held the statue of the goddess.

"Marpessa, don't!" cried Haleia.

"It's all right," Marpessa reassured her. "I can't see anything. And I'm not going in." But she looked toward the sanctuary and asked silently, *Oh, Athena, how long can I endure this servitude?*

Gazing into the darkness she saw the faint glow of the burning coals on the altar before the goddess. She imagined the tall statue behind it, the stern warrior figure. Floating in the darkness above the altar she saw twin points of light, perhaps only the daylight catching in the statue's eyes.

Or perhaps a sign. *Oh Goddess, help me, guide me!* she prayed.

In her mind she heard the goddess saying, *Do it, my child. Go!*

Marpessa's heart surged. For the first time in many weeks, she smiled.

# XIV

## NIGHT VENTURE

Marpessa, having gone to sleep early, awoke and stole out of bed in the deepest part of the night. She glanced at Haleia, a motionless hump in the dark, breathing evenly. Then she peered out of the window into the shadowed courtyard. Stillness all around. She listened to the profound silence, her head lifted, ears straining like an animal's to catch any sound, anything stirring. Nothing. All was well. She would go out for a nighttime adventure. She had done this several times now, but she would not abandon caution. She knew it was not wise to go too often. She swung her legs over the window ledge, her bare feet finding the cool flagstones below. A wan half-moon hovered near the horizon. She glanced back at the temple, a huge forbidding edifice at the upper end of the sloping courtyard, its stone walls black in the starlight. The wide blockish columns that spanned the shadowed entrance looked like the huge teeth of a grinning maw. The world took on a mysterious identity in the night, she thought. Shapes were different, presenting themselves as looming, living things, hiding their daytime forms. As she crept from shadow to shadow along the perimeter of the courtyard toward the gate, she began to hear the soft sound of the priestesses' snores through the windows of their sleeping chambers.

Then—a faint noise. She went still and flattened herself against the wall. A rustle, the squeak of wood. *There! Across the courtyard.* Her body tightened in fear. She willed herself to become part of the shadow. A ghostly figure, a priestess, was coming from the direction of the privies. Coming her way. She stopped breathing. Then the pale-robed figure shuffled to a chamber door, opened it, and went inside. Marpessa's breath slipped out. Her heart slowing, she waited long moments after the soft thud of the shutting door. The fear, the relief, the excitement—all were like wine in her blood.

When she felt it was safe to move again, she slipped along the wall toward the greatest obstacle—the gate, beyond which lay the streets and houses of Troy. None guarded the gate. There was no need. It was twice the height of a man, built of roughly hewn timbers, tree trunks from the rich forests of the mountain slopes, and it was barred from the inside. Marpessa kilted the skirt of her loose garment and pulled herself up to cling with her toes to the first crossbeam. Her fingers found the spaces between the vertical timbers and gripped hard. She heaved herself upward, handhold to handhold, foothold to foothold, until she reached the top. Then she swung her legs over. On the other side, she hung by her hands, looking down. The distance to the ground was higher than a tall man. Below was hard-packed dirt. She drew a breath and let go.

She landed in a crouch, knees absorbing the impact, and stood a moment to catch her breath. A wild, rebellious joy washed through her. Each time it was like this: once outside the walls of the temple, she felt alive. She was the old Marpessa again.

With an effort she reigned in that hot surging tide. The gate closed off the upper end of a narrow, sloping street, bordered by the walls of small, crowded houses, all connected. She could hear occasional sounds, the scrabble of a rat searching for food, the distant bark of a dog, but otherwise the city was silent, the inhabitants asleep. She began to walk, luxuriously inhaling the cool night air and her stolen freedom. A scent of flowering herbs wafted over the wall of a courtyard, and she heard the chirping of crickets, a sound she had always loved, but it made her think of autumn nights. Looking up, she saw the stars that represented Pegasus and Andromeda high in the sky. Did that mean that autumn was already far advanced?

She walked all the way to the bottom of the sloping street, farther than she had previously walked, and came to a corner where the narrow street was crossed by a wider one, which, she guessed, led to the great outer wall. She yearned to see the walls of the citadel but dared not go on. Those walls were guarded from several crumbled lookout towers.

Reluctantly she turned to retrace her steps—and stopped. A faint shout came somewhere, perhaps one of the towers. She frowned, listening.

Another shout, louder this time. Then distant pounding feet. Several men running, shouting frantically.

*"Invaders! Barbarians! Coming this way!"*

# XV

## ATTACK

Marpessa stood frozen. The words had no meaning. Then it hit her. Barbarians pillaged and destroyed all in their path. Her blood turned to ice. A voice quite near shouted, "To arms, to arms!" Her heart nearly leapt out of her chest. She spun around the corner of the narrow street and hid in the shadow of a recessed doorway.

A more distant voice called, "They're here! The east gate! They'll breach it!"

Urgent pounding feet ran past her down to the wider street. The night came alive as men burst out of doorways, some with flaring torches. Marpessa shrank down, tried to make herself invisible. She dared not move.

"Arm yourselves!" someone shouted. "Fetch help! From the barracks!"

*She must get back.* If she could just reach the temple, she would be safe. She could see the temple gate, a large black square at the top of the sloping street, impossibly far. Many people swarmed in the darkness, panicked women milling about, men moving swiftly toward the walls. When Marpessa stepped out of her doorway, no one paid her any mind. She burst into motion, dodging through the crowd, running.

Just then a terrible roar split the air—a many-throated bellow of challenge, of triumph. The invaders had breached the walls. Their barbaric war cries grew louder with every instant, their heavy tramping feet pounded like the hooves of horses galloping nearer, nearer. She heard fearsome thuds and clangs of metal on wood as the Trojan men ran to meet them, armed only with staves and clubs, and fell back with terrible cries. *Wounded, dying.*

Unstopped, the invaders swarmed up the street—toward her. All the breath was squeezed from her lungs, her heart beating hard enough to split her chest apart. The temple gate was close, a hundred paces, but too far, too far! The barbarians were almost upon her. Even if she reached the gate, she'd have to climb it, making herself as conspicuous as a spider on a wall. She flung herself against a house on the side of the street. Miraculously an alley opened to her right, a pitch-black crack between houses. She dived into it and found it very shallow, barely the length of her body. Not much of a hiding place. She flattened herself against the ground, willing herself to become part of the paving stones, part of the shadows, and peered out. Barbarian shouts drowned out all other sounds. Monstrous dark forms were running past, some holding flaming torches aloft, a stream of men, a raging torrent, all shouting, a roar of noise as they ran toward the temple gate.

From all around her came smashing sounds and screams like those of animals at the slaughter. Some marauders were breaking into houses, and she heard their harsh menacing cries from within as they killed the hapless inhabitants. The greatest mass of invaders pressed on toward the temple. Now she couldn't see the gate, so many forms were massed in front of it. There was a commotion amongst the dark throng, a steady pulsing movement, and she heard a deep, booming sound loud enough to hurt her ears. They were wielding a massive battering ram, bronze on wood, striking again and again, relentless, rhythmic blows. Then came a crack like a thunderbolt, and more deafening cracks as timbers were torn asunder. Marpessa envisioned the men pulling the gate apart like a child's toy. A guttural roar of triumph erupted from hundreds of throats, and she knew the gate had given way.

A rush of wind swept her skin. The barbarians were racing past her as if sucked into the ruined maw of the temple gate. She lay flat against the ground, her heart beating into the earth until the last of the invaders had run past her. Then she eased her cramped legs under her and stood up. Her whole body shook. Her legs wouldn't move. She couldn't think.

She began to hear terrible screams coming from the temple courtyard. *Haleia*, she thought. *I must find her!* But moments passed before her weak legs at last obeyed her will. She forced herself into a stumbling run toward the shattered gate. *Athena*, she prayed, *let Haleia, let the priestesses be safe.*

Just inside the gate she stopped. A scene of horror met her eyes. Garish orange light from torches, billowing smoke and flames where one of the buildings had been set on fire. The courtyard was aswarm with the solid bulky shadow-forms of barbarians crouching, bending, stooping, stabbing. They made hoarse grunts like rutting animals. They shouted, jeered, laughed demonically as the women let out piercing screams.

*Rape.* Invaders raped, then killed. *Zeus! Let it not be!*

A dark form stood too near, his back to her. He started to turn, and Marpessa dived into shadows. She stumbled over something soft, wet, and sticky, and looked down. A face, eyes wide, blood dripping from a mouth open in the rictus of death. *One of the priestesses—Hyrmene!* She shoved a fist into her mouth to stop her scream. *I must find Haleia.* Trembling, she backed against a wall, then realized she could be seen in the light of the torches. As she darted behind a column, one of the barbarians hovering over a fallen body saw her. He straightened, started toward her.

*Oh, gods, I must get away. I'll come back for Haleia when it's safe.*

She turned and ran toward the gate. He was behind her, but fear gave her feet wings. She looked over her shoulder, and her foot struck a fallen timber. She fell, her ankle twisted under her. A wrenching pain shot up her leg. She gasped, then glanced back. In the confusion she could not see her pursuer but she couldn't be sure she had lost him.

No time for pain. She pulled herself to her feet. Hobbled out of the gate, down the street, creeping from shadow to shadow. *All too visible.* Many of the raiders, finished with their business in the temple, started roaming the town. *Footsteps behind her.* Wild with pain, she sped up, half running, half hopping to spare her injured foot. The steps behind her—closer, gaining on her. *Zeus, Athena, help me!*

She looked for the alley where she'd hidden before—couldn't find it. She must have missed it. The footsteps—louder, faster. She saw a deep crack of darkness just ahead. *The alley.* With a last burst of strength she flung herself face down into it and lay still, holding her breath, trying to become invisible, non-living, a sack of grain in the shadows.

The footsteps stopped just outside. She smelled heavy, rancid sweat. Menace loomed. Her heart froze.

The man lunged and struck her in the side with something huge and hard. Pain flared, red lightning. She cried out.

The club crashed down on her skull. Darkness. Nothing.

Arion set down his adze, straightening to mop his brow and drink from the water jar. It was early morning, the sun not yet over the horizon, and already he was sweating from the hard work. He was building new stalls in the stable of a prosperous horse breeder whose lands lay near the western edge of the plain. He had started yesterday and was grateful to have mastered the skill of it, for this job would last several more days. He wiped his mouth and hefted the adze once more.

At that moment he heard a frantic shout, the thud of running feet approaching. The owner of the stable was currying a horse just on the other side of the wall, unseen. Someone had run up to him, bringing urgent news.

"Barbarians from the east—the Trares! They're raiding and killing!"

"Where?" the stable's owner asked.

"They attacked Troy last night. They plundered Athena's temple—the riches, the women."

Arion froze. His knees wavered like columns of sand. *The girls.*

"Now they're roaming the countryside," the messenger continued.

"Coming this way?"

But Arion didn't wait hear the rest. There was no time to lose. He dropped the adze, slipped through the rear door of the stable and started running in what he hoped was the direction of Troy.

After a time he had to stop to catch his breath. He slowed his pace to a brisk walk. The sun had barely risen when he forded a stream and scanned the wide, flat plain, green and marshy, dotted with grazing cattle. Pale sunbeams highlighted Mount Ida and its surrounding foothills to his right. Far ahead was a low bluff, barely distinct in the growing light. Atop the hillock he thought he saw a pale glimmer of walls though he could not be sure it was the citadel of Troy or even if he was even going in the right direction. If only he had paid more attention to the landmarks when he and Gortys took the girls there—but then he had been too intent on the danger.

Now this danger was far deadlier. *Athena's temple—the riches, the women.* The words repeated themselves urgently in Arion's head. As the sky lightened, he continued toward the distant hill. A pall of smoke hung over it. His heart sank.

He quickened his pace. There was no trail. The tall marsh grasses slowed him down, scratching his ankles. Again and again his feet sank into muddy water. He pushed on, pausing only to catch his breath and drink from the streams that crossed his path. *Those girls.* Let them not be hurt or ravished or dead. Let him not be too late to help them. He hurried on, running whenever he could, paying no heed to the exhaustion of his body.

The hillock grew bigger. Uneven walls crested the top. *Troy.* With a frantic burst of energy, he ran until he came to the ring of tumbled boulders that surrounded the citadel, fallen from the oft-repaired walls. He slowed his pace then, careful not to turn an ankle on the uneven ground. From where he stood, all seemed quiet but for that dissipating cloud of smoke.

The sun had risen a short distance above the citadel, blinding him. He scanned the walls, trying to remember where they had found the secret way in. Farther on, surely. The wall made a huge oval, looping around the crest of the hillock. He walked to his right along it, searching the uneven rock face above him. Many stones had crumbled away, leaving dark holes. He examined them all to make sure that none was the secret passage. How far had Gortys taken them around the wall?

When he came upon the opening, deeper, darker than the others, he knew it at once. As he climbed up the wall and scrambled into the passage, the sun was high in the sky. *Late morning.* Arion cursed. A night and almost half a day had passed since the raid. *Too much time.*

He crawled through the passage with urgent haste and came out on the street he remembered. Straightening, he stretched his cramped legs. He looked around for any sign of the marauders. But they were long gone. The messenger on the plain had said that they had looted Troy and moved on.

He began to run up the street toward the temple. After a few paces he came upon an old woman huddled in a doorway holding the body of a young man in her arms. Arion saw a horribly crushed head, a chest covered with dried blood. The woman, rocking and weeping, paid him no heed. He paused, hesitating, but he could do nothing for her. He went on.

Farther up the street lay two—no, three men's bodies. Dried blood, flies swarming. A few paces away was a woman lying on her back, legs spread, eyes open. Flies lit on her eyes.

All around him were broken doors, houses that had been invaded. Many more dead lay inside them, he was sure. He forced back sickness, went on. He must find the girls. The temple had a huge timber gate. Perhaps it had protected them. He began to run toward the looming temple.

Then he stopped. Where the gate should have been was a huge heap of demolished timbers. A body was sprawled across one of the broken beams. A woman, her thighs spread. Just beyond her lay another—and another. He fell to his knees and spewed sickness. *I can't,* he thought. *I can't go on and find them like that.*

He took deep breaths, trying to steady himself. Barely aware of what he was doing, he staggered upright on wobbly legs and walked part way back down the street. Then something made him look to his right.

The body of a boy was huddled motionless in a small space between two houses. Arion stared at the dried blood matted in the brown hair that lay in wisps around the head. Near the hairline was a huge raised bruise, deep purple. He couldn't tell if the boy was alive or dead. He was wearing some sort of rough sackcloth garment, bunched up to his knees, revealing slim calves, bare feet.

Arion took a step nearer. The legs were smooth and hairless—feminine. This was no boy, and he had seen those legs before, when Marpessa vaulted up the mast of the ship. His eyes flew to her face. It was the color of parchment, the mouth slack, the eyes closed.

Dropping to his knees, he leaned over the crumpled form and reached a trembling hand toward the delicate neck, deathly afraid that he would find no pulse.

# XVI

## FLIGHT

*Darkness.* Her head was being crushed by rocks. A fierce pain cut through her chest with every breath. But through it all she felt a touch, a presence. A gentle hand on the side of her neck, her face. She heard her name. With great effort she opened her eyes. A man's face was bent over her, his eyes full of fear. A familiar face—but it couldn't be. That face belonged far away, in Naryx. With effort she called forth the name of her home. But she couldn't remember the name that belonged to the face.

She tried to lift her head. Sickness surged up, spurted out. The man deftly turned her head to the side and wiped her mouth with a strip of cloth. All at once his name came to her lips.

*Arion.* She wasn't sure if she had made a sound, but he responded at once.

"Marpessa! What happened?"

*Marauders*— she tried to say, but it came out unintelligible, more a groan than a word. She struggled up, fell back. "I must find—" *Haleia.* But she couldn't say the name aloud. Tears formed in her eyes.

Arion knelt at her side, unable to afford even a moment of relief. Marpessa was seriously hurt, barely alive. Where could he find help for her? He scanned the streets and saw only dazed survivors wandering among the dead. No one paid him any heed. No one would offer him aid. Perhaps he should take her out of the citadel? But she couldn't make the trip through the secret passage in the wall, the long walk across the plain. And even if she could, he had nothing, no way to heal her. Better to return her to the temple, try to find someone there who would care for her. Although from what he had seen—

"Are all in the temple dead?" he asked.

Her body shuddered. She whispered so low he had to bend close, "Don't know."

He feared the worst. The whole citadel was in disarray, many injured, many more dead. "There must be someone here who can care for you." He took off his cloak and carefully wrapped it around her. "I'm going to carry you." When he scooped her up into his arms, she flinched, gasped silently in pain.

As he staggered to his feet, she stirred feebly against him and spoke. "Must go back."

"I have to find help, get you to safety—"

But her fist gripped his tunic. "Haleia," she whispered. "Must find."

Arion stopped, appalled. For the moment he had forgotten the other girl. "I'll look for her," he said quickly, thinking, *If by some miracle she survived.* If so, he would find help for her as well. A fierce determination drove him. After his long loneliness on the plain, he felt desperately alive, full of purpose. He searched for a safe place to hide Marpessa while he ran to the temple. But there was none. It was too risky to leave her here—or anywhere. Grimacing, he turned and trudged up the street toward the temple, carrying her.

Gently though he held her, his steps jounced Marpessa as he walked. Everything hurt. The sight of the gray sky, the swaying walls, dizzied her. She closed her eyes, fighting nausea. Her head rested against the warmth of him. She focused on his solid chest, his heart beating against her ear, strong and steady. He would care for her. She was safe.

But she needed Haleia to be safe too. She tried to move, tried to lift herself, but the effort was too much, and everything went dark again. *Never mind.* Arion would find her. He would take care of her too.

She turned her face inward against his chest and sank into the darkness.

When Arion reached the temple courtyard, the sight that met his eyes choked off his breath. Bodies were strewn everywhere. People wandered among them with dazed, slow movements.

*Where was Haleia?*

He stood still for long moments. His arms ached from the weight of Marpessa. He shifted her body gently. She was unconscious—or asleep. He was glad she couldn't see the scene before him. He noticed a purposefulness to the movements of some in the courtyard. Men were gathering up corpses and putting them in rows; others were building a huge pile of stacked timbers.

A funeral pyre to burn the dead priestesses.

Shielding Marpessa in his cloak, Arion hurried to the pyre. He had to see if

Haleia was among the dead. As he stepped forward, a couple of men glanced at him incuriously. He advanced until he could walk along the row of corpses and look at each pale, dead face. Some had their eyes still open as if in shock. Sickness rose in him, but he forced it down. There were so many—close to fifty, he guessed, their robes torn and spattered with blood. He walked along the line, stopping whenever a young face made him think it was Haleia. *Not her...not her...not...*Here was one with long straight hair like Haleia's, the features too bloody for him to tell if— Then he remembered. Haleia's hair would be cropped short like Marpessa's. All these others had long hair. *No Haleia.* He felt a tiny hope.

As he started to walk away, awkward with his burden, two men were crossing toward the gate carrying a corpse between them. There was something familiar about that body. Then he saw short dark hair—and Haleia's dead face.

He ran toward them before he could stop himself. *"Where are you going with her?"*

The men paused. Two numb, weary, grimy faces looked at him. "This one must be taken outside the walls," one said. "Burned on unfruitful wood."

"The ritual," muttered the other man. "We must, even now—"

"Ritual?" Arion breathed.

"This is one of the sacrificial maidens. We must find the other also—"

*Marpessa.* Without looking down, he felt her face buried in his chest, hidden under his cloak. He turned away quickly, glanced over his shoulder. The men had barely looked at him. They walked toward the colonnade and set down their burden for a moment.

*Haleia—dead.* Arion drew in a ragged, painful breath. Nothing he could do to help her. The defilement demanded by the ritual didn't matter now. What mattered was Marpessa.

*I'll have to care for her myself.*

As soon as the men were well on their way, he would get her to the secret passage and somehow through it, if he had to drag her. He must carry her across the plain and hide her in his rough shelter.

Here inside the walls of Troy, her life had no value.

Carrying her in his cloak, Arion hurried down the street toward the secret way. Mercifully all those around him were too immersed in sorrow, shock, and the painful duties of survivors to notice him. Mercifully, Marpessa remained limp and unfeeling and made no sound. Once he felt her breath catch. He stopped, eased her face away from his chest so that she could breathe more easily.

At last he reached the opening to the passage, a deep pool of blackness against the rough walls lit by the noon sun. He looked around. The street was empty. Quickly he bent and laid Marpessa on the dirt of the street. He arranged his cloak under her and set her feet in the opening of the passage. Then he crawled in. Reaching back to support her head, he began to ease her into the tunnel.

At that moment he heard male voices, footsteps. Looking up he saw two men far up the street, coming from the temple—carrying a body. He knew them at once—the two men who had taken Haleia. They must have been delayed at the temple, and somehow he had gotten ahead of them. *They mustn't see Marpessa.* He tugged on the cloak with both hands, dragging her into the darkness.

She came awake with a cry. Arion slid his hand over her mouth. He pulled her farther down and flung himself over her, praying they were both completely concealed and that the men hadn't heard her. Their slow footsteps came abreast of the tunnel—halted. Arion stopped breathing.

A voice said, "—something moving. Did you see something?"

"No. But isn't this the opening to the old cistern?"

Silence. Then a scraping noise, a footstep—another. One or both might stoop to look into the tunnel. But to do so they would have to lay down Haleia's body. He waited, not breathing, his hand pressed over Marpessa's mouth.

They did not set their burden down. One of them said, "Nothing in here. Let's go—get this sorry business over with."

Their footsteps moved away—stopped again. Arion's hand hovered above Marpessa's mouth.

"Let's hope the others have found the second girl," said one of the men. At last the steps started up again, began to fade. Arion pulled himself forward to peer through the opening. They were farther down the street, probably heading for one of the gates.

He bent over Marpessa and held own his breath until he heard her breathing, shallow, barely audible. Relief filled him. But she lay very still, senseless. A trickle of new blood ran down from her hairline. *Oh, gods!* She must have struck her head on a rock when he pulled her so quickly into the tunnel.

If only he could carry her! He took a moment to study the passage by the dim light from the opening. It was a round bore carved through the rock, barely wide enough for a large man to crawl through. Not high enough to stand in. He eased Marpessa's body around so that she lay head first in the tunnel and he could protect her head as he pulled her. Then he began creeping backward on his knees, lifting the cloak to keep her head and upper body from the floor, stopping often to rearrange the cloak under her. Near the opening the floor was of sandy dirt, but this soon gave way to solid rock. His progress was agonizingly slow. Even though the passage sloped downward, his effort was as great as that of Sysiphus in Hades, pushing a huge boulder up a mountain. The heat and the darkness were stifling. Sweat poured into his eyes.

He stopped for breath and bent close to her. "Marpessa? Can you hear me?" A small, stifled groan answered him, filling him with relief. "Be brave," he whispered, "just a little while longer. We're almost there." The lie tasted bitter on his tongue.

He continued to ease her down the passage, paying no mind to the burning ache in his muscles, the knifelike pains in his knees. All his attention was focused on Marpessa. He felt they had been buried forever in this tomb of rock. His eyes strained against the blackness. Surely it was lightening up ahead, or perhaps he only imagined it. He plowed on until at last he was surrounded by deep gray instead of black. Up ahead was a rough circle of blinding light—the outside world at last.

Near the opening he stopped in case danger lurked, perhaps from those who were seeking Marpessa for the completion of the ritual. He bunched up his cloak to make a pillow for her. Then he crawled forward. Peering out, he couldn't see much, just the steep slope of the wall.

"Stay," he whispered to Marpessa. "I'm going to make sure it's safe."

He slipped down the wall. At the bottom he stood straight, drew a deep breath, shook the stiffness and pain out of his cramped muscles, all the while looking around. Nothing but fig trees and scrub oaks, dark against the dried grass. No sound but the chirping of crickets, the calls of birds hidden in the trees. How strange to hear these normal sounds of nature after such a massacre in the world of men! The sun was just past its zenith. Hours had elapsed. He felt a trickle down his shin. His knees were torn and bloody from the crawl through the passage in the rock. He had no way to wash them, nothing to bind them with. His stomach growled. No food, no drink.

It couldn't be helped. Only Marpessa mattered.

He walked a short distance around the wall in both directions. To his right, the way was clear. He would follow this way around the wall and back to the plain. To the left the wall curved, and he could not see around it, but he suspected that not too far away there was a gate. Suddenly he heard a noise. He jumped, then froze. A man, clearing his throat just beyond the curve of the wall. Arion flattened himself against the rough stones and crept forward to a shrub that would conceal him as he peered through it. Several paces away from the wall someone had made a huge pile of dead branches, and a corpse lay sprawled on it. Arion recognized the white-clad dead body, the shorn head. *Haleia.* The pyre of unfruitful wood.

A man, his back turned, was standing guard. Heart pounding, Arion backed away until he was out of sight. Soundlessly he made his way back up the slope to the passage. He bent over Marpessa and listened to her shallow breathing.

"We made it through the tunnel," he whispered. "But we dare not go on. We'll have to wait, I don't know how long, until it's safe." She made no sound. He did not know if she had heard. He crouched uncomfortably next to her. What seemed like hours passed. His legs cramped, then ached, then screamed silently in pain. His thirst was fierce. Once he heard a tiny sound from Marpessa's lips, a broken word that sounded like "water".

Twice he made his way out of the passage and around the wall to peer out at the pyre. It was unchanged, save that a different man sat next to it. The sun began to slip down the western sky. On his third trip down the wall he smelled smoke. When he crept forward stealthily, the pyre was alight, the flames a pale thin orange in the sunlight, four or five men standing around it. Arion backed away and said a silent prayer to the gods for Haleia on her journey to the underworld.

On his fourth trip down the wall, the pyre was a smoldering heap of ashes, and unguarded.

He returned to Marpessa and took her up in his arms. The only way to climb down the wall with her was to put her over his shoulder like a sack—as he had done an age ago, climbing up the same wall with Haleia. Easing his way backward down the steep slope of the wall, he felt sadness for Haleia and for all who had died such cruel deaths in the raid. For Marpessa, who had climbed so nimbly and so gallantly up this same wall with him that long-ago day, her steps springy as a mountain goat's. He wondered if she'd ever be able to climb again.

At last he stood on the path beneath the wall. The sun was far down the sky, its rays deep gold, the shadows around him lengthening. He made a sling from his cloak to help him bear Marpessa's weight. Then, awkward with his burden, he began the long walk back across the plain.

# XVII

## ON THE PLAIN

Darkness fell as soon as he left the citadel, making it impossible to see landmarks or a trail. He lost his way almost at once and had to guess at the general direction of the shore. His arms and back ached unbearably. He had to stop often and lay Marpessa on the ground while he fought off tiredness and waited for his breathing and heartbeat to slow. He was hungry and thirsty. There was water aplenty if he didn't mind stooping to drink from muddy marshes, but his hunger raged. Each time he stopped, Marpessa lay inert and senseless. Even when he picked her up, shifted her, or lost his footing in rough terrain, she did not stir. Once in a while, just often enough to let him know she was still alive, she gave a small gasp or moan. Just when he thought his hellish journey would never end, he stumbled on a stream and followed its course by starlight. By the good will of the gods it was the one that led to his hut. When he reached it, he had no idea how many hours had passed. Staggering from exhaustion, he lowered Marpessa onto his pallet and drew the sleeping rug over her. Then he sat slumped on the floor at her side, too weary to even light a lamp.

A few moments later he bestirred himself to fetch water from the stream. Mostly by feel, he lifted her head, held the cup to her lips. She coughed and sputtered, then roused just enough for him to get a few drops down her throat before she sank into sleep again. Exhausted, he went to lie outside, wrapped in his cloak and an extra rug, for there was no room stretch out on the floor of his hut. He thought his fear for Marpessa would keep him awake, but he fell deeply asleep the instant his head rested on the ground. Once only he awoke in the night, straining for any sound through the thin wall. Should he look in on her? He was terrified of what he might find. He wanted to go to her, but his spent body would not obey his will, and he drifted into sleep again.

In the wan light of dawn he arose and crept into the hut. She lay so still that his own breath stopped. When he saw the rise and fall of her chest, his knees gave way in relief, and he sat on the floor at her side.

What to do next? She needed the care of a healer, but he didn't know how to find one. He would have to care for her himself. But how?

He took up the water cup and held it to her lips. "Drink," he commanded gently. She opened her lips and swallowed several times. He stopped when water ran down the sides of her face. Then he went outside to look around, belatedly worried about the marauders. But all was quiet. He had seen no sign of them yesterday or last night. They must have moved on, or returned to their homeland glutted with the spoils of Troy.

He washed in the stream, then ate some bread and dried fish from his store of food. There was little left. He would need more for Marpessa. He remembered the stalls he was building when he left to go to Troy. Maybe the owner of the stables would hire him back when Marpessa was better. The man's farm was not far, no more than an hour's walk north. *I'll go today and ask him, but I'll have to leave her alone*, he thought uneasily.

He went into the hut. She lay still except for her shallow breathing. He laid his hand on her cold, damp brow. "Marpessa, I must leave you, but I won't be gone long." She didn't move or open her eyes, but he continued, "I'm just going to see about some work. I'll come back as soon as I can. Here's water if you need it." He set the refilled cup beside her, though if she awoke thirsty she was too weak to help herself. Then he let himself quietly out of the hut.

"You!" The owner of the stables, a portly man in his middle fifties, looked at him with hostility. "Where have you been? You left yesterday without saying a word."

Arion told a partial truth. "When the marauders raided Troy, sir, I had to go. I have a young cousin there apprenticed to a tanner."

The horse breeder narrowed his eyes. "A cousin!" he said as if naming a noisome pest.

Arion persisted. "By the grace of the gods I found him, alive but grievously hurt. I brought him back to my homestead."

"Well! You'd best get to work at once."

"I can't, sir. There is none but me to tend the lad. But when he's better I can come back to finish my—"

"I don't care about your *cousin*." The horse breeder emphasized the word contemptuously. "I just need my stalls built."

Desperation grew inside Arion. "I'll come back in two days," he said recklessly, praying that by then Marpessa would be well enough to stay alone.

"Why should I have you back at all? If some other handy lad comes along, I'll—"

"I can work hard, sir!" Arion interrupted. "I do good work, you said so yourself."

The man shrugged. "We'll see. But no promises. Go! You've wasted enough of my time." Turning away, he waved his hand in dismissal.

And Arion had to be satisfied with that.

When he returned, Marpessa was conscious but very weak. He gave her water and some bread, but she took only a bite of the food before she slumped back on the pallet. The small effort drained her. Her breathing, so much more labored than this morning, took all her strength. The rasping noise of her breath alarmed him. She met his eyes and clutched her side, letting him know that it hurt to breathe. *Broken ribs*, he thought. The nasty purple swelling in her temple was going down, the bruise yellowing around the edges. Her head wound, serious as it was, would most likely heal. So would her bruised, swollen ankle. It was the injured ribs that filled him with fear. He had heard of men dying from such chest wounds, the pain slowly stealing their breath until they drowned from the water in their lungs.

*What can I do?* he worried. *What would a healer do?* He remembered a thing from the long ago days with the elderly couple who had been his first owners. When the man was ill with lung fever, the woman had propped him up in bed to ease his breathing. *I can do that,* he thought. He could also bind her ribs. A few years ago when a worker in Thrasios's warehouse had broken a rib, a physician had wrapped a wide strip of cloth tightly around his chest.

Outside, Arion found some boards left over from building the hut. He wrapped them in his extra sleeping rug. It meant that he would sleep with only his cloak for a cover. But no matter. Inside the hut, he arranged the board behind her head.

"Come, little one! I'm going to move you. Best not sleep lying flat until you can breathe easier." He gathered her in his arms, but as he pulled her up, her whole body clenched and she gave a cry. Quickly he arranged her in a reclining position against the backboard. As he straightened, she bit her lower lip, tears welling in her eyes.

He felt a stab of pain in his own chest. "I'm sorry, Marpessa!" But he would have to cause her further pain. He tore a long piece of cloth from his one extra tunic. When he turned back to her, her eyes were closed. "Can you sit up?" he asked. "I'm going to bind your ribs." She stirred, made a vain effort, but didn't have enough strength. So he pulled her gently forward and slipped the cloth behind her back. As he wound it around her ribcage, she made sharp gasps. Before he was done, she slipped into unconsciousness.

He watched her helplessly. *Zeus and all gods, let her live!* he prayed.

He did little that day but hover near her, offering water and small bites of bread whenever she roused. She seemed suspended in a dream state, opening her eyes at times, giving cries of pain whenever she moved. Arion wished he could breathe for her. He wished he could take away her pain. There was a potion made from poppies called *nepenthes* that he had heard could bring sleep and forgetting, but where and how could he get such a thing?

The second day by late afternoon her breathing was slightly easier. Seeing her asleep, he slipped out of the hut to fish in the stream. When he returned with two small fish, her eyes were open. She seemed stronger. He sank to his knees beside her in relief. "Look, Marpessa!" He held up his catch. "Fish for dinner."

Her eyes fixed on his, suddenly wide and clear with a look that pierced him. "Haleia?" she croaked.

The question caught him unprepared. He turned away, fumbled for the goblet. "Here," he said, "drink some water."

She took a quick sip, then pushed the cup away. She sat up, catching his tunic in a weak grip. "Haleia," she insisted.

"Dead," he whispered helplessly.

"*No!*" Tears sprang from her eyes. She gave a sob that turned into a gasp, and soon she was coughing, crying, and holding her side. Her eyes showed agony.

"Marpessa, Marpessa!" His hands on her shoulders eased her back into a reclining position. "Rest, there is nothing you can do." He heard the uselessness of his own words. But she subsided at last into some private nightmare.

He cursed himself for his bluntness. *I shouldn't have told her until she was stronger.* As he sat by her side, his resolve, the strength and will that had driven his efforts to save Marpessa, drained away. He did not move for a long time. Then he looked down. The fish he had caught lay on the floor. *I should cook them,* he told himself. Still he didn't move.

*You must not give up.* The thought sprang into his mind. He wasn't sure where it came from, but he stood, full of determination. There was nothing he could do at this moment for Marpessa, but those fish should not go to waste. He went outside and began gathering twigs and wood to make a fire. He cleaned the fish, spitted them, and hunkered down to cook them over the flames. When they were done, he took them into the hut. Marpessa's eyes were open.

"Here, eat a little." He held a piece to her mouth. When she did not respond, he said, "Take it! Haleia would want you to get well, to live." He held his breath. At last she reached for the fish with a weak hand. "That's it, that's it!" Excited by this small victory, he gave her a smile of encouragement.

Then he felt his smile vanish. Tomorrow he would have to leave for the whole day to work for the horse breeder—if the chance hadn't already slipped from his grasp.

How would Marpessa fare without him?

# XVIII

## THE HERDSMAN

Marpessa shut her eyes, wishing she could shut out her thoughts. Haleia—dead. *And why am I alive?*

She struggled to remember. *I wasn't with her. I was on the street.* The flaring torches, men shouting and running. The acrid smell of smoke. Monstrous barbarians wielding knives and cudgels. *But how was I on the street?* Useless tears burned through her closed eyelids. *I left the temple. Just because I wanted a bit of freedom.*

She felt a searing shame. *I should have stayed by her side. I should have died with her.* Now Haleia was dead, while she was alive—safe. *I don't deserve life.*

Bit by bit her memory came back. *I returned to the temple.* Screams of the dying in the temple courtyard. The dead woman she had stumbled over. Had Haleia had looked like that in death? Too vividly she imagined Haleia's last moments—mind-numbing terror and agony. *Oh, Athena!* she prayed, *if only Haleia was senseless at the end and felt nothing!* But it was most likely a vain prayer.

Faces appeared in her mind. All those she had known at Troy: the Head Priestess; the Mistress of Discipline; the priestesses who had walked past her and Haleia daily as they scrubbed the steps; the drudges who worked in the storeroom and the kitchen. She could see all their dead faces, hideous, twisted. And Haleia. *Oh, Haleia!* she sobbed. So much death could not be real. Yet the cold emptiness her heart told her that it was.

Pain brought her abruptly back to the present. Her head throbbed and her chest and side ached, though not as much as before. How weak and helpless she felt! Arion had left a cup of water and a round of bread at her side. She ate and drank to pass the time. Where *was* Arion? He'd said something about going to earn their bread. If he had left her here in this small hut, she was surely safe. But where was *here*? Somewhere on the Trojan plain, she guessed. How had he known to come to Troy and save her? How was he here at all? She had no answers, and she couldn't think. Sadness swamped her. She wept for Haleia until she fell asleep.

Arion returned just after twilight. He looked in on her quickly, then went outside. She heard him rustling around. Soon she smelled wood smoke and something cooking. When he brought in rounds of bread, goat cheese, and a cup of barley gruel, she managed to sit up. At the welcome sight of his face, she managed a smile.

Arion lit a small lamp and set it on the storage chest so that he could see her. Her pale face was not as waxen as yesterday, and her breath no longer rasped and strained as much. Feeling hopeful, he set some food before her. She took small bites. For a while they ate in silence. Then she turned to face him. "Arion, how did you come to be here and not in Naryx?"

He thought about telling her how he had planned his escape, how he had swum from the ship, letting them think he had drowned. But this was Thrasios's daughter and he had best be cautious. He only said, "I—I did not go back with the ship."

She seemed to accept this, for she asked no more. Silence fell between them. Then she said, "What will happen to me now?"

"First you must get well. That will take time. Then, somehow, we'll find a way to get you home."

Marpessa smiled wanly but slumped down. Arion realized that she was exhausted from the effort of eating, talking.

"It's late. You must rest." Gently he pulled her up on the board so that her chest was raised. She drew a sharp, silent breath but made no other protest. Her eyes started to close. "Sleep well! If you need me, I'll be outside."

But he did not leave at once. He sat by her side in the flickering light, thinking over the day. He had finished building the stalls for the horse breeder. Though well off, the man was a miser and gave Arion only two coppers and the bread, cheese, and barley meal that had been their supper. But Marpessa needed hearty food in order to heal, and Arion wasn't sure when he would find more work. "Have you any meat?" he had asked.

The man shook his head dismissively. "Only enough for my household." And that was that.

A muffled sound came from Marpessa. Arion turned swiftly. She was twitching and moaning, her face a grimace of fear. *A nightmare!* The gods knew he'd had some after what he had seen in Troy. How much worse it must be for her! He shook her shoulder gently. "It's all right, Marpessa!" he whispered. "All's well." That quieted her. As her breathing grew even again, Arion's eyes traveled over her face, her closed eyelids, the shadows of her lashes, the soft round chin and tender neck. Her skin would surely feel smooth, warm, soft to the touch. His hand came up, fingers reaching— *No!* He stopped, straightened sharply. He felt an ache deep inside. *Think of something else,* he told himself. He drew a deep breath and made his mind dark and blank. Yet he stood looking down at her for several moments before extinguishing the lamp.

Time to sleep. As he went to his bed outside, he thought, *I must find work. Tomorrow. Find a way to earn some meat.*

But several days passed during which he had no success. Those early days he did not want leave Marpessa any longer than necessary. She was breathing better, growing stronger. She could sit up and even walk around for short periods. But their food was almost gone, and though she did not complain, Arion knew she was as hungry as he. He had heard that people recovering from wounds needed meat. She could stay alone all day now if need be. More than his presence, she must have food to regain her strength.

The next day he set out in search of work. *I won't return without meat,* he told himself. He walked a long way across marshlands and came to grazing grounds, where he offered himself for hire to several herdsmen, each time receiving a refusal. Then he came close to the shores of the Hellespont. He glanced at the sky. Noon. *I won't go back empty-handed.* But he couldn't wander for days as he used to. *Zeus and all gods, let me find work,* he prayed, scanning the landscape. Along the bleak meadow near the shoreline was a small hut with a lean-to and a fenced pasture—a farm, the dwellers eking out a meager existence. Not promising, but when he knocked on the door, an elderly man with a crippled leg answered.

"I have no sons to help me," he responded to Arion's query. "If you repair the sheep pen and chop and haul wood, I can spare some bread my wife baked."

"Have you any meat?" Arion asked without much hope. "Some game you trapped? Dried fish?"

The old man shook his head. "We rarely eat meat or fish."

Arion wondered if the old man was telling the truth or merely being tight-fisted. Still he worked until the sun dipped close to the sea. "You'll come back?"

the farmer asked. "I have more jobs, there's so much I can't do anymore." Arion nodded and left with his bread. Trudging homeward, he was filled with discouragement.

On his way, he passed one of the homesteads belonging to a herdsman. He had come here once or twice in search of work, always careful to approach from a different direction. Though this herdsman did not know it, he was Arion's nearest neighbor. The man, his wife, a child or two, and a couple of servants lived here. The homestead lay directly in Arion's path. He did not want to attract notice nor give away his own dwelling place hidden in the reeds of the riverbank. He started to skirt far around the place, careful to stay out of sight.

Male voices came to his ears. Ducking behind shrubbery on a low hillock, he peered out. Two men stood just outside the house. They had slaughtered a sheep and hung it upside down on a frame to drain and butcher. Arion cursed his luck. The sun had set but it was not yet dark. If he stood up now, they would see him. He would have to wait until they were done and then hope they went inside. He settled down to wait, watching them through the branches of the thicket.

One of the men took his knife and made a cut down the belly of the sheep. Working expertly, the two men took out the organs and removed the skin. Then they began to cut the carcass into pieces. Arion had seen this many times and had done it himself. As the men separated the meaty leg quarters from the body and laid them on a rough table, he imagined cutting the strips of meat, spitting them and placing them across the hot stones of a fire, sprinkling them with salt. His mouth watered. He could almost smell the grilling meat.

At last the men finished their work. While one went inside, the other bent over a fire pit and began laying out wood. Then he too went into the house.

Arion leapt to his feet. He ran as fast as he had ever run, right up to the table, grabbed one of the haunches, and ran on without breaking his stride. He heard a shout behind him. "Stop, thief!" He did not pause, only changed direction, running toward a point on the river upstream from his hut.

The two men gave chase. Arion plowed on, breathing hard. When he came to the river, far inland from the hut, he dared a glance over his shoulder. His pursuers were three hundred paces behind, indistinct in the twilight. He splashed into shallow water, then sank in a deep spot, almost losing his footing. Wet to his chest, he held his precious burden above the water and surged on to the other bank. Here the ground was flatter, more open. Arion raced ahead until he could no longer hear the men behind him. He came to a pile of rocks and sank behind it. The air tore through his lungs in gasps. When at last he caught his breath, he peered cautiously around the rocks. Nothing. No one. No sound but the wind, the far-off waves on the shore. Perhaps they had not even crossed the stream. He dared hope they had given up and gone back to safeguard the rest of meat. After all, only a haunch was gone.

*Unless they knew where he lived.*

Arion turned cold at the thought of Marpessa alone in the hut. He sped back along the river, crouching low, keeping to the cover of the bushes and reeds that lined the bank. When he came within sight of his hut, all was quiet. He opened the door. "Marpessa!" he called.

She was sitting up, waiting for him in the dimness.

"I've brought you meat." A smile lit her face, and he couldn't bring himself to tell her that it had been a theft. Later, perhaps. "I'm going to make a fire," he said. It was a risk, but he would keep it small and extinguish it as soon as the lamb was cooked.


Late that night, Arion lay on his bed outside the hut, his mind filled with worries. Perhaps the herdsman and his servant had not given up. Alerted to his presence on the plain, they might find the hut—and Marpessa. Tomorrow he should move her. Abandon the hut and hide their traces. Find somewhere else to build a shelter, perhaps in the hills. But she was in no condition to flee, hide, sleep outdoors.

She had no place in his precarious world. He should get her away from here and find a way to take her home. But what if she wasn't strong enough to withstand the journey? *Oh, gods, send me a sign! Tell me if it's the right thing to do,* he prayed. There was a seaport he'd heard of called Troas south of this barren shore. News and goods traveled back and forth between Lokris and Troy, at least when the weather was fair enough for sailing. Perhaps in Troas he would find a ship bound for Lokris. He could buy passage with the silver pieces saved from Marpessa's mother, whose fierce whispered words came back to him now: *Take care of her. Protect her well.*

A feeling of desolation filled him, a feeling he did not care to explore. He drifted toward sleep. Half awake, his mind wandered back to that day so many years ago when his own mother had left him with the seafaring merchants who had bought him as a slave. As he had stood on the shore, she had bent to kiss him stiffly, pressing so hard into his forehead that if he concentrated, he could still feel the burning imprint of those hot dry lips. Then she had turned and walked away, while he made such an effort to control his sobs that his lips trembled and runnels of tears seared his cheeks. Bent and slow though she was with her wasting illness, she had gone swiftly away, her movements jerky, her head down. She had not even looked at him again. *Why?* he asked in the darkness. *Why did you not turn back for one last look at your son?*

He had not loved anyone in his life since that moment when she had walked out of it. He would miss Marpessa dearly, but after he had seen her safely home, he would abide in solitude as he had always done.

# XIX

## THE SHORE

In the early morning, Leonteus, the Prince-Governor of Troy, leaned on a crumbling parapet and gazed westward toward the coast. Clouds were massing in the sky. Even without being able to see the water, he knew what it was like: dark gray, immense waves racing toward the shore, their white foam whipped by the wind like the manes of horses. *Poseidon's horses of the deep.* The season of storms had come early this year. Soon no more ships would make the crossing from the port of Troas to Hellas.

Leonteus' heart was heavy as he contemplated the disaster that had struck the citadel. Since the raid, Troy was a sad and diminished place, weakened by the deaths of so many and the theft of most of the grain from the harvest. The temple had suffered the heaviest losses. Almost all the priestesses had been killed. *Sacrilege.* But no matter the cause, the goddess would be offended if not given her due. He must make sacrifice to Athena and find new priestesses soon so that they could continue to honor the goddess.

There was also the troublesome matter of the two virgin temple slaves from Lokris. He would have to send a report to the temple in Lokris. Since one of the maidens was dead and the other missing and presumed dead, the Hundred Families would have to hold another drawing and send two more maidens to Troy in accordance with the terms of the decree. The slaves would have to be sent immediately, before the seas became impassible. Or else the consequences of Athena's wrath were not to be contemplated.

The problem was that only one of the temple girls was clearly dead, her body identified and burned on unfruitful wood outside the city gates in accordance with the goddess's decree. The other one had never been found. Leonteus rubbed a hand through his bristly gray hair and beard. What had happened to that other girl? His men had searched the city thoroughly. Her body had not been recovered among the dead within the walls, and she could not have escaped the citadel. The day after the raid, the bodies of the dead had been burned in mass funeral pyres. In the confusion not all of the bodies had been identified.

The bereaved had claimed their own, but there were always itinerant herders, peddlers, and other visitors passing through the city gates, spending a night or several. Leonteus recalled that the missing girl was not full-figured, but rather slender and wiry. With her cropped hair, most likely she had been mistaken for a boy. It was more than probable that the girl's body had been burned without anyone knowing who she was. In any case, there was no way she could have survived or escaped. For, if she had survived, where could she have gone?

*Nowhere.* Leonteus sighed. It was a loose thread, but an insignificant one. He clapped his hands for a servant and ordered a fresh clay tablet. When it came, he set it on the parapet. He stared off into the distance for a moment, then pressed the point of the stylus into the firm red clay. In bold strokes he wrote his report to Lokris. The two Lokrian maidens had been killed in the raid by the Trares. Two replacements must be sent at once. *Before the seas become impassible,* he thought as he imprinted his seal in the damp clay and summoned the servant for further orders.

It was just past daylight when a noise jolted Arion awake. Voices. A crackling in the bushes. Footsteps. He held his breath. Still far off. He shot to his feet and lunged into the hut. Marpessa, wide-eyed, sat up and stared at him.

"We must flee," he whispered.

As she pulled herself to her feet, he grabbed his carrying sack. Into it he threw the remains of the meat and bread, the cup, his knife, and all the loose possessions he could find. He reached into the dirt in the corner for his store of silver pieces and flung those in. Then he bunched up the sleeping rugs and stuffed them in too.

Slinging the sack over his shoulder, he took Marpessa's arm. "Can you walk?" He paused to kick the pallet and the boards on which she had reclined so that they no longer looked like a bed. Then he led her outside, where he scattered the stones and ashes of the fire pit with his foot. He stood still, listening. Over his ragged breath he heard nothing. After a moment came a faint shout. *The herdsman.* He knew that voice from yesterday. They were far upstream of the hut. He tightened his hand on Marpessa's arm—peered around the hut. The way to the shore was clear. "Follow me."

Keeping to the cover of the reeds that lined the river, they started toward the shore. *Where to go? Where to hide?* He tried to remember what he knew of the coastline. *South,* he decided. *Away from the plain.*

As she followed him, her steps were slow, tottering, painful, and he had to rein in his urge to walk fast, to run. They trudged into a strong wind as they approached the shore, then paused behind some tall shrubs while he looked around and listened. He heard nothing over the crash of waves on the shingle. "They're hunting me," he whispered. "We must hide." *Zeus!* he prayed silently. *Let there be some cover on the shore.*

Farther down were rocky outcroppings. If they could make it there—

They came to another stream and splashed across the wide shallow ford where it met the sea. Too much open ground. They would be in plain sight if the men appeared. "Can you run?" He broke into a slow jog, leading her by the hand, but stopped when her breathing began to sound harsh and painful.

At last they made it to the pile of rocks and crouched behind on the leeward side. Marpessa was gasping for breath, her face as pale as it had been when he found her in Troy. She was biting her lip as if from pain. Silently her eyes looked questions into his.

"We'll wait here," he told her, "until they're gone." Glancing down the barren shore, he could see nothing else that would offer shelter or even cover. He prayed the herdsman and his servant wouldn't come this far.

They would surely find the hut. *They won't believe I've gone for good,* he thought. *Even if we outwait them, they'll come back.* "At least they don't know about you." His words to Marpessa were no more than a breath.

He would have to return to the hut when it was safe, to gather the rest of his belongings, to be ready to move somewhere else. In the meantime they must wait here, poor shelter though it was. Marpessa's lips were blue with cold. He wrapped one sleeping rug around her, the other around himself.

The dark sky was overhung with clouds. Waves boomed on the shore. A freezing wind gusted, stinging his skin with drops of salt spray.

A storm was coming fast.

# XX

## THE STORM

It was another nightmare—the marauders attacking, she fleeing from her bed into a storm. But as she huddled behind a pile of rocks on the bleak shore with the rain falling in icy drops, Marpessa shivered, her teeth clacking together violently. The rain stung her face, the cold bit into her bones. Never had she felt more wretched. *This is no dream*, she realized.

His eyes anxious, Arion took the second sleeping rug from his shoulders and draped it over her head to keep out the worst of the rain. "I don't want you to get sick."

But she pulled the blanket off and handed it back to him. "You're wet and cold too. Put it over both of us. And this one around us. We'll sit close for warmth."

They wrapped one blanket around both of them, draped the other over their heads as a cover, leaving an opening for air and light, and leaned into each other's warmth. The thickly woven sleeping rugs, smelling of wet wool, gave some shelter from the rain. The rocks protected them from the roaring wind. Marpessa stopped shivering at last. But she was uneasy. In Naryx young unmarried girls were kept from contact with men. It felt strange to be sitting so close to Arion with his body touching hers from shoulder to knee and his warm breath mingling with hers. Even after all they had been through together, Arion was in many ways a stranger. *I don't really know him at all*, she thought. And why had they fled the hut? She turned to study his face. "Arion, what happened?" she demanded. "Why did we have to run away?"

"Two men came looking for me," he answered, "because I stole the meat."

"The meat we ate last night?" Was *that* how he got their food? She was so startled that she blurted out, "I thought you worked for our food. You *stole* it?" Her voice quavered. "And now we're in danger!"

Arion's body went rigid, and he sprang up so suddenly she was thrown off balance. The two blankets landed on her as he threw them off and strode into the rain. Stunned, she stared after him. She was afraid he would leave and not come back, but he stalked around aimlessly, making violent movements with his arms. Clad only in his tunic, he must have been cold. But he seemed heedless of the water pouring on him. At last he returned and flung himself down next to her, not touching, not making any move to get under the blankets. He was dripping wet and plainly in a rage.

"What did you expect, Marpessa?" he burst out. "We were starving. We had to survive."

Remorse flooded her. She wished she could unsay her heedless words. "Arion, I'm sorry, I thought—"

"You thought! You thought I never worked, all I did was steal!"

"No, Arion, I—"

But he cut her off. "Well, that's not how it was! I worked 'till I was ready to drop—and for nothing but crumbs of bread and cheese or a measly sack of grain! What was I to do if we weren't to starve? You had to get well. I did it for you. *You*, Marpessa!" The "you" came out with the force of the vilest insult.

"Arion, I'm sorry," she tried again when she thought his anger was spent. But what a weak word it was! When she glanced at him, his face was closed, his eyes averted. A gulf had opened between them. "Arion, there was no shame in what you did."

"Shame!" He was off again. "You have no idea, do you? You've been sheltered, cared for all your life!"

*I can't help my past*, she thought. *How will I ever make it right with him?* "Arion, you're wet, you're cold. Come back under the blanket." With a pang she remembered the mouth-watering grilled lamb they had eaten last night. "Is there any meat left?" she asked. "Let's at least enjoy it while we wait out the storm."

He tossed her the sack. "Help yourself." Miserably she reached in. There was a generous portion. She tore off a piece, handed it to him. A peace offering. Apparently he saw it as such, for he took it and said, "You have some too." They ate without speaking. Then Marpessa spread the blankets over him again. She pressed as close as she dared. His nearness sent a warmth through her like embers coming alive in a cold hearth. "Surely the storm will make those men give up," she said.

She thought he wasn't going to answer, but at last he grunted, "Perhaps." And then, "Are you warm enough?"

Her hopes rose. "Aye. Thank you, Arion. For everything." She felt his body relax slightly next to hers. "Arion, please forgive me," she said in a small voice. He did not answer at once, and she held her breath, watching him. At last he nodded. Then silence fell between them.

His rage might have passed, but the gulf was still there.

Arion had asked the gods for a sign, but the sign came from Marpessa. Her words had cut deeply. *How quickly she assumed I was a thief! She thought everything I brought back to her was stolen!*

At least it made things very clear. As soon as possible he would send her back to her world, the one where she belonged and where he himself had no place. At what point had he started to see himself returning on a ship with her? *How stupid to think I could go back, just because I'd saved her and was bringing her home!* Now he knew. They would all see him as Marpessa had: a criminal, a thief. They'd probably even think he'd abducted her and seduced her. *If I go back to Lokris, they'll kill me,* he realized.

He glanced at the sky. The clouds were so thick and dark that he could not tell how far advanced the morning was. When the rain stopped, he would slip back to the hut, gather the rest of his belongings, and make it look abandoned. Then they would go in search of a ship.

*If we walk south,* he thought, *we'll surely reach Troas.* But he had no idea how far it was, nor how often ships sailed to Hellas. And there were other problems. Marpessa would need a female chaperone. He could not send her alone among rough sailors. He hoped to find a companion for her—perhaps a traveling matron or someone who knew Thrasios or one of the families in Lokris—if his silver was of enough value to buy the services of such a one.

*But one step at a time. First, the hut. Then get to Troas.*

His legs were cramped from the cold. The rain had slackened, and when at last it stopped he said to Marpessa, "I'm going back to the hut. To get what I left there. You stay here." He stood up. "It won't take long."

Her eyes grew wide, alarmed. She reached out but stopped just short of touching him. "Don't go! It's dangerous. The men—"

"I'll make sure it's safe," he assured her.

She scrambled to her feet. "Let me go with you, Arion."

He nodded. When he put her on a ship, he would miss her staunch spirit, her courage. He swallowed past the knot in his throat. He found that all his hard anger had melted away. *She can't help what she is,* he thought. *She's Thrasios's daughter.*

He spread the blankets and his cloak on the ground to dry. Then he emptied the carrying sack of his possessions, hiding them in a crevice under one of the rocks. He left his silver and coppers in the bottom of the sack, and they clinked together as he slung it over his back. The sound gave him a small measure of comfort.

As she followed him, Marpessa found that her ankle no longer hurt so much, and she could breathe with only a small catch of pain. When they came to the willows that lined the stream near the hut, he led her to the cover of a large tree. "Wait here," he whispered and vanished between the trees.

She wanted to go with him to the hut, but she was afraid of making him angry again. She sat behind the tree, listening to the burbling of the stream, the dripping of water from the leaves, the tentative cry of a bird emerging from wherever it had sheltered during the storm. Moments stretched out. Why was he taking so long? What if the men had waited? Taken him captive? The wind gusted, blocking any other sound. Marpessa drew deep breaths to calm herself. Arion could take care of himself. He wouldn't walk into a trap. The wind stopped, and she heard the chirping of crickets, the splash of a small fish jumping in the water. *We're never coming back here,* she realized. *Where will we go? Why hasn't he told me?* At last she heard his steady footsteps and a rustling as he came through the reeds. Her knees weakened in relief.

"I found all my things," he said.

"What things?" she asked, pleased that he was speaking to her.

He showed her. "My other knife. An axe. An extra cloak and a tunic. Also a small javelin and a fishing net—which I kept hidden in the reeds. And these!" Reaching into the carrying sack, he held out a pair of ordinary-looking rocks. "My fire-starters. We'll need them."

"Arion, where are we going?"

His lips formed what might have been a smile, though there was sadness in it, and something held back. "A place called Troas," he said, "a seaport." She started to ask more but the look in his eyes warded her off.

*Never mind,* she thought. *I'll find out soon enough.*

Arion stuffed the almost-dry blankets into the carrying sack and hefted it over his shoulder. Then, remembering it was her first day up from her sickbed, he turned to Marpessa. "It's a long way. Will you be able to walk?"

She nodded. As they set out, clouds covered the sky, hiding the face of Helios and mirroring the gloom of Arion's mood. He kept thinking of the parting that would come as soon they found a ship. He couldn't bring himself to tell Marpessa, for he knew she was relying on him to go with her and protect her. He walked in guilty silence and only grunted in reply whenever she spoke. But with his whole being he was aware of her presence behind him, her footsteps, the sound of her breathing. After a time that breathing grew rapid, strained. He stopped and studied her, his gaze drawn to the pulse beating in the side of her slim neck, the delicate hollow at the base of her throat, and lower to the top of her gown. He tore his eyes away. "Are you tired?" he asked more brusquely than he intended.

She shook her head, and they went on. They saw a few homesteads, a few boats bobbing in the surf, and a very few wanderers on business of their own. "Keep the blanket over your head," he told Marpessa. Whenever someone appeared in the distance, he blocked her from view with his body. Fortunately they managed to avoid close contact.

When at last they stopped, it was late afternoon. Tomorrow they would try to reach Troas. His stomach growled. Marpessa too must be hungry and exhausted, though she had not complained. Hours had passed since she stopped making cheerful attempts at conversation. Her face was pale, her eyes ringed in shadows. Her thin arms hung wearily at her sides. She took an unsteady step and stumbled. He reached out to catch her, then held back. *I've been too hard on her,* he thought remorsefully, *making her walk all this way, not even talking to her. And none of this is her fault.*

He pointed to a rocky outcropping a short distance away. "We'll stop there for the night." To show her that he wasn't angry any more, that he didn't blame her, he forced a smile, which was probably more of a grimace. "Come. I'll make a fire and we can eat."

Marpessa sank gratefully to the ground. Arion, sitting on his heels, took out his firestones and uttered a brief prayer to Hephaestos, god of fire. She watched, fascinated by the strength of his hands and their skill as he struck the two rocks together repeatedly, holding them over a small pile of wood he had shaved from a fallen log. A shower of sparks flew. He bent and blew softly into the tinder. Nothing. "It's too damp," he said. "Hephaestos, send us your fire!" He began again, repeating the process with great care and patience until at last a small wisp of smoke rose from the wood shavings. Bending low, he blew on the smoke with a long, soft breath. Soon she saw a tentative orange flame, which he fed with twigs and more wood shavings, then small branches. His face tense with effort, he nourished his small fire as tenderly as if it were a living thing. At last it grew into a blaze. He built it up with pieces of driftwood.

He straightened and met her eyes. The wind ruffled the hair on his brow. Her heart leapt when, for the first time all day, he gave a genuine smile.

As night deepened, they sat by the fire in silence, their stomachs full of lamb. Arion watched Marpessa covertly as she reclined under a blanket on the other side of the fire. The flames illuminated the planes of her face and threw golden gleams into her eyes. She had not questioned him further, perhaps because she was tired, but eventually she was going to ask why they were heading to a seaport. And he was going to have to tell her—

He let out a hard breath and got to his feet.

Her eyes followed him. "What is it, Arion?"

"Tomorrow I hope we'll reach Troas."

"You haven't told me why we're going there," she said.

*There's a lot I haven't told you*, he thought. "To find you a ship, Marpessa."

She sat up, her face alight. "That means we're going home!"

He turned his back on the fire, staring sightlessly at the dark sea. Then he faced her again and sat down.

"Not we, Marpessa. You."

Her mouth opened. Her eyes grew shiny and wet. She pressed her lips together, but one teardrop spilled.

He could not take his eyes off that tear. Something twisted inside him. A log sank into the glowing fire with a soft crack, and a shower of sparks shot upward. "I never told you why I was here," he said at last. "I jumped ship—I made it look as if I drowned. I ran away." She was silent, her eyes unreadable. "That means," he added, "that I can never go back to Lokris."

She whisked the tear away and knuckled her damp cheek. "Of course, how stupid of me! I thought maybe my father had asked you to stay here, to keep watch. I should have known better." Her eyes glittered with more tears, but these, as if by an act of will, did not overflow. She straightened and lifted her head. "Thank you, Arion, for all you've done. Without you I'd be dead. I can never repay you." Each word stabbed him. She gave a small, pained smile. "So I won't ask any more of you. We'll say farewell in Troas."

# XXI

## TROAS

They slept in the shelter of a bluff. Marpessa dreamed she was nearly home; she could see her house in the distance, hear her mother calling, and almost see the beloved face, but her legs would not move, and a fearful darkness grew until it blotted out everything. Her home was lost to her forever. She awoke so filled with grief she could not move.

As they set out again, she trudged a pace or two behind Arion, engulfed in dread and fear. She longed to plead with him. *Arion, I've never had to fend for myself. How will I manage? Without you I'll never see my home again.*

*But I've already been too much of a burden,* she reminded herself. *I can't make any more demands on him.* Still, after a while she broke the silence to ask, "Arion, will you at least help me find a ship?"

He stopped so abruptly that she almost ran into him. "Of course—I said I would. I won't leave you until you're in safe hands."

Marpessa felt some relief. *But I'll still be alone among strangers,* she thought.

Later when they sat down on a pile of rocks to rest and eat some of their remaining bread and meat, Marpessa pondered what he had said yesterday: *I ran away. I can never go back.* She wanted to tell him, *I can make it right. Father will take you back if I tell him how you saved my life and cared for me.* But she was not sure this was true, and besides his eyes had gone far away again, staring out to sea.

As if thinking aloud, he said, "The ship isn't the problem."

"What do you mean?" she asked.

"You can't travel alone. You'll need a chaperone—a protector."

"A replacement for you," she said.

He shook his head. "A female."

She could not imagine how they would find such a person. But there was an even more pressing problem. "What will we do when we get to Troas? You're a man and I a maid, alone together, and—"

His brow creased. "I've thought of a story. We'll say that I'm your family's slave, taking you to relatives in Lokris because your family died—killed by the marauders. You had a female companion who was also killed, and we're looking for another to escort you."

"But don't you see? We can't be seen together! If they find out what we are, *who* we are, I'll be taken from you. You'll be killed!"

Arion sat up sharply. When he said nothing, she realized that he didn't have an answer for this. *We're doomed before we even find a ship*, she thought in despair. *Oh, Goddess Athena, what can we do?*

And then the answer came into her mind, so simple, so obvious that she was stunned by its brilliance. "Arion, we can avoid the whole problem if—" She paused dramatically, waiting for him to ask.

"If what?" he prompted.

"If I am disguised as a boy!"

His smile was like sunlight breaking through clouds. "By Zeus, that might work!"

They stopped by a large rock that offered concealment so that Marpessa could effect her transformation. Arion gave her his extra tunic and cloak. In privacy behind the rock, Marpessa doffed her filthy, ragged slave's robe and donned the tunic, which was much too large for her. That was well, because it hung loose around her chest, concealing her breasts. She pulled up the extra length of it and tied it in folds around her waist with an improvised belt torn from her old gown. She had no sandals, but she had gone barefoot since the day she became a slave in Troy. She fastened Arion's cloak over one shoulder and ran a hand through her hair. Her short curls must look boyish enough. Putting a finger in the dirt at the base of the rock, she smudged her upper lip to make it seem as if the hair had darkened there with the first signs of a man's beard.

She started quickly back to Arion, eager to show him. Then she slowed, changing her steps into the long, loose-jointed stride of a boy. When she reached him, she hooked her thumbs in her belt and tried to look brashly confident. She spoke in a lower, huskier voice. "My name shall be Teukros—your younger brother. Will I pass?"

She was gratified by his grin of surprise. He nodded. Then he sobered. "But what will you do on a ship where there's no privacy?"

That problem had not occurred to her. "I'm good at slipping away from people. I'll find ways."

Arion looked troubled. "I hope you're right."

*

*It's full of danger,* he agonized as they resumed their journey. Troas was turning out to be farther than he thought, giving Arion too much time to worry. The heaviness in his heart was like an anvil. It had been one thing to plan this when the ship was only an idea and the town far away. Now that they were on the verge of arriving, he was afraid. And he knew that, with all her courage and bravado, Marpessa was too. Even if as a "lad" she wouldn't need a chaperone, how could he leave her on a ship full of men? *Anything can happen,* he thought. *She could be sold into slavery, raped, killed. What if she never reaches home? I can't do this.* But as their steps brought them ever closer to the town, he saw no other choice.

The sky was colored with the bruised tints of twilight when at last they began to see signs of Troas: huts and small farms on their left and more boats on the sea. Marpessa's jaunty boyish gait had become a limp again. He didn't have the heart to push her any further. She was clearly on her last reserves of strength.

"We'll go into town in the morning," he told her. It felt like a reprieve. He pointed to a rocky outcropping that jutted into the sea. "Tonight we'll shelter there." They still had food left. He would build a fire for warmth. No one would question two fishermen cooking their supper on the shore.

Marpessa awoke at first light with a knot in her stomach. This day would decide her fate. The pale sun rose above massing clouds. As they approached the town, they saw small knolls with wooden and stone houses around them, smoke drifting upward from hearths. Atop the highest knoll was a long building with a pitched roof and thick stone columns in front—most likely the temple of Zeus. Around it were several smaller shrines to other gods. Wondering which one was dedicated to Athena, Marpessa sent up a desperate prayer. *Please, Goddess, don't let Arion desert me here!* They waded through a wide, sluggish stream that flowed across the muddy shoreline. A few fishing vessels were drawn up on the sand, and two or three larger boats rocked at their moorings on the choppy waters. No boat looked large enough to cross the sea. On the shore, several fishermen labored over their nets.

They stopped. She wondered if Arion felt the same terrible fear that gripped her, the realization that they were fugitives without a home, possessions or friends—without even, when it came down to it, the right to stand on this shore as if they belonged here. It hit her for the first time how flimsy her disguise was and how dangerous it would be if anyone saw through it. And Arion, if they found out he was a fugitive slave—

*Even if we both survive,* she thought, *I'll never see him again.*

She cast a look at his grim profile. Perhaps they should abandon this scheme and flee before they were seen. *Too late.* A couple of men on the shore looked up and noticed them.

"What shall we do?" Marpessa whispered.

"We'll ask what ships will be sailing for Hellas in the next few days." Arion spoke calmly, but there was a telltale catch in his voice. She had to clench her fist to stop herself from grasping his hand. She wanted to hold on and never let go. She was afraid she would cry. As if he sensed it, he laid his hand gently on her shoulder. Her skin warmed. They had not touched since they huddled from the storm. "Come, Teukros." He gave a faint smile. "Let's go talk to them."

He led the way, and she followed half a pace behind, trying to control her trembling knees and walk with a carefree, boyish stride. They approached the nearest fisherman, a man of fifty or sixty years with a leathery brown face and a rag tied about his head, who was caulking the hull of his upended boat. He straightened slowly and looked them over, his eyes full of suspicious questions. His gaze slid past Arion, lingered longer on Marpessa, and focused on her face, then her chest, making her heart pound. She hunched her shoulders and took a step back so that she was half-hidden behind Arion.

"Good day, sir!" Arion greeted him.

"Good day, strangers," the man replied. "Who might you be?"

"My name is, er—" Arion cleared his throat to cover the slight hesitation. "Lykaon. This is my young brother Teukros. We are come from Troy in search of a ship." Marpessa hoped he would not say too much and get entangled in a web of lies. But he added only, "We are returning to our home city in Lokris."

Her heart jumped at the "we." Had he changed his mind?

"Lokris!" the man exclaimed. He was silent for a moment, and his gaze seemed to bore into Marpessa. "Is that so? Well, you're a bit late, my friends! The last ship to Hellas—to anywhere—sailed yesterday."

As if she had been struck hard in the stomach, Marpessa couldn't breathe.

"What!" Arion exclaimed, staring at the man.

"It's the storm season," The fisherman pointed at the huge mountains of dark clouds piling up along the horizon. "No more ships will be sailing over these seas 'till spring."

# XXII

## WRATH

The last ship to cross the sea to Lokris ran swiftly before the wind and brought a man bearing a clay tablet from the Prince-Governor of Troy to the High Priestess of Athena in Naryx.

The High Priestess lived in a well-built house near the temple. It was evening, and she had removed her headdress. Her graying hair fell about her shoulders. She held the tablet close to the lamp, squinted, then read the news with growing horror. Her knees gave way, and she sat down abruptly. She was completely at a loss. The situation was unprecedented. Occasionally one of the girls had been killed by the Trojans on the way to the citadel, and they'd had to send a replacement girl immediately. But never both girls! And never had there been killing in the middle of their servitude.

The priestess decided to consult at once with two of the elders of Naryx, the most important oligarchs. She called her servant. "Go and rouse Klonios and Archippos and bid them come here. It is of the utmost urgency." Quickly she replaced her headdress and smoothed her gown. Then she waited, impatient yet nervous, for the two men to arrive. She would be glad of Archippos' counsel. He was the oldest oligarch and the most levelheaded. She wished she had not had to summon Klonios, for she did not trust him. But since he had recently returned from his trading voyage, she'd had no choice. He was the wealthiest and most powerful man in Naryx, perhaps in all of Lokris. He used his power to gain what he wanted, by means fair or foul. Many times in the past he had gotten her to do his bidding in the matter of temple policy, or sacrifices, or festivals, or who should or shouldn't be elevated in the ranks of priests and priestesses. Just because he contributed generously to the temple treasury, he thought he could—

Her musings were interrupted by the arrival of the oligarchs. The servant led them to her hearth. When they had sat down and declined her offer of wine, she showed them the tablet.

"It says we are to send two replacements at once," she told them. "As soon as—" She broke off. Klonios's face became suffused with rage, his eyes narrow slits, his sharp teeth bared in a beastlike grimace. She watched as his fists clenched and unclenched, the knuckles white.

"*Both* girls?" he snarled at her.

Her heart gave a jolt of astonished fear. She compensated by straightening her shoulders. "Aye. My lord, what is it?"

Instantly his face went as smooth as if someone had passed a hand over it to wipe away all emotion. The change was so quick that, if she didn't know better, the High Priestess might have thought she imagined the whole thing. "Nothing at all," he said, and continued in a level tone, "Two replacements? That's impossible! The Hundred Houses would never agree to such a thing."

Still shaken but refusing to show it, she lifted her chin. "I think they must!" she said sternly.

Archippos pointed out, "During the season of storms, most would be unwilling to risk a ship, but—" He broke off. Both he and the High Priestess looked at Klonios, who was known to undertake trading journeys up the coast and often beyond, even during winter.

Guessing their thoughts, Klonios stared back, his eyes cold and hard. "Absolutely not!" he said. "I will have nothing to do with this wretched business."

The priestess sighed deeply. "Well—" she began.

"Sending two replacements in the middle of the year was never part of the agreement," Archippos temporized. "Once those girls reached Troy safely, they became the Trojans' responsibility, and—"

Klonios's mouth became a thin slit and his eyes turned adamant. "If the Trojans couldn't protect the girls in their own temple, that's their affair. We will not bear the cost!"

"Perhaps we could wait until spring—or even the next drawing," Archippos suggested mildly. "We're halfway through the year anyway."

Klonios drove his point home. "They can't expect us to do the impossible."

The High Priestess hesitated. Whenever Klonios mandated something, she always wanted to do the opposite. Yet she knew it was not wise give in to that impulse. "Then we'll wait," she said at last.

"So be it. If there's no more to be said—" Klonios started to rise.

But Archippos ignored him. "Of course we risk offending the goddess," he pointed out.

*Athena's wrath.* There was a moment's silence as all three of them remembered the tales of famine and pestilence that the goddess had wrought on their land hundreds of years ago. Then Klonios, who had sat down again, slammed his fist against the arm of his chair. "By all the gods, what of it? Make sacrifice to Athena then! That's why we have this temple! That's why I keep you well supplied with riches!"

The priestess heaved a deep sigh, knowing she could not argue. "Very well. We will offer reparation in advance. I'll arrange a large sacrifice to remind the goddess of our promise of two more maidens in the spring. I don't know what else we can do."

"Then it's settled." Klonios rose abruptly, and Archippos got to his feet more slowly. The High Priestess escorted them to the door. "I thank you, gentlemen. Good evening. Now," she added sadly, "I must send a message to the families of the girls who died."

Outside on the dark street, Klonios went in swift strides to his house. Only when he was inside did he give in to his rage. He let out a sound like a fierce animal on the attack. He hefted a large decorative urn as if it weighed nothing and threw it against the wall, watching in satisfaction as it shattered. Then he yelled for an attendant. "Bring me wine!" When it came, handed to him by a timorous slave, he downed it in one gulp.

The servant hovered. "My lord, will there be anything else?"

"Begone!" Klonios roared.

Hastily the man backed away, bowing.

*That girl! Thrasios's daughter.* Klonios leapt to his feet, paced like a leopard in a cage. *I meant to have her, Athena or no Athena, when all this was done! It's Thrasios's fault for letting her go. He'll pay for this! I'll ruin him.*

Then another thought struck him. *We risk offending the goddess,* Archippos had said. A lot of people in Naryx would begin to fear Athena's wrath. Klonios found pleasure in the idea. It presented interesting possibilities. He smiled as a scheme began to form in his mind.

At about the same time, in the courtyard of the house of Thrasios, a messenger from the temple pounded on the door. When a maidservant answered, he told her, "I must speak with the master. I have news for him and orders to deliver it personally."

Thrasios came to the door. "What is it, man?" he demanded in his usual harsh manner.

"This was brought to the temple of Athena. The High Priestess bade me take it to the house of Polites, father of Haleia, then bring it here. It concerns your daughter Marpessa." He thrust the clay tablet in Thrasios' hands and bowed briefly. "Now I'll take my leave."

Thrasios was left staring at the clay tablet. His hand shook and his breathing quickened. Amaltheia had followed him out to the courtyard, her face white. "What does it say?" she whispered.

After the first glance he did not deign to look at her. "Terrible news! The goddess Athena is wroth with us. I fear she will send us doom and destruction." He slammed the tablet down. It broke into jagged pieces as it hit the ground. "Our daughter—" His voice choked with impotent anger. "Athena didn't find her worthy of fulfilling her obligation to the temple. She's dead!"

Amaltheia stood still as stone. Then she fainted.

# PART II

# XXIII

## SHIP AT ANCHOR

After shouting orders for his men to drop the anchor, Klonios paced furiously up and down the gangway of his ship. He was glad he had sailed away, glad to be quit of Lokris. With their accursed ritual, the citizens of Naryx had stolen his fair young bride, and now she was dead. *A pestilence on them all!* he thought. All they cared about was Athena's wrath. What about *his* feelings? He would show them wrath. After he had arranged certain vitally important and secret things, he had sailed away on his largest trading ship, up the coast to the peninsula of Mende, a small settlement where he had holdings. The arrangements he had made before leaving caused him to smirk. *They'll be sorry they trifled with me,* he thought.

"You there!" he shouted at a passing crew member. "A goblet of wine and be quick about it!" When the wine came, he sat on the stern deck, drinking.

Though it was autumn, the beginning of the season of storms, the sky was a high, bright blue, the sea calm. The weather was as unseasonably warm and dry here as it was not far away in Lokris. Earlier there had been a wild but brief storm, but the rainfall had mostly bypassed Naryx. There were reports of storms elsewhere, but none came near Lokris. It looked to be a drought year.

Klonios laughed aloud. Though droughts occurred every few years, the timing of this one was incredibly fortuitous. Events were playing right into his hands. He imagined the Lokrian farmers looking at their fields, worrying about their crops. As for the vintners— Klonios smiled. Thrasios would be expending precious well water to irrigate his vines. *Thrasios, Thrasios, you spineless excuse for a man,* he thought. *Little good it will do you!*

And this was only the beginning. What had started as a simple drought over which he had no control would change, through his careful planning, into something so much worse. He had laid the groundwork. Now all he had to do was wait.

He just might winter here or, if the weather continued mild, head out on another trading journey. There was money to be made when lesser merchants were afraid to leave their home ports. Klonios smiled again and lifted his wine goblet to the sky. *Thank you, Athena, for the boon of this drought,* he thought. *You and I are partners now.*

*Partners in vengeance.*

# XXIV

## THE WARNING

The first birdcalls awakened Arion. He sat up and groaned, still tired, then came out of his cave into the early morning mist. He stretched. The sun had not yet risen, and no sound came from the cave where Marpessa slept. He dipped his hands in the water jar and dashed the sleep from his eyes, then helped himself to bread from their small store of food. As he ate, he looked around the glade where they had made their camp. They'd been lucky in finding this spot on the wooded slopes of Mount Ida. It was bordered by a steep wall of rock indented with caves where they could sleep and store food and belongings. Not far away was a deep, cold spring. With luck they could stay here until the warm weather returned and they could find Marpessa a ship. The fact that it was so high in the mountains, so far from dwellings and villages, was both a blessing and a curse. Here they were safely hidden from strangers. Yet when he had no success hunting, he had to trek great distances in search of food and work.

Arion stepped to the opening of the cave where Marpessa slept. "Teukros!" They'd agreed that he would continue to call her Teukros. If strangers ever came upon them, they could pass for two brothers living together. But in his most secret, unguarded thoughts, she was always Marpessa. "I'm leaving now," he called, softly enough so that she would hear him only if she was awake. He worried about her during the long hours she spent alone each day. Uneasy, he uttered a silent prayer: *Athena, keep her safe while I'm gone!* wondering if the gods heard, or even concerned themselves with the troubles of men, especially those of a lowly slave with no wealth who had never had the means to offer a single sacrifice.

Then he slung his sack over his shoulder and started down the trail. *One more day of building a fence for that farmer*, he thought. *Then what?* As he walked he continued to worry about Marpessa. She'd seemed so despondent and homesick ever since they came to the mountain. Yet he was secretly glad that they would be together through the winter. And at the same time terrified. There were many dangers in the mountains: starvation, wild animals. The yoke was heavy on his shoulders—the burden of their survival.

Walking down the slope was easy. Daylight grew, and he followed his markers, torn rags and strips of hide tied to branches. He'd put them along the trail to guide his way down the mountain. The hard part would be climbing back at the day's end with darkness falling, when he was exhausted. And with autumn far advanced, night was closing in ever earlier.

Marpessa lifted the bow, nocked an arrow, then sighted along it and shot. The arrow went on a short, wobbly trajectory, missing the tree at which she had been aiming. *Gods! Will I ever learn to do this?* Arion had made it look so easy. Sighing, she retrieved the arrow and tried again. It was mid afternoon, and her innards cramped with hunger.

She tried to ignore not only her empty stomach but her heavy heart. In Troas she had prayed to Athena not to let Arion desert her. The goddess granted her prayer but took away all possibility of going home. Now Marpessa was afraid she'd never see her family again. Never had she felt so isolated. No one save Arion even knew where she was, for her mother surely believed her still safe in Troy, faithfully serving the goddess at Haleia's side. The thought made her unbearably lonely.

Though Arion had not deserted her, he left at daybreak every day, often not returning until after dusk. When he did return, he was often so tired he barely spoke as he shared a brief meal with her before going to sleep in his cave. She never complained, for he put all his energy and strength into assuring their survival. But the days without him were long and empty. She had never minded solitude—had sought it even, in Lokris when she left her home to wander in the woods. But now her aloneness was so unremitting that often she spoke aloud to herself just to hear a human voice.

Learning to use this bow might take her mind off her troubles. Arion had bartered for it a few days ago. She'd been practicing for hours. Her growling stomach reminded her that their store of food was almost depleted. How surprised and pleased Arion would be if she learned to hunt!

Just then a large deer streaked across the edge of the glade. A sign! *I'll go into the woods and try my luck right now,* Marpessa decided. But as she slung the bow and quiver over her shoulder, she thought, *I'm not ready!* Shooting at a tree was very different from hitting a moving target, a living creature. And trying to kill it. *I can't!*

*You must,* she told herself.

She crept up the slope following the deer, her bare feet finding places that made no sound. Little sunlight penetrated the deep gloom of the forest. Her eyes searched the leafy shadows while her ears strained for any sound beyond the birdcalls and the wind in the trees. But the deer had vanished.

Suddenly a loud, high-pitched, quavering cry rang through the trees. Marpessa froze. The haunting call reverberated again, raising her hackles, sending chills down her spine. The songbirds fell silent. The forest had suddenly gone cold and dark. She stood still, looked around. Then it came a third time, a long drawn-out, unearthly keening. Her eyes searched and found its source. A tawny owl, taller than her forearm, sat on a branch, transfixing her with its unblinking black gaze. She could not move nor tear her eyes away. What was an owl, predator of the night, doing here in daylight?

The answer came: *It's Athena's messenger.* Marpessa couldn't draw a breath. Legs trembling, she dropped to her knees. The bow fell from her hands. She tried in vain to form words of prayer, supplication. But after another moment of its cold indifferent stare, the owl lifted from the branch and glided away through the trees on silent wings. She groped to her feet, prickles all over her skin. *Oh, Athena, what do you want me to do?*

Then, as if the goddess had sent the thought into her mind, she suddenly knew. *Get away from here. You are in danger.*

Danger from what? And where could they go? Arion might know what to do, she thought. If only he were here and she didn't have to wait to talk to him. She picked up the bow and quiver, realizing she'd forgotten her hunger. Never mind killing an animal today. Feeling a slight relief at that, she started down the slope.

A deer—a small doe this time—came soundlessly through the trees not twenty paces away. Marpessa's arms were heavy as she raised the bow, nocked an arrow, aimed. The doe stood motionless, its beautiful amber eyes looking right into hers. Her fingers trembled. She released the arrow clumsily and it went awry, landing far from the deer, which sprinted into the trees.

Tears of shame scorched her eyes as she retrieved the arrow. *Arion, I've let you down.* If his own quest for meat was fruitless, they'd go hungry again tonight. Then a small sound made her look up. A plump rabbit crept from behind a tree. Without letting herself hesitate, she lifted the bow, nocked the arrow in one smooth movement, and shot. This time her aim was true. The rabbit rolled on its side, dead. But instead of triumph, she felt an empty sadness.

Back in the camp, she forced herself to skin the rabbit. Its little body was still warm, and its eyes, dulled by death, seemed to stare at her in reproach. Tears slipped down her cheeks. *Artemis, forgive me for taking the life of one of your creatures!* She understood the need to kill animals for food, but she would never get used it, never!

While she was working to free the hide from the body and remove the slippery innards, the weather grew dark and cold. She shivered, wishing she had a warmer tunic. The sun vanished behind clouds before it set, and twilight fell without warning. The wind quickened. She wished Arion would come back.

A sudden loud thrashing in the woods at the edge of the glade sent her to her feet, her heart beating painfully. A large animal, she was sure, but she could see nothing in the shadows. There were wolves, bears, mountain lions in this forest. She grabbed the bow and stood frozen, peering into the trees. She felt stillness and menace. Something was watching her. She thought she saw a pair of eyes in the dark foliage, catching the last light. Large eyes, set far apart, predator eyes. Terrified, she couldn't move. But she must. She waved her arms and sprang a short way forward, bellowing with all the force of her lungs. A sudden, intense silence answered her. Then came the rustlings, growing fainter, of a reluctant retreat.

Marpessa's knees gave way and she sat down suddenly. Her eyes fell on the small pile of entrails from the rabbit. The smell of the kill had attracted the predator. Leaping to her feet, she grabbed the entrails and sprinted down the slope, stopping when the foliage grew too thick and flinging them as far as she could into the trees. She washed the gore from her hands in the small nearby stream. Then she ran back, remembering she'd left the rabbit carcass on the frame. By the grace of the gods it was still there. She picked it up, frame and all, and put it in the nearest cave. Dark shadows were closing in from all sides. Rustling noises came from the woods. She went to the fire pit to build up a fire, but the last of the embers had gone out while she was in the woods. *I'll make a new fire,* she decided. *Arion showed me how.* But though she'd tried, never before had she succeeded. She found his precious rocks, gathered tinder, shaved some bark off a dead branch.

*Hephaestos,* she prayed, *help me drive back the darkness.*

She struck the rocks repeatedly. Nothing. Arion had made it look so easy. She *would not* give up. Her hands were bloody when at last there was a shower of tiny sparks—then a small flare. The shavings ignited. Desperately, prayerfully, she fed it with twigs, dead leaves. When the fire came to life, she felt a fierce elation. She added wood and set the cooking frame over it. Luckily she had a pot full of water from the spring. Soon the pot was over the fire and the rabbit cooking. The predator couldn't steal it from the boiling water. She threw in some wild onion and herbs she had gathered and dried. They would disguise the smell of the meat. *I need a weapon*, she thought. The bow would do no good if the animal attacked.

Then she remembered—she *had* a weapon! Arion had fashioned a club from a large fallen branch, and she'd forgotten about it. What a fool not to have kept it at her side! She fetched it from the storage cave and sat by the fire, the club on the ground beside her. Where *was* Arion? It was fully dark now, and he'd never been this late before. What if something had happened? She suddenly couldn't catch her breath.

*Stop it! It does no good to panic*, she thought. But fear had stolen into the glade, its evil presence a black shape teasing the edge of her vision, disappearing when she confronted it directly, sneaking back when she became unwary. Soon it gripped her whole mind. She saw Arion set upon by robbers, lying bloodied in a ditch, Arion falling in the dark and breaking his leg, Arion mauled by a wolf or a bear.

*Stop it!* she told herself again. *Arion can take care of himself.* If he lost his way in the dark, he would simply shelter for the night and come back in the morning. But the voice of common sense did not stop the gnawing and twisting of her innards. She got to her feet, shivering. She strode purposefully around the glade, fed more wood into the fire, then sat again, wrapped in her blanket, trying to keep the darkness as well as her dark thoughts at bay.

Suddenly there was a crashing in the underbrush. A looming shadow appeared at the very edge of the circle of firelight. She grabbed the club in shaking hands and sprang to her feet.

# XXV

## THE DARK WOODS

Night had fallen. Arion had left the farmstead too late and become hopelessly lost. He couldn't find his trail markers on the wooded slopes and wandered around the mountainside for what seemed like hours. At last, by pure luck, when a branch lashed him in the face, he found a leather strip tied to it. *His trail!* He followed it mostly by feel. Then when he was nearing their camp, he saw a flickering light coming through the trees and smelled smoke. *A fire.*

He froze. *Strangers. Have they found Marpessa?* Heart pounding, he raced toward the glade. When he reached it, a slight figure came hurtling at him, shouting and wielding a club. He leapt out of the way. "Marpessa!" he yelped, just in time to stop her from bashing him on the head.

The club fell to the ground. She threw herself into his arms and burst into tears. He was engulfed in her warmth, the feel of her, the sunshine smell of her hair. Heat swept through his blood. For a moment he closed his eyes and gave in to it, tightening his arms about her. Then he forced himself to pull back. He was breathing hard. As her sobs quieted, he felt her staring at him. "Arion, what took you so long?"

For a moment he couldn't speak. Then he mumbled, "I lost my way. In the dark. Couldn't see my markers."

"I was so frightened! Wait 'till I tell you what happened. But first, I've made us supper." Her voice held pride. In the age-old gesture of a host leading a guest toward the hearth, she grasped his hand, her strong, slender fingers entwining around his, and drew him to the fire. When she let go, he ached with emptiness. He was silent while she busied herself over the pot. Then she placed a trencher of rabbit stew in his hands and smiled up at him. "Eat!" she said, and he realized he was ravenous. He ate.

Afterwards, as they were licking the last delicious juices from their fingers, he said, "Tell me how you did this. The rabbit, the fire." He listened in amazement. None of it could have been easy. There were bloody scabs on her knuckles. He longed to take those hands in his, to soothe away their hurts, but he held still.

At the mention of the wild beast, he tensed, pulled the club to his side and surveyed the black woods all around them, his ears tuned to any sound beyond her soft voice, the crackling of the flames. He wanted to tell her that the courage of the ancient heroes ran in her blood, but all he could say through the sudden thickness in his throat was, "You did well, very well." Woefully inadequate words, but a glowing smile transformed her face.

Then the smile faded, and she said, "I almost forgot to tell you the most important thing. The owl, Athena's warning." Arion listened uneasily as she talked of her encounter in the woods. She finished by asking, "What are we going to do?"

He gathered in a deep breath and said, "We stay here. There's nothing we can do. There's nowhere else we can go."

"But what if it means something terrible is going to happen? Something almost did. That wild animal—"

"Hush, Marpessa!" Her name sprang to his lips without his will. "You did all the right things, and now you know how to build a fire. Wild beasts usually stay away from people. With luck we won't see any more." To calm her fears, he tried to quell his own misgivings. But the question insinuated itself into his mine. *Can we survive the winter here?* "Keep the club handy," he added. "I'll build a storage chest for our meat and weight down the lid with rocks."

When she still looked anxious, he said, "We don't know that it was a message from the goddess. Once when I was a boy I saw an owl in the daytime. My master at the time told me that sometimes they come out in daylight. It may mean nothing. How can you be sure this owl was sent as a warning?"

"I felt it! It was as if I heard the goddess's voice." Her eyes came to his face. "Arion, maybe she wants me to go back to Troy and finish my servitude there."

"No!" The word burst from him. "It's not safe! I told you what they did to Haleia's corpse. Besides, I'm sure they think you were killed. Likely they even sent a message to Lokris, before the seas grew too stormy, and—"

She gave an anguished cry. "You think they sent a message?" Too late he realized that the thought had not occurred to her.

*Oh, gods!* he thought. *I only wanted to comfort her, and now I've made it worse.* "Perhaps I'm wrong. With all the looting and robbing, the dead to be buried, they probably didn't think of sending word until the seas grew too rough for travel."

But Marpessa shook her head. "There are many Lokrians in Troy. They would have sent a message right away. Stupid of me to think they wouldn't." She added in a broken whisper, "My mother will die if she thinks I'm dead!"

Silence fell.

Then Arion said quickly, "I almost forgot. I brought you something—a woolen tunic." He had bartered it off the farmer's wife, along with a sack of barley.

She forced a small smile and cast aside her blanket to pull the tunic over her head, covering the old one. "Thank you, Arion! I was cold today, and this one will be so much warmer."

"I'm glad." He stood. "It's been a long day, Teukros, and you're tired." *So am I,* he thought, *down to my bones.* "Go to bed. Don't worry. It does no good." His voice sounded rougher than he intended. To atone, he reached down to help her to her feet. It was a mistake. At the touch of their hands, his breath quickened, and his blood heated again. He led her to her sleeping cave, managed to mutter, "Good night," and went abruptly to his own cave.

But tired though he was, he could not sleep. He tried to distract himself from his thoughts, which all had one name, one face. *Marpessa.*

*In my slave's life, I saw so few women,* he thought, tossing about in his sleeping rugs. *But I could control desire.* It had not always been so. As a lad toiling in Thrasios's vineyards at the harvest, when he'd looked at the servant girls' bare legs beneath their kilted skirts, the muscles of their haunches bunching as they worked to press the grapes, his lust must have been obvious. The grown men had laughed at him, humiliating him. By the time he was twenty, he'd had a few groping encounters with an older slave woman from a neighboring farm. He remembered her heavy breasts, her wide hips, the farmyard smell of her. He'd never learned her name. When she stopped coming to meet him, he found it best never to think about women.

Now, with Marpessa, his control had deserted him.

*She can be nothing in my life, nor I in hers,* he reminded himself. He flung off the sleeping rug and went outside where the night wind struck his skin and cooled his blood. He breathed deeply. Between the branches of the trees a myriad stars gleamed, making him feel small and insignificant.

Here on the mountain their lives could end in a moment. They could starve or be found by hostile Trojans glad to turn in an escaped slave for the reward. Or be killed by wolves or bears. So what was to stop him from going into the

122

cave where she slept?

He made no move.

A young girl who lost her maidenhood was despoiled, ruined. There was also Athena, who demanded virginity in her servant Marpessa. *I may be a fool*, he thought, *but I won't do anything to harm her.*

*I love her.* The thought jolted his heart. It changed everything, and yet nothing. His next thought was, *She must never know.*

That meant he had to keep his distance. Never touch her again.

He returned to his bed, wishing for oblivion. From afar came the long, lonely howl of a wolf, filling him with a strange mixture of sadness and fear.

# XXVI

## THE VINEYARD

Thrasios walked slowly around his ruined vineyards, moving from one plant to the next, touching leaves that were brown around the edges. The grapes were stunted on the vine. Though he felt like closing his eyes in despair, he forced himself to stand straight and look around.

Row after row, as far as he could see, was the same. Withered leaves. Bunches of grapes the size of tiny pebbles, wrinkled, green, dying unripened.

*Klonios,* he thought. *He promised me ruin.*

Even before this, merchants had stopped buying his wines. That was Klonios's doing. But could Klonios have wrought a disaster of this proportion? It was not just his vineyards that were dying. Other vintners had reported failures—some form of rot that attacked the vines. Other crops were dying in the fields, and most of the barley and wheat had not even sprouted.

To make matters worse, the rains had not come. All of Naryx, all of Lokris itself, was falling into ruin. Dying. And he had no power, no knowledge, nor even the will to fix it.

These worries were too big for him to think of when all was not well in his own domain. Amaltheia walked through her days like a living ghost, her eyes hollowed in dark circles, the flesh dropping from her bones. She performed all her household duties but never looked at him nor spoke to him. That made little difference in his life since he rarely occupied her bed. But there was the matter of his own failure. He no longer visited his favorite *hetaira* in Naryx, for he could not trust himself to perform as a man should. These things could only be happening because of the wrath of a god. Or a goddess.

It did not take him long to see which goddess.

His mind turned to the daughter who had previously occupied so little of his thoughts. All at once he was angry. Marpessa was chosen, and it was her chance to uphold the family's honor. It should have been a simple enough thing to go to Troy and do the goddess's will. *Unworthy. Athena found her unworthy. Or there would have been no raid. She would not have been killed. And none of this would have happened.*

As he walked back through his vineyards to his empty warehouse, he felt his shoulders slump and his steps drag like those of an old man.

# XXVII

## THE SPRING

Marpessa knelt in front of her flat stone grinding the barleycorns Arion had brought last night. It was hard work, clean, pure, uncomplicated, and it left her mind free to think. As she fell into the rhythmic, back-and-forth motion, her thoughts flew to her home. Her parents believed her dead. She imagined her mother broken with grief. *Oh, my mother! If only I could go home to you now*, she cried silently. That made her think of Athena's message. *What should I do?* But there was no answer save Arion's: *There's nothing we can do.* The words repeated themselves senselessly in her head until she thrust aside the grinding stone and leapt to her feet.

She went restlessly into the woods, hoping for comfort or even another visitation from Athena that would make the goddess's will plain. But she saw no owls or any other beasts, only birds clamoring in the trees. Athena, as the gods often were, was elusive, absent.

She came to a rocky promontory from which fell a beautiful waterfall. She sat for a time listening to the music of the water and watching the crystal falls, the rainbow spray where sunlight seeped through the trees. The beauty of the forest soaked into her soul. Her thoughts came clear like the water. *Mother, I will accept whatever fate the gods send. I will be strong as you are strong. For it was you who taught me strength. My mother, you be strong too. For me.*

Much later when she returned to the camp, she was at peace. She knelt in front of the flat stone again to finish grinding the grain.

Arion finished his repairs for the farmer in the valley while it was still light and trudged up the slope, his anxious thoughts dwelling on Marpessa. Thanks to his blunder, she now knew that her parents most likely thought her dead. He had to find a way to comfort her. Yet he worried about keeping his feelings concealed. He wanted to devour her with his eyes, to caress the gentle slope of her cheek and kiss her lips.

Last night at times he had been almost speechless in her presence. Now he was weary, thirsty, begrimed with sweat and dust. He needed to renew his depleted strength. *I need to prepare myself before talking to her. I'll go wash first*, he decided. When he reached the glade, he greeted her briefly and laid down his earnings—a jar of olive oil, some onions and beans, some more barley grain. Then with a muttered excuse, he headed for the spring.

The spring, one of many on the mountainside, was small and almost perfectly round in its nest of rocks. Craggy rock walls sprang up around the point where the icy water gushed from the ground. A huge ancient oak had thrown down gnarled roots to grip the rock and suck the water from its source. Arion gave a sigh that was almost a groan. This was a place of tranquility. For a moment he forgot his worries as he flung off his tunic and sank into the life-giving waters.

Marpessa remembered that she needed water for cooking. Arion had gone to the spring without taking the caldron to refill. "Arion!" she called, but he was too far to hear. She picked up the empty pot and followed him.

Their frequent trips had worn a path through the underbrush to the spring. As she walked, she listened to the piercing sweetness of a bird's call—probably a hawk. She stood still, recalling the owl. But there was nothing out of the ordinary here. She wiped dampness from her brow. The air was sultry. A storm was probably on the way.

She stepped out of the underbrush at the edge of the spring—and froze. Arion, his back to her, stood naked in the water. A hot flush rose to her face and neck. The caldron fell from her hands. At once he turned to face her. For too long, though it was probably only a few heartbeats, they were both unable to move or speak. Her eyes came up to his face, which had paled. In the greenish twilight, with his wet hair dripping over his brow, he looked beautiful, his eyes bright in the dimness and achingly vulnerable. All at once Marpessa's legs came alive with a will of their own, and she turned and bolted like a frightened deer, never stopping until she reached their camp.

There she paced around vehemently, her face hot. How could she have so stupidly blundered upon his privacy? He must hate her for it. What would she say when he came back?

There was a tight feeling in her chest. She could not wipe from her mind what she had seen. After a few more turns about the camp, she remembered that Arion had brought more grain to grind. The task was exactly what she needed so as not to think about what had just happened. She fetched the new sack of barley, then squatted before the flat stone. Pouring out several handfuls, she picked up the grinding stone and began the vigorous back-and-forth movements of stone against stone, pressing down hard, putting all her strength into it to relieve her pent-up feelings. But the more she strove to avoid thinking, the more the image of Arion crept into her head.

*What's the matter with me? I have brothers*, she reminded herself. The men of Lokris were quite casual about their bodies, and several times she had glimpsed her brothers bathing or stripping down for athletic contests. But with Arion it was different. That moment at the spring had been a personal exchange between them that had felt—intimate.

She paused to wipe her brow, then went back to work with renewed energy. Why could she not make his image go away? Why this strange weakness in her knees? To distract herself, she imagined herself at home in Naryx. What would her life be at this moment if her name had never been drawn on that fateful day? With another set of threads on the loom of the Fates, her parents might by now have arranged a marriage for her. She'd always feared they would choose some old widower who wanted her only for the bearing of sons or somebody hard and cruel with little patience for women. Like her father. But what if they chose someone young—and handsome?

Unbidden, the image of Arion crept into her mind. She had taken him as much for granted as the trees, the rocks and stones of the mountainside. Why had she not noticed his beauty before? If the Fates had placed different threads on their loom for him, he might have been a free man with property—the very husband that her parents would choose.

In her mind she could see the wedding ceremony and even hear the wailing of the flutes, the steady beat of the drums and tambourines as the procession began. She saw herself veiled and decked in gems and garlands of flowers, being led forth between her parents toward the sacred moment when at last she would stand before her husband. And she saw him so clearly: Arion, wearing the long chiton of the bridegroom, his eyes meeting hers, looking not too different from the way they had just now at the spring: solemn, mysterious, full of deep feelings she could not read.

*No!* She flung the grinding stone aside with a force that sent barleycorns flying, and rubbed her eyes to shatter the images that could never be. A taste of bitter gall filled her mouth. *Unjust Fates!* There would be no marriage of any kind for her even if by a miracle she did reach home. And Arion, who could be nothing to her, who probably didn't even like her, would leave her life forever when this time of isolation on the mountain was over. He had told her so.

She heard a stirring behind her. Arion reappeared, clean and damp and strangely subdued. He was holding the filled caldron. Without meeting her eyes, he set it on the ground near her.

He said only, "Here's the water you needed for cooking."

# XXVIII

## THE RIVER

On the morrow it rained. Tired of his long treks to the valley, Arion took his bow and went hunting. He hoped to kill something big, a boar or a deer, that he and Marpessa could live on for days, but after hours in the woods, he came back wet and cold with only a pair of squirrels and a small partridge.

The next day was dry, and he took a different route, heading south down steep slopes to where he had glimpsed the blue waters of what he'd learned was the Adramyttenos Gulf. It took hours to reach the base of the mountain. There he found a fishing village, a few huts clustered around a shallow cove. He approached a group of men who were repairing some weatherworn vessels.

"Who are you, stranger, and what do you want?" one of them asked warily.

Arion answered in the rough Ionian dialect he'd spoken in his childhood. "I'm a carpenter from a village yonder." He gestured vaguely to the east. "I usually find work in Troy. But since the raid—" He shrugged. "Now I work where I can. I'll lend you a hand if you can spare some food and fishing nets and lines." The man who had spoken gave a silent nod.

Arion set to helping them, mending nets and boats, gutting and cleaning fish. Around mid-afternoon one of the men gave a shout. Looking up, Arion saw a huge, fast-moving ship with two tiers of oars. The men stopped their work to watch its passage north past the mouth of the gulf.

"I've never seen a such a big ship," Arion said. "Where's it from?"

The oldest man, looking troubled, said, "That can only be a Phoenician ship."

"I've heard of the Phoenicians." In fact Arion knew almost nothing about this alien people. "Two tiers of oars," he added wonderingly.

"Aye, their ships are powerful. They command the seas," another man said. "We rarely see them here, though. Most of their trade routes lie to the south."

"They sail where they please, even to the edges of the world," a third man added. "They don't believe in our gods."

The oldest man spat. "Certainly they have no regard for Poseidon! They cross the seas all year as if they owned them, with no fear of his wrath or his storms."

"Are they marauders?" Arion asked.

"Not often," came the reply. "They can be hostile, but they're more interested in trading."

*Ships that cross the sea in winter!* If he could find the Phoenicians, there might be a way to take Marpessa home.

Later, as he trudged up the mountain with dried fish, some precious salt, and fishing nets, lines, and hooks, an idea came to him. Tomorrow he and Marpessa could go fishing in the streams on the lower slopes. *Perfect!* he thought. Easy food, and a way to take her mind off fear and worry.

The next morning the air was heavy and the sky cloudy. Dark clouds rested on the mountaintop. As Marpessa crouched over the fire pit, trying to coax a flame from the embers, Arion came up to her, eager, smiling. "Marpessa." She stared at him, astonished. He even forgot to call her Teukros. Now that she thought of it, he had not called her Teukros since the day at the spring. "Let's go fishing. We'll follow the stream down the mountain. It's a long walk, but—"

Marpessa banked the fire and leapt to her feet. "Let's leave at once. There's some leftover bread. We can eat it on the way."

Thunder rumbled in the distance. She thought about being out in the open in a fierce storm. Looking at the sky, Arion said, "The storm is far away. I don't think it'll rain soon."

"We'll come back if it does," she answered. "What does it matter if we get a little wet?"

Carrying the fishing equipment, they set off down the slope, following the stream bed lined with moss-covered rocks and boulders, overhung with pines and firs, ancient oaks, chestnuts and alders whose trunks were covered with climbing creepers, their crimson and gold leaves aglow with sunlight. Several times they had to ford small streams that joined the flow of the larger one. Arion, walking behind her, said, "Yesterday I saw a Phoenician ship, a large one that can cross the seas in winter. If we could find these Phoenicians—"

Filled with sudden hope, she turned to face him. "Oh, do you think we could?"

"I don't know," he admitted. "I don't even know where to start." A cloud covered the sun and painted the world gray again. "In the meantime you must keep your spirits up," he urged. "Your mother would want you to be well and happy." Then he added, so softly she barely heard, "As I do."

Her heart gave a jump. *I* am *happy,* she realized, *happy just to be with him.* When she shot him a glance, his eyelids dropped, but the very air between them had changed. Her pulse quickened.

The sun came out again. Birds chattered in the trees. Once a partridge shot across their path, and Marpessa grinned at Arion, glad that he had not brought the bow. She heard scurrying overhead. Red squirrels leaped from limb to limb, carrying nuts and seeds to store away for winter. At times she and Arion heard, deep in the forest, the thrashings of larger animals, but none came near. When the sun grew hot, they stopped at the stream's edge to scoop up mouthfuls of icy water. As they finished the bread, their eyes met in a solemn silence deeper than any words.

They walked on, Arion at her side now on the narrow animal trail. His arm brushed hers, and the touch sent warmth flooding through her. When she paused to look up at him, he stopped too, and something flashed in his eyes. *He's going to take me in his arms,* she thought with a shiver of joy. But he only gave a little half-smile that made her heart catch, and as they continued down the trail, she felt a strange desire to brush up against him again to feel his warmth filling her with happiness. The trail narrowed so that they could not walk side by side, and he slipped behind her, but she was excruciatingly conscious of him, his breath, his every step. She felt his eyes watching her. She wanted to turn and look at him but dared not. An expectancy grew in her, deep in the core of her being, an excitement as keen and pure as the sun on the water, the wind in the trees. A loud rustling startled her, and a huge heron lifted from its concealed spot on the riverbank. As she watched its flight, her heart pounded with sudden, frightened joy.

At last the slope flattened out and the stream slowed. They came to a place where the river widened into still deep pools, a tamer place with less boulders, more spaces between the trees, and slender willows overhanging the banks. *A place of peace,* she thought. "Here," said Arion, "we will find fish."

Arion dropped the poles, nets, and hooks on the bank. The thought of teaching Marpessa to fish made his heart quicken. He would let himself touch her because he would need to place his hands over hers as she held the pole. *Here is how you do it,* he would say. But even as he imagined it, she reached down swiftly, picked up a net and a small sack, and said, "I'll set a trap for minnows. We'll need them for bait."

His surprise must have shown, for she laughed. "My youngest brother, Diores, taught me when I was a child." She strode to the river's edge.

The sunlight vanished. More clouds were gathering, some gray and menacing. Arion saw a distant flash of lightning, heard thunder rumble from the mountains. He glanced toward the summit of Mount Ida, hidden in its crown of cloud. Gray lines slanted down from the clouds. *It's raining up there,* he thought. *Maybe has been all day.* But the mountain peak was far away. *Father Zeus,* he prayed, *withhold your storm from us!* They would have to be quick about their business, for they were a long way from their camp.

He looked toward where Marpessa crouched. He could not take his eyes from her slight form in the wool tunic, her curls tossing in the breeze. He imagined caressing the sun-warmed nape of her neck. Her hands made swift scooping motions. She turned to smile at him. "I've got some, Arion. Maybe enough."

He snapped out of his trance in a hurry, and as she came back to him, he busied himself with lines and hooks to make it seem that he had not been watching her. He divided the fishing equipment, then said, "You fish here in the shallows. I'll go a bit upstream. I saw some bigger pools there."

He headed up the bank to a deep green pool, its waters barely rippling in the breeze, the sun kissing each tiny wave with dazzling light. He baited his hook, dropped his line, and gave a sigh. It was the most perfect day he could remember. As his eyes wandered downstream to Marpessa, he felt lifted into some realm of gold. Then thunder rolled again, louder now. Zeus's terrible voice coming through the clouds. *A warning.* There was tug of unease, almost of dread, in his stomach. A chill ran along his skin. The gods were reminding him that they could snatch all this away in an instant.

Standing under an overhanging willow that cast its shade on the water, Marpessa saw the lightning and heard the thunder. Gray clouds covered the sun, making the river look choppy and angry. Lightning flashed again suddenly, and thunder rolled just a few heartbeats after, threatening, ominous. But when the sun came out again, she sighed with relief. *It's still far away,* she told herself. She waded in, catching her breath at the cold of the river, and cast her line. Arion gave a shout and held his arm high, dangling a fish. She smiled and waved. Whenever she thought he wouldn't notice, she glanced at him, thigh-deep in the middle of a pool some distance away, his tunic hitched up to keep its edges dry. Her line jerked. She felt Arion's eyes on her. As she pulled a trout from the water, she tried to make all her movements sure and skillful.

She rebaited her hook and went back, deeper this time. The breeze freshened, and the river sang its lapping melody. Its song seemed to grow louder, more intense—even urgent.

"Arion!" she called. "The river is singing to us!"

But he was staring up-river, his body rigid. Then he whipped around.

"Flood!" he bellowed. "*Run! Get out!*"

A roaring filled the world. Marpessa looked up in terror and saw a monstrous white-topped wave swelling and churning down the river toward them.

# XXIX

## THE FLOOD

For an agonizing moment she was paralyzed. Then she ran splashing to the willow, pulled herself out of the water, and clung in its branches, her gaze fixed on Arion as he raced for the opposite bank. Before he got there, the flood engulfed him. Her heart squeezed and seemed to stop. Then she saw his head and arms. The wave hurtled him toward her. She stretched an arm out. *"Arion! Here!"*

His eyes wide, he raced closer, out of control. He reached toward her, desperate fingers spread. Legs and one hand gripping the tree, she flung herself far over the water. Their fingertips grazed.

He shot past her.

Marpessa gave an anguished scream. She let go of the willow and launched herself into the flood. Icy water closed over her head. She came up gasping. The speeding current gripped her, sucked her into its churning waters, broken tree limbs all around her. A log struck her back, knocking the breath from her lungs. She wheezed, choked. Where was Arion? *There!* She stroked hard, adding her strength to the current. She went under, swallowed water, came up, caught a breath, swam harder. *God of this river, save us!* she prayed.

Almost there. But then he vanished. *Oh, gods, help me!* A leg appeared. She lunged, grabbed his ankle. Held on. Fought to keep her head above the flood. Tried to reach his head to pull it up. But she couldn't. For many heartbeats they raced on the swollen river with all the other things torn loose from the mountain—roots, branches, the carcass of an animal. Downstream a deer was swimming with desperate strokes. A tree limb crossed their path, collided with them. For a moment they slowed, and she reached higher on his body, found a grip on his tunic. She grabbed the tree limb. Broken branches stabbed her. She felt a sharp pain in her arm—almost lost her grip.

Suddenly Arion's head came up. He took a choking breath, caught the trunk, and pulled her arm over it. Their arms were linked. He tried to call out, "Hold—" But he was nearer the middle of the river, getting the brunt of the current. His words were washed away.

Something struck the log. His head vanished, reappeared. He gave a coughing breath. Waves splashed over his face. Marpessa tried to move closer but got jabbed in the ribs by a branch. She could only grip his arm, anchoring him to the log. His head was swamped. *Oh, gods, how can he breathe?* The roar of the flood filled her ears. Arion's face was completely under, she couldn't reach him. *Arion, Arion! God of this river, save him!*

Then she felt a tiny slowing of the current. She searched the shore—or where it should have been. The terrain had flattened, and the water spread out, murky and shallower. She tried to steer them in the direction of the land but made no gain. She stretched her foot downward, seeking the bottom. Nothing. She kicked frantically toward the shore on her right. Arion's head came up. His eyes were closed. At once he went under again.

*Oh, gods, he's dead!*

She touched solid ground, groped with her feet—was swept on. She tried again, found a grip. Planted both feet. She grabbed his hair, pulled his face out of the water, pushed against the current with all her strength. They inched toward land. Waist-deep now, she towed the log, holding Arion's head up. At last she ran their log aground. With her final strength she pulled Arion onto dry land.

She lay at his side gasping for air. The moment she could breathe, she shook him. He was senseless, maybe not even alive.

"Arion!" she screamed. She rolled him on his side, pummeled his back. Water spurted out of his mouth, but he did not stir. She tore at his tunic, baring his chest, pounded on it. "Arion, Arion, breathe!"

No response.

"Oh, gods! Don't let him be dead!"

As if a god had answered, she knew what she must do. She put her mouth over his, forced her breath into him. Again. And again.

On the fourth breath he gave a terrible lurching cough. His body heaved and he was sick. Then he drew a shaking breath. Another. He shuddered. But he was breathing.

She fell against him sobbing. Her cheek rested on his cold chest, his heart beating in her ear. Her body shook with his trembling. She reached her arms around him as far as they would go, scooping through mud, weeds, debris, it didn't matter. She held him as close as anyone could hold another. It was not close enough. She must stop those terrible tremors that wracked him.

She covered his chest with her own body. She pulled her legs over his to give him all her warmth. After a long time his shudders lessened. His eyes stayed closed. She listened to his every breath, breathed in rhythm with him, murmured in his ear, "Arion, Arion! You're on land. You're safe now."

She could lie there forever with him, they need never move again. They were both alive, and it was enough.

His senses returned slowly. Each breath seared his chest. His body was still in the cold grip of death. As he came awake, his eyes were closed and he saw nothing but the churning brown waters that had so nearly swallowed him. He remembered gripping the log, waves swamping him until he couldn't breathe, his lungs filling with water, pain crushing his chest. He remembered seeing sunlit flashes from his life, the vineyards, the workers toiling, Thrasios's harsh face; then his mother's, bending over him; the old couple who had owned him when he was a boy. Then everything vanished in swirling blackness, and just before it closed in, he thought, *This is death.*

Now the coldness and horror would not go away. He trembled uncontrollably. *Cold, so cold.* Gradually he became aware of the heat and pressure of a body next to his, arms holding him tightly. He opened his eyes, then closed them against the sun's blaze.

*Churning brown waters. The current sucking him under. Death.*

He saw other things. Marpessa clinging to a tree. Safe. Then launching herself into the raging river.

He opened his eyes in a panic—and saw her face next to his, her eyes looking at him anxiously. She was alive. And somehow she had pulled him out of the flood.

He tried to say her name, but no sound came. He tried to lift his arms to put them around her, but they would not move. "Marpessa," he managed at last. It came out as a croak. "You saved me. You could have died!" She said nothing but gave him a smile of pure wonderment.

He made a Herculean effort to lift his arms, and this time put them around her. His eyes fell shut. He drifted.

It began with her fear of losing him. His shivering and her unendurable longing to comfort him. It continued as they came awake together, eyes opening and meeting with the knowledge that life could be snatched away in an instant. Each moment was precious. All this flowed between them without words. For a long time they lay still, her face on his bare chest, her arms around him, legs over his, skin on skin, absorbing the warmth of each other and the sun.

Then she felt him start to tremble again, only now it was different—vibrant and urgent. His yearning swamped her and became her own. All she wanted in the world was to fuse her body with his, her soul with his, to not be parted from him ever again. She tightened her arms around him and found his lips with hers.

As they lay together on that ruined shore littered with wreckage, they were borne away on a force greater than any flood.

# XXX

## RUIN

All the radiance of the sun filled Arion and brimmed over. He had never known such joy, never imagined it could be like this. If he kept his eyes closed and didn't move, he could focus his whole being on the feel of her arm across his chest, the hand that rested lightly on his collarbone, the warmth of her body against his side. He could believe it wouldn't vanish like a dream. He could pretend it was all right. Then she gave a sigh and stirred. Her body disjoined from his. He let his arms loosen, but he didn't want to let her go.

He opened his eyes, and remorse fell on him like a shadow, a darkness with weight and substance. His happiness fled. *I had no right. I let it happen. I've despoiled her.* He tried to throw the ugly word from his mind, but it remained lodged there. He was afraid to look at her. But when at last he turned his head, she smiled, lowered her eyes shyly and moved close again.

"Marpessa, we—I shouldn't have—"

She slid her fingers over his lips. "Don't say that!" She tightened her arms about him. "We are alive, and the gods have given us this. It was meant to be."

He was silent. His heart lightened a little. If she was right, gifts from the gods were to be accepted with gratitude. He took a deep breath, but a harsh cough tore his throat. All at once he felt the pain of his bruised and battered body. With a groan he sat up.

The clouds had gone. The storm had passed. A few birds chirped, shrill and outraged at the horror the gods had wrought. A flapping noise from the reeds startled him, and a duck took flight, its wings drinking the wind like thirsty tongues. Next to him, Marpessa sat, then stood. She reached down to help him to his feet. When he swayed dizzily, fighting the weakness that swept through him, she put her arms around him. A cold breeze stirred. He held her, feeling the dampness of her tunic, the shiver that ran through her body.

"We must go, Marpessa. Back to our camp."

"Can you walk?"

He nodded with more confidence than he felt. As she brushed the dirt and leaves from his sodden tunic, he noticed that his belt was missing, and his knife too. And of course their fishing gear and the fish they had caught. He wanted to hunt for these things, but one look at the wreckage all around told him it was useless. Likely their possessions had been washed as far as the sea. And what of their camp, high on the mountain, near the streams that fed this river? He pushed the worry aside and took Marpessa's hand, feeling the delicate bones beneath her skin. "Let's go, my—" But he could think of no endearment tender enough to express what he felt. Instead he willed his eyes to tell her all that he could not say in words.

Their progress up the steep slope was agonizingly slow. Arion had to stop often to catch his breath, and each time, Marpessa listened anxiously to his painful wheezing, then reached for his hand. They went on. She was only vaguely aware of the changed landscape they passed through—uprooted trees, rivers of mud covering the undergrowth, a terrible absence of birds, of any sounds of life. When Arion's feet slowed, she put her arm around him, hoping to give him strength. "Come, Arion! Only a little longer." It was a lie, but he managed the next step and the next, his face drenched with sweat. The sun was sinking in a fiery glow, and the air was cooling sharply when they finally reached their camp.

They stopped at its edge, and Marpessa gave a cry of horror. A wasteland lay before them. The flood had raged through the glade with devastating force. Rocks, boulders, fallen trees were strewn about as if thrown by the hand of a Titan. The open area was littered with debris: branches, torn-up shrubs, the swollen carcass of an animal she could not identify, probably a fox or a weasel. All the things they had acquired to make survival possible were gone: her grinding stones, the fire pit, the cooking pots, the ropes Arion had strung between trees, the garments and blankets they had hung to air out, the javelins, bows, and quivers of arrows he had stowed on the branches of an evergreen oak.

Marpessa's knees buckled. "The gods—they're angry! Athena—" Her voice broke. "Athena tried to warn us this would happen."

Arion gently turned her to face him. "Let's look in the caves," he said. "Maybe some things were spared."

They made their way to the storage cave. It was a sodden wreck, its floor a swamp, the stores of grain and salted meat swept away. There would be no supper tonight, no breakfast tomorrow. Her own cave had fared no better. Gone were her bedding, her extra tunics, the small store of rocks, feathers and other keepsakes she had gathered. She gripped Arion's hand as they moved on to his cave. Its floor was muddy, but there was a crevice where he had stowed a sleeping rug and other things. By some miracle the soaked rug had stayed wedged in place. Arion reached his hand along the crevice.

"The dried meat! It's here, and also my fire-starting rocks. We'll eat tonight," he told her, then added in a shaky voice. "But my silver and copper pieces are gone. Every single one."

As they stepped outside, Marpessa turned away, determined that she would not cry.

Arion saw her shoulders quivering. Over his own despair came a gladness that he had earned the right take her in his arms and cradle her head against his chest. "Marpessa!" he whispered. *At least we're alive*, he wanted to say, but she might not find immediate comfort in this. Instead he said, "Let's search around to see if any more of our belongings have survived the flood." It might be futile, but it would occupy them, give them a purpose.

As she walked around the edges of the camp where the woods infringed, he went to the massive evergreen oak into which he had thrust his second-best knife and wound a rope securely high around the trunk. Looking up, he gave a crow of triumph. They were still there! At that moment Marpessa came running back, holding an iron vessel aloft. "Look, Arion, my cooking pot! It was over yonder, caught in the branches of a tree."

"See, now we can collect water, we can cook, and I have found my rope and knife."

She gave a small smile. "I'll fetch us some water." She winced at the word. "If you can make a fire, we'll warm the meat and dry the blanket."

As she started for the spring, he listened to the sound of her footfalls, light as dried leaves blown against the forest floor. An odd fancy, since all around him the ground was damp, the torn branches wet and dripping. There would be no fire. The evening chill crept in. All he could think of was his need of rest. He found armfuls of leaves and branches that would shield them from the puddled water. With these he made a makeshift bed on the floor of his cave and over it spread the rug that had survived the flood. Wet though it was, the wool was thick enough to keep some of the cold away.

Marpessa came out of the shadows, water slopping from the vessel she carried. Night was falling swiftly. They sat on the ground and devoured the cold meat. She was shivering. He pulled her close. He too was shaking with cold. At last they arose and went into the cave.

In the darkness, Marpessa felt his shuddering. "Your tunic is damp. Take it off." She pulled it over his head, then doffed her own. "Come," she murmured. "We'll warm each other." She arranged the blanket so that they lay on half of it and pulled the other half over themselves as a cover. When she crept next to him, his shaking was still violent. "Arion! Are you ill?"

"I'm well enough," he muttered.

*You're not*, Marpessa thought. He had taken water into his lungs. *What if he dies? Oh, gods! Oh, Apollo, god of healing, help me!* She entangled her limbs with his and blew warm breaths on his neck where the blood pulsed beneath the skin, until at last his body relaxed and his breathing deepened. She reached up to caress his hair, his cheek. Tightening her arms around him, she kissed him.

His bones melted like iron in the forge. He had thought that they would lie together only for warmth. Yet why not accept this wondrous gift of the gods, who had robbed them of everything else? *Marpessa, my love!* He took her in his arms.

Afterwards, he thought, *I should not have. She can never be mine.* His happiness fled, and again he ached with guilt. Yet as she lay trustingly at his side, her breathing becoming rhythmic with sleep, a larger question loomed in his mind.

*What are we going to do?*

Only by chance or the will of the gods had they survived this flood—because they happened to be downstream. But now they had lost everything. With winter coming, there would be more storms, perhaps more floods. Before long, snow would come to the mountains. He flung an arm over his brow. "We can't stay here."

He did not realize he had spoken aloud and awakened her until he heard her soft question in the dark. "What shall we do?"

Holding her close he whispered, "I'll think of something." Wild thoughts raced through his mind. *Take her away to the far ends of the earth. Start a new life together where no one can find us.* Yet it was impossible. All his earnings were gone and he had nothing. Their attempt to survive in the wilderness had failed. The flood had shown them they could lose their lives at any time. And if he became injured or ill and died, she too would perish, with no one to provide for her. Another unwelcome thought came. *If I had gone down the mountain leaving her alone as I so often did, she would have died here.*

*I can't care for her.* Of what use was his love for her—his hopeless, helpless love—if he could neither protect her nor provide for her?

*She can never be mine.*

His duty was clear. *I must get her to safety.* That meant taking her home. And there was only way to do it. Seek the Phoenicians, whose ships sailed across the seas in winter. *If we go south we can surely find them. I can work as a sailor, earn our passage.*

*I must give her up.*

Her arms tightened around him. She lifted her head. He felt her soft lips on his neck and her breath warming his skin. She whispered, "I love you, Arion."

The words stabbed his heart. The pain went sharp and deep. His throat tightened so that he could not speak. *No, no, you mustn't,* he thought. *You'll be hurt.* As he struggled to keep his breathing even, he was glad she couldn't see that his eyes had filled with tears.

# XXXI

## AMALTHEIA'S GRIEF

Each morning Amaltheia would lift the small silver mirror from her bedside stand and stare at her face with a kind of wonder. The features were all there, older, sharper, the eyes deeply shadowed, the hair grayer, but recognizably her own. How could it be so when her heart had died?

She would pull herself slowly to her feet. She must somehow get through the day ahead, a succession of endless, repetitive chores performed by rote from long experience. Often she was barely aware of her own actions or the words she spoke. In the same way each tomorrow must be faced anew.

Amaltheia was no stranger to loss. She had buried her parents, a sister, a brother, and her first child, a baby girl. Each death had torn a hole in her heart. The empty spaces were still there, scarred over by time but never mended. Each grief had its own shape and color. Her first baby left a deep hole, pale lavender, cloudy and blurred around the edges with what might have been. Her mother's loss was a chasm, gray and formless, so wide that the young girl she was then had not been able to see across it. The loss of her unloving father was a small, shallow gash like one made by a spear, an angry red in color, emitting twinges of bitterness and regret.

The wound from the loss of Marpessa was so great, so deep that all the other losses blended into one massive crater. Once she had been terrified by how much she could lose. Now the gods had done their worst. Nothing else could touch her.

*Be strong for me*, Marpessa had said the day she left, the last words she ever spoke to her mother. Now Amaltheia repeated the words mindlessly to keep at bay those other thoughts, the ones that would drive her mad, such as how Marpessa had died and whether she had been ravished by the barbarians. She saw her absence from Marpessa's side during the last moments of life as her own failure. *How I wish I could have held you in my arms. If only I could have died for you!* But in order to get through each day she must not let herself think these things.

In the future she would come face to face with Marpessa in the underworld.

Until then, her daughter's words were a lifeline to her: *Be strong. For me.*

*For you, my darling.* If she had failed her daughter in life, she would not fail her in death.

# XXXII

## THE JOURNEY SOUTH

The next morning, with nothing to eat, nothing to do but leave the ruined campsite behind, they made a pack of their few remaining belongings and set out down the slope along a narrow animal trail. As their walking fell into a rhythm, Marpessa ventured to ask, "Arion, where are the Phoenicians to be found?"

"South," he answered, "I don't know how far. We'll ask along the way. In fact—" She heard his hesitation. "I don't know anything about them, only that they have big ships and enough skills to get us home in winter."

*The Phoenicians*, she thought. They would speak a different tongue, worship different gods. A whole world of fear opened up in her. "Arion, must we?" she asked in a small voice. "Must we seek them?"

He said abruptly, "We don't have much choice."

His words brought no comfort. She skirted her fear and forced herself to think of their goal. *Home!*

Once she'd wanted that more than anything. But now she was no longer an innocent child longing for her mother. She was a woman, joined to Arion for life. She'd been taught that losing her maidenhood outside of marriage was wrong—a fatal mistake, a sin in the eyes of the gods. Yet how could something be wrong that felt so right? She belonged to Arion. Together they would overcome every obstacle.

But what would happen when they reached Lokris? Runaway slaves were severely punished, often maimed or put to death. He would also be blamed for ravishing her. Her heart pounded out of control and her knees turned wobbly. She almost stopped walking. Then she quickly put the thought away from her. *When I tell them how he rescued me and saved my life, they'll reward him, not punish him.*

Yet sudden doubt assailed her. *Father—the members of the Council—they might not listen to me.* She gave a cry of anguish, stopping on the trail.

Arion, two paces behind, came up next to her. "What is it?"

She flung her arms around him. "What if they kill you when we get to Lokris?" Her head against his chest, she felt the sudden jerk of his heart, but he stood so still that she knew he had already accepted this possibility. His hand came up to stroke her hair, perhaps to calm himself as well as her. She raised her head to look at his pale, resolute face. "We'll stop them. When they see that you've saved me, brought me home— And my mother will help us."

He was silent for so long that she didn't think he would answer. At last he murmured, "No use speaking of it. It changes nothing."

"But, Arion, what will we do? We must—" she began, but he thrust her gently from him and turned her onto the trail once more.

"We'd best go on."

After that she was as silent as he. Her mind whirled in a blind panic. *We can't risk it. We mustn't go back to Lokris. Then where will we go?* But there was nowhere else.

A while later they stopped at a stream. As she bent to scoop water into her mouth, Arion walked a short distance upstream to a deep green pool. He crouched over it, intent and still. Suddenly he made a lightning-quick movement that produced a flash of silver and sent a fish flopping onto the bank—a fish almost as long as his hand. He gutted it and divided it. When he handed her half, she was too famished to care that she was eating it raw. The texture was slippery, but the taste was good. As they resumed their journey, she pulled a few small bones from her teeth.

At last the trees thinned and the mountainside opened out onto a wide space. "This is where we drop down to the coast," he said. They stopped to look. Far below lay a calm blue expanse of water shimmering in the sun like liquid light. She could see fishing vessels, tiny in the distance. "The sea!" she exclaimed.

"Not the sea." For the first time that day, he gave a small smile. "The Adramyttenos Gulf." He pointed across the water. What she had taken for a cloudbank was a long, uneven landmass on the far side. "I came this way the day I brought back the fishing lines and nets." A lifetime ago. Before the flood. *Before we became lovers,* she thought. "That was when I learned about the Phoenicians," he said.

Marpessa felt his preoccupation. "Arion?"

"We'll have to cross the gulf. There are villages down there—boats. I'll earn our passage." *Villages,* she thought. *The world of men.* The silence between them was filled with thoughts of the strangers they must confront, the lies they must fabricate, the effort needed to earn their way. "I'll have to start calling you Teukros again." He spoke firmly, almost brusquely. "You must *be* Teukros. All the time. And you mustn't look at me, Marpessa."

"Look at you?"

"The way you are right now. We must be as brothers. Have you ever noticed that men—lads, companions—don't really look at each other? They—*glance*." He added, his voice unsteady, "And we can't be—together any more, as we have been."

She gave a cry of protest. "Why not, Arion, if we are careful, if we are discreet?"

"It's too dangerous. I must do you no further harm."

She was at a loss. "But surely afterwards, Arion, once we're—"

"Once we're what? Safe?" He was suddenly rough. "There is no *safe*, Marpessa. Not for us. Never again."

The words were so final. *He can't mean—* A sudden terror came over her. She remembered another journey, to a town called Troas. And he had said—

"Arion!" Her voice sounded strange in her own ears. "You won't leave me, will you—alone among the Phoenicians?"

He smiled, a smile of unbearable sadness, and gently kissed her brow. "Marpessa, I swear by the gods. I will see you safely home."

But she heard what lay unsaid behind his words. And she knew. He would keep his promise. But once they reached Lokris, he would leave her forever.

# XXXIII

## ANTANDROS

They stopped to rest at a rocky promontory from which they could see the gulf. Arion sat on top of it, his legs dangling. The sight of Marpessa sitting slumped on a log below, her head bowed, made his heart constrict. *She knows,* he thought, *but she doesn't understand. She's still an innocent.* She expected that, once they reached Lokris, she had only to ask for his life to be spared, and those in power would grant her wish. But he knew better. "Oh, gods!" he breathed, sinking his brow into his hand. How unfair the decrees of the gods and the laws of men! A slave could never have the rights that a freeborn man took for granted.

*I* must *leave her. I can't let myself be killed before her eyes.* But it did not good to dwell on that now. He pushed the thought forcefully away. *Concentrate on getting her home.*

But how he would accomplish it? The difficulties were overwhelming. How to find the Phoenicians and gain passage with them. How to keep them from learning that Marpessa was a woman. *And when we reach Lokris, I'll have to devise a way to get her into safe hands and still make my escape.*

He drew a deep breath. One step at a time. The first thing to do was to find food, clothing, shelter, supplies for the journey. How? Alone he could easily earn his way from village to village. But with her at his side— Could she play the part of a young man, working, acting, and speaking as young men do?

He had a sudden thought. He scrambled down the rock, jumping the last distance to land at her feet.

"Marpessa, could you be—a simpleton?"

Her hand came up to wipe the telltale signs of tears from her face. She didn't answer at once. Then her face went slack, her lower lip hung open, her eyes glazed over. "What?" she mumbled with such convincing vagueness that Arion laughed aloud in surprise.

"Wonderful! You could be a bit of a mute, someone who never learned proper speech. My poor, simple little brother, who can only perform very easy tasks!"

The fire of her spirit blazed in her eyes. "Be careful, Arion, lest you go too far!"

Heartened, he reached down a hand to help her to her feet. Then he enfolded her in his arms and pressed her close, breathing her scent, memorizing the feel of her body against his. He wondered if this was the last time he would ever hold her. He could not control the quiver in his hands as he released her.

His sadness flooded through Marpessa. As they started down the slope again, she was too shaken to speak. Why didn't he see that they belonged to each other? *You think you will leave me,* she said to him in silence. *But I will not let you go.*

Then another thought stopped her cold. In holding onto him she would be the cause of his death. *I can't be that selfish. Even if my heart breaks at losing him.* She looked at his broad shoulders, his arms swinging as he walked, the breeze lifting the dark brown hair off this neck. Her insides twisted.

At least it was long way to the ports of the Phoenicians. *A lot can happen before we find them—if we find them. Maybe by the will of the gods we'll never get there.*

She stumbled over a small rock and looked down. Lying across the trail was a large feather, tawny with brown stripes. The feather of an owl. She stopped. A chill ran down her spine.

"Arion!" she cried. "Look!" He picked it up and studied it. "An owl feather. It's a sign. Athena is angry," she whispered.

"Nay!" he said with a note of conviction. "It might just as easily be a sign of her favor. It was pointing west toward the sea. Toward Lokris, showing us the way."

"How do you know that?" she asked.

He answered with a half-grin and a twinkle in his eyes, "I'm an augurer!" And he handed back the feather.

Hope soared in her heart. If Athena *was* helping them, they could prevail in Lokris. *Please help us, goddess,* she prayed. *Show me the way to save Arion's life.*

But what if he was wrong? Despite his jest, he wasn't an augurer. And even augurers weren't always right, except in the old tales of heroes. Her mind flew back to the owl in the woods. *Athena is angry,* she thought. *And why not? I broke my oath.*

The feather seemed to burn in her hand. How much greater the danger from the goddess that from the men of Lokris! *Oh, Athena,* she prayed, *do not turn your wrath on Arion. He swore no oath.* She thought of the moment of their joining on the riverbank. *It's my fault,* she said in her mind. *Forgive me, goddess, and guide me. I will obey your will.*

But if Athena tried to destroy Arion— *I won't let her.* Marpessa's fist clenched around the feather. *I will fight the gods themselves for him.* Then she could hardly breathe. That was defiance, which the gods punished like no other sin. She remembered stories from her childhood. Tantalus in Hades, doomed to have food and drink dangled before him and forever snatched from reach. Sisiphus pushing a boulder uphill, only to have it crash down again each time. Defiance of the gods was punished for all eternity.

But eternity was far away. Nothing mattered so much as Arion here beside her. *His life.* As they resumed walking, she fought to keep her steps even, her breathing regular, so that he would not read her fear.

Marpessa was nearly dropping with exhaustion when they reached a town called Antandros not far from the shore of the gulf. After knocking on several doors they found a household willing to honor the sacred laws of hospitality, however grudgingly. A severe, silent man with leathery skin and iron gray hair opened the door and gestured for them to join the group eating the evening meal. At the table were three younger men, clearly his sons, who looked them over suspiciously before continuing to mop the food off their trenchers with coarse brown bread. A small, stooped woman hovered in the background, muttering querulously as she set out extra bread and a platter with remnants of a bean and onion stew.

It might have been a rough, plain meal, but to Marpessa it was nectar and ambrosia from the gods. As she gulped mouthfuls of bread and stew, she glanced covertly at Arion and saw that he was eating with the same satisfaction.

As the law of hospitality dictated, their host waited until they had eaten their fill before asking, "Who are you, strangers? And where are you bound?"

Arion finished chewing his last piece of bread. "I am Arion, and this is my brother Teukros. He's a bit simple and has been in my care since he was a small boy." Marpessa felt glances coming her way. She kept her head down, shoved a crust of bread into her mouth, and said nothing. "We went to Troy seeking work," Arion continued. "But after the barbarian raid there was no extra food or silver for strangers. Then we lost our belongings in a flood on the mountain, so we're returning to our village across the gulf."

Marpessa hoped their host wouldn't ask for the name of the village, but he nodded and made no comment. "We're destitute," Arion continued. "I'm willing to work hard for you to earn our bread for the next few days."

Their host poured himself another goblet of the weak, sour wine. He offered some to Arion, who declined with a gesture of thanks. No one else spoke. At last their host said, "My name is Epistrophos. These are my sons, Aphareus, Pheidas, and Drakios." He did not name his wife. Marpessa raised her head and made herself stare in a wide-eyed, childish way at each face. Aphareus and Pheidas looked as if they had passed thirty years, their faces almost as austere and leathery as that of their father. Drakios was younger, not many years older than Arion. He was shifty-eyed, with a smooth face, hardly any beard, and burnished locks that hung to his shoulders. *He is vain of his looks*, Marpessa thought. He stared at her penetratingly, and she turned away, uneasy.

At last Epistrophos said, "Your visit is timely. We are cutting trees for an order of lumber that must be delivered across the gulf by the next full moon. We are behind and need extra help." He paused and his eyes fell on Marpessa. "We have a small flock of sheep. Could young Teukros be trusted to take them up to the meadows during the day and bring them back at night? If Drakios could be freed of that duty, he could help us cut the trees."

Marpessa's eyes met Arion's, but she knew better than to speak. "Aye!" he answered for her. "Teukros watched our sheep at home. He can be trusted and understands well what to do."

"Then it's settled." Epistrophos gave a thin smile and poured Arion a glass of wine, brooking no refusal. "There is a small shed behind the house with clean straw. We use it at lambing time if the weather is bad. You may make your bed there. My wife will give you extra sleeping rugs."

*Perfect!* Arion thought. It was halfway to the full moon. That would give him work for many days. With any luck he could barter for a few supplies or some coppers to buy them with. And when that load of lumber crossed the gulf, they would go with it. His heart was lighter as he and Marpessa carried the sleeping rugs to the shed.

Epistrophos had even given them a lamp. Inside the shed, Arion set it down carefully on a patch of bare ground and stole a glance to see where Marpessa was placing her rug. He ached with wanting her. He regretted his earlier words.

Surely it was private enough here to take her in his arms and— As he spread his own rug over the straw, he kept his eyes lowered. But when Marpessa came close, his hands fumbled, and he straightened, looked up. Her eyes were shining in the lamplight. She gave a tremulous smile that made his knees go weak. "Arion," she said softly, shyly, holding out her arms to him, "let's enjoy the time we have together."

His heart leapt. *I don't have to give her up yet. Not yet! Maybe not for a long time,* he exulted, and kissed her with fierce tenderness.

Much later, when her head was resting against his chest and her soft, deep breaths told him she was asleep, he cursed himself for his weakness. There was another concern. If he couldn't resist her, he'd best make some changes. So long as a man's seed didn't enter a woman's body, there could be no baby. *If there isn't a baby already*, he worried. *If only I'd thought of this before!*

Sitting on the edge of a spring, Marpessa gave a sigh of contentment. The job of tending the sheep was ideal. It took her away from prying eyes and gave her freedom to roam the hills in the company of the animals: the sheep and a scruffy black and white dog whom she had promptly named Herakles. She had been tending the sheep for many days now and had given them all names as well. The old ram was called Odysseus, his favorite ewe was Penelope, and all the others had names befitting their age and status.

How good it had felt to be clean, to be wearing a tunic that was not a filthy rag! Epistrophos' wife had reluctantly given her a much-mended tunic that had belonged to one of the sons. When Marpessa had led the sheep high into the hills the first day, she had found this isolated spring surrounded by tall reeds. The water was icy, but she hadn't been able to resist plunging in to scrub her hair and body clean. Now the bath had become an almost-daily ritual.

The sheep had been grazing calmly. Suddenly their bodies became taut and all their heads swung around as one to stare through the reeds. Marpessa sprang to her feet. Something had startled them. She strained to listen. *A stirring noise.* The breeze? Or footsteps through foliage? She walked toward the sheep, becoming Teukros again, speaking to the animals in a broken mumble. The noise came again, louder. A crashing through the reeds, now retreating. She ran forward, parted the reeds.

A man was running down the slope, long, burnished hair flying. *Drakios!*

What was he doing here? He should be with the men in the woods. A thousand insects seemed to be crawling over her skin. She did not trust him—she had not from the first day. Had he spied on her? When she bathed in the spring, had he seen her?

Nausea rose in her throat. She forced herself to draw a deep breath. *Be calm,* she told herself. *Surely the sheep would have alerted you, as they did just now.*

But this spot was too isolated. And now that he knew where she brought the sheep, he might come back. Though the sun was only halfway down from its zenith, she clucked to the sheep and began to drive them down the slope.

That night as she lay next to Arion, she told him what had happened. "I'm worried that he knows I'm a girl," she said.

Arion sounded troubled. "I'll try to keep a watch on him as we cut down trees. But it's hard. Epistrophos sends us to different parts of the woods. Drakios works with the oldest brother, and I almost never see him." He gave a sigh. "Luckily we'll soon be done with the wood-cutting. We can board that ship in two days. Still—" He got up, fumbled in the straw. "Take my knife tomorrow." He reached for her hand, curled it around the wooden haft. "Hold it thus. Keep your fingers out of the way of the blade. Go for the weak places—the eyes, the neck under the jaw." His voice hardened. "If need be, don't hesitate to use it."

# XXXIV

## BATTLE BY THE STREAM

*One more day,* Marpessa thought as she trudged up the hill with the sheep. *If I can just elude him today—*

When they came near the spring, the sheep, drawn there by habit and the lure of the tender green shoots near the water, started to stray toward their usual spot. But she veered away and drove them onward with firm prods on their haunches from her staff. "Herakles!" she called to the dog. "Here! This way!" And with his energetic help, she led the flock higher up the slope. As she walked, her hand went to her belt and found the haft of Arion's knife. *I don't know if I could use it,* she thought. Yet its presence reassured her.

She paused behind a shrub to survey her surroundings. They had climbed high enough to look down on the rooftops of the houses in the village below and the broad sweep of the gulf beyond. She could still see, faint in the distance, the small flock of goats with their drowsing goatherd that she had passed some time ago. The slope lay open below her without much cover except for the occasional olive tree and scrub oak. She had been careful as she set out, and she did not think she had been followed. But the sheep were noisy with their bleating, their hooves swishing through the grasses. It would be far easier for Drakios to track her than for her to be aware of his presence. Her stomach tightened.

"Herakles!" she called. "Here!" The dog trotted to her side. As she reached down to scratch his ears and slip him a piece of dried meat, he gazed up at her with loving eyes. He had become absurdly loyal to her. Probably no one had ever treated him with kindness before, or even paid him any notice. She bent to rub the fur behind his ears. "Herakles, my hero! Stay by me. Be my eyes and ears!"

Continuing up the slope, she veered northward, straight toward the mountains, in the opposite direction from the woods where the men would be cutting the last of lumber and carrying it down to the shore. She walked farther than ever before, until she came to a huge rock jutting out from the slope, surrounded by a stand of pines. Climbing around the rock, she found flat space behind it, and a stream bordered with willows and reeds. There was a grassy meadow by the side of the stream, where the sheep started to graze. She peered around the rock, her view of the slope obstructed by trees and shrubs. The landscape seemed unthreatening. She had not seen any people since the goatherd.

She sat on the bank of the stream, listening to its burbling and the murmur of the breeze through reeds and branches. Birds chirped in the willow overhead. She feared she would not hear if anyone approached. Then she remembered how the sheep had alerted her yesterday. *Artemis,* she prayed, *watch over me as you surely watch this lovely spot.* She felt a surge of guilt. No longer a maiden, she could not expect Artemis' help. *Still, all will be well if I just stay watchful.* She cupped her hands full of clear water, said a brief prayer of thanks to whatever naiad lived in this stream, and drank deeply. Then she reached for the bread and cheese she had brought.

As the day passed, she paced often around the grassy area, pausing to gaze down the slope. Nothing. *Perhaps I was overly fearful*, she thought. *Maybe Drakios just spied on me because he was curious.* The shadows were lengthening when she rose slowly and stretched.

At that very moment a shape loomed over her from the uphill side of the slope. Before she could cry out, Drakios barreled into her, knocking her down. The knife flew from her belt and skittered to the ground. His weight crushed her into the dirt. His hands held her wrists at her sides. She couldn't breathe or move. He leered into her face.

"You can't fool me, pretending to be a boy! I saw every bit of you when you were bathing yesterday!" He was breathing hard, his words spraying her face with spittle.

She forced down fear and tried to kick him, but his legs pinned hers down, immobilizing her. His breath, reeking of wine and onions, was hot on her face. She smelled his acrid sweat. As he reached down to raise her tunic from her thighs, she clawed at his eyes. He slapped her with massive force across the face.

Everything went black, shot with sparks of light. Stunned by the pain, she felt a trickle of blood from the corner of her mouth. His hand curved around her thigh, inched upward. Her skin crawled.

Suddenly she remembered the dog. "Herakles, to me, to me!" she screamed. Drakios's hand clamped over her mouth, forcing her head painfully upward and to the side. She saw a bright glimmer in the grasses. *The knife.* Out of reach.

Herakles circled them, barking wildly. Then the sheep bleated and the dog ran back to them. The bleating and barking grew fainter. They were scattering. Herakles must be running after them, leaving her alone. Marpessa's stomach sickened with fear.

Drakios' hand probed her inner flesh, making her nauseous with revulsion. *The knife.* It was behind her right shoulder. She couldn't reach it even if she could extend her arm. She dug her heels into the soil and thrust against them with all her strength. Arching her body up, she managed to scoot herself and Drakios closer toward the knife. The movement dislodged his legs. She crossed her ankles and clamped her knees together. He was breathing hard, trying to get her legs apart. Now both her hands were free. She reached backward over her head slowly, slowly, groping toward the knife. Not close enough. Her fingertips just grazed it. She was terrified he would notice. To distract him, she gasped out, "Arion will kill you!" And pushed off again with her heels.

It made him focus on her face. He loomed over her, laughing contemptuously. "Nay, I'll kill *him*. Playing us for fools, sleeping with his whore under our very noses. Now I mean to have what *he* has every night!"

"I'm his *sister!*" Marpessa hurled the words with explosive force. Her eyes locked with his as her fingers closed around the knife.

# XXXV

## SEARCH FOR MARPESSA

The shadows were lengthening, the sun's light deepening to orange. Arion, working with Epistrophos and his sons to carry loads of lumber from the woods down to the shore, stopped to wipe sweat from his brow. His gnawing anxiety was rapidly growing into panic. Drakios had disappeared. All afternoon Arion had tried to watch him, but his work often took him down to the shore while Drakios remained in the woods.

"Where is Drakios?" He shot the question at Alphareus, who was preparing another load to carry.

Alphareus replied, "He went farther into the woods to see if there were any cut trees we left behind."

Pheidas, the middle son, said, "That was some time ago. It wouldn't surprise me if he went home. He's a shirker!"

The words struck Arion like a blow. He flung down the log he had lifted. "I'll go see if I can find him." He strode off before they could object.

The strength of a Titan flooded his veins. He ran through the woods, calling Drakios's name. No answer. Drakios had gone—he was sure of it. Avoiding the place where the others were working, he raced toward the family's dwelling.

When he arrived out of breath, the door stood open. Epistrophos' wife sat at her loom. Drakios was not there.

The old woman gave him a surprised glance. Before she could speak, he set off at a run up the slope in the direction Marpessa usually took with the sheep. She'd mentioned a spring up the hill and to the west. He ran until he was out of breath.

"Teukros!" he called, turning in a circle to send his voice in all directions. No answer but the wind. He ran again, weeds and thorn bushes scraping his legs, but he barely noticed. He saw a stooped old goatherd heading downhill. "Have you seen a lad with a flock of sheep and a dog?" he asked. The old man gave him a vague look and shook his head.

At last Arion came to a spring, perhaps the right one, but there was no one there. He saw signs of cropped grass and sheep droppings, but these were old. No sheep had been here today. The fiery disk of the sun slipped behind the top of the hill. "Teukros!" he called over and over, listening after each call for a faint answer or perhaps the baahing of the sheep. No sound but the whisper of the wind. At last he stopped and looked to his left up the mountainside, where the terrain became rougher and more overgrown. To his right the land rose steeply, strewn with boulders. There was no way to tell which way she had gone, or if she'd even come this way at all. The sun was gone, the wind brought a chill to his bones, and twilight deepened swiftly. Perhaps she was far below him on the slope. Or she'd returned to the dwelling. His heart froze at the thought of her alone with the family, or worse, alone with Drakios.

He must go back. If she was able, she'd return there. If not, he'd find Drakios and force him to tell what had happened.

"Teukros!" he called one last time. And then, his voice rising in agony and desperation, not caring who heard: "Marpessa! Marpessa!" But there was only the silence of deep twilight. Even the wind had died.

"Zeus, help her!" he prayed. "Athena, as she honored you and served you in your temple, be merciful to her now!"

Filled with urgency, he started back toward the house. He had been gone a long time. Perhaps she'd returned there while he was searching, and was waiting for him. But when he opened the door, only Epistrophos, his wife, and the two elder sons were sitting by the hearth. Fear squeezed the breath from his lungs.

Their heads swiveled toward him. "Where is Drakios?" Epistrophos demanded. "We thought you went to seek him, and—"

"Where's *Teukros?*" Arion interrupted roughly.

"Your simpleton brother has not returned with the flock," the wife retorted. "You should know better than I what trouble he's got into. He'd better not have allowed the sheep to come to harm."

*The sheep.* He'd almost forgotten them. *Surely she'll be with them.* "We must find them!" He started for the door.

But just then it was flung open, and Drakios staggered in, his hair disheveled, his tunic torn and dirty. A bloody rag was tied around his neck. He was alone.

Arion lunged, knocking him to the floor, seizing him in a chokehold. *"What have you done with Teukros?"*

"Let go!" yelled a voice behind him. Rough hands grabbed his neck, tugged his hair. But Arion had never felt such fury—or such strength. He was barely aware of their efforts. He closed his hands around Drakios's throat and at the same time shook him. "*Where is he?* Tell me before I kill you!"

"Get your hands off him, you monster!" Epistrophos bellowed, but Arion tightened his hold until he was squeezing the windpipe. Drakios's pulse beat against his fingers. The man's eyes bulged in terror. His mouth worked as he tried to form words. Arion fought off a savage desire to strangle him and loosened his grip just enough to allow Drakios to speak.

"Up the slope," Drakios gasped. "Very far. There's a big rock surrounded by pines, a stream and—"

A blow from behind struck Arion on the side of the head, stunning him. Two of the men hauled him away, dragged him to his feet. They held him while the third man, Alphareus, swung his fist and drove a mighty blow into Arion's belly just below the rib cage. Arion fell like a dropped sack of grain.

He couldn't breathe. He was in agony. He made groaning sounds beyond his control. At last he caught a breath. Another. Slowly he dragged himself to his feet. Epistrophos, at Drakios's side, shouted over his shoulder to his sons, "Hold him!" but Arion, lurching like a drunken man, pushed past them and managed to reach the door.

"She'd better be safe!" he snarled, and flung himself out into the night. Then he stopped. *Oh, gods, I said "she"!*

It didn't matter. Nothing mattered except finding her. Outside he tried to recover his strength. His head throbbed. When he put a hand to his temple, it came away bloody. He drew several deep breaths. Then he started up the slope.

It was not yet fully dark. Far up the hillside he saw the outline of a huge rocky outcropping, surrounded by a black fringe of trees. His breath tearing painfully, he made himself trudge uphill until at last he reached it. On the far side of the rock, just as Drakios said, there was a stream. And not a living soul was near.

He felt an enormous relief. He'd feared he would find her dead. Or too hurt to move. But she must have fled. *If* Drakios was telling the truth and she'd been here at all.

He began zigzagging down the hill, calling her name, trying to imagine where she might be. As darkness fell completely, his despair grew. He was nearing the house when he heard a faint bleating. He ran, following the sound. Soon a small flock of sheep emerged from the fold of a hillock, followed by a dog and a bedraggled figure trailing behind.

*"Marpessa!"*

He ran to her, enfolded her in his arms. For long moments he couldn't speak. At last he loosened his grip to peer into her face. "Are you well? Are you—are you—?"

"I am—unharmed." But she buried her head in his chest and burst into sobs.

He held her against him for the rest of the walk down the slope. When they reached the sheepfold, he helped her secure the flock for the night. At the door of the house they stopped. Arion hesitated. He was not ready to confront Epistrophos and his sons, but he and Marpessa needed food.

"Go to our shed." He swung Marpessa gently around by the shoulders and pointed her toward it. "I'll get us what we need."

He entered the house, and before anyone had time to speak, he said, "Your sheep are safe." He glared around the room at all of them, defying them to stop him. Deliberately he went to the pot on the hearth and filled a trencher with enough food for two. Then he took a clay lamp and a jug of water. He fled before anyone spoke.

After they finished eating, Arion said, "Did he hurt you? Tell me what happened."

Marpessa told of the sudden attack, the struggle, the knife. "When I got my hand on it, my nerve failed and—" She stopped.

Arion put his arm around her and held her close. "Tell me."

"I—my grip loosened. I aimed for his jugular but only made a shallow gash. I thought he would come at me again, but he fell away. I leapt to my feet, scrambled away from him, and then Herakles returned." She gave a shaky laugh. "He saved me! He growled ferociously and lunged. I lifted the knife, and Drakios jumped up and ran away."

"Then what?" Arion asked. "You were gone a long time."

"The sheep scattered. It took me hours to find them."

Not satisfied, Arion put a finger under her chin and turned her face up to inspect it by the dim, flickering light of the lamp's flame. When he noticed the bruises on her cheek, the cut on her lip, dark rage filled him again. He jumped to his feet. "I'm going to kill him!"

*"No!"* She scrambled up, grasped his arms. "There are four of them. They'll kill *you.*"

Arion shook her off. "No matter! He hurt you. He tried to force you." He grabbed the knife and started for the door.

Marpessa flung herself on him, pushing him back with all her weight. "Arion, listen! It's past. We're finished here. All we need to do is get on that ship tomorrow."

Arion's muscles were tensed like springs. His hand clenched hungrily around the knife. He moved her aside and reached for the latch.

Marpessa gave a sob. The sound of it stopped him. He saw fear in her shadowed face. Breathing raggedly, he forced down his rage. "Aye, the ship. That's all that really matters." He slipped the knife back into the sheath at his belt.

Marpessa slumped against him and buried her face in his chest. As his arms closed around her, his knees weakened with the thought of what had almost happened today. It had been too close a call. A warning. He touched the hair that fell in soft, feminine curls around her face.

"You look too fair!" he said. "No wonder Drakios noticed. Before we leave I'll cut your hair, make you look more like Teukros. But now you must sleep. We'll go to the ship at dawn. Before Epistrophos and his sons are awake."

As soon as Marpessa settled down in the straw, Arion went to lie across the threshold. Drakios would not catch them unawares again.

# XXXVI

## PERGAMOS

They left at first light and made the long journey across the gulf. Then they found passage on fishing boats that plied the coast to the south, with Arion working as a fisherman to earn their way. Many days later the boat that carried them arrived at a sandy harbor near the mouth of a river. After the men ran the vessel up onto the beach, Marpessa waited, sinking her feet into cold, damp sand, while Arion thanked the fishermen who had given them transport and then had further talk with the owner of the boat. She could not catch every word when Arion spoke the Ionian dialect of his childhood, but she guessed that he was asking for information.

As they left the shore and headed toward the village, Arion said, "There's a big, rich town just inland, up in the hills—Pergamos. Their merchants trade with the Phoenicians, who come here often. This is where we will find our ship. And," he added with a grin of triumph, "the man told me of an empty shack up the shore where we can live until the next ship arrives. *And* there'll be work for me while we wait."

Arion had a few coppers in his belt. When they reached the marketplace, Marpessa's mouth watered at the smells of food offered at the stalls. Arion bought them each a round of bread and a stick of grilled goat meat which they ate as they walked. With her hunger assuaged, Marpessa stopped before a booth selling trinkets of copper and silver. She picked up a copper mirror, then put it down as if it had burned her fingers. Teukros would never touch a mirror. But Arion guessed her intent. After a swift glance to make sure they were unobserved, he took the mirror and held it before her.

Marpessa stared. It was a lifetime since she had last seen her reflection. Now she barely recognized herself. It showed the face of a lad hardened beyond his years. A sun-browned, wind-roughened face smudged with dirt, its sharp cheekbones hollowed out by hunger, the hair roughly shorn close to the scalp. When Arion had cut her hair, he'd spared no pains in taking away her femininity.

As he put the mirror down, she looked up at him. His eyes were deadly serious, speaking to her without words. The role of Teukros was no mere game. It was an identity she must adopt completely, every moment of every day. Her survival—and possibly his—depended upon it.

As they walked away from the booth, she was already cultivating a scowl and a boyish squint to further disguise her girlishness.

The shack was in sad condition, a dirt floor, walls made of thin boards with cracks between them and some boards missing. Marpessa's heart dropped at the sight, but she knew they were lucky to have even this much.

The next day, after Arion set off down the shore to join the fishermen, she explored the hills behind the village; they were barren with their cover of dried winter grasses. There were no woods or streams. After a day of wandering, she found a few nuts and late berries. She returned to the hut weary, wondering what she would do during the long days.

Arion came back in the evening with coppers in his belt and goat meat for dinner. "I'll make enough to buy our food and even have a few coppers left over for other things we need," he told her as he prepared a small fire in front of the hut. "And the men are very friendly."

Marpessa felt a pang of loneliness. "I could work too," she offered, but he shook his head.

"It's heavy work. We've forever pulling boats out of the water, repairing hulls, mending nets, hauling in fish, cleaning them."

"I can repair nets and clean fish," she pointed out.

"Marpessa, there are lots of crass jokes, men's talk. I wish to spare you that."

*He's scared, after what happened with Drakios*, Marpessa realized.

The next day she went to the river, which they had learned was called the Kaikos. She followed its course inland and caught several fish, which she cooked and had ready when Arion came home. "Freshwater fish tonight!" she said proudly, thinking he'd be pleased.

But he frowned. "Be careful! Stay away from people. Don't speak to anyone."

"I *am* careful!" she protested. "I avoid places where I'm likely to meet anyone."

"It's just that I worry. The fish is very good," he told her.

The next day brought a storm. Winds lashed the hut and drove the rain in icy spears. Marpessa huddled miserably inside the hut. The roof leaked, and she had no way to repair it. The rain did not stop for days. Arion continued to work with the fishermen, who lent him a hooded cloak of oiled canvas. He brought back oakum and driftwood to plug the worst holes in the roof. At night when they lay together, Marpessa drew comfort from the warmth of his body. But when morning came, the rain still fell.

She spent long, empty hours in the hut. The inactivity drove her wild. Her muscles twitched with restlessness. She paced the confines of the tiny space. She even ventured out into the freezing rain but soon came back shivering. *I can't stand it,* she thought.

Yet there was no end to it. No Phoenician ship came.

One morning when the rain slackened, she said, "Arion, I'm going into the village. Just to look around."

The thought of her venturing among strangers filled him with alarm. *What if someone guesses? Like before, in Antandros. What if she doesn't come back?* "You mustn't!" The words burst from him.

"But I've been confined here for days!"

"It's not safe anywhere else," he snapped.

"I must practice being Teukros. How do you think I'll manage on a Phoenician ship?"

"On a ship you'd never be out of my sight." There was a harsh edge to his voice. He paused, drew a breath, and tried to speak calmly. "Stay here, where nothing can happen to you."

"Arion, I must get out or I'll go mad!"

The rage and pain, the fear he had known on the day when Drakios nearly raped her rushed through him anew. "By the gods! Why won't you understand?" He heard his voice snap like a lash. "This is for your own safety!"

She flinched as if he had struck her. Turning away from him, she burst into tears. "No, it's for *your* peace of mind!"

"Marpessa—"

He reached out to her, but she fended him off with an out-flung hand. "Very well, I'll stay here. Don't worry about me!"

He hesitated. "Go!" she cried. "Your friends on the shore are waiting for you."

Arion left. Just outside he stopped, sick with remorse. *I'm stifling her.* With the rough haircut, the loose tunic that hid her figure, he'd made her as plain as possible. Yet every time he looked at her, he could only see her beauty: the bright eyes, the smile that lit her whole face and made his heart jump. He worried that everyone would see what he saw. *She must stay hidden*, he thought, but now he had opened a rift between them. *Oh, gods, will we be trapped here forever? Let there be a ship soon!*

Yet the thought of a Phoenician ship caused him fierce pain, for its arrival would bring him closer to the time when he must leave her forever.

As he set off for the shore, he felt torn in two.

When he joined the other fishermen, he heard some unexpected news. "Tomorrow we don't work. There's a festival honoring Zeus, Apollo, and Athena, up in Pergamos."

His heart lifted. A festival meant food and drink, song and dance. It was just what Marpessa needed. *We'll make a sacrifice to Athena and beg her for a ship to take Marpessa home.* He remembered Marpessa's worry that the goddess was angry. *I'll plead to be forgiven for taking Marpessa's maidenhood*, he vowed.

On the following morn, when they climbed into a small boat whose owner, for a copper piece, ferried passengers up the river Kaikos, Marpessa's heart was still bruised from their quarrel. Other than Arion telling her about the festival, they had barely spoken since.

The boat was crowded with other festival-goers whose loud, jubilant mood was in no way dampened by the rain. Marpessa and Arion sat silently on a plank near the stern. She was aware that they must behave as brothers who rarely looked at each other and spoke mostly in monosyllables. Still, she ached for a word or a look from him. When the others on the boat broke into raucous song and Marpessa felt sure she would not be noticed, she peeped at him, willing him to understand that her anger had passed. After a moment he returned her look, the briefest of glances, but she read in his eyes his apology and his desire to take and squeeze her hand. Happiness came alight inside her, a small, cautious flame. She had to restrain herself from touching him.

They disembarked where the river curved to within a league of Pergamos. Walking with a growing crowd, they climbed a rocky slope and found themselves in a marketplace three times the size of the one in the village on the shore. They threaded their way among the stalls, looking for something to sacrifice to Athena, and settled on a large honey cake and a flagon of wine that cost several of Arion's hard-earned coppers.

High above the town was the acropolis where the festival would take place. Following throngs of people, Arion and Marpessa trudged up the path. At the top they stopped to admire the panorama that lay below: coves and inlets on the coast and, in the distance, the island of Lesbos, half-hidden in clouds. As the crowd dispersed in search of various entertainments, Arion and Marpessa went to find the sanctuary of Athena.

It was a simple stone building with four granite columns adorning the entrance. A small crowd had gathered there. Marpessa and Arion had to wait as each group took time in private with the goddess. At last their turn came, and they entered the sanctuary. Inside, behind a low altar on which many offerings were laid, was a life-sized statue of the goddess. As Marpessa looked into the graven face of the helmeted Athena with its huge empty black eyes, all her memories of the goddess flooded back—the choosing, the ceremony of dedication in Naryx, the oath, the long days on her knees scrubbing the porch of the sanctuary in Troy—the raid. Her heart ached with remorse as she thought of Haleia. Then she remembered the owl in the forest, and she was afraid.

She tried to compose her thoughts into a prayer. But she wanted two irreconcilable things: Arion and home. *Athena, release me from my servitude and let me be with Arion in Lokris*, she begged. *I promise to make offerings to you for the rest of my life.*

As she gazed into those fathomless black eyes, words formed in her mind that seemed to come from the goddess. *You are mine to do my will. And you do not even know my will.*

Marpessa started in surprise. *But I belong to Arion now.*

*Then you must be willing to pay the price.* She was not sure if this was her own thought or the goddess's answer. Then all at once the altar before her seemed to fade, and she saw a different altar, a larger one, outside, with smoke rising. A knife flashed, and just before cold darkness closed over her, she saw it enter her flesh.

She heard a muffled, agonized cry, barely aware that it came from her. The ground dropped away, and she realized she had fallen. Strong arms gathered her up. She could not stop shaking.

"Marpessa, Marpessa!" She felt the heat of him, his breath in her hair as he held her close. "You're pale as a ghost! What is it?"

The vision had faded. Gradually some warmth came back to her, but she

167

could not form words or thoughts. Nausea rose in her throat as she put all her effort into standing on shaky legs. The cold would not leave her heart.

Arion was looking at her with anxious eyes. "What happened?"

She managed to shake her head. "It's nothing. I felt faint. Hunger, I think."

To her relief, he seemed to accept that. "Come then, my love," he said. "If you've made your prayer, we'll give our sacrifice to the goddess. Then we'll find you something to eat."

As they walked forward together to lay their offering on the altar, she averted her face. He mustn't see, he mustn't guess that she had just seen her own death.

# XXXVII

## STILLBIRTH

Amaltheia lit the incense she had placed at the foot of the small statue of Hera, patroness of childbirth. Then she knelt beside the bed of one of her servants, a woman far advanced in labor who writhed and cried in agony. But it was much too soon. There was scarcely a bulge in her belly. She could not be more than four or five months along.

Amaltheia had no means of stopping the birth. She muttered soothing words and rubbed a damp cloth over the woman's brow. Then she signaled to another servant to bring her what she needed. Just as in a full-term birth, the woman's breathing quickened, and her body tightened to expel the infant.

Amaltheia's hands caught the tiny, grotesque body, already dead and putrefying. An odor of decay filled the room. The servants quickly carried the corpse away, and Amaltheia worked through the night trying to save the woman's life.

It was futile. She died before dawn.

Amaltheia sat back with a deep sigh. A slight breeze stirred in the room. She looked over her shoulder at the shrine of Hera. The incense had gone out. A wisp of smoke obscured the goddess's face. A chill went through Amaltheia. She had heard of two stillbirths in the next village, and on the other side of Naryx a babe born with a huge opening in its belly leaving its entrails exposed. And one of the goats in their own pen had been delivered of dead, malformed twins.

Death was all around them. There could only be one reason. A powerful god or goddess was angry.

# XXXVII

## THE ARRIVAL OF THE PHOENICIANS

Days had passed since Pergamos, but an unremitting knot of dread stayed lodged in Marpessa's stomach. It immobilized her. It made breathing difficult. The rain had stopped, and on most days she sat huddled outside the hut, too listless to stir. She longed to speak to Arion about the terrible vision in Athena's temple, but she could not. She could barely speak at all. When he came home in the evening, she tried to smile, tried to listen as he talked about the events of the day, tried to act as though nothing were wrong. This took all her energy when all she wanted was to be left alone. And when she was alone, all she could do was turn the questions over and over in her mind. *How will it happen? And when?*

If she could only speak to Arion, he would surely take her in his arms and comfort her, and she longed for comfort. *Maybe it's not a message from the goddess at all,* he might say. *Sometimes people imagine their deaths. It doesn't mean anything.* And perhaps that was true. Marpessa remembered a serving girl at home who dreamed that she would die at the next full moon. She cowered and wept and carried on, but the moon grew full and waned, and at last she realized it had just been a fancy.

Yet try as she would, Marpessa could not shake herself out of this terrible state of lethargy. Sitting outside the hut, she buried her face on her drawn-up knees. It was cold. She should get up, stretch her legs, wrap the blanket around herself. She should start the cooking fire. But she couldn't bring herself to move.

The Phoencian ship arrived without warning as Arion was working on the shore. The fishermen stopped to watch its approach. When it came in close, two sailors dropped stone anchors, one from the bow and one from amidships, for the ship was far too large to be run up on the sand. Its great round hull loomed out of the water. A high beam, topped with the carved head of a sea horse, curved above the prow. Attached by a rope to the stern were the two smaller vessels used to ferry the sailors to and from the shore. The ship was twice as long as the one that had brought them from Lokris, and much wider and deeper. As Arion's eyes went to the brown-skinned men who lounged at the oars or stood at the rails, he felt a chill at the foreignness of them. They wore tight, knee-length kilts and round caps. Their black hair and long beards were oiled and curled. Sounds of the strange sibilant Phoenician language wafted across the water.

Then, at a shouted order, several men brought the rowboats around to the side of the hull and began loading amphorae, bales, and bulky canvas bundles into them. As Arion watched them row the loaded boats toward the shore, his thoughts flew to Marpessa. He carried her unhappiness within him, though he didn't know what was wrong. She had been so silent and withdrawn since Pergamos. Maybe she would be happy now. Then his stomach tightened. *How will I protect her from these aliens? How will I even get them to take us to Lokris?*

*Lokris.* The end of their journey. Their final parting. He had avoided thinking of it these past weeks. Now the pain of it struck him in the gut with a sickening jolt. *Oh, gods! How can I even consider leaving her?* He couldn't breathe. *How will I live without her?* He closed his eyes for a moment, then looked again at the Phoenician ship rocking at anchor. *I have to take her home,* he told himself. *We can't stay here. This is no life for her. She's sad all the time.*

He inhaled deeply and forced his thoughts back to the present.

The Phoenicians made a massive heap of their assorted goods on the shore. This took several trips from ship to shore in the small boats. Then they built a large bonfire a short distance away, piling it with driftwood and dried seaweed, making a fire big enough to be seen from Pergamos. *To alert the townsfolk of their arrival,* Arion guessed.

There was a chill in the wind, and when flames leapt skyward sending the smoke billowing, the Phoenician sailors stood on the leeward side of the fire, near enough for warmth. Now was the moment to approach them. But Marpessa must be with him. He ran to the shack and found her sitting just outside. She looked up in surprise.

"The Phoenicians are here!" he told her.

She scrambled to her feet in dismay. "So soon?" How long would the journey take? Days? Weeks? Too short! Her homecoming might mean her death. And even if she lived, she had thought of no plan to save Arion and no way keep him at her side. *We'll both die,* she thought.

"I was hoping you'd be pleased," he said. She saw the puzzlement in his eyes, the silent questions she couldn't bring herself to answer, the rift between them that had never quite closed. He reached toward her with both hands. "Come with me, my love," he said gently. "We'll ask them for passage—together."

She couldn't resist the appeal in his voice. As if he had called it forth, her courage came rushing back. *Long ago I promised myself I wouldn't live in fear. I'll make the most of what's left of my life.* She smiled and put her hands in his.

At the shore Arion approached the nearest Phoenicians, who stopped talking and stared at him. He quailed before the blank, dark gazes of so many foreigners. Then he asked, "*Adon?* Where is your *adon?*" One of the fishermen had told him that this word, which meant "lord," would get him speech with the Phoenician captain.

Someone gestured toward a broad-shouldered Phoenician of middle years who stood with his back to the fire looking out to sea. Arion and Marpessa approached him. "*Adon.*" Arion made a shallow bow, then gestured toward the big ship. "Are you bound for Hellas?" He pointed to himself and Marpessa, "We seek passage to Lokris in Hellas."

The man shook his head, muttering something in his own tongue. He turned and called out to one of his men. Amidst the flood of Phoenician words, Arion caught the repeated word *hamilcar.*

Hamilcar turned out to be the name of a short, stocky man with a lined face who came quickly toward them. Smiling, he pointed to himself. "I Hamilcar. I talk Greek."

Arion repeated the name, then pointed to himself and Marpessa. "Arion—Teukros."

The captain watched impassively, but Hamilcar's smile widened. "Good, good! What you want? I tell captain."

"Is your ship going to Hellas?" Arion asked again.

A speaking glance passed between Hamilcar and the captain as the little man translated. The captain replied in Phoenician, and Hamilcar turned back to Arion, grinning hugely. "Oh, aye, Hellas! Captain say aye."

Arion drew a deep breath. "We seek passage—to Hellas. To Lokris." Again he pointed to the water. "I'll work."

"You want come on boat?" Hamilcar's face clouded, and he turned to his captain. A long conversation ensued. Arion could guess nothing from the tone of it. He and Marpessa exchanged an anxious glance. At last Hamilcar turned back to them. "Captain not take Greeks on ship. Not ever before."

Arion's hopes sank. "I'll help," he said emphatically. "Work hard." He pantomimed energetic rowing, hauling, hammering. "I also help with speaking Greek."

Again there was an exchange between the two Phoenicians. At last Hamilcar pointed to the ship and said, "We have man hurt. Break arm. He very strong rower. You strong rower?"

Arion nodded vigorously.

But Hamilcar gestured at Marpessa. "What about friend?"

"Brother," Arion corrected. "My brother's not strong. Can't row. He can do other work."

The captain, watching closely, evidently caught the gist of this. He made a sharp comment, and Hamilcar gave an appreciative laugh.

"Captain say aye. We have work for brother. We sail morning."

*Tomorrow! Too soon!* As he and Marpessa walked silently back to their shack, Arion was filled with misgivings. He didn't trust the foreigners, hadn't liked that final exchange between Hamilcar and the captain. *What work will they expect Marpessa to do?* he wondered.

# XXXVIII

## NEWS FROM NARYX

Klonios was in his warehouse in the settlement of Kysikos when a messenger arrived with the news from far-off Naryx. The cowering messenger handed him the clay tablet, fearing the temper of his master when he read what was happening at home. "The news is bad, my lord," he warned.

Klonios took at the clay tablet. The man hovered uneasily in the doorway, awaiting dismissal. Klonios looked up. "What are you doing here? Begone!"

The messenger was only too glad to obey.

When the man left, Klonios perused the tablet. His wife had died, and there was drought in the land of Lokris, the worst in memory. Bad news? That depended on one's perspective.

Klonios gave a harsh laugh. His wife's death was good news. He had expected it, of course. He was now free to remarry, but his thoughts flew to that girl, Thrasios's daughter. *Dead.* And why? Because instead of giving her to Klonios, Thrasios hadn't had the manhood to stand up to the priestess. He had allowed her to be sent to serve the goddess, who had evidently deemed her unworthy, unfit.

The drought seemed to be continuing, even worsening. Klonios had promised Thrasios ruin. Now even the gods were playing into his hands.

Inevitably some of his own vines had withered and several of his crops had failed with the lack of rain. It mattered not. He was far from ruined. He had vast holdings in Ionia and other colonies. He prided himself on being too smart a man to keep all his eggs in one basket.

Klonios read on avidly. More bad news. Crops were withering on the vine. Sheep and goats were dying, the ewes miscarrying, the mares producing stillborn foals. The people believed that Athena was angry and had cursed them. Particularly hard-hit was the vintner Thrasios.

Klonios smiled. *It's working!* he thought.

He pitched the clay tablet into an urn near the wall and left the chamber, his steps almost jaunty.

Amaltheia stared at the vineyards extending beyond sight behind their house. Where there should have been new shoots and green leaves on the vines, all she saw was brown stubble from autumn's harvest. She glanced at the cloudless sky. How often she had chafed at the icy rains of winter, at being confined indoors! Yet now there was no pleasure in the sunny weather, for without rain the vines were dying.

*We're all dying,* she thought, *cursed by the Goddess. For me it doesn't matter.*

But it mattered to those in her care. To her three sons and her grandchildren. To the citizens of Naryx.

She whispered to the lifeless fields, *Oh, Goddess Athena, wise one, show us your will.*

# XXXIX

## ON THE SHIP

In the darkness of their shack, Marpessa's and Arion's lips came together with infinite longing and tenderness. Their arms enveloped each other and held fast. Then, as searching hands touched warm flesh, their breath quickened and they lay entwined on the rugs, clinging to each moment of the passing night. *Perhaps never again*, each thought but dared not say.

In the morning they walked toward the shore, each carrying a small pack with their few belongings. They stopped just before they reached the strand. Through a mist of tears, Marpessa's eyes devoured Arion as he stood looking back at her in exactly the same way. She managed a brave smile, then turned aside. Their bodies separated ever so slightly, and for the eyes of the world they became brothers, Arion and Teukros.

They found the Phoenicians in the midst of final negotiations with men from Pergamos who came to gather the goods offered for trade and give payment for them. Although Hamilcar lent his services as an interpreter, his efforts were largely ignored, and the negotiations took place in pantomime. The spokesman from Pergamos gestured to the proffered payment, and the captain of the Phoenicians turned away in a grand gesture of scorn. More silver and gold were added to the heap at the feet of the spokesman until finally the captain indicated with a magnanimous sweep of his right arm that he was satisfied.

Marpessa and Arion stood with the onlookers until the transaction was completed. Then Arion advanced toward the captain, Marpessa at his side. Hamilcar, who stood to the left of the captain, gave her a broad smile. She forced herself to grin in return. The captain gestured them toward one of the boats at the water's edge. As Arion stepped toward it, she followed with a boyish stride.

On board the ship, one of the men pointed Arion pointed toward a rowing bench. Marpessa's heart sank. That quickly they were to be separated. Arion shot her a quick glance with pain and worry in his eyes. She could not muster a smile as he turned and toward his place on the lower level, disappearing from her sight.

Left alone among the foreigners, Marpessa looked long at the spot where Arion vanished. At least he was near. She found comfort in that. But what was the good of it if she never saw him? Her throat tightened. Men were moving about the ship, stowing belongings, settling onto rowing benches, calling out to each other in so strange a tongue that she could not begin to guess what they were saying. She and Arion were at the mercy of these Phoenicians. Anything could happen on the journey ahead—a journey that might end all too quickly. *Zeus, father of the gods, and Athena, goddess of wisdom,* she begged in silence, *send me a sign that you will help me.*

It did no good to give way to fear—and the foreigners might be observing her. She straightened and forced herself to inspect her surroundings. *Two banks of oars!* she marveled. *And the hull—so thick! But where should I go?* The only space not occupied by rowers was the small triangular deck at the prow. The front of the ship. She did not want to be there before so many staring eyes. But there was nowhere else. And the men, as they settled at their rowing stations, for the most part ignored her. She went to the foredeck and crouched down, making herself as inconspicuous as possible. Another occupant sat on the deck: Hamilcar, too slight a man to be a rower. He met her eyes with a squinty-eyed, lopsided grin and motioned her to sit down. At least he seemed friendly—and could speak Greek.

Feeling not quite so alone, Marpessa watched as the captain shouted orders. The huge stone anchors were hauled up on ropes, and, on each side of the ship, two banks of dripping oars were lifted from the water and held poised above the curving hull. Then, at a shout from the captain, the oars were thrust into the water as one, and the ship swung away from the shore. Someone was beating a drum to keep the rowers in rhythm. Marpessa started at the familiar sensation of a swaying deck beneath her. She watched the shore dwindle away. Their journey had begun.

When they were underway, Hamilcar said to her, "I show you your work." He gestured her to follow him along the gangway to a ladder that led to the hold. As they climbed down into half-darkness, a familiar smell assailed her nostrils: the earthy odor of farmyard animals. Hamilcar led her toward a penned-off area near the fore. In the pen were the sheep and goats that would provide meat on the long journey.

"You take care animals. Food, water." He gestured toward piles of fresh excrement in the sawdust and straw on the bottom of the hold. "You clean up mess two, three times day." He pointed to some wooden pails and a shovel. As she hesitated, he gave his friendly grin. "You clean now. Later I show you ship." Then he left her.

The stench and the mess were overwhelming. She longed to be up on the deck as close as possible to Arion. Then she took heart. The great Herakles himself had not been too proud to clean the Augean stables. She loved animals, she did not mind hard work, and she would be out of the sight of these rough, foreign men. Below deck she would have privacy and less chance of discovery.

She laughed aloud. This might be an answer to her prayer. Perhaps one of the gods was helping her after all.

Her work in the hold finished, Marpessa went to the rail amidships, not far from Arion's rowing bench. Though she strained to look for him, she couldn't see the lower level where he sat. It was a blustery, cloudy day. The land lay far to their right. *We're heading north*, she realized. With the wind southeasterly, a group of men loosened ties and hauled on ropes, and gradually the huge square sail unfurled from the yard. The captain shouted an order from the foredeck: the rowers shipped their oars, letting their tired arms go limp.

The sail bellied out. The ship swung in an arc to catch the wind and pranced through the waves like a frisky horse. The deep blue water churned restlessly, flinging up spray. Resting against one of the beams that supported the rail, Marpessa watched the sea gulls gliding in the ship's wake, dropping away one by one as the land receded to a brown haze. She licked her lips and tasted salt.

It had taken many days for the ship that brought her from Lokris to reach the Trojan shore. But with this huge ship cutting through the open sea, with a favorable wind— *We might reach Lokris in five days,* she calculated. Five short days during which she might never see Arion, and then he would leave her. *Must I let him go?* Aye, she must, if it was the way to save his life. She thought of her premonition. If her return to Lokris meant her death, it would be best to let him go at once, so that he would never learn of it. A tear slipped down her cheek. At that moment a shadow fell over her. She wiped her face surreptitiously and turned.

Hamilcar, smiling as usual, stood at her side. "Come, Teukros!" he said. "I show you ship."

Marpessa straightened eagerly, glad to banish her dark thoughts. Anything she could learn about these foreigners might be useful. She forced an answering smile and followed him along the gangway.

"Sail, ropes, pulleys." With his wide grin, he pointed out the obvious. It seemed he wanted to practice speaking Greek. "Captain lead, helmsman steer, men row." He pantomimed vigorously. "But I, Hamilcar, take care. I lookout man for ship," he said with pride in his voice. His broad gesture encompassed the whole of his world. Halfway along the gangway, he pointed down into the hold where, in the dimness, she could see a large storage area. "Things for trade," he explained. Near the mast was a small tent like structure. "For captain sleep." They continued down the gangway. But when they came to a spacious aft deck covered with canvas that she hadn't noticed before, he made no comment about it and hurried her past. He pointed out the helmsman and the steering oars.

But Marpessa stopped and gestured toward the covered deck. "What's that?"

Hamilcar's eyes evaded hers. "Only things for ship." He did not offer to let her see them. "Come, I show you where food cooked, and where we worship gods."

The helmsman was looking at her, an odd, flat look. *Because I'm Greek—and less than human to him.* But at least he did not seem to have penetrated her disguise. Then his eyes shifted and something unspoken flashed between him and Hamilcar. Hamilcar looked away too quickly, his smile suddenly shallow and forced. A shiver ran along her skin. She longed for Arion.

As she followed Hamilcar down to the stern of the hold, she thought. *I'd best keep my eyes open and my wits about me.*

At sundown at the end of the first day's sailing, they dropped anchor, not far from the land to their right. The oarsmen spread out about the ship to rest. Some straddled the rowing benches and leaned their heads back over the rail, eyes closed in exhaustion, while scents of cooking meat wafted from the stern.

His body unused to the hard work of rowing, Arion arose painfully from his bench. He flexed his fingers and shook out his tired arms. Blisters had popped out all over his hands, some open and oozing, some bleeding. He'd only had time only to wrap a thin band of cloth around the worst ones. Stretching his cramped legs, he climbed to the deck level and sought Marpessa, who stood near the stern. She gave him a huge smile. As she started swiftly along the gangway toward him, he lifted his fingers in a gesture of restraint.

They met amidships and stopped just short of touching. As much as he dared, he drank in the sight of her. He could find no words. Aware of glances that might come their way, he turned toward the rail, indicating with a quick glance that she should join him. Side by side, they rested their arms on the rail and looked into the deep orange sky in the west.

"Are you well?" Arion whispered at last.

"Aye. Arion, they've given me the job of cleaning the pens of the animals," she told him. He felt rather than saw her grin. "It's perfect!"

An enormous relief came over him. He ventured a sidelong glance. "The hold is a place where you can have privacy and be safe."

They were silent, staring out to sea. He edged as close as he dared, his forearm near enough to hers on the rail to feel the warmth from her flesh. His body was starved for her. The desire to touch her, to engulf her in his arms throbbed through him. She must have felt it, for she crept closer until her arm brushed his skin.

He jerked back as if scalded. "You mustn't," he said, barely moving his lips.

She lowered her gaze, moved away. He felt the pain of even that small separation like a sharp wound.

The second day, when the ship dropped anchor in the evening, Arion rose and stretched. They were somewhere north of Troy, and soon they should be heading west. He and Marpessa ate the evening meal together: rounds of bread and cooked lamb seasoned with spices strange to their tongues but not unpleasant. All too soon they parted, Marpessa going to the hold, Arion lying down uncomfortably on his narrow rowing bench. All around he heard unintelligible, murmured conversations, short sharp comments, bursts of laughter. He could not shake the feeling that some of those comments were about him, the laughs at his expense. *Ridiculous!* he told himself. Still, he didn't trust the foreigners.

Another oarsman nudged him awake at dawn. The rowers were handed a quick meal of bread and cheese and summoned to their oars. The helmsman shouted commands that Arion could not understand. He'd become used to being surrounded by a strange tongue, although he still jumped if someone shouted or something unexpected happened. Now he guessed that the ship was making a tricky maneuver. He followed the motions of the other oarsmen near him, holding his oar aloft while those on the right side of the boat rowed furiously. Then it was the turn of those on the left, Arion's side. It was barely light and he could see nothing through the narrow opening for his oar.

Then for a long, exhausting time with the wind unfavorable, they pulled on their oars without respite. Arion had never rowed so hard. Sweat poured down his back. His arms ached. The men around him were working equally hard, some grunting in agony. A current surged against them, pushing them back, impeding their progress. The voice of the helmsman lashed them like a whip, exhorting them to pull with greater strength.

At last Arion felt a breeze on his neck. A sharp command from the helmsman caused the men to cheer. They were allowed to ship the oars. Arion heard the creaking of rope through pulleys, and the sail rose. As the ship leapt forward, he looked through the oar opening and saw gulls skimming over the water. Land was not far away. He lurched upright in shock. He was on the left side of the ship. If they were heading west to Hellas, he should see nothing but open water.

*Surely I'm mistaken*, he thought. They were probably passing an island he hadn't remembered from the earlier trip to Troy. Soon the breeze died, and he was commanded to row again, his arms protesting at the pain. He had no more time to look or even worry.

When evening fell and the anchors were dropped, he scrambled from his post below the deck, and even before searching for Marpessa, his eyes found the setting sun. Behind him! The shock buckled his knees.

There was no doubt. They were heading east, away from Hellas.

The Phoenician captain had lied to him.

# XL

## ANGRY SEAS

He dreaded telling Marpessa. Sailing with the Phoenicians was a reckless plan, he saw now, which he had leapt into too precipitously. "Marpessa," he began when she came to the rail where they met each evening. He kept his tone expressionless, his eyes fixed on the sea. "The Phoenicians—that is, the ship is going—" His voice stumbled.

She sidled close to him. "I know."

Surprised, he risked a look. "How?"

"I saw where the land lay and where the sun set."

In an undertone he voiced his vehemence. "I shouldn't have trusted them!"

To his surprise she did not look worried. "I don't like it any more than you," she whispered. "But what are we to do? If we left the ship, we might land in worse trouble than we are in right now. At least here we have food and shelter."

She was right. For the time being they were reasonably safe. But what lay ahead? "There are Greek colonies along this coast," he pointed out.

"We still wouldn't be able to cross the seas to Hellas," Marpessa said. "The Phoenicians can't go east forever. Who knows? Perhaps the captain was telling the truth and they intend to sail to Hellas after they return from the east."

He thought about how hard things had been for her in the fishing village. At last he said, "We may as well stay with the foreigners, then. At least for now."

The ship rocked on great swells. He had grown used to the constant rolling motion, the straining and creaking of ropes against wood, the frequent bouts of queasiness, but there was an urgency to the ship's movement now. A surging current was pushing them back. The ship strained against the anchors. A cold wind from the east blew against them.

A sudden clanging of the ship's gong called sailors to the evening meal. As men went toward the stern where trenchers of grilled meat and dark, flat rounds of bread were handed around, Marpessa and Arion followed, always under the rude scrutiny of the foreigners. *As if we're some strange kind of animal—or their prey. But do they know Marpessa is a woman?* He tried to read those blank eyes. *They don't know,* he guessed as a familiar anxiety gnawed at his heart. *Yet.*

The next morning he awoke to a ferocious bucking of the ship and the bellowing of the helmsman. He understood the Phoenician command: "To your oars, men!" They rowed against a mighty current. The muscles in his arms seemed as if they would break, but there was no respite. They were traveling northeast. Through the opening for his oar, he caught glimpses of low, barren hills.

As they rowed endlessly, Arion noticed an idle man wandering about, his arm in a sling. This man looked at him in a smug, gloating way. *This must be the one I've been hired to replace,* he realized. He also saw that there were more Phoenicians sailors than oars. Tired rowers around him were replaced with fresh ones. This happened more often as they rowed against the current. Arion, exhausted, looked around for relief. But no one came to take his place. The only rests he had were those that everyone got, when the rowers stopped briefly for food and water.

A rough, surly man named Barekbaal, a kind of foreman, arranged substitutions on the lower level. The next time Barekbaal directed a man in front of him to be replaced, Arion called out, "Barekbaal—" and pantomimed tiredness. Barekbaal looked at him, eyes narrowed, then made a show of not understanding and turned away, shaking his head. Arion was furious. His meaning had been perfectly clear to the Phoenician. But he was granted no relief.

A while later Arion, yielding to a moment of weariness, lost the beat of the rowing and his oar crashed against the one in front of him. Shouts rang out. Out of nowhere Barekbaal appeared and swung a great blow that struck Arion across the face and nearly knocked him from the rowing bench.

He caught the bench for balance and wiped the blood flowing from his lip. Barekbaal dragged him from the bench and another took his place, but only for the moments it took to regain his breath. Then Barekbaal shoved him back to his place, snarling at him.

*So that is how it is!* Arion thought. Yet he dared not protest. Not only would it would be useless, it might put Marpessa in danger. *Zeus, Poseidon, help me endure,* he prayed. *And send us a wind from the south.*

When Marpessa saw the blood on his lip that evening, she asked him about it, but he only shrugged. She handed him a rag to wipe his mouth. *I can't tell him about Hamilcar*, she thought. Not that there was anything to tell. Only that Hamilcar's easy grin had become oily and familiar. He winked at her in a way that made her shudder. His hand would swing as if accidentally and brush against her side, her hip. Had he guessed she was female? There was no suggestion, when he called her Teukros, that he knew this was a lie. She was puzzled, dismayed. He was her source of information, her ally, yet now she looked for ways to avoid him.

Still, he gave her tidbits of knowledge, and she was able to tell Arion that evening that they were traveling through a strait the Greeks called the Hellespont.

"The rowing will be hard, Hamilcar says."

"I already know that!" Arion answered ironically.

The next day the boat rocked and swayed as it never had before. Marpessa grew queasy. The stench of the animals in the hold made it worse, as well as the smell of blood, the spill of entrails when an animal was slaughtered. Knowing that she loved the animals and had given them names, Hamilcar made her watch so that he could taunt her. Last night, grinning hugely, he'd said, "Tomorrow we kill the goat—what you call her?—Nenni. Good eating. Much meat."

Marpessa had turned away, refusing to be drawn. No, she would not tell Arion. Not when his lot was so much worse.

Now Hamilcar climbed halfway down the ladder, leaned into the hold, and called, "Come up moment. Come see."

She dared not defy him. Staggering to keep her footing, she pulled herself up the ladder and followed him to the stern deck. The sky was gray and the ship was surrounded by waves the size of small hills. She gasped.

He laughed. "This nothing! Wait and see." He pointed astern. "We leave Hellespont." Behind them the strait receded. Ahead it widened into a sea. "Now we sail—" He said a name in Phoenician, then added, "Propontis in Greek. More winds." He gave a wicked grin. "Storm coming soon! We go out to sea to avoid wrecking. Look!" Marpessa followed his pointing finger. Along the lee shore, black rocks stuck up like jagged monster teeth. She felt sick with fear as she crawled back into the hold.

The first blast of the storm flung Marpessa against the hull. She cried out, bruised and shaken, and crawled to her feet only to be knocked down again, her ears filled with the din of waves crashing on the hull, shouts from the men, their feet pounding on the gangway as they ran to pull down the sail, turn the ship, lash everything down. Suddenly Hamilcar's head appeared above the ladder.

"Come help, boy!" he shouted urgently. As she climbed halfway up the ladder, he reached down to haul her the rest of the way. He pulled her along the gangway toward the stern.

The canvas that covered the aft deck was loose and flapping in the wind, about to blow away. "Quick!" Hamilcar yelled. "Grab! Hold!" She leapt up in the dark of the storm, gripping a rope for balance, and seized the billowing canvas. Under the canvas she saw a bunch of mysterious objects that Hamilcar fought to keep from rolling away and falling into the bilge. There were coils of rope, indistinct bulky shapes, stacks of clay tablets, and several large baskets. One of these fell over, and as Hamilcar flung his body over it to catch what spilled out, she caught a sudden glimpse of—*gold!* Many ingots of gold, several fortunes worth in this basket alone. Then a great wave struck the stern, drenching her. She fought to keep her footing and lost her grip on the canvas. For several moments she was busy catching it, pulling it down to secure it. When she glanced at Hamilcar, all the gold was hidden from sight. As they secured the covering, he shot her a sudden, hard glare.

*I wasn't supposed to see that,* she realized. *Pray Zeus he didn't notice me looking!*

But he didn't seem to have. Once the canvas was secured, his mood changed abruptly. "Thank you, my boy! You very quick—very good!" He grinned at her. "And very wet! Come. I have blanket." Before she could escape his touch, he swept her along the gangway, both of them swaying like drunks. He pulled her down the ladder.

"Come. My boy." His voice caressed the word. His eyes gleamed moistly. Shudders snaked down Marpessa's spine. This was even more ominous than if he had found out she was a girl. He grabbed a blanket, wrapped it tightly about her wet shoulders. "You spend night with me, little lad. I keep you warm." He reached for the hem of her garment. "Now take off wet clothes."

"No!" Marpessa managed to jerk away. "I must see my brother!" Heart pounding like a drum, she bolted for the ladder before he could move.

When the storm struck the ship head on, Arion was nearly knocked into the bilge. He let go of his oar to grip the bench. Icy rain poured down his chest and back. At shouted orders from the helmsman, the rowers on the left side shipped their oars, and the ship swung in a great arc. They were heading out to open sea.

The wind was a steady roar. It was impossible to gain a purchase with the oars in the seething waves. The helmsman bellowed again. All the men lifted their oars and pulled them inboard as far as they could.

A wall of water washed over them. The men hunkered on their rowing benches. Several were sick. A brigade was handing bucket after bucket up from the bilges, the buckets pitifully small. Another wall of water struck. The ship lurched. The clouds were so dark Arion could not say if night had come. Soaked to the bone, he lay on the short plank, knees pulled up to his chest, muscles so stiff and aching he feared they would snap. He was surrounded on all sides by oarsmen on their own benches, probably as miserable as he. He gripped the wet, slippery wood with icy fingers. His head plunged downward with each wave and up again. His stomach heaved; he spewed sickness. *We're going under,* he thought, almost past caring. *I'll die without seeing Marpessa again.*

Suddenly a warm body was squirming onto the bench next to him. His arms shot out to catch her just as a wave nearly knocked them off their perch. She gave a breathy little gasp. Quickly, before she could speak, he covered her mouth with his. The darkness was now complete. So long as they made no noise, the Phoenicians all around them would know nothing of her presence. Joy flooded him. How she had dared come here? They clung together barely moving, kissing in silence. The danger, the unseen men around them breathing in the dark, only added to their excitement. When at last the storm diminished, they drifted into sleep. And when he awoke near dawn, she was gone, leaving only the taste of her kisses.

The first daylight showed a sullen world of gray skies and roiling, angry seas. There was no sight of land. The oarsmen brought the ship about. Without the sun it was hard to gauge direction, but Arion guessed the storm had blown them north, far from the shore, and they were now heading southeast. The Phoenicians raised a tattered sail, and as the ship limped forward, men made repairs to the loose ropes and damaged gear. When night fell and stars appeared through the clouds, Arion expected they would ship the oars and drop the sail. But instead the helmsman raised a curious instrument made up of a long beam of wood and a shorter piece. He pointed it to a bright star and appeared to take some kind of measurement. By the light of a lamp he consulted a clay tablet. Then he shouted orders. The ship changed heading.

Arion, leaning his back against the rail, looked closely at the star. It was near a constellation the Greeks called the Great Bear. *It must give them a clue as to direction,* he thought. *That must be how they navigate at night so far from land. Unlike Greek ships.* It was not just the size of their ships, but their superior knowledge, that gave the Phoenicians mastery of the seas.

Suddenly the helmsman turned his way, and even in the dark Arion could feel the man's hostile eyes boring into him. Raising his free hand, the helmsman jerked it in a slashing motion across his own throat. There was no mistaking the threat. When the man barked a harsh command at him, Arion went hastily back to his oar bench.

Days later the ship sailed into a small harbor. As the oars were shipped and the anchors dropped, the Phoenicians began loading goods and clambering into the shore boats. A rest stop to replenish food and water, and perhaps also a trading stop. Arion got to his feet and stretched with an enormous sigh, flexing his cramped hands. He felt as if he had been rowing his whole life. He wanted nothing more than to set foot on solid ground. Looking around for Marpessa, he saw her head emerging from the hold.

"Teukros!" he called joyously. "Let's go ashore."

Together they approached the rear of the ship where Phoenician sailors were forming into a line as the shore boats were being lowered. But an abrupt gesture from one of the sailors stopped them. Holding a short javelin, which he shook menacingly, he shouted, and Arion understood the harsh Phoenician *"No!"*

He froze. He dropped his eyes. As he fought to control himself, he could not look at Marpessa.

She touched his arm. Her hand was trembling. "Arion, we're prisoners," she whispered.

# XLI

## THE STRAITS

Arion smashed the railing with his fist—two, three, four times, until Marpessa cried, "Stop! They're watching us!"

Two men had stayed on board to guard the ship—and keep an eye on the prisoners. He felt their flat black eyes staring at him. "By Zeus, what a fool I was to have trusted these accursed foreigners!" he whispered fiercely. But he was furious at himself. *I did this*, he thought. *I put us at their mercy.* The full force of their plight struck him like a blow in the gut. *They're going to kill us.*

The knowledge came to him with certainty. He remembered the helmsman's threatening gesture when Arion saw him charting the ship's course from a star. He remembered Hamilcar saying that the captain never took Greeks on board. Then the captain had changed his mind because one of his sailors was injured. *They took us on because they had a use for us*, Arion thought. *Lucky for us, we're still useful—but for how long? We know too much about their ship, their navigation secrets. From the beginning they never intended to let us live.*

Next to him Marpessa said with a quiver in her voice, "Arion, we must escape them." He turned to her. *I can't let her know*, he thought. *She's already afraid enough.* He wanted to take her in his arms and tell her that he would protect her. But at the moment he was as powerless as she.

His fist struck the rail again, this time with determination.

"We'll find a way," he said. "I'll think of a plan."

He would begin right now. He would devote all his thoughts to it. He glanced covertly at the two Phoenicians left behind to watch them. *If they always leave no more than guards on board, we might be able to fool them or elude them.* The ship was anchored not far from a small cove surrounded by a cluster of huts. One of the shore boats had been pulled up on the beach. The other was moored to the side of the ship, in plain sight of the guards. *But we can both swim*, Arion thought. *Next time they make port, I'll have a plan.*

"Marpessa," he said, "you must find out from Hamilcar when we'll be stopping next. And if it's a Greek settlement. Then we can—" A small, sharp indrawn breath drew his eyes to her face, and he saw a fleeting look of fear, a mere shifting of her gaze. It melted him with helpless tenderness. "What is it, my love?" he asked, barely moving his lips yet caressing her with the word.

"Nothing, Arion. I—I will do my best."

*Arion, you don't know what you're asking!* Marpessa thought. But she shoved aside her memory of that terrible moment in the hold when Hamilcar had almost stripped off her tunic and taken her to his bed. At all costs Arion mustn't find out. He would kill Hamilcar. And get himself killed. Only she could gain the information they needed from Hamilcar. And only if she kept her secret.

She would worry about that later. Now she basked in the pure happiness of being with Arion on a nearly empty ship. Never mind the danger. They could speak freely, for the two guards understood no Greek. She savored the caress of Arion's words, the more guarded caress of his eyes.

As soon as the ship was underway again, Marpessa's dread returned. During the day she avoided Hamilcar as much as possible and answered tersely when he spoke to her. Strangely he seemed unaffected by her rudeness and distance. After the storm, she had moved her bedding to a far corner of the animal pen, hoping that if Hamilcar came in the night, the sheep and goats would give warning. But surprisingly, he never came near. As before, he often sought her out to chat or assign her chores. Only now he was almost diffident, all too eager to please. He started bringing her gifts—a small jar of olive oil, a warm blanket, a half-filled wine skin. "To help you sleep better," he said. He even stopped taunting her and forcing her to be present for the butchering of animals.

Marpessa was puzzled. At times she could see a greedy desire lurking in his eyes, but he seemed to be holding back. Then she realized. *He knows he frightened me. He's trying to win back my trust.*

However long this lasted, it could be put to good use. She plied him with questions. "Hamilcar, where are we going? Is it far?"

He seemed gratified by her curiosity. "We go to great sea. Greeks call Euxine. But first must go through long, narrow strait. Big current. Bigger than last one. Very difficult for rowers."

Marpessa felt a pang for Arion, but said brightly, "When are we stopping next? I'm so tired of sailing!"

"Ah! Next trading stop after straits. In Euxine Sea."

Marpessa tried to make her voice casual. "Does it have a Greek name?"

"Aye. Greek settlement. Heracléa Pontica."

Since he seemed so willing to answer questions, she asked, "How far?"

He shrugged. "After we leave strait? Maybe five days sail."

When Marpessa reported all this to Arion, he smiled grimly. "Good! By the time we reach Heracléa Pontica, we'll have an escape plan ready. One that won't fail."

*Or they'll kill us*, Marpessa added silently. She suppressed a shiver. "At least it's a Greek settlement. We might eventually find a ship to Hellas."

"But this strait we must go through first—" He broke off with a sigh.

Marpessa asked, "What is it?"

He gave her a slight smile. "Nothing—just that the rowing is already very hard."

When they reached the strait that Hamilcar spoke of, Marpessa knew it at once. The huge ship bucked. She struggled to the deck and saw great swells striking the hull, all but stopping their progress. The ship was heading north, and a northerly wind was beating it back, a wind so strong that Marpessa could barely stand against it. Churning, hurtling, white-capped waters surrounded them, flinging salt spray in her face. The land was close on both sides. The helmsman shouted furiously, a word that sounded like "Hup! Hup! Hup!" *Pull! Pull! Pull!* He loosed a stream of Phoenician curses, then resumed his exhorting chant. The oarsmen were rowing with all their might, faces contorted, sweat rolling off their bodies. She ached for Arion at his hidden oar.

With progress at a standstill, the helmsman shouted orders that sent the ship heading toward the farther shore instead of up the strait. Though the low-lying hills across the water seemed close, the rowers fought many hours to reach it. At last the ship lurched to the right. They had caught a counter-current carrying them northward. The tired men slumped at the oars and let the water bear them forward.

All day the ship followed a zigzag course from one side of the strait to the other to catch what eddies and counter-currents it could, for it was impossible to row directly into the surging current and the north wind.

When evening fell, the ship pulled in close to the lee shore and dropped anchor. Marpessa hastened up to the spot where she met Arion and found him slumped over the rail. His face, resting on a limp arm, was sweaty, deathly pale. His eyes were open, but he did not seem to see her. His left hand lay in a smear of blood. She lifted it gently and saw a mass of fresh, oozing blisters torn into his callused palm. His right hand was the same. Her stomach turned over. She felt his pain flash all the way down her spine.

She left him and ran down to the hold, where she sheared clumps of wool off one of the cleaner sheep. She collected strips of cloth, a jar of water, her vial of olive oil. Going back to Arion, she took each hand tenderly in hers, cleaned it and rubbed oil into the skin to keep it from drying. Then she made pads with the wool. She wound the cloth around them, bandaging each hand gently yet securely. Through it all, Arion lay unmoving, his eyes closed. She thought he was unconscious, but when she finished, he gave a small smile without opening his eyes and whispered, "Thank you!"

She wiped his brow, then lifted his head to give him water. Eyes were watching her, but she didn't have a thought to spare on whether she was being brotherly or something more. "I'll get you some food, my love." She fetched meat and bread from the galley. When she returned, he revived enough to open his eyes and eat.

"What happened?" she asked.

"The rowing," he breathed. He fell silent, then gathered the strength to continue. "The others," he whispered. "They all get rests. I...never."

Anger coursed through her, but she helped him gently to his rowing bench and covered him with the blanket she gotten from Hamilcar. After a quick glance to make sure no one was looking, she bent to kiss his brow. He smiled with closed eyes. "Sleep, my love," she murmured.

When his breathing grew even, she left him and went swiftly down the gangway to find Hamilcar, too furious to be afraid.

He was on the stern deck with the helmsman. Before she reached him, she stopped, her rage replaced by icy fear. The foreigners could simply kill her—and Arion. She drew a deep breath, approached slowly. The two men watched her in surprise. She looked directly into Hamilcar's eyes, then went down on her knees before him.

"Hamilcar, we Greeks believe a suppliant is sacred to the gods." She bowed her head. "I come before you and your god Baal as a suppliant. I beg you. Please go to your captain and ask that he let my brother Arion rest from the oars as the others do. My brother is near death from exhaustion. I, Teukros, without my brother am nothing. I will be alone, and I too will die. Help me," she pleaded.

Hamilcar exchanged a glance with the helmsman, then gave a twisted grin. His black eyes shone with gleams of triumph that filled her with dread.

"I can help you, boy. I can save brother," he began softly. He shot a glance at the helmsman, who lowered his eyes discreetly. "But if I do, what you give me? Too long I be kind to you, I spoil you. But no more sly games, my lad. No more run away. If I save brother, you give what I want."

Marpessa, still on her knees, straightened, her arms limp at her sides. Her eyes closed. She felt as if she were dropping straight down into a dark pit, her heart and stomach left far behind. Her words came after a long, shuddering breath.

"Save my brother!"

# XLII

## THE HOSPITABLE SEA

That night as the ship lay at anchor, rocking in the current, Marpessa, in her bed, heard footsteps shuffling through the animal pen. *Hamilcar!* He carried a lamp and approached without a care how much noise he made, shoving sheep and goats aside, muttering in Phoenician. When he stood over her, the lamp's flame distorted his face, giving him demon features.

Her heart pounded like the hooves of a runaway horse. As Hamilcar hunkered down on the bedding, her throat closed with fear. She reared up and backed as far as she could against the curving wall of the hull, clutching the blanket to her breast. Then, realizing what a feminine gesture that was, she let it fall.

Hamilcar, almost conversationally, said, "I do what I say. I speak captain. Brother can rest, heal. When he row again, he have rests like others."

"Thank you," she breathed almost inaudibly—and waited.

"This bed not comfortable. Too close animal stink." He leaned closer and inspected her in the light of the lamp's small flame. She saw the twin gleams of that flame in his eyes and smelled his rank breath. "You come my bed," he said.

All the air left her lungs and for several heartbeats she couldn't speak. At last she blurted, "What do you want, Hamilcar? It's late. I was sleeping."

Her weak pretense of ignorance angered him. His voice roughened. "You beg, beg, and I keep promise. Now you come my bed."

She said, "I can't, Hamilcar! I'm sick." In fact this was not a lie. Bile rose in her throat. She retched suddenly, loudly.

There was silence. At last he said, "Tomorrow night," the words dragged out reluctantly.

She heard his footsteps stomping off, eloquent of his anger. Shaking with horror, for a moment she couldn't move. Then her mouth filled with sickness. She crawled quickly to a mucky corner of the pen and vomited.

Back in her pallet she was weak with relief. But it was short lived. *A one-day reprieve*, she thought. Not enough. It might take days to get through the strait, and after that five more days to reach Heracléa Pontica. *How will I avoid him for that long?*

When she awoke the following morning, she could tell by the movement of the ship that they were already underway, the oarsmen fighting the current. For a moment she lay still, too full of dread to move. But she must see Arion to learn if Hamilcar had indeed kept his promise. When she climbed out of the hold, she found Arion lying near the aft deck, eyes closed. He looked exhausted, but his color was normal.

"Arion!" she cried joyfully.

He opened his eyes and smiled.

"Did you sleep well? Let me see your hands." She inspected the bandages. There was some seepage, but his wounds looked clean.

"I slept well. I'm much better," he said. "How did you arrange it?"

Marpessa felt her smile slip away. She lowered her eyes and forced herself to speak lightly. "I asked Hamilcar to convince the captain."

But Arion had always been able to read her. "Marpessa? What is it?"

"Nothing. I...I just don't want him to suspect me."

"And does he?"

"No, not yet." At least this was the truth. And it struck her as so ironic that she managed a grin. "Arion, I came to see you even before tending the animals. But I must go now." She got to her feet, turned toward the ladder. She felt his puzzled gaze on her back. Never before had she avoided him. But if she stayed in his presence he would probe her secret. Her dread returned, draining strength from her legs.

Then, as she backed down the short ladder to the hold, her gaze fell on the aft deck with the canvas cover and the mysterious things hidden under it. The gold. If she and Arion escaped, they would have use for gold. A thought began to form. And at the same moment an idea sprang into her head about how she could keep Hamilcar at bay—at least for a while.

Arion knew at once that Marpessa was hiding something. She looked drawn and sick, her eyes hollow from lack of sleep. It must have something to do with Hamilcar. Had the Phoenician discovered her secret? When he asked if Hamilcar suspected her, her answer had the ring of truth. Then she had made an excuse and left before he could ask anything else. So what was it? A terrifying thought came to him. Was Hamilcar one of those men who liked boys? Arion sat up, ready to spring to his feet and find Hamilcar. But he would be stopped, maybe beaten or even killed. There was nothing he could do that wouldn't put her in greater danger. His helplessness nearly sent him mad. He tried to comfort himself with the thought that somehow Marpessa must be keeping Hamilcar at a distance. Or perhaps he was wrong, and it was something else entirely.

Soon he was called to his station once again. Wearily he took up his oar. As he bent his back into rowing, blood oozed from his blisters. But this was a small thing compared to their other troubles. The men around him also had bleeding blisters. And as the day wore on, he was given periodic rests as often as the Phoenician rowers.

When night fell, the ship once again maneuvered over to the shore and dropped anchor, and Marpessa came as usual to the railing where he awaited her. He moved forward eagerly to greet her—then drew back in shock. An overwhelming smell of the animal pen enveloped her. There were streaks of dirt along her arms and legs.

"Teukros—" he began in dismay.

Keeping her distance, she said, "I'm sorry, Arion. I had no way to wash. No water." Yet she had always washed before, staying clean even under the most difficult circumstances. He gave her a skeptical look, but she offered nothing more. Instead she asked, "How are you faring, Arion?"

"I'm tired," he said, "but much better."

"You're rowing again? You have rests?"

He answered abstractedly. He did not want to talk about the rowing. He wanted to find out what was happening with Hamilcar, but she clearly wasn't going to tell him. A silence fell between them, making him at once worried and sad.

As darkness closed in, men sought their berths. Normally at this time Marpessa would return to her pallet in the hold, and he would go to his rowing bench to sleep. But instead she turned toward a narrow ledge near his bench, under the gangway. "I'm going to sleep here, Arion. I'll stay near you—make sure you're all right."

"I'm fine, Teukros. What will the Phoenicians—"

But she did not let him finish. "We're brothers, Arion. Surely I should watch over you when you've been ill."

"But that shelf is very narrow and uncomfortable."

"It's wide enough for me."

He was glad to have her close to him.

The next day it was the same. But Arion was determined to learn more. When she came to meet him that evening, he said firmly, "Marpessa. What's the matter? Tell me. Is Hamilcar—"

She cut him off. "All's well," she said insistently and gave a fleeting smile. "I'll explain it all when we get off the ship."

And he had to be content with that. *If we ever get off alive*, he thought grimly.

As the ship continued to struggle up the strait, Arion noticed that, while he was still given periods of rest, his were shorter and less frequent than the other rowers. It took almost four days to get through the strait, but at last the water ahead opened into a wide sea, gleaming beneath silver clouds. The Euxine! Its name meant "hospitable sea," and Arion, exhausted, had never seen a more welcome sight. As the current ceased and the sail opened up to the wind, he stretched his cramped body and lifted his arms to the sky in gratitude. He guessed that the roughest part of the rowing had passed. Marpessa was still acting strange and distant, but without her help as they rowed through the strait, he would certainly have died.

Five more days to reach their goal. They stretched ahead of Marpessa interminably. The situation with Hamilcar, the tug of wills between them, became ever more unbearable. The first day when she had spread the animals' filth over herself, he had hissed, "You wash! Plenty water in buckets. You filthy!"

She had ignored him. Had slept on the narrow, uncomfortable plank near Arion's rowing bench.

The next day he shouted, "Why not sleep in own bed?"

"I must keep an eye on my brother. He's not well."

"Brother fine! Stop avoid me. You sleep where you belong!" She said nothing, and as Hamilcar stood looking down at her, something changed in his face as if he had had a revelation. His eyes darkened with an even greater rage, but he left without speaking.

After that Hamilcar had no more words for her, only fuming silence, stares of hate, and threatening gestures—a lifted, clenched fist, an ominous hand drawn across his throat.

She did her best to ignore him. She concentrated on her plan to steal some gold. Sometimes with a favorable wind the ship sailed through the night. When this happened, there were too many people about. But on nights when the ship dropped anchor, there would be only one or two men standing guard. While Arion, exhausted from rowing, slept deeply, Marpessa restlessly left her uncomfortable perch and prowled the ship in growing desperation. By her calculation only two more days remained until they reached Heracléa Pontica.

On the fourth night after leaving the strait, she knew it had to be now or not at all. As she slipped off the sleeping ledge, she said a silent prayer: *Athena, help me.* But Athena seemed very distant, as if she had turned her face away. And Marpessa thought she knew why. Even though she had acted out of desperation, she had made a tacit bargain with Hamilcar and failed to keep it. In the eyes of the gods that was a sin.

Still, fortune seemed to be with her. She noticed that the two Phoenicians on guard duty were sitting on the foredeck, a lamp between them, deep in a quiet conversation. Silent as a stalking cat, she crept to the stern deck, out of their line of sight, and with deft fingers unfastened the ropes that held the canvas covering in place. Her groping hands found a basket and selected by feel three sizeable ingots of gold. Glancing furtively over her shoulder, she shoved these down the front of her tunic, just above her belt. The guards had noticed nothing. Then she felt some square clay tablets. *Charts. They use these to navigate the ship,* she realized. These might be useful when they reached Heracléa Pontica. *Tomorrow—surely tomorrow.* She grabbed one of the tablets, stashed it with the gold, and, after fastening the canvas back in place, ducked down the ladder. She planned to bury the stolen goods in the straw behind the animal pen. But she dreaded going into the hold, where she would have to pass the sleeping Hamilcar and possibly others who sometimes slept there.

Part way down the ladder, she stopped. Listened to the creaking of the ropes, the splash of waves against the hull. Heard snoring from the hold. She continued down, one hand pressed against her tunic to keep the ingots from clanging together. Moonlight made a bright square on the floor of the hold. Hamilcar's bedding was in a corner. Three other dark shapes lay half in shadow. She tiptoed around them, not breathing. One of them stirred, muttered. She froze. He slept on. She crept to the pen, climbed over the rail, made her way past goats and sheep that raised heads to look at her. At last she reached her bedding. She buried her plunder a short distance away under layers of straw.

She was just straightening when a stirring made her look over her shoulder. A dark shape loomed. *Hamilcar!* How had he gotten here so fast? She turned quickly from her buried goods, praying he hadn't seen her hiding place.

But he didn't even look. He came right up to her, so close she smelled wine on his breath. "You fool me! You lie to me!" he raged. "No more fooled! Now I know."

Her eyes fell in horror on the object he held. Moonlight glinted along a cold, shiny blade. "Brother not your brother! You his lover boy!" He lifted the knife. "I kill you first, then him!"

# XLIII

## HERACLEA PONTICA

Marpessa leapt up like a deer, sprinted across the pen, and vaulted over the rail almost before Hamilcar could react. As she sprang up the ladder, she heard his shambling pursuit, but she was faster, more agile. She raced along the gangway to the spot near Arion's rowing bench. Here she stopped, heart hammering. She tried to quiet her breathing. On the foredeck, the two guards were standing in the moonlight, looking her way. The wind hissed through the ropes; the quiescent ship rocked on a sudden series of waves. Crouched on the gangway, her body taut, her eyes fixed on the opening to the hold, she waited for Hamilcar's head to appear. If he came, she would scream, she would wake the ship. But he did not come up the ladder. The wind gusted, quieted. Perhaps he wouldn't dare attack her in the open.

Her heart slowed and her knees went weak. One of the guards said something to her in a low voice that might have meant *Go to bed*. Then he turned away. Carefully she climbed down to the second tier.

She crawled along the planking to her shelf near Arion's bench. He stirred, raised his head groggily, looked at her with unfocused eyes, and immediately went back to sleep.

"Arion," she whispered, then stopped. He was always so tired from rowing that she wouldn't wake him. *I'll tell him tomorrow.* Tonight she would keep watch. She positioned her body between him and the gangway. If Hamilcar came, he could not get to Arion without waking her.

Arion woke early to find Marpessa lying asleep half on her ledge, half on his bench, one arm out flung toward him. The gray light showed lines of strain in her face. At once she opened anxious eyes.

"Arion—" she began, but a shout called the men to their oars. Around them, the Phoenicians, grumbling, scrambled onto their benches. Giving her a rueful glance, Arion took up his oar and began rowing. No chance to talk now. After a moment she left him and crawled up to the gangway. When she returned a short while later, she was breathing hard and holding an awkwardly shaped bundle tied in a cloth, which she slid onto the small shelf where he stowed their possessions. He noticed that she had washed herself. As she squeezed onto her sleeping shelf, her face was pale and she was trembling.

"What is it?" Arion whispered between oar strokes.

She opened her mouth. "H-Ha—" she began, then cast a look around at the other rowers so close behind and in front of them. She shook her head and said nothing more.

*Hamilcar what?* Arion worried. Around them, the sailors had begun to sing a loud, rhythmic chant as they sometimes did when the rowing was tedious, and he couldn't ask her what Hamilcar had done. Angry, frustrated, he could do nothing except continue rowing.

It was late morning when shouted orders directed the men on the right to ship their oars. Those on Arion's side continued rowing, and the ship swung in an arc toward an unseen destination. There was an excited buzzing among the men. Could this mean they had reached Heracléa Pontica? The ship slowed, Arion heard the order for the dropping of anchors, and the men around him began pulling their oars in-board, stretching, and rising.

His heart quickened as he shipped his oar. He exchanged a speaking glance with Marpessa. *Escape!* His mind went over their plan. Everything depended on the Phoenicians leaving only two men to guard the ship. *Let there be nothing unexpected*, he prayed as he followed her up to the gangway.

They went to their usual spot near the middle of the ship and looked over the water at the small village spread out along the shore. A few fishing boats bobbed in the surf, and some lay on the sand. Curious on-lookers had gathered on the strand, and more came out of houses to stare at the ship. The Phoenician sailors formed into lines near the stern to board one of the two shore boats, some chatting eagerly, some staring out to land, their backs to Arion and Marpessa. "Now—tell me!" Arion said.

"Hamilcar—he pulled a knife—said he'll kill us—"

Rage exploded in Arion's head. "I'll kill *him*!"

"Hush!" Marpessa looked around anxiously, but no Phoenicians were nearby. The first boats started ferrying men to the shore. She quickly told Arion what had happened. He said nothing, but grimly tightened his hands into fists. "That bundle I put on your shelf," she whispered. "I stole three gold ingots and a clay tablet that looked important from that secret area on the aft deck."

"Well done—you're a wonder! We need the gold." Arion grinned at her, then returned his gaze to the boarding Phoenicians. At his feet, concealed against the hull, was a broken oar the Phoenicians had never gotten around to repairing. He'd also collected some rags and coils of rope tucked into his belt. "Soon now," he murmured.

Boatload after crowded boatload rowed to the shore, while one Phoenician stayed on board. *To guard us*, Arion thought. He watched to gauge how long each rowboat trip took. According to his memory from the first stop, when the last of the Phoenicians were on land, a single shore boat would be rowed back to the ship, leaving two men aboard to stand guard. When the last boatload of Phoenicians left the ship, he'd have to be quick to knock out the remaining guard, bind him, gag him, and hide him before the second man came back.

While they waited, he kept a wary eye on the man, who crouched at the stern, his back to them, doing something with the canvas that covered the mysterious storage area. Arion's stomach tightened. *Oh, gods, let him not discover Marpessa's theft!* He couldn't breathe until at last the guard closed the cover. The man stayed where he was, staring at the land. Less than a dozen Phoenicians were left on board. Arion, following his gaze, saw a boat coming back. *This would be the last boatload.*

He drew a deep breath. The boat bumped up against the ship. *Ready.* The Phoenicians crowded into it. One of them shoved off. Less than a *stadion* separated the ship from the village—enough so that the figures on land were indistinct. He would have to wait until they were almost at the beach and wouldn't see or hear anything. As the oarsman began rowing, Arion's fists were clenched, his whole body taut.

At last the men in the boat appeared no larger than locusts. *Now.*

Signaling to Marpessa to stay where she was, he crept up silently behind the guard, lifted the oar, and swung a mighty blow that cracked against the man's skull. He fell senseless, one of his legs half off the deck. Arion bent and awkwardly rolled him over, shoving him fully onto the deck. He bound his wrists and ankles tightly. The man's limbs twitched. *Quickly, the gag.* Arion tied a cloth securely around the man's mouth, then lowered him none too gently into the hold. Arion glanced at Marpessa and raised a fist to signal success.

He waited in the stern, ready with his club, for the rowboat to return. As it came closer, he drew in a sharp breath of dismay. *Two men were in the boat!* Then he recognized them. *Hamilcar and Barekbaal.*

Every muscle in his body tensed. His hand tightened around the broken oar. "Hsst!" he beckoned to Marpessa. She came running. "Quick! Get Hamilcar to go with you—that way!" He nodded toward the forward deck. "Distract him— I'll come back as soon as I can. Here!" He handed her his knife and hid the club nearby, ready for Barekbaal. Then, feigning boredom, he strolled a few steps away, leaving Marpessa to meet the men. His stomach knotting with tension, he pretended to look abstractedly out to sea.

Marpessa slipped the knife under her belt at her back and pulled a fold of her tunic over it to conceal it. *Athena, help me!* she prayed as she watched the two men scramble up the boarding plank and walked to meet them. *Don't let me have to use this knife!* Barekbaal's face was blank, Hamilcar's grim. A chill slid down her spine.

"Hamilcar." She tried to keep her voice normal, but it cracked with fear. "I must speak to you. About last night." She pointed toward the forward deck. "Alone."

Hamilcar glared at her. With difficulty she forced a smile. "It's been a—a misunderstanding." Hamilcar said something tersely to Barekbaal, who turned away. Trying to keep her knees from trembling, Marpessa walked the length of the ship to the bow, glancing only once to see if Hamilcar followed. On the foredeck, she faced him, hiding her fear.

"Hamilcar—" she said softly, dropping her eyes, trying to look inviting. He stepped closer. She backed away, involuntarily, thinking, *Arion, come quickly!* He grabbed her, pulled her to him, and clenched his mouth over hers, his loathsome hands groping down her body. *Arion, help*— But she was on her own. Rage drove her, and she reached for the knife, pushed it with all her strength into his side. It went in only a short way and struck something hard.

Hamilcar jumped and released her. He gave an angry cry, then a laugh filled with hatred and cruelty. Blood trickled down his side where the knife dangled for an instant, held by its tip only, then clattered to the deck. "You miss!" he gloated, and pulled out his own knife.

Marpessa shrank back. Arion was creeping up silently. To distract Hamilcar she cried, "Don't hurt me!" Just as he raised the knife, Arion lunged and swung his club. Hamilcar fell, and Arion, his face contorted, struck him several more times until he was senseless.

Marpessa couldn't stop trembling. Arion tossed ropes onto the deck. She crouched down to help him tie the bonds though her hands shook so violently they were almost useless. At last he straightened and pulled her to her feet.

Pent-up fury filled him. He felt Marpessa's trembling and took her in his arms, whispering soft words into her hair, as much to calm himself as to soothe her. Then he let her go. "We must hurry."

They gathered their belongings and the stolen treasures. As Arion wrapped them in the blanket and bound the pack with rope, he was grimly silent. It was life or death. The Phoenicians would mount a massive search for them. They'd have to swim a long way up the coast and hide until the foreigners gave up looking for them. What to do about the pack? Suddenly his eye fell on the oar he had used as a club. He lashed their belongings to it. He would tow it as he swam.

When they were ready, he pointed to a deserted stretch of shore with sheltering reeds and trees. "We'll head there."

On the seaward side of the stern deck, where they wouldn't be seen from land, they lowered themselves down a rope. Arion dropped their pack into the water, then let go of the rope. The choppy water was so icy cold it cut off his breath. He heard a splash behind him and Marpessa's gasp as she hit the water.

"Quickly!" he said as they started to swim. "We haven't much time."

# XLIV

## THE SHIP FROM HELLAS

Beneath sullen clouds the water was deep green, almost black. As she sank into the freezing sea, Poseidon's realm, Marpessa quailed at its enormous depth, where unseen things lurked beneath. Her bones hurt from the cold as she fought her way to the surface. Large waves assaulted her, swamping her face. She couldn't breathe. Arion was shouting something, but she couldn't hear. He was in front of her, his dark head bobbing in the surf, and she began stroking after him, fighting the waves. In no time she was exhausted, Arion drawing ever farther away. She panicked, tried to cry out, and a wave splashed her, choking her.

Arion turned to check and swam back swiftly. "Roll on your back and rest," he told her, his eyes anxious yet reassuring. As she did so, his hand came up under her head to lift her face out of the water. When her breathing came even, he said, "Don't fight the waves! Let them do the work."

The shore seemed impossibly far, but Arion swam beside her, calming and encouraging her just the way he had soothed the injured Haleia all those months ago when he led them to Troy. *I barely knew him then. How everything has changed!* Her thoughts served as a distraction from the freezing water and the chore of swimming, and at last the land grew closer. She could see the rocks and black shingle of a beach. Her foot reached down to nothing but icy depth. She started to panic, but Arion said, "Almost there," and soon her feet found the bottom. She pushed forward and staggered onto land. A wind from the sea gusted. She collapsed on a soft pile of brown grass a short way up the shore, shivering so hard her bones rattled.

"We can't stop here—too close to the village." Arion looked around anxiously, then scooped her into his arms and set her on her feet. He pulled her soaking blanket from his sodden pack, shook it out in the wind, and wrapped it around her shoulders. His hand on her arm, he led her up the shore.

They found a trickling river and followed it upstream through thickly wooded hills into ever-rougher terrain. As they pushed forward, Marpessa wasn't cold any more. "Just exhausted," she muttered. "You're a hard task master, Arion!"

"I'm better company than Hamilcar!" he retorted.

After climbing into wilder and wilder undergrowth, they came to a rocky outcropping and clambered to the top. "Look, the coast!" Arion said. "See the Phoenician ship?"

It was tiny in the distance, but Marpessa shuddered. "Do you think we're far enough away?"

"I hope so." He found them a hiding place in the center of a thicket and tore loose branches to conceal the place where they had crawled in.

It was late afternoon. Their clothes were still damp, and as soon as they stopped moving, Marpessa shivered uncontrollably. Arion pressed his body close to hers to warm her. There would be no food until they could go safely to the village. At last night fell, and they slept fitfully. Marpessa woke often, hearing noises, perhaps animals stirring or the wind, but she imagined the Phoenicians searching, drawing ever closer. She felt Arion next to her, alert and listening in the dark.

When daylight came, they crept cautiously from the thicket and climbed the rock. Barely breathing, they gazed out to sea.

"Look, Arion!" Marpessa cried in excitement. The Phoenician ship was bearing eastward, fading into the morning mist.

Arion wasted no time on relief. His mind was already on the next stage of their journey. He gathered their belongings, ready to trek down to the village. "We begin again," he said softly.

She gave a weak grin. "Aye, and I shall have to be your *simple* brother again!"

Although it had looked inviting from the ship, "village" was too grand a word for the collection of shabby huts they found clustered around the shore. There were no temples, no marketplace. A few rough men, working with fishing nets or upended boats, watched curiously as they approached the nearest resident, a grizzled man of middle years.

When Arion introduced them as brothers from Hellas, the man looked them over, eyes narrowed with suspicion, before replying that he was Thoas, from Megara, as were the others from this place, a recent settlement no more than two years old.

"How did you come here?" he asked.

"We've left the Phoenician ship," Arion said.

This drew a sharp gaze from Thoas, who must have seen the Phoenicians searching. "Why were you with them?"

"We were told they were going to Hellas."

"Indeed!" muttered Thoas. "They were sailing east."

"So we found out!" Arion gave a grin that seemed to lift some of the man's suspicions. Then he asked, "What work do you do here?"

"Anything and everything. Most have families in Megara they'll send for some day. We have farms, grazing lands. We look for iron and copper rocks. We fish and dry our catch to trade with the people of this shore. When ships come, Phoenicians and others, we sell our goods to them."

"We're seeking a ship returning to Hellas," Arion said.

Thoas scratched his beard. "Not many ships will come before spring. But there is one. The captain is a rich trader, a hard man who dares to sail in winter. He makes short runs between the colonies along this coast. He comes through here now and again."

"Perhaps he'll take us on," Arion said. "Until then, can we stay and help the settlement? I can do any sort of work." He cast a glance at Marpessa, who kept her head down, shuffling her feet in the sand. "My brother wanders in his mind sometimes. But I'll work for both of us."

"There are no extra houses," Thoas replied. "I can loan you materials to build a small lean-to, but you'll have to repay me with work. Hard work," he added sternly.

The day Marpessa saw the ship belonging to the Greek trader Thoas had spoken of, she felt relief. Their life in Heracléa Pontica was hard. Arion had built them a small shelter using one wall of Thoas's shed, but the boards were thin and the winter wind whipping off the Euxine went right through her bones. There were frequent storms with icy rain. They had neither extra clothes nor the means to acquire them. She saw too little of Arion, for every day in all kinds of weather he did heavy work for Thoas, clearing fields of rocks to create the farmlands so precious to the Greeks, plowing, going far afield in search of suitable lumber for building.

Thoas, a widower, had a twelve-year-old son named Eurypylos. Since everyone presumed that Marpessa was a boy of more of less the same age, she and Eury spent a lot of time together. Thoas often sent Eury fishing in their small punt or up into the hills to collect rocks with iron, and Marpessa went too. He was a friendly lad who liked to talk, and while she listened, nodded, and managed to smile, she often let his chatter roll over her. Her mind was far away, filled with dark thoughts. Had Hamilcar or the other two Phoenicians died at their hands? She hoped not, and Arion had said likely not. But if they had died, would the gods punish her and Arion for their murder? *We were only defending ourselves,* she pleaded silently. Those men were merciless predators. Arion had told her he was sure that from the beginning the Phoenicians had intended to kill them. She, who would never hurt an animal, felt little remorse for hurting them. This shocked her. *I would stop at nothing to defend Arion,* she realized. What a long way she had come from the carefree girl who had roamed the woods of Lokris rescuing orphaned baby animals! She felt years, centuries, older than the boy at her side.

The ship arrived just after noon when Thoas and Arion were plowing a field at the farthest end of Thoas's holding. Marpessa and Eury ran down to the shore. It was a large ship by Greek standards but still small enough to be run up on the beach. Marpessa and Eury watched the men haul the ship onto land and prop it upright with timbers.

"It's the ship from Hellas," Eury told her in the superior tone of an expert. "The rich merchant. We've collected lots of iron rocks, and he pays well for those. Father will be happy."

When Arion returned in the late afternoon and learned that the captain was on the deck, he decided to speak to him at once. He had some silver pieces, hard-won from working for Thoas, but negotiation would be tricky. How would he isolate and protect Marpessa on a small ship with a Greek-speaking crew? As he approached the ship, he prayed, *Zeus and all gods, send me an idea.* He glanced down the shore, where Marpessa and Eury stood side by side, skipping rocks into the water. Arion had shorn her hair as soon as they reached Heracléa Pontica, and from here she looked every bit the boy.

The captain was a sturdy man of medium height, his face as brown and tough as leather, the skin pulled tightly over his cheekbones. His narrow eyes, squinting, scowling, looked on the world with superiority, disdain, or disillusion—or perhaps all three. There was something familiar about him that nagged at Arion. He could not think where he might have seen this man before. But the captain showed no sign of recognizing him.

Arion introduced himself, at the last moment giving his name as Lykaon, "I'm seeking passage to Hellas for myself and my young brother." He gestured down the shore toward Marpessa and Eury, but the captain did not bother to shift his gaze. "Will you be going to Hellas?"

"It's still winter. There are storms, rough and unpredictable." The captain gave him a hard stare. Arion waited. "As it happens, I do plan to sail to Hellas on this trip." The man spat. "I do not fear Poseidon, nor any god. If the Phoenicians can sail these waters, so can we."

*Hubris!* Arion thought. The gods punished this kind of arrogance. He hoped they wouldn't strike the man down while they were sailing on his ship. But he said, "I can pay our way. What will you ask?"

The captain's eyes showed a gleam of interest. "Ten pieces of silver."

Arion raised his brows in outrage. "A man cannot earn that much in half a year! I've only been here a short while." He reached into his belt and produced a few lumps of copper and three silver pieces of varying size. Two more remained nestled in his pouch. "This is what I've earned. This is what I can pay."

"No."

Arion thought of the treasure Marpessa had stolen from the Phoenicians, which they kept hidden among their meager belongings—enough gold, with any luck, to buy a future. No way was he going to offer them to this miserly captain. He pulled out one more silver piece and stated firmly, "I can offer you this and no more. And I can help with the rowing and any other work."

Without committing himself, the captain asked, "Where in Hellas are you bound?"

Arion hesitated. "Lokris."

The man gave him an odd look, and Arion at once regretted mentioning that name. As he quickly prepared to change his story, the captain frowned and said, "You'd be ill-advised to go *there*."

"Why?"

The captain only shrugged. "Not for me to tell a man his business."

*I'll find out later.* Aloud, Arion said, "It doesn't matter. I just want to get around the island of Euboia and land on that coast. It's to Delphi that we're heading. To consult the oracle." He was pleased with his lie. It gave them a reason for traveling that no one would question.

The captain gave a slight nod. "We will be making stops along that coast." A pause. "And what of this brother you mentioned? Can he work too?"

Arion felt a flash of panic. "He's only a lad, and frail. He has bouts of illness and weakness," he invented. "On our last journey he spent lots of time lying on his pallet in the hold. In fact," he added on sudden inspiration, "that's why we're going to Delphi, to—"

But the captain cut him off with a wave of his hand. "Very well, I'll take you on. We sail in two days."

"Thank you, sir! You won't be sorry." The captain only regarded him with a cold, indifferent stare. As Arion turned away, he suddenly knew where he had seen this man before.

It hit him like a blow.

This was the merchant who had viciously kicked him in Thrasios' warehouse in Naryx all those months ago.

# XLV

## KLONIOS

"If we go on this ship it will be a great risk," Arion said. "The captain's name is Klonios. I found out from crewmembers. Do you know him?"

Arion had kindled a fire outside their lean-to, and they were sitting by it, sharing a supper of bread and dried fish, although "bread" was too fine a name for the hard lumps of crushed grain and water they had browned over the fire. Marpessa was heartily sick of dried fish, and she suspected Arion was too. The wind gusted, and the thin flames did nothing to stop her shivering.

"No," she said, "I never heard that name."

"He may have seen you in Naryx." He paused. "I wonder if we should even go on this ship."

"Not go?" Sudden tears sprang to her eyes. She, who did not cry easily, was often on the verge of tears these days. It was this place, she told herself. This miserable, dreary place. The ship offered an escape, a hope. For a moment her worries about what would happen when they reached home seemed very far away. She felt a great longing for her mother. If only they could reach her, Amaltheia would find a way to protect them. "Arion, there may not be another ship for months!"

"But this Klonios might recognize you."

"I'm sure he's never seen me. And I don't look like myself. But what of *you?*" she demanded. "He saw you in my father's warehouse. And today you must have told him your name."

He shook his head. "I gave my name as Lykaon—you must remember to call me that. And he didn't recognize me. I was a slave, a nothing. Someone like him wouldn't even see me as a man. It's you I'm worried about. He has dealings with your father. Did Thrasios ever mention him?"

"No. My father never spoke to my mother or me of his business dealings." *My mother!* A great sorrow settled on her heart. *Will I ever see you again?* Arion must have sensed her thoughts, for his eyes, as they met hers in the twilight, reflected sadness. Silence fell like a shadow between them. He reached out and took her hand in his.

At last, letting go, he said, "I told the captain—" He hesitated, tossed his fish bones into the fire. "I told him you were sickly. That you would spend much of the voyage lying on your pallet in the hold."

Indignation flared in her. "I've never been sick in my life, except when the marauders hit me with clubs!"

"But it's a way to keep you out of his sight."

"For the *whole* voyage? It would be unbearable!"

"This trip will be much faster. We won't be going against the current. Instead, it will speed us on our way."

Still, she'd spend all her time in the dark, smelly hold to satisfy his need to keep her safe. Worse, she would not be near him. Then the realization struck her. In a few short weeks, perhaps less, they would reach Lokris, and he would leave her. Or be killed, unless she could find a way to prevent it. The fear loomed like a boulder atop a precipice that threatened to crash down on her. The image of her death that she had seen in Athena's temple came back to her. Her skin went cold. The Fates were pushing them relentlessly toward some terrible end in Lokris. She knew her mother would be powerless to save them. For a long time she could not speak. At last she heard herself say, "Very well, Arion, I will do as you wish."

Two days later, Arion carried their belongings and a pallet for his frail brother Teukros to the ship. Then he went back for Marpessa, who walked in slow steps, feigning weakness and holding a cloth to her forehead, which worked well to conceal her features. He installed her in the hold. As she crouched over the pallet, he could see, in the dimness, the fierce gleam of her eyes.

"My love!" he whispered ruefully. "I'll come to see you as often as I can."

She glared at him. "Go to your oar. I hope the weather is terrible and the rowing is hard!" Then she reached a quick hand to grasp his arm. "I don't mean that!" she amended.

He returned to the deck. He had already struck up an acquaintance with the crewmembers. "My young brother," he explained as he settled among them, "has always been sickly." He affected a sorrowful look, hoping to discourage their interest in Teukros. "Also weak in his mind."

As the journey began, a fresh breeze was blowing astern. The sail went up, and the men relaxed at their oars. Arion sought a way to ask for information about the captain's warning not to go to Lokris. He glanced around at the men on the rowing benches. "Are any of you from Lokris?"

Several surprised looks came his way. "Most of us are, including our captain. Why do you ask?"

"The captain hinted at trouble."

"Aye! There is drought, the crops are failing, and there have been reports of more than the usual numbers of stillbirths and deformed babies. They say Lokris has been cursed by the gods."

Arion digested this in silence, wondering what it could mean for their return.

Lying in the hold, Marpessa felt listless and queasy. If only she were free to move about, to stretch her muscles, to breathe the fresh sea air! The waves of the current propelled the ship forward on great, even swells. Instead of soothing Marpessa, they made her sicker. Surely it was a punishment from the gods. Boasting to Arion that she had never been sick was hubris, and the gods detested hubris. *Athena, forgive my false pride!* More and more often she prayed to Athena. Ever since the Phoenician ship, she imagined that all the other gods had deserted her, and Athena was a lone, distant presence who sometimes watched over her.

When Arion came down to see her in the evening, bringing food, she said, "I can't eat. I'm sick. The gods are punishing me."

"Nonsense! It's just seasickness. You'll feel better if you eat."

She took the proffered meat wrapped in bread. But she heaved and gave it back to him hastily. "This is what comes of having to lie in the hold all day." Seeing his stricken look, she added, "Arion, I'm sorry! Tomorrow I'll be well. You'll see."

For Arion the trip was the complete opposite of the outbound voyage with the Phoenicians. With the current and prevailing winds carrying them most days, sailing was easy, and there was much less rowing. Though the captain was an unpleasant man, the crew treated Arion with friendly camaraderie.

But he did not enjoy it long, for the next day Marpessa was worse. She could barely sit up. When she tried to eat the goat meat he brought, she vomited, then lay with her eyes closed, her pale face covered with a sheen of sweat. He cleaned up the sickness, then laid his hand on her hot brow. *Surely just a passing fever*, he prayed. With an ache of guilt he wondered if she had indeed fallen ill from being confined to the unwholesome hold. Perhaps he should bring her up onto the deck. Klonios treated his sailors as menials and paid them little attention save to give orders. He probably wouldn't have noticed Marpessa had she paraded right under his nose. Arion tried to remember the lovely young girl in Naryx that Klonios might have seen, with her long, flowing, burnished tresses, her quick, graceful movements. Now she was thin, ragged, her hair roughly shorn.

*Ah, gods, what have I done to her? I've brought her nothing but harm.* Perhaps he should leave her now and turn her over to Klonios, telling him that she was Thrasios's daughter. As her father's business associate, Klonios might be willing to escort her home. *At least he'll feed her properly,* Arion thought. *Better than I've done.*

But Klonios was a cruel, unscrupulous man. Too well, Arion remembered that vicious kick that had knocked him from his feet. Whatever it took, he would deliver Marpessa safely to her mother's arms.

When he returned to his place on the deck, the men were muttering, going silent as he passed by. One of them said, "Maybe a plague." Someone else said the word *contagion.* He felt a flicker of fear. If they thought that, they would dump Marpessa on land at the earliest opportunity or even throw her into the sea.

He stopped and faced the men. "My brother does not have a plague," he said, turning about so that all could hear. "It is as I told you. He's been an invalid since he was a child. That's why we are on this journey. We are going to the oracle at Delphi to see if Apollo can heal him."

Doubtful stares met his eyes. One of the men said, "We'll see. But if you or anyone else sickens—" He didn't finish his sentence.

"Look at me," Arion challenged. "I'm healthy, and I've been with him night and day." The man shrugged. Something made Arion look over to the captain's spot at the helm, and he felt the coldness of Klonios's malevolent stare. Surely the man was too far away to have heard the exchange. Arion prayed that no word of it would reach his ears. *Maybe I should bring Marpessa on deck,* he thought. *Just briefly. To prove she doesn't have the plague.*

Hours later, with the wind astern and the sail up, Arion, freed of rowing duties, went down again to the hold, this time bringing bread, olives, and a delicacy: fresh shellfish. He found her lying still, her eyes closed. With a pang, he saw that her hand was clasped around the owl feather she had carried with her from the mountainside.

He held out the food and forced heartiness into his voice. "Look, my love, these are much better than anything we had in Heracléa Pontica, or even with the Phoenicians."

To please him, Marpessa made a huge effort and sat up. But a mere whiff of the food was enough to make her heave emptiness and bile until at last she lay back weak and gasping.

"Perhaps you could come on deck for a brief time, as long as we don't let the captain see your face." She heard desperation in his voice, but she shook her head. The concern in his eyes was too much to bear. It demanded effort when she was sinking into a whirlpool of lethargy. She wanted him to leave her alone.

She said faintly, "Just let me rest. I'm sure it will pass, and—" But she closed her eyes, too weak to go on.

A cold, heavy fear weighed him down. Not only the crew was still talking about contagion, Marpessa was weakening. He thought of the wasting sickness that had taken his mother. Marpessa had something like it, he was sure. He would be helpless as she wasted away before his eyes.

After they glided almost effortlessly through the strait that took them out of the Euxine, Klonios walked to the center of the ship. "We'll be stopping at Kysikos," he announced. "I have many holdings there to deal with." His manner was abrupt, inviting no questions. He glared around at the men and added, "We'll be two days there. You have leave to go into the town, but do not cause trouble."

The men glanced at each other, pleased with this news, but none dared show it openly. Klonios's eyes fell on Arion, and he frowned. A shiver ran down Arion's back. *Does he know something?* he wondered, but the captain's gaze moved on as if Arion were no more than a repulsive insect.

When they reached the town, the ship was run up onto the beach. As the other men clambered down the gangplank, Arion hurried to the hold. He found Marpessa on her feet, pacing. At first he was encouraged. Then he saw her face. She was flushed, her eyes feverishly bright. Her fists kept clenching and unclenching.

"What is it?" he asked in alarm.

"I'm so stupid!" she cried. "I don't know how I could have missed it!"

He caught her in his arms and whispered, "Tell me, my love."

She leaned against his chest, trembling. She said, so low he barely heard, "Arion, I'm with child!"

# XLVI

## KYSIKOS

>>><<<

The words struck him with the force of an avalanche. For a moment he couldn't breathe.

There could be no good outcome for this.

They sat side by side on her pallet in the hold. The stillness from above told them they were alone on the beached ship. Arion put his arm around her.

"There are people who know how to get rid of a baby," he said at last. "But I don't."

She too seemed to have trouble breathing. "Our baby!" she gasped out. "I don't want to get rid of it."

They were silent, Arion trying to peer into a future where he could see nothing. Then he had a sudden thought. "We'll have to leave this ship at once!"

"Why?"

"Well, everyone will know you're not a boy."

Marpessa gave a broken laugh. "Nonsense! Nothing will even show for months. I can still be Teukros."

"Then we can stay on this ship until we reach the coast of Lokris."

She shook her head. "I can't go home. My life is over. My parents will be disgraced. They would rather I was dead."

"But you must go home. Your mother could not wish you dead. She'll know what to do."

"My mother! How do I know she's still alive?" Marpessa's voice fell to a whisper, and he heard the longing in it. Tears filled her eyes.

Those tears pierced Arion like shards. "Your mother is strong, Marpessa. I'm sure she's alive." He reached for her hand and held it. Then he was silent for so long that she asked, "What are you thinking, Arion?"

He did not answer. A furious battle was raging inside him. *Get off this ship,* he was thinking. *Take her to the far ends of the earth and start a new life somewhere.* He had thought about this before. But he had failed miserably in caring for her. He had not provided her with safety, a roof over her head, or enough food to eat. Now that she was with child, his vow to take her home was all the more important, so that her mother could care for her. Against his will, his own eyes burned with the sting of tears. He was thankful that she did not look at him.

"Arion?"

*I'll honor my vow*, he thought. Aloud, he said, "We must stop troubling ourselves with this now. It does no good."

"But we're still continuing our journey home?"

"I don't see a choice. We'll pray to the gods and see if their will becomes clear, but—" He sighed and didn't finish. "Come now." He stood up. "Let's get off this ship and walk on land. The evening air will make you feel better."

She got to her feet, and they climbed out of the hold. But when she stepped onto the plank that led to the shore, her weakened legs buckled, and he had to help her down.

Klonios owned a large house that overlooked the harbor. He sat at ease in the front room, a full goblet of wine in his hand, listening with half and ear to his overseer's accounting of the year's profits. But his eye was caught by the spectacle before him on the shore. The mysterious young man who had recently joined his crew was helping his sickly, feeble-minded brother down the plank onto the beach. There was something so solicitous and tender about the man's behavior toward his brother that it riveted Klonios's attention. The boy was pathetic and weak, rather feminine really. Klonios focused on the lad's slender, hairless legs and thought how well they would have looked on a woman. And the ankles, small and pretty, almost like a girl's.

Something was not quite right. Klonios narrowed his gaze on the pair. The man—what was his name? No matter. Names meant nothing, but Klonios prided himself on never forgetting a face. He had seen this man in the past, he now realized.

*Lokris. They wanted to go to Lokris.*

Klonios tried to recall where had he seen the man. Somewhere in Naryx. He was an underling, Klonios was sure, else he would have remembered him more clearly. Perhaps a slave?

He sighed, let it go. It would come to him. Then, with sharpened focus, he remembered Thrasios's warehouse. This man had been there. Was he a slave of Thrasios?

Suddenly Klonios was almost sure of it.

What was he doing here? Escaped? And the lad? His catamite? The crew might know. They were all from Lokris. He would see what he could learn from them.

The overseer's voice was droning on, but Klonios leapt to his feet. Something could be made of this. As yet he did not know what, but it would come to him.

"My lord?" the overseer said.

"Later," replied Klonios. "We'll finish the accounts after supper."

As he continued to watch the man and the boy, he realized that he would have to show the man another face, pretend to respect and even trust him in order to allay his suspicions during the rest of the voyage. A steely smile hardened his lips. He was good at this game. The journey ahead had suddenly become interesting

# XLVII

## A PLEASING SACRIFICE

Every event in Naryx gave further proof of the wrath of the gods. The drought continued. There was a blight on the barley crop. Somebody's wife had miscarried. Someone's prize brood mare had dropped her foal early and it had died. Knots of angry men gathered in the agora. Late one evening the knots coalesced into a mob. There was shouting.

"Athena has cursed us!"

"The priestesses of Athena are to blame."

"The High Priestess—"

"She offered sacrifice. It did no good."

"It's the dead maidens. If we had sent two more—"

"Will you offer your daughters?"

"No one would risk a ship."

"Perhaps someone should try."

A man leapt up onto the plinth of one of the temple's columns. "Hear me, men!" he shouted. He had to try several more times until the crowd quieted.

He cupped his hands about his mouth and raised his voice. "We can't go on like this! We're becoming paupers, our crops and animals dying, and the High Priestess sits in her fine house getting rich off temple offerings and doing nothing. We must force her to act."

"How?" a voice shouted out.

"We'll go now! To her house. To demand that she find a solution."

"Aye, a solution!" Someone took up the cry.

At once the disorderly mob charged up the hill toward the house of the High Priestess. As they marched, the chant swelled their throats. *"Find a solution! Find a solution!"*

The High Priestess, forced from her bed, stood at a window on the upper level of her house. An attendant behind her held a blazing torch that cast eerie shadows over the priestess's white face. She raised her voice to the crowd. "What do you want?"

"Find out why the gods have cursed us. Then take action," the leader shouted back.

"It's not always possible to know the will of the gods." The High Priestess's voice carried across the crowd. "We have offered sacrifice to Athena, Apollo, Zeus. But they've turned their faces away."

There were angry shouts and mutterings. "Not good enough!"

"We have even sent envoys to the oracle at Delphi," the priestess shouted over them. "They've recently returned."

This got their attention. "And what did the oracle say?" asked the leader.

"As usual the oracle has given us an enigma. Something about birds—turtledoves—not being a pleasing sacrifice to the goddess." The priestess shook her head. "We could not make any sense of it. We will reward the one who can offer a correct interpretation, but so far no one no one has found the answer."

An angry, puzzled half-silence fell. Suddenly the leader cried out, "Then do something else! Find out who offended the goddess. And put that person to death!"

Someone else shouted out, "Aye, death! Sacrifice the guilty one to Athena! Surely *that* would please her!"

The mob came alive again, chanting, "*Put the man to death! Put the man to death!*"

"Or woman," somebody shouted.

All they needed now was a culprit.

# XLVIII

## PREY

Two weeks later, as evening fell and the crew rested, the ship rocking at anchor in a small cove, Klonios sat on the foredeck. Praise the gods, the journey had gone well and swiftly so far, he thought. In just a few days they would round the island of Euboia and make land on the coast of Lokris. Now Klonios watched curiously as the newest crewmember walked with his brother along the gangway. With his narrowed eyes and detached gaze, Klonios could observe their every move without the appearance of watching. He had learned nothing of the man from the crew, only that his name was Lykaon—"wolf-like." Indeed there was something feral about him. This made Klonios believe he was a runaway slave. The more he thought about it, the more certain he became that there was a bounty on this man's head, a reward for his capture. When they made land, he could put the man in fetters until he found out the truth.

He smiled to himself at his own cleverness. He was sure the man had no suspicions. Klonios had cultivated his trust by consulting with him about Phoenician navigation, had even pretended to listen to his opinions. He'd learned that the man had gotten some kind of chart from the Phoenicians. The chart might even be useful, and Klonios planned to get it for himself. Getting his hands on it would actually serve two purposes.

He turned his attention to the brother. According to the crew, there had been rumors that the lad was ill with a plague; now Lykaon paraded him up and down the ship almost nightly, as if to dispel those rumors. He was just a weak, spiritless lad with no more stomach for the sea than a girl. Look at him now, holding a cloth to his brow, leaning heavily on Lykaon's arm as if his legs wouldn't carry his own weight! Klonios's predator instincts were aroused. When the man was in bonds, he could have some sport with the boy.

As they stood on the Lokrian shore at last, watching the crew unload the cargo into wagons, Arion felt numb. The long journey was all but over. They were close to the town of Naryx, no more than a few hours even if they had to walk all the way. It was early afternoon. With luck they would make it by nightfall. He'd worked long and hard for this moment, but now he wanted to postpone it forever. He could no more imagine turning Marpessa over to her mother and walking out of her life than he could imagine his own death.

He glanced at her, but her head was lowered, her face hidden from him. She shivered. "What do we do now?" she asked.

"Come," he said. He hefted the pack that held their belongings, heavy with their stolen gold, and led her away from the windy shore to a sunlit spot near a stand of pines. He set the pack down at the base of a tree, then pulled out the clay tablet. "The captain asked me to wait. He wants to buy the Phoenician navigation chart. He'll give us eight pieces of silver for it. After that," his voice shook a little, "we'll find a way to get you home."

He looked back at the ship. The captain, about to step onto the gangplank, turned to give instructions to a pair of crewmembers. As he began his descent, Marpessa stepped a little to the side and lowered her face so as not to attract attention. At last the captain came up them. He was smiling—a shark's smile. Two men followed him, both holding something concealed behind their backs. The hairs on the back of Arion's neck rose. He dropped the clay tablet so that both his hands were free. At the same moment he became aware that a third man had circled around behind him.

Over Klonios's shoulder, Arion saw the two closing in, menace in their faces.

Arion smashed his right fist into Klonios's face and drove his left as hard as he could into the captain's gut. Klonios doubled over. One of the men swung a club. Arion dodged it. The other grabbed him, wielding a rope. Arion tore himself loose, hitting the man in the jaw. All three men closed in, seized his arms, and wrapped them in ropes. Arion kicked at the men with all his might, landing several blows. A club came crashing down on the side of Arion's head. Pain exploded behind his brow. His knees gave way like columns of sand.

As he went down, his eyes fell on Marpessa, frozen with horror just a few paces away.

"*Run!*" he hissed.

Marpessa bolted into the piney woods that bordered the shore.

Klonios, one hand held over his bleeding nose, the other cradling his gut, saw her run. He bellowed in rage. "Secure this one! Then go after the lad!" The three thugs bound Arion's wrists and ankles so tightly the rope bit into his flesh. Then they slung him violently into a wagon and took off after Marpessa.

Arion's head throbbed. There were bruises all over his body, and blood ran from his mouth. But he barely noticed. All his being was focused on one anguished prayer. *Go, my Marpessa!* he exhorted her silently.

In one instant she understood two things: they were not going to kill Arion, at least not right away, or they would have done so at once; and if she didn't escape, she didn't have a prayer of helping him. So she ran as fast as she could, her chest bursting, until she could run no more. Then she found a depression behind a rock and burrowed into it like an animal, pulling handfuls of pine needles and dead branches over herself. She concentrated on quieting her gasping breaths. She lay still for a long time, managing not to move, not to make a sound. When heavy footsteps crunched the ground not far from where she huddled, the blood left her head, making it ache. At last the footsteps retreated. They hadn't seen her.

Her whole body shook. She had forgotten to breathe.

She waited until silence returned—dared not wait too long. She must risk going back. She had to know what they'd done to Arion. They were taking him somewhere. She must follow. Pushing her face through the foliage, she looked out. *No one.* She got up cautiously. Crept from tree to tree until she was near the spot where they had attacked him.

When she reached the place, she hid behind a thick trunk and peered out. She saw a train of wagons harnessed to horses. They were preparing to set out. At once her eyes found Arion, bound hand and foot in one of the wagons and guarded by the three brutes that had attacked him. His face was bloody, his body slumped, but his eyes were open. Marpessa went so weak with relief she had to hold onto the tree. Then she remembered the pack that held their belongings— and their treasure. He had dropped it behind one of the pines. She found it, scooped it up, and silently backed deeper into the woods. She would keep out of sight until the wagon train set out. Then she would follow.

Klonios shook with fury. His nose was broken, his gut horribly bruised. For a moment he thought of having this Lykaon, this rogue slave, killed outright. But no, it was better to wait, prolong it, and see what reward the slave might bring in Naryx. Surely a generous one, since he was strong and in his prime. No matter if it took a little longer; Klonios would have his revenge. Meanwhile he raged with impatience, waiting for his men to catch the boy. When they returned empty-handed, he bellowed at them, "Where is he?"

One of the men muttered, "Master, we ran far and searched in all directions, but we found no sign of him."

"What kind of men are you that can't outrun a sick lad?" Klonios lashed out.

"Who would have thought that weakling could run like a deer and hide like a woodland animal?" retorted the man.

"Never mind," Klonios snapped. He couldn't wait here any longer. He had his quarry, the one that mattered, in the back of a wagon. He climbed into his own wagon and they set off. The thought of revenge gnawed at him like a hunger. Even if the slave was punished, even if he was put to death for escaping, he was going to pay an even heavier penalty for what he had done. Nobody struck Klonios and got away with it. There was a satisfaction to having the slave in his power, bound and bleeding. Klonios's groin tightened with excitement at the thought of what was to come.

But after a time, during the long, jolting ride, his thoughts turned to the "brother" who had escaped. Something didn't make sense. Was the brother really a catamite? The fugitive slave had been so anxious to protect him. And if the lad was sick, how was he able to escape and hide?

Klonios wracked his brains. Something eluded him, something he should have noticed. Then all at once he remembered the moment when he saw the boy run off. So swiftly. But not like a boy. *Like a girl.*

Klonios sat bolt upright. *By the gods, they made a fool of me!* What better way to hide a girl than to disguise her as a sickly boy and keep her concealed in the hold? And he had fallen for it. He almost ordered the driver to turn back, to look for her. But the girl was surely already far away.

They were illicit lovers for certain. And he remembered that the girl's "seasickness" usually afflicted her in the mornings. The slave must have gotten her with child. But why had the two been traveling in the far reaches of the Euxine? And who was she? If Lykaon—by now Klonios was convinced this wasn't his real name—was from Naryx, the girl might be too.

What if she was one of the two girls who had been sent to Athena in Troy? What if she was *the* girl—the one he wanted—Thrasios's daughter? No, not possible. She was too scrawny and plain to be the glowing girl he had coveted. It must be the other one, whom he had never observed closely. Klonios's thoughts raced. What if this girl had somehow survived the massacre by the marauders and Lykaon had rescued her? Hadn't Thrasios sent a slave to accompany the girls? Klonios wondered if that slave had ever returned, and cursed himself for not bothering to find out.

Suddenly he was almost sure. It must be the very same slave, the one he had seen in Thrasios's warehouse. Nothing else made sense. But he had to make certain. Torn between outrage and elation, he ordered a halt. Climbing down from his wagon as fast as his injuries would allow, he went to the wagon where the accursed slave lay trussed like a sheep awaiting slaughter. Klonios smiled at the sight of him. "Your whore won't get far," he taunted. "I know who she is. And she'll pay the price for defying the goddess. Just as you will."

The slave's control was good, but the merest flicker in his eyes betrayed him. Klonios's smile widened. *I knew it!* he thought. He could continue to the town with his captive, secure in the knowledge that the girl would follow. She would not abandon her lover. Once in Naryx, he would find her.

He couldn't wait to reach Naryx. Thrasios, the slave, and the girl would dance like shadow puppets at the movement of his fingers.

A black beast was devouring Marpessa's heart, urging her to go faster, faster. But even as she ran, exhausted, panting for breath, the speed brought no relief. More was needed. She was too far away, it was too late, he might be dead by the time she found him. Shadows were falling, evening dropping around her like a cloak. *Hurry!* urged the voice in her head. Carrying the heavy pack, Marpessa drove herself ever harder, gasping and wheezing until she could not get enough air into her lungs. She stopped, dropped her burden and rested, hands on her knees, until her breath caught up with her. The pack was too hard to carry. It was slowing her down.

*Leave it,* an inner voice urged.

Their hard-won fortune? Something that might buy a future, Arion had said. But what was it weighed against his life?

*Athena, help me!* Looking around desperately, she found an oak with a large knothole that might once have been the burrow of an owl. She shoved the pack into it, paused for a moment trying to memorize the shape of the oak and its surroundings, and then ran on, pressing her hand against the tearing pain in her side.

Stars sprang out in the sky and began to swing in their stately arc before she at last caught sight of farmhouses, their white walls faintly visible in the deep of night.

*Naryx, at last.*

# XLIX

## HOME

Amaltheia dreamed that someone had come into her room and was shaking her. A figure bent over her in the dark, a hand caressing her face. "Mother, Mother!" Harsh breathing, an insistent whisper. "Mother, it's me. Marpessa!"

Amaltheia knew that beloved voice. Her daughter often came to her in the night. Amaltheia floated, waited to see what this visitation would bring. But the girl was demanding action. "Hurry! Light a lamp! Quietly!"

Reflexively Amaltheia rolled to her side and reached toward the table that held the lamp, but her hands moved slowly, refusing to obey her commands. Then she heard the strike of flint on iron, a fumble, another attempt. She dreamed that someone else was lighting the lamp and taking a long time about it. When a small flame glowed, she saw in its light a thin, dirty boy bending over her, his bare arms scratched and bleeding.

She sat bolt upright. "Who are you?"

"Mother, it's me." The boy spoke with Marpessa's voice, and the lamp moved upward so that it was beside the face. Amaltheia saw beyond the shorn hair to the eyes, Marpessa's clear eyes, but they were enormous, swollen with love and grief and terror. "Help me, Mother!" The lamp disappeared with a clunk on the wooden table, and strong arms closed around Amaltheia, the slight body shaking, sobbing.

Amaltheia put her arms around her daughter and surrendered to the embrace. Never before had Marpessa's presence seemed so solid. Never again would Amaltheia let her go. But Marpessa was tearing herself loose. "Mother, I need your help! *Hurry!*"

Almaltheia reached for her. "My daughter, are you come back from the dead? Tell me—"

Marpessa tried to pull her to her feet. "Later! We must rescue Arion before they kill him!"

"Arion? Who—? Will you stay this time, Marpessa?"

Marpessa sat down on the bed as tensely as a bird poised for flight and shook

227

her arm. "Mother! Wake up!"

*I'm dreaming,* Amaltheia thought. Then she felt the cold floor beneath her feet, saw the flame gutter slightly, and smelled the burning lamp oil. These things seemed solid, real. Yet so many times before she had been betrayed by a dream into thinking Marpessa had come back. "It couldn't be," she muttered.

"Mother, listen! You're not dreaming. I didn't die. Arion saved my life and risked his own to bring me home. Now Klonios has him, and we must help him."

Amaltheia tried to shake the confusion from her brain. "Arion the slave," she said. "Klonios the merchant? This is men's business. I'll talk to your father in the morning—"

"*No!* Father mustn't know! Arion—he's hurt. Klonios's men beat him. We must go to him now." Marpessa's voice sank to a trembling whisper. "Mother, you must help me! Klonios will kill him."

The desperation in her daughter's voice cleared Amaltheia's mind. This was impossible, but somehow she accepted it. Even if it was a dream, her daughter needed her. Strength and purpose flowed through her. Swiftly she got to her feet. "I know the way into the women's quarters of Klonios's house, and I know one of his serving women who can be trusted."

Marpessa slipped her hands into Amaltheia's and held on for dear life. "Can we go there at once?"

Fully awake, Amaltheia stared at the wan, ragged figure before her. "Nay. First I must send a message to the serving woman. And you, my darling, you must eat, rest."

The cage that held Arion had been built for livestock. It was not big enough to stand up in nor stretch out completely. It seemed that Klonios expected to keep him alive at least for a day or two, for there was hay strewn on the floor, a slop bucket and a jar of water. But no food. The door was held shut by a large wooden lock on the outside. After the men threw him into the cage, Arion watched as Klonios twisted a wooden key that dropped pins into place, then removed it. When Klonios left, Arion shook the door and the bars violently. Nothing loosened. He reached through the bars and grabbed the wooden lock, twisted, pulled it with all his strength. It did not move. He looked around. The cage was on a patch of hard dirt, probably behind Klonios's house. A guard was seated on the ground a short distance away, watching him impassively.

Arion felt like cursing aloud, shouting, sobbing like a broken-hearted child. Why had he trusted Klonios and waited for him after getting off the ship? His jaw throbbed, his head, arms, and shoulders ached with bruises, but these things did not matter. Klonios knew about Marpessa. In his mind he saw again his last sight of her, fleeing into the woods. *Marpessa, please be safe!* He had nothing to offer the gods except his silent supplication, but he begged them, *Athena and all the gods, let him not find her! Please protect her!*

But even if she reached safety, he would never see her again.

When night came on, he fell into an exhausted daze. Suddenly, a sound. He jerked awake in complete darkness, his pulse pounding. Then he saw a tiny bobbing lamp flame. He could just make out two figures on either side of the lamp, trailed by a third, shapeless in the dark. As they drew near, the flame shone upward on the lined face of an older woman. The figure beside her was small and slender. His heart leapt.

"*Arion!*" came her whisper. His whole being flooded with joy. His hands shot out through the bars of the cage. She brought them to her face, and he felt her smooth cheeks against his fingers. Her tears rained down into his palms.

Another hand touched him through the bars. He looked into the shadowed face of Amaltheia. "Thank you for saving my daughter," she said.

*She doesn't know about the child*, he thought with a pang of guilt.

The third shadow came forward, a stooped and shriveled crone. "Be quick!" she hissed. "The guard—I drugged his wine— but he may wake soon."

Amaltheia asked, "Where is the key to this cage?"

"Locked in his strongbox. Only the master can get it," the crone answered.

Arion's hope ebbed. He said, "Then you can't get me out of here." His voice shook, and he fell silent.

Marpessa's hands quivered in his. "Oh, Arion, what will he do to you?" Behind her, the crone was clucking with impatience.

But Arion cut them both off. "*Listen*," he insisted. "Klonios has guessed everything. He said he'd make you pay for defying the goddess. I don't know what he means to do, but I fear the worst. *No one* must know you're here in Naryx—not even Thrasios." He reached through the cage, grasped Amaltheia's cloak, and looked urgently into her eyes. "You must hide her. Klonios'll look for her. He won't give up." He paused to let his words sink in. "Dress her as a servant. Don't let *anyone* in your house."

A sudden swishing noise made them all freeze. But when it came again, it was nothing but the night wind. "Hurry!" the crone hissed in panic. "He'll kill us all!"

Marpessa straightened, withdrew her hands. He felt her reluctance, the warmth slipping away. "What about you?" Her words trembled. "My love, we'll find a way to save you," she whispered.

Arion shook his head. "It's hopeless. Save yourself, my Marpessa. That's all that matters now."

The next morning, while his minions were combing the town for the girl, Klonios went to the agora so that he could look, listen, and gauge the temper of the townspeople. He prided himself on his ability to do this. *A sacrifice to appease Athena,* he heard them saying. Well, if that was what they wanted, he had the perfect victim. It would be most satisfactory to turn over to the High Priestess the man who had defiled one of the maidens sent to the temple in Troy and consecrated to the service—*virginal* service—of the goddess.

It would also take care of Klonios's revenge on the lowly slave who had dared attack him. It was a nice touch that Klonios needn't soil his own hands.

As soon as possible he would have audience with the High Priestess. He could hardly wait.

# L

## FAILURE

>>>×<<<

In the servants' quarters of the house of Thrasios was a small hole of a room with a dirt floor and space for only two pallets. It was unoccupied, for with the failed crops, Thrasios had been forced to let some servants go. It became Marpessa's hiding place. Amaltheia told the serving women, "She's in danger. *No one,* not even the master, can know that she's here." She added, "Don't let her go out."

Marpessa heard but lay without speaking on her pallet curled in a ball, knees against her chest. She couldn't move. She could barely breathe.

She remembered her vision in Athena's temple. The altar and the knife. They were for Arion, not her. On the morrow they were going to kill him.

If only Athena had chosen her as the victim instead.

A human sacrifice to propitiate Athena!

Notices were posted in the agora where men read them aloud in incredulity, in growing excitement. A culprit had been found: the slave who had been sent to escort the temple girls to Troy last spring and who had never returned. By the merchant Klonios's heroic intervention, he had been captured. It was revealed that he had ravished and defiled one of the girls, getting her with child and bringing Athena's wrath upon the town. Now, with his death, Lokris would be saved.

Rumors swept through the agora like a wind. Klonios, watching half-hidden in the shadows of the temple's columns, listened with satisfaction to the buzzing of small knots of men who gathered, dispersed, formed into other groups.

"—one of Thrasios's slaves!"

"I know who he is, used to see him around—"

"A surly fellow. Kept to himself."

"How do they know he ravished the girl?"

"Klonios swore to it, he said—"

"The slave got her with child. He *should* be killed!" At that there was an angry buzzing and mounting outrage.

"And where is the girl?" someone shouted.

"—seems to have disappeared."

"I'll wager Klonios knows. He'll bring her out of hiding in time for the sacrifice."

Klonios smiled to himself. *That I have every intention of doing*, he thought.


Amaltheia stood over the bed, looking down at her daughter. Marpessa loved Arion. That was evident from all the girl's actions, even before she confessed this to her mother. But it came as a shock that Marpessa was with child. *How can any good come of this?* Amaltheia worried. She would do anything to ensure her daughter's happiness. *But I can't worry about it now*. Amaltheia looked at Marpessa's pale, clammy face, her closed eyes ringed in shadows. Amaltheia didn't think Marpessa was aware of her until the girl whispered, "Mother, if he dies, I'll die too."

*Then we must save him*, Amaltheia thought. *But how?* Could she persuade or bribe the High Priestess to stop the sacrifice? She had no means for a bribe since she had parted with the last of her dowry months ago when she gave it to Arion to watch over Marpessa. *What, then? Think!* She wracked her brains.

The oracle—could it work in their favor?

Amaltheia went down on her knees and took Marpessa in her arms. The girl's body was quivering with frenzy. Amaltheia held her tightly. Then she got to her feet, backed away. Somehow she had to break through Marpessa's despair. She made her voice deliberately harsh. "Get up, girl! Why are you lying here? We must do everything we can!"

Marpessa looked up at her mother, her eyes wide and dark with fear. "What can we do?"

"Some weeks ago the High Priestess sent envoys to Delphi. The oracle they came back with is an enigma. It's posted on a column of the temple with a reward to be given for the correct interpretation. If we can find a solution that might help Ar—"

Marpessa sat up at once. "What does the oracle say?"

"The envoys asked the Pythoness at Delphi how to break the curse. The answer was, 'The sacrifice of a mated pair of turtledoves is displeasing to the goddess. They must be set free.'"

Hope flared in Marpessa's eyes. "Mother, I think Athena's been helping me ever since I escaped the marauders." She gave a tremulous smile. "I know the meaning of the oracle."

*I'll go at once to the temple,* Amaltheia decided. But revealing her daughter's presence was risky, and she did not know the High Priestess. Her one friend at the temple was a minor priestess who could not even help her get an audience.

At the temple she was admitted by a priestess wearing a white head cloth that completely hid her hair, a thin woman of middle years with a pinched face. Her body tight and tense, the priestess listened to Amaltheia's request, then shook her head impatiently. "The High Priestess is very busy. She won't see you."

"My name is Amaltheia, wife of Thrasios, mother of Marpessa. It's of utmost importance. Please, you must ask her."

The woman's blank look indicated that those names meant nothing to her. But she said reluctantly, "Very well. Wait here." She led Amaltheia into a small room off the main chamber.

Amaltheia waited, fretting that in her absence Marpessa would do something foolhardy. Amaltheia doubted her servants' ability to keep the girl confined. At last the woman returned—without the High Priestess.

"It's as I told you. Her Eminence cannot be disturbed. She is about to undergo the ritual purification for the sacrifice tomorrow."

"Listen, please! My daughter Marpessa was one of the temple maidens sent to Troy last spring. She has come back, and—"

But the woman cut her off. "What are you saying? Both those girls are dead."

"But my daughter has returned. I beg you to tell Her Eminence and ask—"

"Your story is impossible. You're wasting my time. I have duties to perform."

"Wait, I can prove it—I can bring my daughter—Marpessa—here. And she knows—"

But Amaltheia got no further. The priestess cut her off, her voice rising in fury. "Enough! Leave now!" She picked up a mallet and struck a bronze gong. Two burly male attendants appeared as if they had been waiting just outside the room. "Take this madwoman outside!"

As the men grabbed her arms, Amaltheia burst out in desperation, "But my daughter can—"

"Your daughter's dead. I won't listen!"

As the two men pulled her to the door, Amaltheia said in a muffled voice, "I only wanted to help our city."

The priestess looked slightly abashed. She said reluctantly, "There is a very old tradition. Just before a human sacrifice, anyone may speak on the victim's behalf. If you have something to say, come forward then."

A slight hope lit Amaltheia's heart. "Thank you!" But the priestess had already swept from the room.

The guards showed Amaltheia to the outside door, then left her. She recalled that her friend the minor priestess owed her a debt of gratitude. Amaltheia had nursed the woman's mother through a dangerous illness last winter. Her friend was in charge of incense, and this gave Amaltheia an idea, something that might make Athena seem displeased with the sacrifice. Amaltheia found her friend in her room at the rear of the temple. The priestess, a small, timid woman, agreed to do as she asked.

But Amaltheia feared it wouldn't be enough.

Without much hope, Amaltheia decided to call on Thrasios in his warehouse. Perhaps she could persuade him to use his influence to stop the sacrifice. When she reached the warehouse grounds, a man, one of Thrasios's workers, accosted her. "My lady, a word with you. I dare not go to the master!"

It was unusual for a male servant to address her. Surprised, she asked, "What is it?"

"I beg you, do not tell the master it was I who spoke to you."

"Aye, aye!" she promised. "I'll not mention your name. Now go on."

He hesitated, lowered his voice, looked around. "Do you remember Nikias who used to work in our fields?" Amaltheia had a vague memory of Thrasios's complaints about a man by this name quitting his service abruptly. "Nikias left after he suddenly became rich," the servant said. "I know why."

Amaltheia waited impatiently.

The man continued, "He was bribed by Klonios to perform a service for him."

She caught her breath. "What service?"

"Months ago, Klonios bribed him to bake all our seeds—barley, wheat— before they were put in the ground, so they would not sprout, and to put salt in the irrigation water in the vineyards." The man paused, lowered his eyes. "I also heard that he put poison in some of the wells in town. So that it would look as if the town was cursed, and the goddess angry. But mainly he wanted Thrasios to be ruined. Klonios wanted revenge—I don't know why."

Even with everything else, this news punched the air from Amaltheia's lungs. She thought of the women who had miscarried, the malformed offspring born in sheepfolds and stables. She looked at the man sharply. "Why are you telling me this now?"

"It's been weighing on me. I didn't know what to do. We all feared Klonios. But after this long, I was afraid to go to the master."

She let out a breath. "Thank you for telling me." As the man bowed and left, her thoughts raced. Could this news help defeat Klonios before it was too late? But even if Thrasios publicly denounced him, it would not save Arion's life. Her hopes sank. As she walked into the warehouse, she breathed against a weight of dread.

Thrasios greeted her with exasperation. "Why have you come to bother me?"

"Thrasios, you must influence the heads of the Hundred Houses to stop this sacrifice. Arion is your slave."

He waved her to silence. "Mine no longer. He ran away. Now the temple has him, wants to kill him, and welcome, I say."

Amaltheia appealed to his greed. "If you stop the sacrifice, you could have him back."

Thrasios gave a humorless laugh. "As an example I'd have to punish him harshly for escaping—perhaps cripple him or kill him. On top of that, Klonios would demand a huge reward for returning him. So the slave is no use to me."

"But this sacrifice is wrong. It will be a stain on *your* honor!" Amaltheia lashed at him.

"Not so. He deserves to die!"

"He is blameless!"

"It will save our city. You know nothing of these things. Now go!" Thrasios growled. "I have important work."

Amaltheia pulled her shawl over her head in defeat. Then she told Thrasios about Klonios's treachery.

Thrasios went rigid with outrage. "Klonios did this? *Why?*" he demanded furiously. "I'll kill him! I'll get my sons, and after the sacrifice we'll—" He paced and ranted, oblivious of Amaltheia.

She sank her face into her hands, then turned away.

All day Marpessa waited for the night. She must go to Arion. But she knew the servants were watching her, so she stayed alone in her room. When darkness came, she sat huddled on her bed until long after the household fell silent. At last, when all seemed to be asleep, she stole outside silently. A bright moon lit her way. She needed no guide and no lamp.

As she crept up the alley to the back of Klonios's house, she held her breath, paused—peered fearfully around the corner into the garden. Last time the old serving woman had drugged the wine of the man guarding Arion. This time— But luck was with her. The guard was slumped against the fence, snoring. She inhaled deeply, passed him on silent feet, reached the cage.

"Arion!" It was the softest of whispers, but it brought him instantly upright and alert.

"Marpessa?" He pulled himself close to the bars. "*Gods!*" he hissed. "Why have you come?"

Shocked, she whispered, "I had to see you." She touched his face. His skin was cold, damp. His eyes, their surfaces glistening in the moonlight, were glazed like the eyes of an animal caught in a trap. His breaths were short, rapid, each one cut off before it was complete. He had gone very far to a place where she couldn't reach him. His eyes abruptly swung to her, feral, angry. "It's too dangerous. You must leave." Tears burst from her eyes. His hand came out and traced the line of her cheek. Then he withdrew it as if burned, and she heard his abrupt breath. In a voice she barely recognized as his own, he said, "If Klonios catches you, they'll sacrifice you too."

"He won't catch me. But Arion, we have a plan, and we can—"

He cut her off. "It's no use. You've risked everything—for nothing. Now go!"

She went cold with dismay. She couldn't leave him like this! Just then a noise jolted them. Shuffling footsteps. A quavering voice. "I heard you come."

Only the crone! Marpessa took a shaky breath. The old woman said, "The master's awake. Quickly! Out the back way." She pointed. "Go!"

A thud came from the house. A door opened. A lamp flared. Marpessa cast a look at Arion, but his face was frozen. "*Hurry!*" he said.

Marpessa ran.

A silent shadow detached itself from the deeper darkness of a clump of bushes near the alley and followed her.

# LI

## THE ALTAR

The sacrifice would take place at noon at the altar in front of Athena's temple, and all the people were required to be present to propitiate the goddess. In slowly growing numbers, the entire town gathered in the agora outside the temple. From his spot just inside the temple portico, Klonios watched. Impatience gnawed at him as the sun inched its way up the sky. One of his most diligent servants had followed the girl last night when she sneaked in to see her lover, as he had known she would. Now he knew where she was—and *who* she was. He smiled with satisfaction. *Marpessa*. His men had orders to bring her here so that she could watch her lover die. After that, Klonios would make her pay for defiling herself with a slave. And no one would stop him. Thrasios would not thwart him again. In fact Thrasios should thank him for making sure the harlot got what she deserved.

The crowd grew restive as the sun rose toward its zenith. There were angry murmurings to which Klonios listened anxiously when a dissenter stood on the plinth of a column. "Hear me, men! We must stop this. The gods don't want human victims! Not for untold generations has this happened—only in the far past, when men were barbarians."

An uproar broke out. "He angered Athena. He must die!" And the crowd clamored, "Sacrifice! Sacrifice!"

"Is it a sacrifice?" the dissenter shouted. "Call it what it is—an execution!"

But the mob, impatient for the bloodletting, drowned him out. A voice bellowed, "Call it what you want, so long as it lifts the goddess's wrath."

Another voice shouted, "You saw what the oracle said. The goddess doesn't want turtledoves. That must mean she wants human blood!"

"Aye, aye!" a chorus of voices shouted. "Human blood to appease the goddess!"

"He ravished the girl. Let him die to lift the curse!"

"Hear me, men—" the dissenter tried, but several men threw rotting vegetables at him, driving him down from his post.

And the chant started up. "*Let him die! Let him die!*"

Klonios sighed with relief. His heart raced with anticipation.

In the servants' quarters, Marpessa, ill with fear, could hear the chant. It chilled her to the bone. She wanted to fly into the agora, to demand the silence of the crowd, their help. She wanted the power of the gods to spirit Arion away, as aeons ago the goddess Artemis had rescued the maiden Iphigenia when she was about to be sacrificed, leaving a young doe in her place.

*Athena, help me!* she screamed silently. *Save him!*

Amaltheia came to sit on Marpessa's bed. "My darling, remember, you will have a chance to speak." Marpessa tried to focus on her mother's words, but she was so close to panic she could barely take them in. She forced herself to breathe deeply. "I must go to the agora with Thrasios," Amaltheia was saying. "We don't know what Klonios is planning, so you must go at the last moment only, dressed as a servant. And don't neglect to take two attendants with you."

Marpessa thought at once of the two girls who had sometimes accompanied her on childhood adventures. "I'll take Ianthe and Damaris," she said. Damaris was tall and strong but cautious. Ianthe was slighter and quick-witted.

Amaltheia kissed her brow. "Only make sure you get there in time!"

When her mother and the rest of the household left, Marpessa rose and drew many long breaths. She reached her arms to the sky. She had wallowed in fear; she had been paralyzed into inaction. Perhaps it was thanks to the influence of the goddess, but she now felt almost calm. Everything had come down to an absolute. She would save him. Or she would die with him. There was no other choice.

She stood a moment in thought. She heard Arion's voice in her head saying, *Klonios has guessed everything.* It was as if he were cautioning her as he had so many times. Over and over he had saved her. Now everything was up to her.

"Athena, be at my side," she whispered.

She put on a gown that molded itself to her body, and tied the sash above the small bulge of her belly. She wanted to look fecund in this barren land. She covered her cropped hair with a head cloth. Lastly she flung an old cloak about her shoulders for concealment.

She called the two servant girls who had remained behind. "Damaris! Ianthe! We go together to the agora. I need your help to save my beloved." She gave each a knife. "Hide these in your sashes."

"Why?" asked Damaris warily.

"Klonios may try to stop us. If his men attack, don't let them take us at any cost."

Ianthe's eyes flashed. "Let them try!"

"I've never fought anyone, Mistress," said Damaris staunchly, "but I'll do my best."

"I'm counting on you." Marpessa was touched. "Here's how you hold a knife." She demonstrated, remembering with heightened urgency the feel of Arion's fingers on hers when he had taught her this same skill. "Now let's go!"

As they set out, the very silence and emptiness of the streets frightened her. All the townspeople except themselves were gathered in the agora. Marpessa drew an unsteady breath. *Athena, help me.* "We must hurry!" she told the serving maids, and they quickened their steps. They heard faraway shouts from the crowd. Marpessa's heart clenched, then began to beat with frantic urgency. *Let me not be too late!*

"*Hurry!*" she cried.

Suddenly two men sprang out from behind a wall. One came straight for Marpessa and swung his fist into her temple. Suns burst behind her eyes. When her vision cleared, she struggled free. He punched her hard in the stomach and yanked her arms behind her, pinning her under him. A fierce constricting pain blocked her breath. She couldn't move. She heard gasping, groaning noises— they were coming from her. A moment passed like an hour. She fought to breathe. She had to get up. In the agora— *Oh, gods, Athena, help me! I can't—*

*There is no can't.* She heard Arion's voice in her head, saying those words as he had so long ago on the way into Troy. Her breath returned. She willed strength into herself and thrust her knee with all her force into the man's groin. He doubled over. She rolled away, found her knife. He lunged again and pinned the hand with the knife. She swung her free hand up to his face, shoving the heel of it into his nose, her fingers digging for his eyes. He let go with a cry. She plunged the knife into his neck. As he fell back, spurting blood, she scrambled to her feet.

The other man had knocked Damaris down and was grappling with fierce little Ianthe. Marpessa hauled Damaris to her feet. "Your knife!" she hissed. The girl pulled it out but stood frozen, her eyes full of fear. Marpessa pointed to the injured man. "Stab him if he moves!" She launched herself at the second man, thrusting her knife deep into the soft flesh of his side. He fell. The first man was getting up. Damaris jabbed at him ineffectually with her knife. Marpessa grabbed a rock and smashed it against his head. Ianthe got to her feet and stabbed him under the chin.

"*Run!*" Marpessa shouted. The three girls sprinted toward the agora. As they reached it, Marpessa saw a vast crowd that had fallen silent. She fought down panic. Far across the agora in front the altar stood a tall figure in a white robe, his hands bound behind his back. A man in ceremonial robes approached, lifting the huge sacrificial knife.

*She was too late!*

Icy sweat broke out on Arion's brow. He was cold to the core. He struggled for each breath as if he were underwater. His heart pounded, hard and heavy, shaking his body. As if from far away he heard the High Priestess's voice. "If there are any here who wish to speak on behalf of the victim, let them come forward now." A hush fell over the crowd, and Arion too ceased to breathe. With all his being he prayed to live. He had an absurd hope that Marpessa and her mother would save him. Now moments passed. The silence grew. His hope died.

Arion felt his entrails liquifying, his whole being crumbling. The eyes of the multitude were all fixed on him. He drew breath. With the last of his resolve, he straightened, lifted his head. None should see his fear. He would die like a man.

The executioner came forward. "Does the victim agree to the sacrifice?"

Arion knew that animal victims were made to nod in assent by having water poured over their heads. He would not. He held his head high, but a hand struck him hard from behind. His head jolted forward, giving the appearance of a nod. Sickness rose in his throat.

"The victim agrees," intoned the High Priestess. "Proceed!"

"*Wait!*" screamed a voice from far across the crowd.

Arion's heart jerked. Someone was swimming through the multitude like a fish against the current, parting it, pushing people left and right, shouting, "Wait, wait! I can interpret the prophecy!"

The High Priestess echoed, "Wait!"

But the executioner held his knife high.

The High Priestess lifted her voice. "Stay your hand!" The man's arm dropped.

A breath flooded Arion's lungs as he watched the figure that struggled toward the altar. He thought he would never see her again. At last she reached him, breathing in gasps, and placed herself between him and the executioner. From under the hood of her cloak, her gray-green eyes burned a look into his heart, the briefest look, but it was enough. Then she addressed the High Priestess.

"Your Eminence, I know the meaning of the oracle."

"Who are you?" the High Priestess demanded.

"I am Marpessa, daughter of Thrasios," Marpessa shouted so that her voice carried over the crowd. "I left last spring to serve the goddess in Troy."

There was a stirring, a murmur of voices from the crowd.

"Marpessa?"

"—doesn't look like her—"

"Aye, it's her!"

"How is it you have returned from the dead?" asked the High Priestess.

Marpessa gestured toward Arion. "This man saved me and brought me home. I have come forth interpret the oracle."

The High Priestess looked dubious but said, "Then do so."

"The goddess Athena will be angry if you kill this man." Marpessa's words were breathy with panic, at first barely audible, then gaining in strength. The crowd gasped, and their gazes shifted. Arion turned, saw what they were looking at. The white smoke rising from the censer behind the altar was turning gray.

"Continue," the High Priestess said curtly.

Marpessa threw off her cloak, her body revealed in the clinging gown— widened hips, full breasts, the small but unmistakable bulge of her belly. Some voices exclaimed in surprise. A noise like a restless wind passed through the crowd.

"Athena saved me from death, protected me. She guided Arion to me and helped us on our journey home. She sent me this token of her favor." Marpessa held high the feather of an owl, the one she had carried with her or perhaps another one. Her voice rang out with confidence as she continued. "Arion and I are the pair of turtledoves the oracle spoke of," she said. She took a step backward and threaded her arm through his bound one. "We are mated for life. I am carrying his child. If you kill him," her arm tightened in his, and her voice choked, "you kill me. That is the sacrifice that would anger Athena." Marpessa lifted her free hand toward the ominous gray smoke. "The oracle says that to lift the curse you must set us free."

No one spoke, no one moved or breathed. Time stopped. Then there was a small *poof*, a crackling sound, and the smoke from the incense turned a thick angry black. The small priestess who tended the censer stepped back with lowered eyes. The smoke billowed in an enormous cloud. The High Priestess's eyes followed it to the sky. Some in the crowd pointed. There was a murmur of fear.

At last the priestess spoke. "The will of the goddess is clear. This sacrifice is not to her liking." She waved toward the two male acolytes who flanked the altar. "Set him free!"

Arion's knees went so weak with relief he feared they would dissolve like sand. He felt hands fumbling behind him, loosening the ropes. Soon he could pull his own hands apart.

There was a ferocious shout, and someone leapt from the crowd, wielding a deadly knife. Arion saw the knife arcing toward him and, behind it, Klonios's rage-distorted face. Marpessa flung herself in front of him. The knife struck flesh, not his, and blood burst forth. His freed hands came up just in time to catch her as she fell, her blood soaking into the white linen of his sacrificial gown.

He was only vaguely aware that three or four men had leapt on Klonios with drawn swords.

Arion sank to the ground holding Marpessa as she slumped against him. Her eyes met his for one instant with all the love and all the light in the world. Then they closed.

# LII

## HANDFAST

꘏꘏꘏꘏

Arion's heart became stone. His arms felt heavy and useless as they held her. He sat, unable to move, staring into her white face, until somebody pushed up next to him, and an elbow jostled him.

"Quick!" Amaltheia was pulling off her head cloth, winding it into a long strip. "It's only her arm, but we must stop the bleeding." Just then Marpessa's eyelids flickered, and Arion came to life again. Amaltheia tied the improvised bandage tight around Marpessa's arm, high above the elbow. "Press your fingers here," she directed him. "Press *hard!*" Arion did, and soon the dreadful pumping out of blood eased. "Now—can you carry her? We must get her to the house."

Cradling her, he staggered to his feet. Knots of people milled around, but they were outside of his awareness. From the corner of his eye he saw the crumpled body of Klonios and heard Thrasios shouting. But that too meant nothing. As if in a dream, he held Marpessa tight against him and followed Amaltheia across the agora.

Marpessa came awake at last, lying on her own bed. As Amaltheia and her old nurse Eumene leaned over her, she tried frantically to sit up. "Arion? Where is he?"

"Hush, child, all's well," Amaltheia soothed. "Arion is in the men's quarters." A sharp, throbbing pain ran down Marpessa's arm, and she reached around to feel a thick bandage. "You have a nasty gash, thanks to that villain Klonios!" her mother said. "Your father and brothers killed him, and none will blame them. The High Priestess believes that Athena made you and Arion instruments of Klonios's destruction. He angered her with his hubris, and he tried to ruin the city out of revenge."

All it meant to her was that they were out of danger. "Mother, I must see Arion!"

"Later. After you've rested."

But several days passed, and she did not see him.

"He shan't see her. I will not have it!" Thrasios raged.

Amaltheia bowed her head. "My lord, he saved her life and brought her home. If not for him, she would be dead."

"That's why I haven't punished him. But he's a runaway slave. I don't want him here. I'll sell him as soon as I get the chance."

"He escaped to save her! He risked his life. He should be set free." *As I promised him long ago*, she thought. "You would be dishonored if you did not reward his service."

Thrasios frowned. But the word "dishonor" did the trick, as Amaltheia had hoped. He gave an irritated sigh. "Very well, have your way, woman. Send for him."

Arion had tried every day to see her, only to be turned away by a blank-faced servant who gave him no news. His stomach was knotted with dread. What were they keeping from him?

When he was summoned into Thrasios's presence at last, he saw Amaltheia standing against the back wall, fidgeting with her shawl. His eyes threw her a silent, imploring question, which she seemed to understand, for she nodded in reply. His knees went weak. *Thanks to the gods, she's mending!* he thought.

Thrasios beckoned him forward. "Thank you for saving our daughter, for bringing her back," he said, the words dragged from him. He handed Arion a sack of coppers. "Take this token of our gratitude. You are hereby set free."

Arion bowed briefly, muttered thanks. Thrasios added, "But you must leave Naryx."

Arion gave a start. He glanced at Amaltheia, but she did not meet his eyes. He straightened with steel in his spine and looked at Thrasios in the face. "I want to marry your daughter."

Thrasios gave a growl of outrage. "Out of the question. Did you not hear? You are exiled. Now leave us!"

Amaltheia stepped forward with a muffled cry, her eyes swimming with tears, but Thrasios waved her back. "You have no say in this, woman."

"I want to see her," Arion said. "Before I go. *If* I go."

Thrasios made no reply. Amaltheia mouthed something at Arion that might have been, *Later,* or perhaps *Wait*, but her eyes, meeting his, were full of despair and defeat, and he had little choice but to turn and walk out of their presence.

He went to his old hut at the edge of the woods, where he sat on his pallet. He had no will to move. They might as well have killed him there in the agora for all his life was worth. His whole being and will had been bent on bringing Marpessa home. He had not thought, had not dared think beyond the moment when he delivered her to safety. Then, when she saved him from death and spoke of them as a mated pair, he had begun to hope.

He was furious at himself for being duped. How could he not have known that Thrasios would send him away, considering himself merciful in giving the lowly slave his freedom and a sack of coppers? Arion flung that sack against the wall with all his might. An abyss opened in him, a wide enough maw to swallow his very soul. Without her there was nothing. And who would care for her and be a father to her child?

*Wait*, Amaltheia had said.

*How long?*

"Exiled? *NO!*" Marpessa screamed. "Find him! Bring him back! I haven't even seen him since—"Tears streamed down her face. Amaltheia and Eumene ran to quiet her. "Hush!" Amaltheia said. "Your father will hear and be angry."

Marpessa shook her off. "Where is Arion? Has he gone?"

"He hasn't left," Amaltheia reassured her. "I heard from the servants that he's in his old shack."

But he might leave at any moment, and Marpessa would never see him again. She must hurry. She started violently for the door, but the two older women restrained her, Amaltheia protectively holding her daughter's injured arm, which rested in a sling. "Calm, now! You'll reopen your wound."

"Never mind. I will see Arion. I *will* marry him!"

"Your father won't have it."

"He will. I will talk to him. Now." *Before Arion leaves,* she prayed. *Oh, goddess, let me not be too late!* Marpessa dried her eyes in haste, one-handedly put on her sandals, and straightened her gown.

"Don't be absurd!" Seated by the hearth in the central hall as Marpessa and Amaltheia stood before him, Thrasios glared at his daughter. "He's nothing—a freed slave only through my kindness."

Marpessa quieted the anxiety gnawing her belly. *Arion, my beloved, wait for me!* She clutched the feather of Athena hidden in her hand, reminding herself that she had known since that day by the mountain spring that she would have Arion and no other. The Phoenicians, the gods, the Fates, and Klonios himself had not been able to stop her. Nor would Thrasios. Facing him, she lifted her chin.

"Father, you were there at the altar when the goddess made her will plain. If I wed him, she will lift the curse, and Naryx will flourish." Marpessa narrowed her eyes at her father and lifted her chin. "If you do not grant us permission, we will escape, and none shall stop us. We will wander the world as beggars, as we have learned well how to do. But we will be together, and we *will* wed." Thrasios was silent. "I am carrying Arion's child," she reminded him.

He frowned mightily. "That disgrace changes nothing!"

Marpessa stood like an implacable cliff face. "Father, there's no other life for me. No other man will have me."

"And it's clear from the oracle," Amaltheia pointed out, "that Athena blesses their union."

Thrasios's eyes wavered. "It's out of the question!" he said gruffly, but with less force. "The slave hasn't two coppers to his name, save for ones I gave him."

Marpessa gave a beatific smile. "That's not true. He has a fortune, Father!"

It took Arion and Marpessa all day to scour the woods for the old oak where Marpessa had hidden the Phoenician gold ingots. As they searched, a gentle rain began to fall, the first to touch the parched soil in many months. *A good omen,* Marpessa said. At last they found their treasure—enough to buy Arion a small holding on the edge of town with a house, a few outbuildings, and fields behind.

Enough to buy a future.

On her wedding day, Marpessa, veiled in gossamer and wearing a crown of wildflowers, was led forth between her parents to Arion's house where he awaited her. A procession followed: her brothers with their wives and children, their friends and servants, and a troupe of musicians. The beating of drums, the ringing rhythm of tambourines, and the insistent wailing of flutes quickened her heart as she saw him from afar, her Arion, clad in the white chiton of the bridegroom, waiting for her in front of their new home.

At last came the sacred moment when she stood before her husband. His fathomless brown eyes looked at her the way the first man created by Prometheus must have looked upon the first woman. He spoke not a word—only reached out and, with utmost tenderness, took her hands in his.

# ACKNOWLEDGEMENTS

Thank you to all my family, both immediate and extended, whose unstinting love and belief in me have enabled me to persevere in my writing—too many to name, but you know who you are. Thanks also to the members of my writers' group, who have endured so many drafts of all my novels, and who with your wisdom through the years have taught me everything I know: Pat Elmore, Cleo Jones, Nellie Romero, the late Charlene Weir, and the late Avis Worthington. Thanks to Beth Barany for helping me frame my synopses and queries. Thank you, Dan Levine, for the book jacket photograph; you did wonders! A big thanks to Carol Collier for the wonderful map you made. And above all, thanks to my publisher, Dana Celeste Robinson, for making it all possible.

CPSIA information can be obtained
at www.ICGtesting.com
Printed in the USA
FSOW02n1147270617
35704FS